The Boarder on Monroe Street

by

Rich Polk

Copyright 2012 by Rich Polk

All rights reserved. No part of this book may be reproduced, stored in a retrieval system or transmitted in any form or by any means without the prior written permission of the publishers, except by a reviewer who may quote brief passages in a review to be printed in a newspaper, magazine or journal.

First Printing

ISBN: 978-1-300-08731-1
Published by Lulu Enterprises, Inc.
www.lulu.com
Raleigh, N.C.

Printed in the United States of America

For Kaul, Debbie, Jen, Michelle and Sue

1

Ever so slowly, the two enemy soldiers crept around the side of the house, their rifles at the ready. Craig raised his carbine to his eye, sighting down the barrel, alternating the two targets in his sights. The shots would be rapid and accurate. His victory in this mock battle would be decisive and complete.

As a grim smile found its way across his face, Craig lowered his toy weapon and continued to watch the figures. They turned their attention to the overgrown evergreen shrubs in front of the house. Systematically, they began to search around the trunks of the shrubs. Certainly this was the best hiding spot in the entire yard, and a thorough search of the back yard having yielded nothing, they were confident they would find their prey amongst the ewes and hemlocks. Craig's smile grew as he recognized their frustration increasing. He could predict their complaints of how he surely had left the boundaries of the yard in violation of the rules of engagement for these war games for nine year old boys.

Baffled and annoyed, the two continued their search around the house in the direction of the back yard, as Craig relaxed in his position behind the scrawny boxwood elder planted at the very corner of the property for no other purpose save to mark the end of one parent's lawn and the beginning of another. His hiding place was just barely within the boundary and was such a pathetic planting that it offered little cover. But the bush's lack of presence was so outstanding in its absence that it did not attract the searching eye for a fleeting instant. Thus had been found the perfect hiding place.

2

The sunlight dims, almost imperceptibly at first, then finally succumbs to the encroaching cloud cover. The clouds, in turn, change in color, becoming an increasingly darker shade of gray. What warmth the sun had provided is gone, and a noticeable chill is now pervasive. The alarms of raucous jays and the guttural croaks of crows sitting high in the trees go silent, and then the birds seem to vanish. Vultures descend from their high orbits to seek a roosting place in the pines, the boughs of which sag beneath the large birds' weight. There is no doubt now, the snow is coming.

Softly, silently, the flakes begin to fall, dancing on the wind which brought the storm eastward. As the storm intensifies, there is less dancing. The flakes, larger now and more numerous, take a direct diagonal route to earth. In no time the ground is covered, and the limbs of the trees greedily grab all they can, not stopping even when their spines begin to curve under the accumulated mass.

For most, this curvature will be temporary, with a return to the normal, skyward pointing attitude coming shortly after the snow melts and drips off the humbled boughs. For others, the deformity will be longer lasting, an osteoporosis lingering deep into the spring season when the more bountiful sunlight will entice the plant, cell by cell, to turn towards its life giving succor. For a very small group, the load will have proved to be too much, fracturing the branch, leaving the extremities without life support, to die and wither. For even a smaller minority, where the break is not fatal, the branch continues to grow, in a deformed, unnatural way.

In similar fashion, human lives are challenged. Naturally occurring events introduce burdens that mental and emotional frames are unable to bear. Rather than improving the chances of weathering such storms, matrimonial unions often prove more fragile than the partners, individually. The relationship so formed frequently provides additional precipitations, which accumulate along with the ordinary fall out of life to challenge the couple's ability to support one another. Should the situation develop where the partners no longer work together as a unit, but follow individual strategies for coping with the load, then the union is seriously threatened. Worse yet, some individuals, weakened by the familiarity of previously proffered aid and support from his spouse, suffer more than would have been expected, with personal devastation a possibility.

It was in such a condition that Craig Miller found himself. The slippage had been gradual, not at all uniform. Decline and doldrums had been intermittently broken with some happiness, even occasions of elation. The good times were convincing in their promise of a reversal of malaise. The bad times were never bad enough to rule out a reversal of the decline. Until one day when an accounting revealed the dimensions of the losses. That day included the admission that prospects for future happiness were diminishing rapidly and in multiple directions. For someone who had been so easily placated throughout his life, who had found a satisfactory level of contentment from even the weakest sources, this was a shocking discovery. Craig had felt something snap deep within his being. The sensation was spurred by hopelessness, magnified by despair, solidified by rejection.

An evening in recent months served as an example of how the marriage had declined. Arriving home after an extended day at the office, Craig, never capable of completely segregating his work from his life, was fully engaged in evaluating the day's events when he crossed the threshold.

Dolores's greeting was not icy, it even hinted at a degree of understanding. "You forgot what we were doing tonight?"

"Huh—err, what? The twelfth…oh! Barb and Allan. Crap! I'm sorry. I got so involved I totally forgot. I'm sorry. I knew you wanted to go to that reading."

"An actors' workshop."

"Right. Darn it. You should have called me."

"I did. Joan said you were in a meeting. I left a message."

"Oh, Dee, things have been so crazy. I've got two big projects coming due this week, and George is falling way behind. I was practically doing his part for him over the phone in a three hour conference call….You should've gone on without me."

"And put Allan in the position of a third wheel? How fair would that be to him? I know you don't particularly like him, but Barb is my best friend. I'd think you might play along once in a while."

"Allan's okay--"

"Oh, *please*, you hardly talk when you're together; like it's too much of an effort."

"Well *excuse me*, but real estate law and that yacht of his are two topics that I can't talk about for too long. And those are the *only* topics that interest him!"

"Like I said, you don't like him."

"Look, Dee, you're pissed, and I don't blame you. But it's not like I sabotaged this date on purpose. Preston is expecting me to make these two projects gel, and it's not going well. I had to invest the time or there'll be hell to pay."

"Here's your dinner," she said, laying a plate of macaroni and cheese before him. "It's not much, but then I was expecting to have the 'catch of the day' at Red Lobster." With that, she left him alone in the kitchen. All there was to say had been said. Craig knew the topic was closed, but not forgotten.

As alien as this condition was to his usual state of being, his reaction was just as abnormal. Craig's thoughts seldom ventured away from analyzing this state of affairs, and despite the amount of time spent thinking, indeed perhaps because of it, the responses so generated passed objective evaluations too readily, weaknesses were excused too quickly, overarching assumptions inadequately vetted. His plans, and soon thereafter, his life, assumed characteristics which, while not necessarily dysfunctional, were outside the realm of normal behavior. As a lifetime introvert, Craig sought no assistance from individuals objectively detached from his situation, neither professional nor from his small group of friends, his sole long-time confidant, his wife Dolores, now resting at the center of his problems.

As a result, he received no counsel advising him when his conclusions were leading in the direction of self-destructive action. When he recognized such elements on his own, Craig dismissed them as not to be unexpected given the frailty of his condition and the trauma he was experiencing. Exactly where Craig fell, within the boundaries of the wide spectrum of mental functionality, he was uncertain. Pinpointing his position was more difficult as his moods, attitudes and cognitive reactions varied, day by day. While positive he was far from the insanity pole, he believed he was being pulled in that direction. This served as a stimulus that empowered his obsessions which in turn energized his strategies and gave life to the courses of action they engendered. Once in place, the power these forces had over his actions was undeniable and unrelenting.

3

Long pink streams of morning sunlight swept rapidly westward across the New Jersey countryside, just above the girdled waistband of the state's mid-section. As a brilliant contrast to the even fill light bouncing off the now starless ceiling overhead, these probing beams brought warm accents and highlights to countless details of the terrain over which they passed. A string of dingy black railroad tank cars resting in a Jersey City rail yard suddenly had their shapeless mass defined, as the warm light outlined their curves. Cattails in the seaside marshes were suddenly bronzed by the piercing rays, and the scarlet epaulettes on the blackbirds' wings shone with new glory as the creatures clung to the reeds' stalks and trilled their piercing calls. Guard rails on the New Jersey Turnpike reflected the sunlight when not eclipsed by the racing shadows formed by the vehicles of commerce that streamed by. Leafless trees were prime targets for the invasion of illumination, especially the upper branches, which even on this early spring morning were selfish in determining how much of the warm glow they would allow to pass to the ground below. Where a clearing would enable the sunlight to strike the meandering Raritan River, the water would sparkle anew, whether rippled wide flow or narrow channeled rapids. Gold crosses atop the highest church steeples experienced a new valuation. And the jaundiced, dew laden petals of the blossoms of early blooming jonquils were intensified into the bold primary color for which they were named.

One such blossom, in one of many gardens in this, the Garden State, was to be found on the Miller property in the small town of Peach Hill. Once orchards covered the rolling hills of this community, and the products of the trees, particularly juicy peaches, would be carted to the railway station to be loaded into freight cars for delivery to Plainfield, Newark, New York, and beyond. But the economics of fruit growing, the introduction of refrigerated box cars, and a demand for residential real estate within railroad commuting distance of the urban zones already crowded upward, had resulted in the orchards' replacement by residential housing. Mr. and Mrs. Miller occupied one such dwelling, a small ranch-style two bedroom home of post-World War II vintage, not unlike a dozen others within their subdivision, although the well tended garden did tend to set it apart.

Dolores Miller, in her "everyday" bathrobe and an old pair of clogs she had relegated to household use, clomped around the kitchen, simultaneously preparing a light breakfast of toast and jam, and returning yesterday's dishes to the cabinets from their overnight berth in the dishwasher. Her motions were heavy and deliberate, and would be until the first few sips of coffee performed their magic. Likewise, her thought processes were heavy and muddled, the routine of making coffee, shaking orange juice and depressing the toaster lever superseding any true cognitive action. This, too, would change after the introduction of caffeine. She would be alert, even perky, for the nine o'clock meeting of the Somerset Garden Club as they solidified their action plans which had been formulated and initiated as a result of earlier meetings this spring.

The garden club had become a predominant activity in her life recently. As her marriage had produced no children and exhibited no extravagance in lifestyle, it had become clear years ago that her job as a secretary at the insurance agency was doing little more than forcing the couple into a higher tax bracket. So she had left the job and now, at the age of forty-five, having bounced around between various civic minded roles, visiting friends, playing tennis, jogging, walking, shopping (but seldom buying) and reading, she was certain she had found the best route to self-fulfillment. Two years ago, an invitation to a meeting of the S.G.C. had led her to where she felt most comfortable, just the right mix of solitude--planting, cultivating, watering, weeding--and membership--planning the annual flower show, staffing the booth at the mid-May street festival, and recruiting a crew to tend the small public gardens planted around town.

Her husband, Craig, sat at the kitchen table, nursing his orange juice. Normally, he would have thrown it down in a few gulps, but today was different. More alert than she, as a result of his shower of a few minutes before, he studied his wife's motions with an attentiveness as though he hailed from a land where breakfast was an unknown custom. For nineteen years he had shared this kitchen with Dolores at this hour of the morning, but today was the first day he seemed to really see her in action, more details observed.

With this study, came a tender warmth to his heart, such as he had felt two and a half decades prior when he had first seen her performing on stage. He recalled how later he had enrolled in a university English class on modern authors just because he knew Dolores was registered for it. Closing his eyes for a few seconds, images flashed by: their whirlwind courtship, the wedding, the honeymoon in the Caribbean, those first few blissful years where it seemed every action was a joint venture. Then came the painful recollection, reviewed repeatedly in recent days, of how they had grown apart. Right behind the recollection he remembered the parasitic bromides that had attached themselves to this painful realization: dedication to career, fatigue, conflicting obligations, his mother's illness, and on and on. All camouflaging the basic truth: that he had stopped treating her as if she were the most wonderful woman on earth. This, despite the fact that he had no evidence to suggest that she no longer deserved such treatment. For this reason he would spare her the pain. He would execute his plan today, as scheduled.

Opening his eyes, he glanced at the kitchen clock. He must be on his way now to meet the timetable. They exchanged the obligatory buss, as he headed for the door. Would she sense that his lips tarried on her lips and then her temple longer than usual?

4

Preston Gilmore turned into the parking lot of Gilmore, Haskins and Cass and could not stop the smile that jumped onto his face every morning at this time. It was more than just pride of ownership. It was pride of accomplishment and constant fine-tuning of that accomplishment. It had been his vision to break away from the huge real estate firm that had employed Walter Haskins and him in their property valuation department. Preston was responsible for convincing Walter to jump ship with him. No easy task was that, either. Likewise, he recognized the capitalization Bob Cass could offer the new start-up company. After Walter lost his battle with cancer, it was Preston who determined that Bob's casual ways were running contrary to his vision and offered Cass a lucrative buy out proposal he would have been foolish to refuse.

Some managers operated their businesses using a day planner. Gilmore's planner was in his head, and was always open. In the shower he laid out the items to be accomplished that day and that week. On the drive in he formulated action plans on how his goals were to be accomplished, and during his initial walk through the office he would briefly communicate the plans to key personnel, scheduling meetings for detailed instructions, should that be necessary. Parking next to Miller's car, Gilmore acknowledged to himself how dependable Craig had been since joining the firm twenty one years ago. Potential partner there, he thought, should the day ever come when he felt inclined to share the management burdens, and the ownership spoils. But today, his task was to finalize the appraisal for that warehouse project in Edison.

Gilmore poked his head into Miller's office, but the chair was vacant, the desk apparently untouched from its straightening the night before. "Must be in the men's room," he thought to himself, almost aloud.

He continued down the aisle towards his office, making less conversation than normal with the staff he passed on the way. He powered up his computer, quickly reviewed the correspondence his secretary had left on his desk, then sat in his chair, grasping his chin with his left hand as he again reviewed his plan of attack for the day. The Edison project was foremost in his thoughts, and there was no way he could move beyond that thought until he was satisfied that Craig had completed his work. He arose and retraced his steps to Craig's office, where he found no change.

"Jerry, do you know where Craig is?" he asked of the occupant of the cubicle opposite Craig's office door.

"I don't think he's in yet, sir."

"His car is here. Take a look around for me, would you?" Preston moved on back towards the entrance way, noting that the men's room was unoccupied as he passed, and still finding Craig's car parked in the lot. He again retraced his steps to his office where, a short time later, Jerry reported that Craig was no where to be found inside or outside of the building.

"Strange," thought Preston, this time aloud.

Preston busied himself with some correspondence. A phone call from an attorney required a prompt response by facsimile copier for a real estate closing within a couple of hours. Normally, he would have assigned the task to Craig, but under the circumstances he busied himself with drafting the response. With that done, he dialed Jerry's extension.

"Any sign of Craig?"

"No sir, it's really strange, he's never this late."

Across town, Dolores had showered and applied the minimal amount of makeup, as was her custom: just enough to show that she cared about her appearance, but no more than her vibrant complexion and healthy good looks required. Her shoulder length brown hair was gathered behind her head, keeping it out of her face and out of her way, no matter what activity she might undertake. A light blue short sleeve shirt and denim skirt adorned her slim figure, and the clogs had been traded for a pair of brown leather sandals. Thus attired for this spring morning in the ides of April, she felt ready to greet her favorite season, encouraged by the recent spell of warm weather. Thus inclined, she thought to herself, the mood would be appropriate when the leaders of the Somerset Garden Club made their appearance later that morning.

She turned her attention to the family room which, being adjacent to the kitchen, was conducive to Club meetings as she could make refreshments ready without either missing any part of the meeting or requiring a pause in the agenda. The room, containing comfortable, practical and modest furniture, was inviting in its creature comforts as well as to the eye, as Dolores had decorated with just a few accent items to attract the eye without overcoming the mind. She was scooping up a number of magazines that Craig, with his voracious appetite for reading material, was constantly introducing into the room as a blight upon her efforts at interior decorating, when the telephone rang.

"Hello."

"Dolores, it's Preston."

"Well, hello. It's been some time since I've heard from you!"

"Yes, I suppose it has. Say, I was just calling to ask if you knew where Craig went this morning?"

"Why, he left for the office, same as usual. Hasn't he arrived yet?"

"Well, that's why I called. His car is in the parking lot, but we can't locate him anywhere. I thought maybe something came--"

"No, nothing out of the ordinary that I'm aware of." Dolores's voice betrayed her concern.

"I don't mean to alarm you. Normally I wouldn't have called, only he was working on a rather large project and it was due to the client today--"

"Yes, he was working on it last night, after dinner. He seemed to be relieved that it was finished about eight-thirty last night." Dolores's mind was racing. It was not like her husband to leave Preston in the dark about anything regarding the job.

"Well, I'm sure there's an explanation. I doubt there's anything to worry about. Forgive me if I upset your morning."

"Don't be silly. Like you said, there's probably a good explanation."

"All right, then. Should he check in, uh, do have him call the office, would you?"

"Of course. Good-bye, Preston."

"'Bye, Dolores."

5

Patrolman Tom Morgan laid his head back against the patrol car's headrest and closed his eyes. Just two more day shifts and he would be off for four days. A smile came to his lips as he imagined he and Jennifer, along with Burt Robbins and his girl friend, Sheila, cruising down I-95 towards Myrtle Beach, taking turns driving through the night so they could pack the most fun into those four days. For a month, he and Burt had been writing their motor vehicle summonses so that court appearance dates would be scheduled after the four day break. They had worked out an arrangement with the court clerk that any previous adjournments were to be scheduled outside of that black out period.

His thoughts then turned to the beach, as he imagined Jennifer and her incredible ass, her long, strong legs, and those breasts-to-die-for, all neatly confined by a skimpy bikini. But confinement that was pure freedom compared to the last seven months of concealment in layered protection against New Jersey's cold, wet, windy excuse for winter weather. He had hoped the southern latitude would provide the necessary warmth to guarantee some quality beach time. On the other hand, should the weather turn rainy or chilly, there was always the motel room where he would bang--

"Headquarters to thirteen-Edward," squawked the radio in defiance of his revelry.

Mimicing the dispatcher, Patrolman Morgan erupted, "Oh, for Christ's sake, what now? 'Thirteen-Edward, take the sergeant's car up to the inspection station.' 'Thirteen-Edward, go to the hardware store and have some keys made for the detective's office.' 'Thirteen-Edward, make a coffee run for the brass, two regulars, one dark and sweet.' I hate day shifts." His stress relieved, he spoke into the microphone, "Thirteen-Edward."

"Thirteen-Edward, 47 Nassau Boulevard, offices of Gilmore, Haskins and Cass, complainant Mr. Gilmore, reference a missing person."

"Thirteen-Edward, 47 Nassau, ten-four."

"Well, now, this call has all of the earmarks of a leaky bag of shit," he thought aloud. "Who goes missing at nine thirty in the morning—from a business, no less?"

Morgan preferred the afternoon tour of duty, when police work was more likely to be meaningful. It was the afternoon and early evening when people returned home from work to find their home burglarized, or after a long day at work, turned their frustration towards their spouse or significant other and eventually escalated an argument into a full-blown domestic dispute. Or, if they didn't go home, but went to a tavern, instead, those frustrations could lead to major league bar brawl. Teenagers, freed from a day of being locked in classrooms, would prowl the streets or gather at convenience stores in small groups, and be subject to disbandment and dispersal by the police, only to coagulate again in another corner of town.

Even midnights were better than day shifts. Rare was the midnight shift where anyone holding a rank higher than sergeant was on duty, which meant much less second guessing of a patrolman's decisions. There were the alcohol inspired problems: drunk and disorderly, D.U.I., horrendous traffic accidents. After two in the morning, just about everyone encountered was somewhat suspicious, just because it was after two in the morning. But Morgan would just have to buck up and suffer through these two day shifts before heading south.

Morgan was greeted at the door by Gilmore's secretary who immediately led him into her boss's office. Gilmore quickly briefed the patrolman: Miller's car was in the lot, but no sign of Miller. His wife had reported nothing out of the ordinary. A major project was due, Miller had completed it the previous evening, and his briefcase was visible on the front seat of the car.

Morgan filled in the details for his report, with specific information on Miller easily obtained from his personnel file. He took a quick look into Miller's office, then, accompanied by Gilmore, walked out to Miller's car in the parking lot. As Gilmore had indicated, the briefcase rested on the front seat of the locked vehicle. All appeared orderly, there was no sign of a struggle or hurried carelessness. After retrieving a tool from the patrol car to help him gain entry, Morgan quickly unlocked the driver's door. Upon entering the car, he spotted a set of keys lying on the floor, two of which proved to belong to the vehicle. Checking the contents of the briefcase, he found only the appraisal which Gilmore was clearly relieved to have in his hands. Gilmore carried the report as he followed Morgan and stood looking over his shoulder as he opened the car trunk. Nothing.

"Does Mr. Miller travel for the company?" Morgan asked.

"Yes, but there are no trips planned for the next two weeks."

"Strange. No evidence of foul play. The keys and briefcase were left to be easily found. How valuable is he to your business?"

"He is a very important member of my team," Gilmore replied.

"Important enough to be kidnapped?"

"I don't know who would benefit from that," said Gilmore. "We deal with real estate appraisals, nothing more exotic than that."

6

When Mr. Gilmore's secretary had ushered the police officer into his office, Joan Bartlett left her desk to investigate.

"What's going on?" she asked of the secretary.

"We can't locate Craig anywhere, but his car has been in the lot all morning."

Joan realized that she had not seen Craig either, and recalled how her first sighting each morning always had the same effect on her. Though never more than a glance, Craig's eyes seemed to burn through her flesh on their way to her innermost soul, a feeling she still found discomforting, although it had been a daily occurrence for the last nine months. Then, just as the discomfort reached its peak, a warmth backfilled her body, its source the comfort of knowing how deeply he cared for her, and the countless ways he showed her kindness and respect. Then, as the warmth spread to her head, bringing a tinge of red to her cheeks and ears, she would, again and again, begin to second guess her decision to discourage Craig's amorous advances.

It was late the prior June, when, as one of the firm's three report writers, she had been assigned to work with Craig on a major project that would require some overtime, with the resultant extra pay being a particularly welcome benefit.

"How're those data tables coming along?" Craig had asked, approaching her desk.

"That's all done, except for the numbers you said were going to change," she had responded. This had been her first experience working directly for Craig, and she was eager to make a good impression on a senior manager.

"Roy should be faxing that info in shortly. Were you able to decipher my chicken scratch?" he chuckled.

"Yes, sir. It's not nearly as bad as Jerry's handwriting."

"Please, drop the 'sir'. There are no knights around here, at least not this late in the day." He had said this with a warm smile as he assumed a seat at a neighboring desk. Reclining the back while elevating one foot against a top drawer handle on the desk, he brought his forearm to rest over his eyes to block out the light from the fluorescent lights overhead.

"You look exhausted," she said. "This project is really taking a toll."

Craig raised his arm slightly to peer at her from under it. After a second, he replaced his arm and answered her, "I'm still suffering from a sleep deficit from before my mother's funeral. Every time I think I can afford a day to try to grab some rest, Preston drops another folder on my desk, and I never say no to him; never have."

"I was sorry to hear about your mother. I'd heard she'd been suffering for a long time."

Removing his arm and facing her directly he said, "Thank you. Yes, she suffered for more than a year. Radiation, chemo, drugs, whatever the doctors threw at it, that damn cancer just came back stronger. The worst part was the helplessness. There was nothing she could do to kick the thing. Nothing I could do to ease her pain."

Joan lowered her head and remained silent, symbolic reverence both for the deceased and the suffering of the survivor. Memories of her own loss were revived and she silently contrasted them with what she imagined had been Craig's experiences. While her circumstances had spared her the long period of suffering prior to the finality of death, the suddenness and unexpected nature of her husband's passing had been traumatic and taxing in its own way.

"When my time comes, I hope I go quick," Craig continued. "Stoic suffering, by the victim—and the family—is overrated for its heroic value."

"Be careful for what you pray for. Sudden death stinks, too. Every night I pray that my husband knew that I loved him, that he now hears the good-byes I was cheated from saying."

Craig sat up and turned to face her directly. "That was insensitive of me. I'm sorry for your loss. I shouldn't have assumed that I had a monopoly on grief."

"That's okay. Your loss was more recent. It's natural that it should be a focus."

"How long ago did you lose your husband?"

"Two years ago. A crash with a tractor-trailer on '78. They told me he didn't suffer, it was all so fast."

"Again, I'm sorry."

She had turned back towards her computer screen, but she had nothing to type until Roy's fax arrived. She felt comfortable talking with Craig. Dare she continue? "That morning had been so typical. We had no hint that things were going to change so drastically in just a few hours. You read of people on airplanes that realize something is going wrong, how they make cell phone calls to their spouses. Pathetic as it sounds, I envy them. I wouldn't have anything more to say than 'I love you', but that would have said everything, meant everything."

Craig sat silently, looking at her intently.

Turning again towards him, she continued, "Were your farewells complete? Were they enough? If you don't mind my asking."

"No, I don't mind. It's funny; we had months to prepare, yet we kept putting an optimistic spin on things. Even at the very end, we'd say. 'See you tomorrow,' as if it were something to look forward to. Even my mother was praying 'Take me already!' She was ready. Much more ready than I was."

"You two were close?"

"In our unique way, I guess we were. She was constantly making sacrifices, I was always the beneficiary. It was much more than a debtor-creditor relationship, of course, but it formed the foundation. There came a time when I realized I could never repay her, even if I had three lifetimes. The result was constant devotion at the very end, 'though I realized how tragically late that devotion came."

"I wonder if my kids will be as grateful," Joan grinned, trying to lighten the tone of the discussion.

"How many do you have?"

"Two. Neal is fifteen, Alyssa is twelve."

"The beginning of the difficult years."

"Don't I know it. You have kids?"

"No. No, I don't." Craig's voice almost sounded apologetic. He had resumed his partly reclined position in the chair.

"Their demands are relentless. But they gave my life focus after Steve's death. If I ever started to feel sorry for myself, there was a hockey practice to get to, a dress to buy for an upcoming party, a meal to be prepared.... Funny how kids can both be a primary focus and a distraction at the same time."

"Lately, I could use either one," Craig volunteered, his eyes focused on some distant vision.

"What do you mean?" asked Joan.

Craig redirected his gaze towards her, started to say something before stopping. "Nothing," he said, again looking away.

"I get the feeling it was something."

He returned his eyes to hers, and for the first time she felt uncomfortable. "I'm sorry," she said. "Too used to cross examining my kids. I've gotta learn when to shut up."

"No," he said. "You're right. I'm just not used to having an empathetic ear to talk to. And I guess that's the trouble."

She turned back towards her monitor, but looked down at her hands. She had overstepped her bounds, something she was inclined to do too often.

Craig continued to speak, apparently recognizing no insult. "You know, most of my friends live their lives through, their kids. They spend freezing nights with their sons at Boy Scout camp outs, re-live, again and again, their son's touchdown run, rave about their daughter's exploits clearing jumps riding high aboard a horse at the equestrian academy, or predict glorious academic careers for their straight A students. I listen, recognizing their obvious pride, but not particularly envious. There are, after all, other paths to fulfillment in life, and I believed I was on several of them."

Craig paused, and Joan turned towards him again, no longer feeling uncomfortable as he continued.

"One of those paths, perhaps the most important one to me, is my relationship with my wife. But lately that relationship has been strained, even before my mother became ill, but certainly becoming worse during that illness. Lately, when we try to talk, rather than a sharing experience, it's become a trial of wills, leading to arguments over the least significant issues. But it's not the issue, but the win/lose contest that becomes important. And the more one party 'wins', the more the relationship loses.

"I cannot pinpoint the moment or event that caused us to put on different colored jerseys. But with this competition comes an adversity, an attack, and defending against that attack through defensive postures or counterattacks becomes an increasingly important goal—even more important than the marriage relationship itself."

Craig fell silent and averted his gaze. "Listen to me," he said, "dumping my problems on you as if you don't have enough of your own. I'm sorry."

"If it helps, I don't mind listening," she said.

The look he gave her was intense, as if he were trying to divine the degree of her sincerity. The look she returned was sympathetic.

"Thanks," he said, "but this is something I need to work out on my own."

"I know it's almost a cliché, but have you tried counseling?"

He smiled at her, but she was unsure whether he was amused at her persistence or the platitude contained in her question. "We went to a therapist once. Neither of us was impressed with his approach. We left closer than we had been for months, united in our agreement not to return to see him. But within a few days that unity had worn thin."

"How about with each other, directly and honestly?" she pressed.

"Attempts to discuss our problems are always initiated by me, and become yet another excuse for blame fixing and arguments. I'm afraid Dolores no longer loves me, at least not as she once did. She'll deny it if I ask her directly, but her actions, her reactions, the whole tone of our relationship, says otherwise. So, yes, we have discussed it directly, but I don't believe honestly."

A ringing phone from another room was just audible.

"That has to be Roy faxing over his numbers," said Craig.

So ended the conversation that would be followed by others, and the beginning of a relationship fired by Craig's outpouring of emotion at last reaching a receptive target. Joan had believed that providing an ear to Craig's concerns might be therapeutic to him and perhaps to his relationship with Dolores as well.

Innocently, and with the smoothness that characterized all of Craig's interactions with her, he had taken Neal to a hockey game. The two of them had seemed to click, and she had seen an improvement in the boy's attitude towards school. This was a drastic improvement in his recent behavior, and she was finding she was arguing less with her son than before. She did nothing to discourage Craig from taking Neal fishing or helping the boy with a school project.

But on the day, several months later, when Craig proclaimed that he was certain his concern was augmented by affection for her, she responded with polite but firm rejection. A number of ill scenarios were much more likely than the one possibility for which, if she were honest, she would confess she had a longing. For Craig Miller had crept quietly, ever so softly, into her heart.

Thus Craig's disappearance was of particular interest to Joan, who now kept alert for any news the office grapevine might provide.

7

As Dolores hung up the phone with Gilmore, her anxiety increased. This behavior was very unusual for her husband. He rarely missed work for any reason, and it was very strange that he had not reported a change in plans, an emergency, or any other situation out of the ordinary.

"Ordinary" was the word that defined Craig. A "B" student in college, non-athletic, not artistic, just handy enough to be useful around the house, Craig had taken a routine job at a stodgy firm in a lackluster field and had performed reliably, in an ordinary way. Dolores recalled how her ambitions had been nullified in exchange for a structured life in this modest house in Peach Hill, the most benign of towns. Once again, as she did almost daily, she questioned the wisdom of her decision to marry the well-grounded man who offered her security. The unexplored alternative was the uncertainty, the glamour, and the passion of a career as an actress on Broadway or perhaps, if fate so dictated, in Hollywood films. The bitter taste of regret coated her tongue as she recognized how quickly safety and routine had supplanted desire and a fiery spirit so that even acting in local summer stock productions was now just too much to attempt.

Even now, with the possibility of Craig's disappearance, something, on occasion, she had privately desired if just to force her to rekindle her passion for life, she found herself worrying for his safety. For by extension, his safety helped insure her own, which had become the narcotic which she craved above all else. A safe state of being which allowed her to tolerate a nearly loveless marriage, a routine existence where a flower garden in front of town hall was her ultimate creative invention. With that thought, the doorbell rang, announcing the arrival of the executive committee of the Somerset Garden Club.

8

Patrolman Morgan was feeling uncomfortable. Everything about this Miller disappearance was wrong. First, the victim was not known for unusual behavior. If anything, his boss's descriptions made him sound like the epitome of routine. Yet here he disappears without so much as an "adios" to wife, boss or co-workers. Then there was the way the car was left, everything secured, but plainly visible and easy to retrieve. This part of the disappearance, at least, was premeditated, and since there was no hint of Miller being coerced, the meditations appeared to be his own. Besides, who leaves behind their transportation when they leave? Unless he was picked up by someone. Perhaps a girlfriend, scooping him up in her sports car and whizzing off to the Marriott for an all day tryst? No, based on the way Miller was described, more likely it was a golf buddy coaxing him to play hooky and eighteen holes. But if that were the case, why not just call in sick? Why perk up everyone's antennae and get the police involved in looking for you?

Morgan was reviewing these thoughts as he cruised the vicinity of Gilmore, Haskins and Cass, in ever increasing radii, the small photo from Miller's personnel file on his clipboard for comparison to any pedestrians he might see. Noting nothing unusual, he decided to turn to Mrs. Miller. More often than not the spouse would know or could guess what was going on.

9

Craig Miller descended the stairs from the platform to the dimly lit concourse of Newark Penn Station, walked past the barber shop, newsstand, and coffee shop squeezed between the stairways, past the battery of shoe shine purveyors, and into the main waiting room brightly illuminated by tall windows on two sides. He was about to check the arrival and departure board for the status of the clocker he would take to Washington, but before he could turn around to look, he became aware of the public address system and the announcer's recitation: "...Princeton Junction, Trenton, Philadelphia, Wilmington, Baltimore aaannnd Washington, Train 137 to Washington, Track Number Three, Allll Abooooooard!"

Retracing his steps, he chose the stairway to Track Three, climbing the moving escalator two steps at a time. He reached the platform just as the train, arriving from New York, came to a stop with an open coach vestibule before him. Stepping inside, he was relieved to see an available seat, for frequently these trains left New York full, requiring some to stand until arrival in Trenton. Stowing his valise and overcoat overhead, he took the open aisle seat next to a man, barely out of his teens, wearing a baseball cap on backwards, eyes closed, his body gyrating to the sounds filling his head from the headphones he wore.

Normally Craig would have privately scoffed at the apparent lack of direction of his coach companion. But today he had to question what direction his own life was turning. Sure, he had a ticket to Washington in his pocket, and when he arrived there he would buy another for a nowhere town in an all but forgotten state. But to what purpose? Escape? Escape from what? A marriage where each partner played a routine part so perfectly that there never were any surprises, only the plain vanilla merging of one day into another and another year into one more? Escape from love for another which had become an all consuming passion that continually occupied his mind? A love which was not returned or hardly recognized, which only further drove him to despair?

This last thought returned Joan, front and center into his consciousness, and again forced nearly all other thought processes to switch to automatic mode. Would he be successful in driving her from his mind simply by putting five hundred miles and a mountain range between them? Would she recognize to what lengths his love for her had driven him? Would she feel remorse for having rejected him? Worst of all, would the pain he was trying to avoid fall upon Joan or Dolores as a result of his effort to escape?

10

Assuming the role of hostess to her friends and fellow club members, Dolores had put Craig's disappearance out of her mind rather easily. Perhaps it was the underlying belief that there had merely been an unexplained deviation from Craig's normal routine, and, as Preston had said on the phone, there was a logical explanation that was not worthy of worry. Perhaps it was the excitement of seeing her friends again, and talk of spring plantings and the beauty of blooming flowers that distracted her. But just as the meeting turned from small talk and catching up on local happenings to the formal agenda, the doorbell again summoned her. She opened the door to find a young uniformed police officer on the front porch.

"Mrs. Miller? I'm Patrolman Morgan, Peach Hill Police. I'm investigating your husband's disappearance."

At first surprised, she immediately concluded that Preston must have called the authorities. If he had done so, he must have been truly concerned, and this elevated her concern.

"Oh, yes, please come in," was her response as she opened the door and backed into the foyer.

Morgan removed his hat as he crossed the threshold, slinging its strap over the handle of his holstered sidearm, leaving his hands free to record notes on the clipboard he carried. Glancing at the guests through the living room doorways, he asked, "Is there someplace we can speak privately?"

Dolores nodded and led him through the family room and the sliding glass door to the attached deck. To her guests, "Please excuse me for just a minute, a little business with this officer, nothing to be concerned about."

They sat on benches on the deck, which received direct sunlight at that time of day, and that heat counteracted what little chill was left in the mid-morning air, so that it was quite comfortable even in shirt sleeves.

"I am sure there is good reason for my husband's absence from work," she began. "Surely you must have more important things to do, officer."

"Your husband's boss, Mr. Gilmore was very concerned. He told me that this behavior was totally out of character for Mr. Miller, and in all the years he had worked for him, nothing like this had ever happened before."

Dolores could not argue that fact, and conceded, "Well let me see if I can help you then, so we can solve this 'mystery' and get everything back to normal."

"Do you have any idea where your husband may have gone this morning, Mrs. Miller?" Morgan asked.

"No, as I told Preston, uh, Mr. Gilmore, he left for the office at the usual time, and mentioned nothing out of the ordinary."

"Did he behave normally? Was he upset or distracted in any way?"

"No, everything was normal."

"His car was parked in the office lot, locked, with his briefcase of the passenger seat and the car keys on the floor in front of the driver's seat. Do you have any idea why he would have locked the keys in the car?"

This bit of news surprised Dolores, and she answered hesitatingly, "No, no I don't."

The officer took a deep breath and continued, "Mrs. Miller, there is no polite way to ask this, but I have to ask, please forgive me. How is your marriage, have there been any problems?"

"I understand, officer. No, there is no problem, our marriage is fine. We have been married nineteen years. I don't believe my husband is having an affair, and I think I would know if he were."

Dolores listened to her answer as if it had been spoken by a third party. It sounded so convincing she almost believed it herself. Impulsively she had begun to immediately lie to this police officer, and she questioned why. Shame? Perhaps that was it, although she wasn't sure why she should be ashamed. Her marital relationship was stable—very stable, nearly unchanged in years, certainly no recent changes. Maybe it did not conform to the expectations of the writers of articles for those magazines by the check out counters at the Shoprite, but she and Craig had an understanding, they had a relationship. Not without stress, but one that had weathered years of storms. Besides, her interviewer was young enough to be her son. What right did he have to demand such personal answers from her?

The interview had just begun and already Dolores was feeling uncomfortable with answering the official's questions honestly and openly. She was aware that the patrolman was studying her face. Did she appear calm, did he believe her answers were truthful? How good was he at detecting liars and evaders? Given that about half of the people he spoke to on a given day were inclined stretch the truth, would he realize that she was being less than honest with him?

"How about financial matters? Is his job solid? Any unusual debts recently? Is there a gambling problem?"

Checking the name plate on the officer's uniform, as she had forgotten his name, Dolores answered, "No, Officer Morgan, our financial matters are in order. As for gambling, my husband is not a risk taker, of any kind, believe me."

"What do you mean?"

"Craig has been at the same job for twenty one years. We have lived in this house for eighteen years. Our investments are all mutual funds. We take the same vacation to Maine every summer. No, my husband is *not* a risk taker."

Morgan smiled meekly and continued, "Are there any children?"

"No." Sensing that this answer was insufficient, Dolores added, "Early on we decided to wait to have kids, then as we came to enjoy our lives, just the two of us, we just ..."

Dolores stopped short. She questioned why she was providing this youngster with such personal details, and she was not at all comfortable admitting that her marriage had been nearly sex-free for the last few years, certain that condition would be attributed to her decision, which was not entirely the case. A glance at the police officer's eyes indicated he was waiting for her to end the sentence.

"...and then, we just never had children."

"Okay," said Morgan. Dolores sensed an uneasiness in the officer's manner and was relieved when he channeled the questions in a different direction. "You mentioned mutual funds. Do you and your husband have sizable investments? Anything that might attract someone interested in kidnapping and ransom demands? Again, pardon me for asking, but how much are you and your husband worth?"

"I have no idea," she responded. Craig handles all of the investments. Other than the refund amount, I admit I don't even read the tax returns before I sign them. Let's see, there's the house, of course. Our mutual funds might equal four or five hundred thousand, maybe a little more. As you can see, we live rather modestly. Do you think he's being held for ransom?"

"I don't believe so, Mrs. Miller. There was no evidence of foul play. Still, I'm just trying to cover all the bases. Have you received any threatening letters or phone calls, or anything out of the ordinary lately? Anything that wasn't normal?"

"No, officer, I am sorry. I can remember nothing at all unusual."

"Would you have a recent photograph of your husband I could take with me? If so, I'll be on my way. I will keep you informed of anything I learn during the investigation, and if anything comes to mind you think may be helpful, please call me at the number on this card."

"I will," she said. "There's a photo of Craig in the living room."

She saw the patrolman out and returned to her guests, frantically fabricating a story to downplay why a Peach Hill policeman should be asking her so many questions.

11

Charlie Padula leaned back in the station desk chair, which groaned and creaked in response. Checking the Seth Thomas clock on the wall against the Hamilton watch on his wrist, he acknowledged the conformity of the latter to the former, as required by the rule book, but more importantly was pleased to see that his lunch hour would commence in less than a half hour, a full six hours since he opened the station at six that morning. He began to debate the merits of ordering, once again, the hot pastrami sandwich at Mabel's coffee shop against choosing her too greasy cheeseburger which he ordered on occasion as a change of pace.

Placing his hands behind his head for support, Charlie was comfortable in knowing that the work for the day was complete. His cash drawer was tied out, bank deposit made, ticket sales accounting completed and sealed in the company mail envelope to be handed to the conductor of Train 622, waiting room swept, rest rooms evaluated as "clean enough", and even the freight waybill for Dingbee Manufacturing, the sole railroad freight shipper left in Peach Hill, had been typed up. All that was left before lunch was to "OS" the morning trains, that is, telephone the train dispatcher giving him the departure times and engine numbers of the fleet of passenger trains that passed eastbound and the few westbounds that sneaked back in the opposite direction. Originally designed to give the dispatcher an accounting of where all his trains were at any given time, the "OS" ritual of reporting each train as it passed a station, had morphed on busy commuter lines such as this one, into a collective cataloging of train times to be entered into a computer for the purpose of calculating an on-time percentage for the division. This ratio would in turn be used to justify capital expenditures for the passenger operations, regardless of its absolute value. A low percentage would suggest new equipment was needed to allow for performance improvements, while a high percentage would serve to vindicate the wise judgment of previous investing and justify more of the same.

The dispatcher on duty this morning was known for his lack of patience. He looked forward to receiving Charlie's OS report about as much as Charlie looked forward to providing it, so Charlie continued to lean back in the chair and procrastinate. It was during this interlude that the waiting room door opened and a Peach Hill police officer entered and approached the ticket window. Charlie rose to his feet and greeted the officer.

"' Morning, Tom. Only got one today, LMS-574," Charlie said, providing the license plate of a car in the parking lot which should be exempt from a parking ticket due to unusual circumstances.

"Okay, Charlie, but I'm here on another matter," replied Tom Morgan. Slipping a photograph under the security bars, he said, "Have you seen this fellow here today?"

Charlie looked at the photograph for a few seconds and nodded. "Yessir, he came in this morning. Bought a one-way to Newark on 612. Carrying a good sized suitcase. And I remember, he was wearing a heavy overcoat, which was kinda odd. Imagine wearing an overcoat on a day like today. What'd he do, murder somebody?"

"No, Charlie, this is Peach Hill, remember?" Morgan grinned. "Was he with anybody?"

"Nope, came in by himself, and I remember watching him getting on the last car, the only passenger to walk that far down the platform."

12

The train emerged from the gloom of the tunnel into the bright midday sun bearing down on Baltimore Penn Station. Craig squinted at the glare as his pupils adjusted to the light suddenly pouring in through the coach windows. All the way from Philadelphia thoughts of Joan had occupied his mind, as was typically the case over the last nine months. Her enchanting smile, furtive glances, even images of her preoccupied with her work, unaware that he was watching, all of these images flashed through his mind only to be recycled again. Like back to back reruns of a less than funny sitcom, the images reappeared, yet he never tired of viewing them, as if he were looking for a detail or nuance that he had missed in a previous screening. As the train hurtled southward, ever farther away from Peach Hill, Joan, and Dolores, Craig questioned the wisdom of his decision to flee. What did he hope to find in the mountains of West Virginia? Would he ever be free of the torment of constantly thinking of a love he could not share? Would he soon miss the familiar ease that was his marriage with Dolores? Though now without passion, he could not deny that the relationship had been built on love, and that love, of an intransigent, immutable kind, still existed.

Was this not folly? Running off, without leaving hardly a word, spoken or written, as to why he was leaving, where he was going, what he was seeking, or even what torments he could no longer endure? He had left Dolores with essentially all of their joint assets, taking just enough cash to enable him to establish himself in the new setting. Yet neither would probably see any of his pension money, and he visibly shook his head as he pondered how shortsighted that decision was. In response to near maddening despair, he had, with minimal planning and little more preparations than stuffing a suitcase with a few articles of clothing, abandoned life as he had known it. For someone who had always been so dependably consistent, this inconsistent behavior was a desperate response to a ponderous stimulus, a mental anguish he could not bear to endure. He was not sure what kind of Social Security benefits Dolores would be eligible for under these unusual circumstances. He had asked no one, as there was none he could trust to keep his secret. No, this adventure was more of a reaction to panic than the execution of a plan. For someone not used to panic, this revelation created more panic still.

Taking a deep breath, Craig began to analyze his state of mind. He recognized that he had been frustrated, as perhaps never before. Frustrated with a wife who was devoted, but not loving. Frustrated with Joan, who, though he believed she possessed the solutions to many of his problems, was unwilling to share them with him. Frustrated with a job which offered little in the way of challenge or promise of advancement. Frustrated that the malaise which his life had become was constantly causing him mental torment. Frustrated that work, hobbies, even his books and magazines, were ineffective in diverting him from this torment for anything but the briefest periods. Finally, he was frustrated with his inability to change any of the elements contributing to his condition.

Next came anxiety. Clearly he had chosen a drastic step, to abandon the only type of life he had known, to quickly and completely cut all bindings to that life, leaving him absolutely, perhaps irreversibly, alone. He was anxious about starting a new life from scratch, but not over concerned with being alone. For in that solitude, in his own self-reliance, he hoped to find the freedom to rid himself of the frustrations which had dominated his spirit for the past months.

He realized that the anxiety led to concern. Concern that his wife would not suffer, for although he was disheartened by her lack of reciprocity, he still loved her, and it was the lack of recognition of that love which had initiated the cascading torrents of frustration into his life. Likewise, he had a similar concern for Joan. Although she had denied any emotional attachment, surely there existed some appreciation for him, for if there were none, how could he explain his attraction to her, an attraction which had matured into a state of love and devotion which was only matched by the feelings he had for Dolores so many years ago?

13

"Mrs. Miller? This is Patrolman Morgan, Peach Hill Police."

"Yes, do you have some news?" Dolores asked, her heart seeming to thrust upwards in her throat.

"Yes, ma'am, I do. It seems your husband was seen boarding a train for Newark this morning at the Peach Hill station. He was carrying a large suitcase and wearing a heavy overcoat."

Dolores was speechless, perplexed by this news.

"Would you have any idea where he might be going?" Morgan continued.

"No. No, I don't," she answered, her mind racing to understand where her husband was going and why.

"Well, Mrs. Miller, my witness says he was traveling alone, without coercion. That means this really isn't a police matter any longer. I'm sorry, but there really isn't much more we can do for you under these circumstances. You may want to consider hiring a private investigator...uh, if you want to find him, that is."

"I understand. Thank you, officer," Dolores answered quietly and hung up the phone. Turning to her guests, who had moved from Garden Club business to unrelated small talk, Dolores made the excuse that she had a sudden headache, and asked her guests to kindly leave her to rest, to which they promptly obliged. Dolores went to the bedroom, threw herself across the bed and began to sob.

14

Preston Gilmore returned to his office from lunch, first checking in with his secretary to ask if there was any news regarding Craig. Receiving none, he closed himself into his office, and turned his chair towards the window. He stared out across the fairway of the golf course which was adjacent to his building, with just a small stream separating the properties. This behavior was so unusual for someone as reliable as Miller, so unexpected. How many times had Craig come into the office on the morning of a scheduled vacation day, to be sure that all was in order before he left for the remainder of the day? On the rare occasions when he became sick, he often had to be ordered home because his miserable appearance was disconcerting to other employees and he ran the risk of infecting the whole office.

If Craig were gone for good, Gilmore would have to make some staffing adjustments to carry Miller's weight. He reviewed several candidates mentally, their flaws quickly outweighing their qualifications for consideration. He winced at the idea of hiring a new replacement, the process being onerous, of uncertain outcome, and often demoralizing to other employees who were "passed over."

A telephone call interrupted Gilmore's thoughts. After he hung up, he summoned John Gibbs, his personnel manager, to his office. "John," he said, "I'd like you to schedule a meeting for three o'clock in the conference room. I want Scott, Larry and Bruce there. Have Andy phone in remotely, too. I want to cover Craig's absence, make sure nothing falls between the cracks."

"You don't think Craig's coming back?" Gibbs asked.

"I'm not sure."

"I mean, if he had some kind of emergency—"

"Then we can undo whatever we do pretty quickly. I just don't want to be exposed if this turns into a long-term absence."

"And you think it might?"

"Craig has never acted like this before. Always, and I mean *always*, reliable. The way he left his car, with the keys locked inside, the H&C file finished and accessible—all of this suggested his usual thoroughness. But there was no note, no phone message. That seems to carry a certain finality with it. Now the police tell me he took a train to Newark with a large suitcase. No, our boy has a plan, and he isn't inclined to let us in on it."

"Wow, that's strange. I'll set up the meeting."

Gilmore figured the meeting would layout interim plans until Craig's status was made clear. It would also serve as a proving ground for his managers. Maybe one of them would step forward and demonstrate some promise against the negative vibes he was feeling. He could only hope.

15

Joan Bartlet cleaned her desk in preparation for leaving for the day. Her productivity this day was certainly below par, as she had been preoccupied with Craig's disappearance. The meeting Mr. Gilmore was conducting in "The Fish Bowl", the nickname for the conference room visible to all through the room's glass walls when the blinds were not drawn, was obviously related to the disappearance, based upon the attendees and their demeanor.

The realization that Craig's disappearance was now nine hours solid, and apparently recognized as such by company management, had a strange effect on Joan. She tried to recreate the sensation of warmth that filled her body when she was touched by his kindness. But she had no success. Instead, she felt an all-consuming emptiness, and this feeling was heightened as she considered whether her rejection had led him to his decision to abandon his job, his wife, perhaps his life.

As she drove home, Joan recreated in her mind the procession of events from that evening when she was assigned to work with Craig on a special project, how she was flattered by his concern for her welfare, not only with the firm, but during some personal crises as well. She recalled how she was impressed with his honesty, his goodness, and typical upbeat personality. She continued to suspect that he was involved with an unscheduled salary increase that appeared in her paycheck three months ago, although he had denied it.

Her husband had been dead more than two years now, and she missed him. She missed his smile, she missed his laugh. Most of all, she missed how he held her at night. Her fear of finding someone unable to measure up to what she once had, was greater than her fear of not finding anyone at all. So she had not made herself available, had made no efforts to begin dating again. It was convenient to fall back on the conventional excuses. The children took so much of her time. She wasn't yet ready. She wouldn't know how to begin to look again. Yet many were the nights when she imagined her pillow was her husband's chest, only to leave it tear stained before finally falling asleep.

She recalled Craig's confession of strong feelings for her, and how she had recoiled at the revelation. With her fears on one scale and the positive feelings she had for Craig on the other, the resultant equilibrium led to confusion and a predisposition towards inaction. When she added the fact that he was still married and all the complications that would surely accompany that circumstance, her fears won out. She told him directly, pointedly, and she now confessed to herself, insincerely, that she wanted nothing to do with Craig Miller emotionally.

Arriving home, Joan fished some bills and junk mail from the mailbox. Buried among them was a small envelope. Although it had no return address, she recognized the handwriting as Craig's from the numerous letters he had sent her protesting her decision and pleading for her to reconsider. She dropped the mail to the ground as she ripped open the envelope to reveal a folded note card, which opened to reveal a single word.

"Adieu."

16

When Dolores awoke, the afternoon sun was streaming into the room. At first she was surprised how long and deeply she had been asleep, considering the circumstances. Next, she considered those circumstances. The fact that Craig had left was surprising primarily because Craig was not prone to do surprising things. As she reviewed their interaction over the past few months, she had to objectively conclude that departure of one of the parties was more than understandable. Indeed, she had toyed with the idea, herself.

She recalled a recent incident, perhaps the event that pushed Craig over the line and led him to choose to flee. He had embraced her from behind, burying his face in her hair as he nuzzled her affectionately. She remembered the coldness she felt and the iciness she in turn directed his way as she squirmed out of his grasp. It had not been clear, and was not clear now, why she felt so cold, so empty. What was clear was his frustrated response and verbal thrust, "What is the matter with you?" as he fled the house, not to return until many hours had passed. She could not identify a single action or omission that could be pinpointed as the root cause or turning point in her feelings for Craig. Rather, it was a long gradual malaise, not so much a slide down a slippery slope as much as an oozing, a glacier-like movement that, although nearly imperceptible, nevertheless led to the same unalterable result.

In some of their sparring matches, efforts had been made to affix blame on the other party. During attempts at reconciliation, blame was magnanimously accepted in a thinly veiled attempt to validate the sincerity of the attempt. Now, in the clarity of hindsight, isolated from her partner who could neither argue against her nor be the target of sympathy seeking gestures, Dolores was prepared to shoulder the responsibility for the failure of her marriage. Clearly she was the first to abandon efforts of reconciliation, whether failing to take action for her sake or dissuading Craig's efforts on numerous occasions.

The lamentable truth was that Dolores could not rationally justify why she had permitted failure to evolve. She had feelings of inadequate fulfillment, it was true, but she had no one in mind who could replace Craig as a substitute, someone capable of improved performance. But he was gone now, and the silence that filled the house screamed at her about her failure. The loneliness sucked away her self-righteousness. She dare not gloat that her stubbornness was responsible for his surrender, her victory. Like a chess player on the run after a surprise move nixed confident plans of checkmate in three, Dolores was flailing about. She desperately sought some indication that happiness was awaiting, improvement in her plight was achieved. Instead she saw that as mundane as the status quo seemed, it was much preferable to such a complete and drastic change.

17

"Charlottesville. Charlottesville is next," the trainman announced as he passed through the car.

Craig had been lulled into a peaceful state of mind by the train's gentle climb into the Piedmont and by a satisfying meal from the dining car to which he had repaired immediately upon boarding No. 1 in Washington. The mad dash of the clocker within the city limits of Megalopolis had ended at the nation's capital, where Craig had changed to a train which understood the southern heritage of its route, and proceeded at a more dignified, relaxed gait. The slight climb to Charlottesville served to reinforce this attitude, almost to suggest that the train was pacing itself for the upcoming climbs over the Blue Ridge and then the Alleghenies.

The station announcement served to jerk Craig back to full consciousness, and he consulted the schedule he carried inside his sport coat, comparing it to his wristwatch. He also became painfully aware of an infant riding the lap of his mother three seats behind him, a child who was not enjoying the ride, but was crying loudly despite the protestations of his mother, who eventually tired of trying to calm him and, thus resigned to the situation, allowed him to bawl.

Craig considered approaching the child in an attempt to calm him. Often the novelty of a stranger's interest had been enough to throw off an upset child and quiet him—at least for a time. But aboard this train the child might feel uncomfortable, as might the mother by unsolicited overtures from a stranger. No, the safer course of action was to remain detached, just like the mother, and hope that the child soon runs out of steam.

It was then that she arrived, front and center in his mind, crowding out most other thoughts, just as she had in nearly every waking hour for the past few months. It was Joan, appearing as usual, a visage no different than he had seen her countless times at her desk, often smiling, occasionally pitching her head to launch her red curls from in front of her eyes, but always, *always*, just beyond Craig's physical grasp and outside the boundaries outlined by strong emotional bonds. As often as she had appeared Craig reasoned that he should have become comfortable with this ghost of the apparently unobtainable, but despite the frequency, each appearance attracted his undivided attention. But not tonight. No, he would cast her aside.

He turned to the window and searched the darkness for a focal point as the train came to rest for the station stop. As he was on the side of the train opposite the station platform, his was a commotion-free view of a brick freight house sitting fifty yards off in the distance. During Woodrow Wilson's administration the structure was probably a center of activity at all hours of the day and night. But tonight its doors were padlocked, and the only light associated with the structure were two security lamps to deter thieves from seeking out whatever stores the railroad had stockpiled inside.

Craig studied the brickwork which was especially ornate for such a utilitarian building. High brick arches rose over each of the numerous doors that opened toward the rail siding adjacent to the freight house's long side. Such craftsmanship was not uncommon for the era, in contrast to today when concrete blocks would be employed to rapidly and efficiently define the structure without a thought as to aesthetics.

How many masons had labored under a mid-summer Virginia sun to build this practical monument to support the premier industry of the time? Had this been their finest hour, the pinnacle of their professional careers? How long had they expected their creation to last? Would they be surprised that less than three quarters of a century after its completion, the structure created by their efforts would stand not only unused, but would stand in the way of developing this prime downtown real estate into yet one more strip mall with its boutique, pizzeria, convenience store, bank and donut shop, just like four other strip malls within walking distance?

The apparition appeared again. Her lips were silent, but her eyes held questions for Craig, which his mind verbalized: So what was the pinnacle of *his* professional career? How could he identify a pinnacle upon a salt flat of consistent, repetitive, uniform achievement? Which valuation of which strip mall had he identified as his masterpiece in his two decade career? Having achieved his ultimate success, he begins an impromptu retirement aboard a series of trains moving deliberately towards....nowhere? Joan was laughing now, and turning on her heel, just as she had on that fateful day when she had delivered the forceful blow of rejection, her red-orange tresses moving with the momentum of her turning head, wiping away the view of her face as she walked away.

Only this time, she turned her head back to look over her shoulder, stopping for a moment to continue the mockery: What's that you say? Work is just a means to an end? What end might that be? The pursuit of happiness? Possibly even its capture? So tell me, are you pursuing it now aboard this daily accommodation? Or have you captured happiness? Is it locked up there in that sorry suitcase over your head? Or are you just a pathetic fugitive trying to escape not from one, but two failed love affairs? With that indictment, the lovely Joan's unrivaled smile transformed into a ghostly, snarling laugh, the sight of which was to Craig like a biting wound to the marrow of his bones.

18

The sound of the phone ringing broke out of the receiver. After six rings, that familiar voice, which might sound gruff to the untrained ear, spoke a flat "hello", which was promptly followed by the high-pitched whistle of feedback from the man's hearing aid.

"Hold on a second. Let me go to the other phone," he said, now clearly annoyed. As he lay down the receiver his voice could be heard trailing off in the distance, "Confounded thing. They can put a man on the moon but...."

"Hello," he said again a few seconds later, this time more resigned.

"Hi, Daddy."

"Dolores! I was just thinking of you! How are you?"

"Not so good, actually. Craig left me."

This matter of fact summary was met by silence from the other end. After a brief pause the man continued, "Left you? You guys had an argument?"

"Not really," Dolores responded. "He just packed up and left, without a word."

"That doesn't sound like Craig. Are you sure? Maybe he's away on business."

"No, Daddy. Craig left the car and a project for work at the office. Gilmore called the police. The police said he caught a train for Newark, carrying a big suitcase. He's gone. I know it."

Silence followed as the father digested the news. A moment or two later he spoke again, "I'm sorry, baby. Have you two been having problems?"

"Not really. No more than usual. Things haven't been good for some time. I haven't been happy. *We* haven't been happy. Not that we necessarily fight or argue, but we just don't agree like we used to, we spend time apart, even when we're together. But I didn't expect this." She paused briefly before continuing, "But you know, Daddy, when I realized what happened, I didn't find it all that surprising."

"Babe, I'm so sorry. Do you want me to come up there? I could be on a plane first thing tomorrow morning."

"No, I'm fine. I mean, there's nothing I need for you to do

here. Just knowing that you are there to talk to, that's important. Let me see how things go. If I need to get away from here, maybe I'll fly down to Boca and stay with you for awhile."

"You're always welcome, you know that." He added, "Craig's a pretty smart fellow. I wouldn't be surprised if he came back to you, hat in his hand. If he's as smart as I think he is, it won't be long before he does."

"I don't know, it seemed pretty final, like he had made up his mind for good. If he came back, I'm not sure what I'd do."

"You need to be ready for that possibility. Decide what you want. If you want to take him back, accept his apology and move on. Don't dwell on the past too much. Seek common ground and build for the future. History can be informative, but once you've identified a course of action to avoid, it does no good to mire yourself in all the reasons it should be avoided."

"I know what you're saying makes sense. It's just so hard to think rationally about something like this. I know I have to decide what I want, something I haven't had to worry about for years. I'm going to concentrate on that decision in the next few days."

"Don't be bashful about asking for help—from friends, professionals, and me, of course."

"I hear you. You've been helpful already. Thank you. I love you."

"I love you, too. Call me anytime."

19

Guilt boarded the train in Staunton, and occupied Craig's seat. What had he done? What had he been thinking? To abandon his wife to whom he had pledged a lifetime commitment, a vow made before God, family and friends, was a failure of character of a magnitude that he had never before approached.

Speaking as his own defense counsel, Craig detailed his justifications. The marriage was over, by her hand, not his. How many times had his gestures of true affection been rejected? How often had Dolores failed to uphold her side of the commitment, to sexually consummate and thereby renew and strengthen the bonds that were to hold him? What of truth? Who benefits from the living of a lie? His departure had been an honest, liberating act, not only for himself but for his wife as well. She was now free to seek whatever it was that he could not provide, and hopefully find the happiness which he repeatedly failed to supply. Finally, how prudent is it to expect, much less to make, promises of servitude that remain inflexible while everything and everyone else changes over time? How naïve to expect a couple with little or no practical experience to adopt a set of vows that will rule their lives far into the murky future without anticipating changes and adaptations despite abundant evidence that such modifications will be required?

But Guilt, as the prosecutor, pressed his case. Craig's justifications were nothing but excuses for his own weaknesses, his feeble commitment, his failure to articulate and make understandable his feelings of love for Dolores. To the extent that those feelings were valid, they were called into question by a mid-life fling, a high risk pursuit of the younger Joan. Now, after making a mess of things on two fronts, the coward skips town so as not to have to face and recognize his failings and certainly to avoid the consequences which reasonably would follow.

Lies! The defense's objection was vehement. He had been and continued to be faithful to Dolores. Joan represented not a "fling" or passing fancy, not some treat from a dessert cart plucked for its freshness or sweetness. His feelings for her were primarily feelings of compassion, isolated and apart from an animalistic sexual yearning. If truth be known, Dolores, the former actress, possessed the extra points in the beauty, erotic and pleasure potential categories. To characterize his actions and motives in such a way cheapened the love he possessed but was frustrated in demonstrating. It suggested motives that were not seriously in play and ignored motives that were honorable and sincere but hardly appreciated by anyone but himself.

Precisely correct! Guilt rejoined the attack. You are the only one with appreciation for this situation because you are the sole intended beneficiary of your actions. It is selfishness. It is about you: first, last and always.

Then pray explain why my misery mounts with each mile I put between me and Peach Hill.

20

The train charged into the night, firmly guided by the rails which followed the route carefully laid out by engineers twelve decades before. Staring out the coach window, Craig became mesmerized by the undulating topography near the tracks. At times the ground would rise high above the train as the tracks entered a cut, only to fall again, this time far below the rails which rode an earthen fill. Never ending, an army of telephone poles marched along in single file, rising and falling with the terrain in a measured gait. Often a road would parallel the railroad, and the train would overtake an automobile, but not before its occupants, silhouetted against the blurred background speeding by, could be observed, appreciated for their anonymous familiarity, and then left behind, transformed simply into two headlights, rising and falling with the road.

In the foreground, glaring rectangles of light projected from the coach's windows would dash along at the speed of the train, sometimes clinging to the ballast along the rails, only to dash to the jagged wall of a rock cut, then back to the ballast, SPLASH!--a quick dip into a meandering stream, WHAM!--the up close and personal attachment to the sides of a box car resting on a siding, then back to the relative calm of skipping along the ballast again.

Craig mused how his life was like that solid earth that followed the tracks, rising and falling, offering alternatively triumph and depression, opportunities and regrets. Further, he smiled to himself as he recognized the fleeting coach window lights as symbols of his personal reactions to all that life had presented him. He recognized how, especially lately, he had dashed about from one extreme to another, bouncing off the hard surfaces of rejection, being swallowed by the mushy contours of the comfortable.

Occasionally, a farm house would be passed sitting off in the middle distance. More often than not, a porch light would be burning, or perhaps a mercury vapor lamp high on a pole in the back yard, giving definition to the details of an otherwise shadowy dwelling. This driveway is occupied by a pickup truck, still warm from its recent return from the local tavern, where its owners had drunk beer to wash down the reality which was their lives, only to take to the dance floor for a ceremonial public affirmation of that very reality. The truck would be ready for tomorrow's sojourn into town for needed supplies, the broadcasting of gossip acquired from the tavern the previous evening, and, perhaps, if luck were to allow it, a pocket knife swap in the shadow of the court house so that pearl handled beauty which had been coveted for so long might finally change hands. At this next house, the porch light spotlights a pair of clay laden boots resting right where they had been removed, their owner too exhausted after a day of early plowing with a stubborn mule to do anything more than kick them off and hobble to the supper table. Here, at this home, a tethered hound dog, restraining chain drawn taut in the direction of the passing train, barks incessantly at the intruders aboard this vehicle which passes by nightly, although his protests were unheard by the isolated passengers this night, as they were every night.

Through these vignettes of Americana Craig passed, his cupped hands against the glass to shade the glaring coach lights and improve his view of the passing scenes. But overlaying his thoughts on the subjects outside the window, were the all too familiar thought patterns, whose rhythms had been pounded into his mind like a street beat for an endless parade. Once again, the theme was rejection.

It was curious what memories popped into his head. How minor incidents foretold major calamities. He remembered the earrings, purchased for her birthday several years ago.

"I hope you like them," he had said, handing Dolores the small gift-wrapped box.

"Oh, nice," she had said, closing the box after viewing them briefly.

"I thought you'd love them. They're not too big, too showy. I thought they're pretty elegant."

"They're nice," she said, emphasizing the repeated word. For an actress, she wasn't playing this part very well.

"Look, we can return them, get something else you might like more."

"No, they're fine." Her eyes were focused on the gift in her hand, making no contact with his eyes.

"Dolores, is something wrong?"

"No, nothing. Come on. We'd better get going or we'll lose our reservation."

And so she had put a chill on the evening before it had begun. They were just a stupid pair of earrings. But he had spent time—a considerable amount of time, given his distaste for shopping—and he had hoped his thoughtfulness would be more appreciated.

Later he would remember the passive rejection of his amorous advances, and finally the hours of silence which characterized their quality time together.

Attempts to discuss the rift in their marriage were, alas, also met with rejection, as Dolores would typically respond in a barely audible voice that he did not understand, punctuated with her leaving the room, even locking herself in a bedroom were he to press further, remaining there until the subject was dropped.

Had he been a fool to stay with her under these circumstances? Had she been signaling that she was through with him, that it was time to move on? Had his stubbornness, his pride, forced him to remain in an unhealthy situation?

Or had he given up too easily? Had he exhausted all possibilities? Most disconcerting, although he felt he loved Dolores as much as he always had, had something been lost? Some spark or other element of combustion missing, which, by its absence, permitted acceptance of a coexistence with progressively less and less manifestations of the love they once shared? When these questions could not be categorically answered, as they never could be, came the follow up question with its associated guilt and remorse: Had his failure to go the distance with Dolores resulted in his seeking solace with Joan?

With this turn of the analysis, the drum beats moved from the persistent reverberations of the snare drum to the beat-setting preponderance of the bass drum and the thunder roll of the timpani. For it was the new love of Joan, the full frontal direct rejection with which she countered that love, and the inescapable obsession that plagued him afterwards that had pervaded his life for the past months. Finding not solace, but yet more rejection, Craig wondered how close he had come to madness, for surely the obsession—the relentless invasion of thoughts of her into his consciousness several times in every waking hour—surely this was not sanity. When the obsession had led to compulsiveness, Craig knew that drastic measures were called for.

This was the ultimate rejection: the rejection of his entire life as he had known it. A rejection of Dolores and the promises he had made to her. A rejection of Joan, and whatever promise she possessed. A rejection of career, income, savings. All replaced by a railway ticket, a few articles of clothing stuffed in a tired valise, a few thousand dollars in his pocket, and whatever promise the impoverished state of West Virginia had to offer.

21

Sarah Stiles stared past Eb Jordan's animated gesturing at the large cross hanging on the wall above his left shoulder. Though clean, modern and sanitized in the Protestant tradition, Sarah nonetheless visualized the life-sized crucifix that she remembered from the Catholic mass she had attended with a friend years ago. The suffering Jesus that she envisioned looked down sympathetically at the minister as he attempted to impress his congregation, roughly half of the church-going residents of Walsh, West Virginia, with the import of his words. The wooden sculpture's unwavering gaze, while seeming to sanction the ministry, nevertheless had no more reaction to the worship service than Sarah's wandering mind.

She vividly remembered the outstretched limbs down to the delicately carved extremities. Surely artistic license, she thought, as no carpenter she had ever known possessed such fragile fingers. Certainly Frank had not. She closed her eyes to more clearly imagine the Christ's face, focusing on the eyes with a strained intensity. What was His will? What was His purpose in introducing such drastic changes to her life? When would her suffering be complete and a new stage of her life begin, a stage where hope would replace despair, and she might again find some happiness?

"The Lord be with you."

"And also with you!"

Sarah turned to her right to receive a smile from Kay, who, with her nearly mute husband Sam, had made it a point of sitting with her at every Sunday morning service since Frank's funeral. Sarah truly appreciated the sincerity of Kay's intentions, but was coming to realize that Kay's unwavering devotion was helping to solidify her status as forlorn widow, a state she was finding difficult to escape even on better days.

22

Craig was jolted awake by two firm thrusts on his shoulder from the conductor's hand.

"Walsh in ten minutes, sir" he whispered.

"Oh, yeah, right, thank you," was Craig's confused reply.

He had fallen asleep faster and deeper than he had expected. The infant towards the rear of the coach had finally stopped the wailing that had begun a few miles out of Washington. Craig had slept through the station stops since Clifton Forge, despite the car knockers' insistence in communicating only with shouting voices. He had also been oblivious to the fact that passengers getting on and off the train did so with little regard for those who were trying to get some sleep. These annoyances were overpowered by the rhythmic rocking and hypnotic rolling as the train weaved its way through the creases in the mountains of West Virginia. Checking his watch, Craig noted that the train had added ten more minutes to the tardiness it had acquired by the time it had pulled into Charlottesville.

Craig donned his overcoat, retrieved his valise from the overhead rack, and made his way to the vestibule. The conductor, who long ago had been convinced that coach step traps were worthy opponents that could only be subdued by brute force, was dramatically applying that principle with an inordinate amount of noise as the train lurched again in response to a second brake application as it began to slow for the station stop. Victorious once again, the conductor descended the steps his battle had revealed, swinging to the ground as the train groaned to a halt to commence Train Number 1's westbound station stop at Walsh, West Virginia. After helping a frail woman of advanced years traveling with three large suitcases, the conductor admonished Craig to "Watch your step."

Reaching the platform, Craig's nostrils were immediately greeted by the pungent odor of urine that had been discharged contemporaneously with his dismount. The contents of the coach's commode had been emptied onto the tracks, as one of his fellow travelers of just a moment before apparently failed to understand the sign posted in the lavatory forbidding such discharge while the train was sitting in a station. The other disembarking passengers were quick to leave the platform to move towards their final destination. But Craig, lacking such a definitive goal, lingered. By the stark light of a few bare bulbs along the platform, Craig took stock of the conveyance which had transported him safely to Walsh. Twin diesel locomotives chanted impatiently awaiting their call to assault the mountains and skim over the flatlands again. Directly behind the engines, the baggage car was a source of its own commotion as two employees muscled a tall crated object clearly of considerable heft. Next, the sleeper, worthy of a name, and wearing "Allegheny" on its flank, was an island of peace in the sea of hustle and bustle that constituted the 3:15 am station stop. Its occupants doubtlessly were relishing air conditioned comfort, crisp linens and light wool blanket in their private accommodations as they dreamed until daybreak. A reading lamp from one roomette revealed one traveler who was clearly awake, the nature of his business tomorrow in Cincinnati being such that there was no point in even turning down the bed, as sleep would not come. Smartly attired in full uniform, the car's porter stood at the ready by the open trap in the event one of his charges chose to step off for a minute to catch some early morning air or a last minute passenger should arrive holding documentation that he had acquired passage in Bedroom C. The porter's black hands, finger tips stained a little blacker by shoe polish, would resume the work of polishing the sleeping passengers' shoes once No. 1 resumed its journey. Next came Craig's coach, and two more like it, presently disgorging passengers who found the Walsh depot to be the closest of the railroad's destinations to their own while swallowing up those who had chosen to forsake the small burg for bigger or better locales. Lastly, the dining car, lights now dimmed as last call for dinner had been more than six hours prior, punctuated the train with fluted stainless steel elegance. In two hours, the cooks and waiters now catnapping in the booths, would begin to prepare eggs, hotcakes, sausage and grits so that all so inclined would be braced for the new day with stomachs well filled.

    Craig saw all of this, not just as a current example of reliable, practical, and often romanticized transportation, but also as the conveyance to the next chapter in the book that was his life. That story seemed to spread across a very few chapters, and he feared, with too little depth. Now he was beginning a new chapter, perhaps even a whole new book. Although the setting was of his choosing, he felt that he would have very little control over the plot, the characters he would meet, the final outcome.

Once again he questioned his choice of West Virginia, and Walsh, in particular, as the stage for his drama. He recalled the desperation that he had felt as his emotional world crumbled around him, be it the loss of his last significant blood relative with the death of his mother, the long term stagnant state of his marriage, the dreariness of his eight-to-five job, the face-forward free fall of his relationship with Joan. To end it all, cut all ties, sever all bonds—that was his goal. Was he suicidal? No. For that end he felt no affinity. As frightening as this little Appalachian town might be, it lacked the ultimate finality of death with its added layer of unknowable mystery. Another train ticket could return him to the life he felt was unbearable, should this new life prove more unbearable still. A different ticket could forward him and his minimal belongings to Maysville, Kentucky, Hamilton, Ohio or Dyer, Indiana, or beyond. Objectively, and with no sentimentality, he understood that he was too much a coward for suicide.

Instead, he had sentenced himself to a kind of purgatory, a waiting room before the next examination. There he would sit, as naked as decency laws would allow, and await the next crashing blow or uplifting tailwind that Fate would bestow. The purging of his past life would be as complete as possible. He carried some wealth, but it was finite, with no ready source of replenishment. He had his emotions, as diced and scrambled as they were, but he remained tethered, as symbolized by the wedding band remaining on his ring finger, to the commitment to a relationship in principle, if not in presence. He had his wits, but with no known history, would need to establish new credibility at every turn. And he had his sense of rightness, bumper posts against which moral collisions would release their kinetic energy along a truer vector toward the ultimate good. It was along such a path that he believed this passenger train had carried him.

As the baggage car door rolled shut, the porter retreated up the steps of "Allegheny", and the conductor waved his signal forward to which the locomotives responded with amplified throbbing and steady acceleration, Craig sensed the loneliness of his isolation, a continuation of the loneliness he had felt back home. As the silver snake, reflecting moonlight from its fluted flanks, glided around the curve and its glowing red markers disappeared from view, Craig felt the emptiness of abandonment and the icy chill of being alone.

Entering the brick station, Craig was aware of the disparity between design and function. Built to accommodate four times the number of trains calling at Walsh today and eight times the number of patrons, the depot's excess capacity was being left undisturbed as much as possible. The baggage room had been converted to storage years ago, and whatever had been stored inside had not been needed for nearly as long, so that the room was all but sealed. The waiting room was crisscrossed with paths from the doorways to the ticket window. The tile floor not included in the thoroughfares was dusty, with detritus accumulating in the corners, having not been seriously cleaned in nearly ten years. Where a mop had contacted the floor in recent days, its visitation had been brief, confined to the walkways and along the four wooden benches which afforded waiting passengers their only alternative to standing. Clearly the janitorial staff had replaced a quest for excellence with a more lax philosophy.

The agent was securing his office for the night since No. 1's departure marked the end of his time on duty. Once the lone passenger in the waiting room made his exit, the agent could lock the doors until his return later that morning in anticipation of No. 2's arrival from the west. Sensing his imposition upon the agent's planned departure, Craig purchased a canned soft drink from the vending machine and left by the door opposite the one he entered and began to walk around the building back towards the tracks.

Adjacent to the station's east side, a stub siding parallel to the main line was occupied by a lone maintenace-of-way camp car. As the track maintenance season was several weeks in the future, the away from home sleeping quarters for section hands was continuing its winter hibernation, a fact confirmed by the rusty railheads and the windblown rubbish that had accumulated along the tracks indicating that the car had not been moved for at least two seasons. With a few furtive glances, Craig confirmed that his presence was not being observed, and quickly stashed his valise under the car near a wheel. Thus freed of that burden, he was set to begin his exploration of this Appalachian town.

The primary highway artery, bearing the unoriginal appellation of "Main Street", snaked down the mountain to the east, paralleled the railroad through town, then made a straight and direct assault on the first hill to the west. Main Street was lined with the typical commercial establishments, most of which were closed and dark at this early hour. Two banks stood directly across from the station, separated by Depot Street, which terminated at its namesake. Adjacent to the First National Bank stood the U.S. Post Office, while the Bank of West Virginia shared a wall with Kaufman's, where local residents could purchase rugged work clothes, or if funds were available, a fine suit to wear to the church whose floodlit spire pointed heavenward two blocks east. Craig also noted Carol's Diner and Degnan's small grocery store in the heart of the commercial district, which would prove useful before the sun was too high in the morning sky. Interspersed throughout the commercial blocks were empty stores, their empty windows like missing teeth in a poorly cared for mouth. Those structures, as well as those occupied by going concerns, in most cases were run down, were in need of paint, or in some other subtle way reflected hard times.

Streets parallel to Main bore the last names of early American presidents as well as that of Benjamin Franklin, who, while not presidential, was revered enough by early town fathers so as to be included not too distant from the street named for the Father of His Country and certainly before the likes of Madison and Monroe. Perpendicular to the statesmen ran the streets named for indigenous trees, with the only exception being the previously mentioned Depot Street which helped delineate the important role the railroad played in Walsh's development.

Last to be mentioned, though first to enter this valley, the Sweetbriar River, whose gentle grade the railroad engineers had followed as they constructed trackage westward. This usually peaceful stream served as the centerline of the valley, and was crossed via substantial bridges by Chestnut, Willow and Oak streets. Maple Street had crossed it as well, until a flood some years past, after which it was decided that barricading the roadway on the abutments where the bridge had stood was the most economical course of action.

Pocketing the canned drink he had purchased, Craig crossed the river on the Chestnut Street bridge, then proceeded to walk the length of each east-west street in alternate directions as he stair-stepped his way up the valley wall. Washington and Jefferson Streets, (President Adams having been excluded from this memorial of American presidents), were nearly of the same elevation, while

Franklin, Madison and Monroe Streets required increasingly steeper climbs up Chestnut or Willow. Property lots became progressively shallower, with less land suitable for establishing yards. The houses on these lots seemed to hold more perilously to the hillside than the residences on the street below.

    Craig's footsteps echoed softly from the sidewalks, one of the few sounds of the night. Midway down Franklin Street, the hoot of a horned owl burst forth from the otherwise silent canopy. Occasionally a truck would grind downgrade into town, storm under the coal conveyor extending over east Main Street, hiss to a stop at the traffic light in the center of town, grumble into motion when the light changed, and then make a charge for the hill on the opposite end of town from which it came. These andante movements would be intermixed with little mazurkas performed by the town's sole police patrol car as it would race from one end of town to the other, then tiptoe down a residential street before roaring onto Main Street again for another boastful display. Footsteps, owl, truck, police car-- otherwise the town was silent.

    After the rather exhausting climb up Willow Street between Franklin and Madison, Craig leaned against a substantial oak tree and drank his soda. While he drank, he reflected upon what his walk thus far had disclosed. Walsh was a tired town, whose boom had come and gone with the success of the local coal mines. The modest one family homes that he had passed were in various states of disrepair. A few lacked only a "CONDEMNED" sign to make them totally unsuitable for human inhabitation. Most were apparently unashamed of a major ailment--a sagging roof here, a disconnected porch there, crumbled steps, tarp covered repairs-no-longer-in-process, "temporary" bracing which had as much chance of fulfilling its mission in the next two years as it had during the last two. Interspersed amongst these dwellings were the occasional homes where pride of ownership was still very evident. Craig wondered what sacrifices had been made--forgone vacations, fewer meals out, more modest Christmas celebrations--to finance these nearly futile investments in real estate. Clearly the lack of commercial vitality in the center of town was not only evident there, but also in the residential section originally built to support it.

    Returning the empty can to his pocket, Craig faced uphill, deciding to skip Madison and get the climb behind him now, while he was refreshed. The street light a block ahead indicated that Willow extended no further than the next street up, which, predictably, was named for the fifth president. Not long after passing the intersection of Maple and Monroe, Craig spotted one of the objectives of this early morning search. In a first floor window of a modest home bearing the number "43", back lit by a table lamp, was a simple hand-lettered sign, "Room for Rent."

    Built practically into the hillside, the two story building was reached by mounting a set of stairs prior to reaching the three steps to the short veranda. To the left of the porch , the house featured two bay windows, one above the other, beneath a front facing roof gable. On the right side of the building, over the front entrance just above the porch roof, a small upstairs window looked out onto the street. The house siding was a pale yellow, discernible from the porch light burning next to the front door. Overall the structure was in good repair, altough a section of gutter had become detached from the roof, and hung at an arrogant angle from its remaining roof attachment into space.

    Craig took all of this in approvingly. His needs were simple, and this dwelling should serve them adequately, provided its inhabitants were as accommodating. Now, with the first light of day beginning to infiltrate the night sky, Craig descended the hill back towards the commercial center of town, in search of a breakfast to satisfy the hunger that the night of hill climbing had fueled.

23

Carol Wilson scraped the sausage patty off the grill and flipped it to reveal the solid black scorched side, the source of the smoke that had caused her to run back to the kitchen. With flip of the spatula she threw the patty into the garbage pail, replacing it with another slice. She couldn't afford such waste of both time and meat. She was tired and the day had barely started. She felt another headache coming and she longed for the simple pleasure of sitting down, a pleasure she must delay until her husband arrived hours from now.

When the bells on the entrance door rang, she looked up to see Dave entering. She grabbed the container of batter and began to pour three flap jacks onto the grill, anticipating his usual order. Using her forearm to brush some stray hair out of her face, Carol quickly wiped her hands before heading back to the dining room to confirm Dave's order.

The sudden departure of Billy, the cook, had thrown the operation of Carol's Diner into a barely controlled tailspin. Carol was attempting to go it alone, but it was a precisely timed ballet with a quick tempo that kept her dancing from dining room to kitchen. Mistakes, like the overcooked sausage patty, were happening more frequently.

Every time Carol was reminded of the situation Billy had created, she cursed him aloud. Even as bad as things were at Carol's Diner, her situation was better than that of Billy's wife and three young children. Billy had abandoned them when he blew out of town following the discovery by his wife of his indiscretions with a young girl not yet out of high school.

24

The air was laden with the smell of fried pork fat as Craig approached the diner. The lights from inside caused the establishment to glow, almost like a beacon, as it was about the only business open in Walsh at this early hour. Through the door, Craig could see about a dozen of the town's denizens occupying about half of the available seating, being served by a single waitress in her late thirties. Her nearly spotless white apron coordinated well with the piping on her salmon colored uniform, her shoes, and the clasp that held her auburn hair tightly against the back of her head. The dining area was buzzing with conversation. Although most of the patrons were seated singly at tables or in booths, most were engaged with fellow diners seated nearby. These repartees were accented by spirited joking and interjections from the waitress, who appeared comfortable with those she served.

All of this came to an abrupt halt, however, as Craig crossed the threshold. All eyes in the room turned towards him. Clearly an intrusion by an outsider was a matter of such novelty as to be of interest to the group. Striding deliberately towards the counter, Craig took a seat at the end opposite the cash register, where a police officer sat finishing his coffee. Once he was seated, the conversations resumed, the stranger having been accepted as such, although Craig was aware that the policeman was giving him a sidelong review from head to toe.

The waitress darted towards the kitchen, throwing a question in his direction over her shoulder as she passed, "Coffee?"

"Tea, please," Craig responded.

The door to the kitchen was propped open by a large bag of flour, and Craig could observe the waitress tending the grill. Momentarily she returned, drew a cup of hot water, and placed it, a tea bag, and a menu in front of him, and then returned to the grill to plate some pancakes and bacon. In the short time Craig scanned the menu and made his selections, the waitress made four changeovers between server and cook, finally returning to him.

"What can I getcha?"

"Two eggs, over light, white toast," he responded.

"Coming right up, " she said.

"You seem a little short handed," Craig offered.

"Yeah, my morning cook left me kind of sudden. Haven't found a replacement yet."

She spun around and entered the kitchen to put his eggs on the grill and plate another order.

The policeman rose to leave, calling into the kitchen as he did so, "Thank you, Carol." Then, as he passed the stranger, he again scanned him from top to bottom, giving him a slight nod and the briefest of smiles. Craig was not particularly uncomfortable with this scrutiny. Certainly he was doing nothing that would require police intervention. No doubt this was the same officer who had patrolled the streets a few hours earlier, but who, as far as Craig knew, had not seen him performing his own foot patrol south of the river. Still, the look served to remind Craig that this was a small town, where the locals knew one another, and where the stranger was quickly identified as such.

Craig took a sip of tea and felt its warmth as it moved down his throat. From over his left shoulder, the voice of a patron stood out from the ambient noise as he proceeded to tell a lengthy joke to the waitress, who had returned to the dining room to clear a table. Glancing into the kitchen, Craig saw a cloud of smoke billowing over the grill.

"Whoa!" he shouted as he jumped off the stool and ran into the kitchen. Grabbing a spatula, he scooped up a burning mass of blackened matter, some of which could be identified as having once been grated potatoes while another part was The waitress appeared, slightly bewildered that a stranger was in her kitchen, embarrassed with her failure to perform two jobs, but appreciative that he had taken corrective action. Cautiously, she offered thanks for his actions.

"What do you say I help you through breakfast this morning?" Craig offered. "I was a cook while in the National Guard, so I have some experience." Seeing her reluctance, he added, "I'll work off the books, just for my breakfast."

"I'd be much obliged," she said, extending her hand. "Carol Wilson."

"I'm Craig," said the stranger as he shook her hand.

25

Sarah Stiles awoke with a start. Instinctively she turned to her left, but the pillow that lay there only served to remind her of what she had forgotten as she had passed from the world of dreams to the stark reality that was her life. All the blood in her heart seemed to be flushed away, leaving an aching void, as she recalled that her dear Frank was gone these six months. The unused pillow reminded that her burly husband, who would bound up a ladder with a beam over his shoulder, the handle of his hammer swinging wildly from its holster next to his nail apron. She remembered how his deep voice and unpretentious bearing would announce his presence so unmistakably. And she remembered how he could also be so attentive to her every need and did so with a gentleness that was so alien to the carpenter's persona which was known to all others. She was reminded that this ponderous hulk of a man, larger than life in so many ways, had fallen without warning to an aneurysm that struck so quickly and completely, leaving her so thoroughly alone.

She embraced the pillow, poor substitute though it was for the man she missed, and closed her eyes in an attempt to remember the better times. But instead the events of recent months flashed through her memory: the debts her husband's business had incurred, how nearly all their savings had gone to pay those debts, and through it all the overpowering listlessness which had become her master. Sarah was fully aware that her grief had very nearly transformed into melancholy, and that the absence of motivation to take realistic action against the negative forces in her life was potentially destructive. Yet she made no attempt to seek employment, as friends had suggested, so that bills could be paid. She took no action to obtain assistance from the county, no matter how temporary, as her minister had urged. She had found no real solace from church attendance, though she now rarely missed a service. In fact the decision to rent out the spare bedroom had not really been reached by Sarah as much as it had been a conclusion of Kay, a church member who had appointed herself Sarah's personal guardian. This appointment was yet another decision Sarah lacked the will to contest. It was Kay who had produced the sign and placed it in the front window, and it was she who had spread the word through town that there was a room for rent at 43 Monroe Street. Kay had even placed the small advertisement in the weekly newspaper.

The replaying of recent history in the theater of her mind only increased Sarah's depression. So, as she did nearly every morning, Sarah arose from bed, not to face the challenges of a new day, but rather to escape depressing reviews of yesterday. She dressed quickly, with minimization as her theme, for she lacked motivation to even consider the choices afforded by her wardrobe. A blouse and a pair of shorts would suffice. Even selecting a pair of shoes was more than she was prepared to consider, so she left her feet bare.

For breakfast, splashing some milk into a bowl of corn flakes met all requirements. She sat quietly eating, the only sound being the crunch of the flakes between her teeth, until the milk had been absorbed to an extent that sound was stifled. She didn't turn the radio on, as she found love songs added to her depression, be they about love just found or just lost. She read no newspaper nor aroused the television from its slumber, for nothing in the outside world was of interest to her. Instead she stared at the stylized rooster on the cereal box which seemed to promise a glorious new day was beginning. She stared, chewed, and doubted the rooster.

26

Stepping out of the diner into the mid-morning sunshine, Craig felt revitalized. Despite the long train ride and being awake through most of the night, then cooking for four hours after that, he felt alert and energetic. Still, he realized that fatigue would soon arrive. He was not keen on the idea of carrying his suitcase up the hill to Monroe Street and then possibly carrying it back down the hill should he choose not to rent the room. But the prospect of climbing the hill twice this morning was even more distasteful. Besides, he had a strong feeling that fate would be on his side today. He had not expected to land a job so quickly, but, partly due to Carol's desperation, and partly due to his cooking skills, Carol had offered him a job just moments before. Her husband, Marc, who worked nights in the repair shop at the coal mine east of town, relieved the morning cook at ten and covered the lunch cooking duties. After introducing him to her husband, Carol had made the offer. It was part time work, from five until ten, but it would give Craig some income as well as help anchor him in the community.

Although the steady stream of customers had left them little time for talking, when she had asked about his accommodations and had learned that he had none, accommodations on Monroe Street at the widow Stile's home were given her endorsement. Armed with this intelligence, and her name as a reference, Craig retrieved his valise from its hiding spot under the railway car, crossed the river and began to climb the hill.

Spring's arrival was approaching in the Appalachian Mountains, and the robins patrolling the yards of Walsh were its most noticeable harbingers. A few sparrows darted about the shrubs and small trees, seeking what few seeds they had missed during the long winter. The arrival of the more vocal birds was a few weeks away, so Craig's morning climb was acoustically little different than what he had experienced the night before. A prominent exception was a lone cardinal singing from the top of a walnut tree, its crisp song standing out as clearly as the bird's crimson feathers contrasted with the cloudless sky. The town had come awake, however, and Main Street traffic noise was more uniform, less individually identifiable. A long coal train was slowly snaking through the valley, each acceleration and deceleration accentuated by the rhythmic, mechanical banging of coupler slack out and in. Houses he passed added their individual solo accompaniments--a radio here, a door slamming there, a dog barking over there. Craig felt a moment of joy when he heard the shouts of children from a playground down Jefferson Street.

Approaching his destination on Monroe Street, Craig was winded by the climb. About two doors away he set down his suitcase and caught his breath. Once recharged, he continued to No. 43. In daylight the house possessed all the charm he had noted by the glow of street lights. This was enhanced by the window curtains, a few rugged flower beds in need of attention, and a small front yard whose new grass complemented the budding trees. Mounting the stairs to the covered porch, Craig set down the suitcase and rang the bell.

27

Sarah had washed the breakfast dishes and returned to the table, only to stare out the window. She saw herself almost as a third party observer, recognizing the absence of drive or direction in her life, feeling as if she should violently shake the woman who sat at the table and bring her to her senses: "Do something. Anything. Stop feeling sorry for yourself." But then came the pangs of recognition as she again found that she lacked the motivation to become motivated.

Sarah lost all sense of time as she gazed out the window at nothing more than spring morning sunshine on a West Virginia hill. She was jolted from this stupor by the sound of the doorbell, an alien sound so distant and unfamiliar that she had to concentrate on how she should react to it. Eventually she rose and proceeded to the front door. Glancing through the sidelight window she saw a man standing outside, wearing an overcoat, a suitcase on the porch next to him. Cautiously, she opened the door a few inches, placing her face in the opening.

"Yes?"

"I'm inquiring about the room," the man said

Sarah began to recall the events of the last two weeks. She vividly remembered Kay arriving with a "Room for Rent" sign, but her memory was unclear about other details, for when Kay began to speak about placing advertisements in the newspaper, about how much a fair monthly rental might be, and about the need to scrutinize potential renters and set clear ground rules, Sarah's mind had drifted off, leaving her head to nod understandingly at all that Kay had said. She now looked at the stranger with a blank expression.

Breaking the awkward silence, the man continued, "Carol Wilson, from the diner, recommended you. I started working at the diner this morning."

With the mention of Carol's name, Sarah relaxed somewhat, allowing the door to swing open a little wider. She began to look at the man in front of her with some interest as she realized his intrusion into her lonely morning would only end with her acceptance or dismissal, and she realized that she would best make that decision objectively. Having not given the rental a second thought since Kay posted the sign in her window, she sensed that she was not prepared for what was now required, but she would make an honest effort.

The man was shorter than average, with intense brown eyes that were slightly bloodshot. His brown hair was just beginning to show gray at the temples, and while not recently combed, it was not disheveled, either. His thin face was covered with stubbly whiskers. The gray overcoat was inappropriately heavy for the weather, and his shoes, while recently polished, displayed some scuffs and a coating of dust that suggested they had not seen attention for a day or so.

As if sensing that the woman's stare and now roving study was for the purpose of determining his suitability, the man spoke in his defense, "I apologize for my appearance. I've been traveling for more than twenty four hours now and could use a shower and shave. I assure you, I do clean up nicely." He said this with a slight grin which served to counter the deprecation his words expressed.

Sarah was keenly aware that the stranger was using the awkward silence to study her, much as she had studied him, from head to foot. For the first time in months, she was now conscious of her appearance within her own home. Her shoulder length blonde hair, uncombed, framed a face that she realized was neither strikingly beautiful nor plain. Had he at first noticed that her hazel eyes had a noticeably detached appearance, as if they were place holders for the true organs which had left on their own mission? She was becoming progressively aware of what was happening, and believed her eyes were coming to life as a result. Her slightly upturned nose was underscored by the thin line of her mouth, which, although it usually offered the promise of a pleasant smile, had not yet been coaxed into one during this short interview. She saw no reason for that condition to change. Today she wore no makeup, and she wondered if her features were much worse for its absence. Her almost athletic figure featured strong arms that terminated in thin fingers grasping the door for support. From a pair of khaki shorts emerged her slim legs, of which she had always been proud, balanced on bare feet that overhung the threshold.

To end the awkward silence, her mouth spoke but her mind listened in astonishment, "Let me show you the room. You can set your suitcase inside here."

What was she doing? She needed no more complications in her life. Surely this strange little man she didn't know would do nothing but introduce complications. She was not mentally prepared to negotiate, much less execute, a rental contract and all of the peripheral obligations that were surely attached. Yet here she was, leading him up the staircase to the bedroom.

"The room is very simple," she volunteered. "There is a separate, adjacent bath. My late husband was a carpenter, and he added the bathroom a few years ago." She stepped aside as he entered the room so he might have an unobstructed view.

Her characterization was accurate. A full size bed with a laminate headboard dominated the room. A chest of drawers was on the far wall while a desk and chair were between the two windows that looked out onto the street. A nightstand and its bedside lamp completed the furnishings. The walls, which were pale blue, were decorated with prints of landscapes in the style of Corot.

"This will be fine," he answered. "What are you asking?"

Sarah had been anticipating this question from the base of the staircase, desperately trying to remember what dollar figures Kay may have mentioned as she had rattled on about how Sarah might garner some badly needed income from this unused room. Sarah blurted out an amount, immediately regretting that she probably had shortchanged herself.

"That would be fine," the stranger said. "May I give you a month's rent in advance?"

"Uh, yes, that would be good," she stammered. Then, in deference to her protesting mind, "Just to be clear, this is just a room. No board. No meals. You use the front door—I'll get you a key, but frankly, few people lock their doors in Walsh—so, you use the front door, the stairs, this room and the bathroom, that's it."

"Okay," was his simple response.

Sensing that she had been a little too curt with the rules, Sarah added, "And the front porch. You can use the front porch, you know, sit out there if you like."

"Okay."

His too easy acceptance was not putting her at ease. "I'll clean the room on Wednesdays, at a time we'll work out later. I'd appreciate it if you could be as neat and clean as possible."

"I will."

His short answers continued to contribute to her awkwardness , which manifested itself again in a much delayed introduction, "Uh, my name is Sarah, Sarah Stiles."

"I'm Craig."

28

    Sarah returned to the kitchen, but not to her seat. She began to pace rapidly across the room, thinking aloud but in muted whispers of what needed to be done. Taking on a boarder was unexpected and disconcertingly complicated. She questioned the wisdom of allowing a stranger to share her house, but fishing the bills he had paid her from her pocket brought to light the relief a monthly infusion of cash would bring to her financial situation.

    Remembering the sign that had drawn him here, Sarah retrieved it from the living room window and stashed it in the kitchen pantry. Now, for the first time in months, she was being stimulated, attacking this new problem with measured thought processes, not just the stimulus/response mechanism that had defined her life. She was amazed at how instantly her lethargy had been curtailed, and was pleasantly surprised how good it felt to be truly alive and engaged again. She was still annoyed that this stranger had so quickly and completely disrupted her life and was disappointed with herself for having been so quick to agree to the rental arrangement. But now her focus was the reaction to these new circumstances and how they would change her life.

    Sarah was also aware she was reacting to the new boarder as well. Who was he? Where did he come from? What was the nature of his character? He seemed polite enough, yet his scruffy appearance, his brief verbal responses, his concentrated glare that seemed to take in all details, these characteristics made her uncomfortable. Why had she rented the room without knowing more about him?

    It was true that the fact that he worked for Carol had disarmed her. Carol was a kind, hard working entrepreneur, who, with her husband, Marc, had purchased that run down diner a few years ago. After they cleaned it up, prepared decent meals, and, most importantly, offered their genuine, good natured hospitality, Carol's Diner had become the social center of Walsh, which, except for the two churches and three bars in town, otherwise sorely lacked such an establishment. So Carol's endorsement was important. Still, it was Carol, after all, who had employed that cad, Billy, who had proven to be the epitome of unfaithful, irresponsible immorality. Sarah determined that she would gather some information about her new boarder, and she would do so right away.

Her plan abruptly encountered an obstacle, however. She wished to dress a little more modestly for a journey into town. To all who knew her she was, after all, still the mourning widow, and she still dressed for the part whenever she left the house. Besides, she would need her pocketbook and shoes from her bedroom. But the thought of passing the rented room on the way to her own chamber made her fearful. She scoffed at this reaction. She would have to get over that fear, and quickly, as this fellow would be in the house for at least another month. Taking a deep breath, she began to creep up the stairs. She remembered, angrily, the seventh step, too late, just as her foot pressed down upon it and it responded with the loud creaking sound as it always did. Sarah froze in place and listened intently. Not a sound came from his room. She resumed the climb, crept into her bedroom where she quickly changed. She then retraced her steps quietly down the stairs, carefully bypassing number seven this time, and slipped out the front door.

29

Craig closed the door as the landlady retired. She had made him welcome in a rather strange way, having laid down the ground rules, collected a month's rent, and conducted the briefest of tours. Still, she seemed pleasant enough, though slightly dour. As tired as he was, he would not permit a first impression to influence his judgment of a situation that might be long running. Certainly the room was clean, provided everything he needed, and with the exception of the climb up the hill, was well situated for someone who traveled only on foot.

He hung his coat on one of the two hangers in the small closet, then transferred the contents of his valise into the chest of drawers. This task completed in less than two minutes, he slid the suitcase under the bed, and feeling fatigue rushing on, quickly stripped to his underwear and slid between the sheets for a midday nap.

No sooner had he closed his eyes than the red haired vision appeared again. This time she sat quietly, apparently seeming to forget the angry taunts of the night before. That only made Craig remember them more vividly, and he began to reexamine his situation.

He had not expected to be anywhere near as comfortable as he now found himself within twelve hours of arriving in Walsh. Not only had he found a place to live, but had secured the room and was already enjoying its comforts. Even more surprising, he had found employment, even if only part time. Some quick calculations indicated that the job would more than cover the cost of the room, the rent charged was below what he had expected, even in a town with such a depressed economy as this. The additional earnings would go a long way towards his meals, especially if Carol would permit him to take small breakfasts and lunches at the diner as part of the compensation package.

Again he saw Joan in his mind, the vision vivid and overpowering his thoughts. Joan's face, and particularly her piercing eyes, captivated Craig, here in his imagination as much as it had when they were together. He found her physically beautiful, based upon subjective criteria which he knew would fail to meet any of the minimum standards of even the least prestigious modeling agencies.

However, it was the purity of her soul and the kindness it engendered that had captured his heart. He longed to be with her, to be in the presence of that soul. Even as he realized the impossibility of that desire, he recognized that it once was possible. That possibility spawned these mental images that plagued his existence, while at the same time they served to define it. So he would bask in the warmth centered in his chest each time these images appeared, and as he did so, he drifted off to sleep.

30

When Sarah entered Carol's Diner, the lunch crowd had begun to arrive, and she regretted the timing of her visit. Still, her curiosity had been piqued, and she was anxious to learn as much as she could, as quickly as she could. This in itself was stunning, as for months now Sarah had had little interest in anything. Her life was merely existence, meals but a sustenance, and sleep, when it came, a dream-free unconscious version of what passed for her normal consciousness.

. Only her Sunday visits to church brought a break from the routine, punctuating the week with regularity, but, unfortunately little in the way of spiritual revival. The words of the hymns had no meaning, Reverend Jordan's sermons droned on as background noise as if they were delivered in a foreign tongue, and the cackling sounds of parishioners before and after the service was like the static she would hear on a radio tuned between two channels. Only the organ spoke to her. Its every note from the shortest pipe to the pedaled notes, all were heard, very nearly the only element of clarity in her life.

And, oh, what the organ would say! Sometimes it was the sobriety of Handel, with the measured chords and stately presentation. On other occasions it would be the lyrical melodies of Purcell. On the best of days, it would be a Bach toccata or fugue with its complexity of counter-melodies. Suddenly, she was alive. Her ears, often deaf even when people were speaking to her, were alert to the melodies, harmonies and rhythms. Her mind was attuned to the dynamics, the resonance or the syncopation and would anticipate and then rejoice in a final chord's resolution. Her heart was warmed by the emotions the songs carried even as it was massaged by her rib cage set to vibrating by the organ's energy. The music would stir Sarah's soul, elevate her spirits, and almost convince her that her life was worth living again. But, inevitably, with the conclusion of the last fermata, her soul would sleep once more, only to be aroused when the organ again came to life a week later. Today in the diner, Patsy Cline's voice from the jukebox was singing of love gone wrong, hardly inspiring in tone.

Now, with the intrusion of this stranger, this boarder in her own home, came a revitalization. It was not her soul that was affected, as was the case when the music moved her, but a more cognitive, thoughtful element of her being which was being shocked into defibulation. Sarah was fully aware of the change, a change she had longed for but had not had the impetus to initiate.

She was annoyed at the intrusion, but at the same time pleased that the imbalance this stranger had introduced into her life had once again set her life in motion. Yet she had little time to enjoy that pleasure as the annoyance triggered actions that kept her focused on matters other than her personal feelings, which in turn accentuated the annoyance resulting in more focus, spiraling her out of the malaise she had known.

"How's it going?" Carol greeted Sarah as she entered the diner, and made her way towards the counter, to the very stool where Craig had sat earlier that day.

"I'm good. A cup of coffee, please?"

When Carol returned with the beverage, Sarah motioned her to come closer. "Carol, I know you're getting busy and all, but I need you to answer a couple of quick questions, if you don't mind."

Carol scanned the patrons quickly, and seeing none with an immediate need, turned back to Sarah. "Shoot."

"I took in a boarder this morning."

"So he did go to you! Well, that's great."

"So you did send him?" Sarah asked.

"Sure. He said he needed a place to stay, and I knew you were trying to rent that room."

"But what do you know about him?"

"Not very much. He came in this morning, ordered breakfast, and within a few minutes had put out a fire in the kitchen, and filled the position of morning cook. He worked at the grill for the rest of the morning shift, and did a pretty good job."

"You hired him, just like that?" Sarah was incredulous.

"Sarah, I was pretty desperate. I haven't had a cook for two mornings now, and I was kidding myself thinking I could run the whole place singlehandedly. It wasn't looking like I was going to find anyone to take the job. Anybody in this town willing to get up at that hour of the morning already had a better paying job over at the mine."

"But what about references? Do you know anything about

him?"

"Pffft. If he shows up tomorrow morning at five, I'll know most of what I need to know. Besides, he seemed to be pleasant enough. Sort of quiet, but eager to please. Excuse me."

As Carol refilled a coffee cup across the room, Sarah sipped her coffee, still surprised at how quickly Carol had hired the stranger.

"Sorry," Carol said upon her return.

"I just can't get over how quickly you offered him a job," Sarah continued.

"Well, how long did it take you to rent him the room?" Carol countered.

Sarah stared into the dark liquid in the cup before her and said nothing.

"Listen," Carol continued, "I can understand you being nervous renting a room out for the first time, but I don't get any bad vibes about this guy, Craig. True, I don't know what brings him to Walsh. Maybe he's running away from something. Truth is, most of us do at least once in our lives. But I don't think he's an axe murderer, or anything. When you deal with the public, like I do, you find that most people are pretty decent. Those with troubles usually don't make trouble for others. Sure, a bunch of them are stupid and can't even figure out our simple menu, but stupid in a harmless way. But let me talk to him and see if I can learn anything. If he says anything that makes me the least bit uneasy, I will let you know right away."

"Thanks, Carol. I appreciate it."

"No problem. But like I said, I think everything will work out fine."

31

"It's *good* to see you again, Sarah," said the grocery store owner. Ralph's usual gruff expression was replaced with a genuine smile.

Sarah picked up on the emphasis in his comment, and had to agree. It *was* good to be alive again. "Thank you, Ralph. You have a good day, now."

Sarah had left the diner keenly alert. Although her fact finding mission had not yielded many facts, she had become keenly aware that her life was no longer on hold. She felt the slightest pangs of hunger, the first she remembered feeling since Frank had died, and then she recalled how poorly stocked her kitchen was. Now that she had some money, she felt not only comfortable, but actually excited, to enter the grocery store a few doors down from Carol's Diner.

She was startled at how quickly her unused skills were remembered. She began meal planning on the fly as she walked through the store, altering the menu as she identified especially appealing vegetables, or particular meat selections the butcher had displayed in the refrigerated cases. She also made the conscious decision not to splurge on account of her newly found funding. As she checked out, she was pleased with the frugal choices she had made, while still sure she could prepare them so that they would be especially pleasing to eat—a new requisite in this, her new life. She also acknowledged, with a wry smile, that she was not yet accomplished at shopping for one, as the portions she acquired were in keeping with the habits acquired when she was cooking for two. Undeterred, she concluded that she would just double the number of meals to be prepared. She was quite content with herself as she left the store with chicken legs and thighs, a good sized rutabaga, fresh green beans, some apples and bananas.

Upon returning home, Sarah found the kitchen in total disarray. Before, when she was but a ghost passing through the room, foraging for sustenance, and sustenance only, the kitchen was more than adequate. If something was left where it did not belong, it was easy enough to work around it. Or what was the problem with shoving items aside to clear a flat area large enough to do the task at hand? But now, her new attitude towards life brought new vision: a clearer, more objective perception of her environment, which demanded that certain things change. Sarah set about organizing the kitchen. She cleared counters, put things away, and rearranged utensils to make them more accessible for the jobs to be performed. She scrubbed with cleansers to add sanitation and sparkle.

When those tasks were done, she began meal preparation, and soon chicken was frying, vegetables were boiling, and her appetite, long dormant, was awakening. Her spiritual revival had reached her stomach, and its response was undeniable: hunger--not just for food, but for tasty food, attractive in presentation, spiced to make the nose and the palate rejoice.

As she worked, she thought of the stranger upstairs. She wished to learn more about him, to set her mind at ease that renting the room to him was not a mistake. Seeing the food cooking before her, a plan developed. She would invite him to dinner—just this once—as a gesture of welcome to her house and her town. Perhaps, as he dined, the quiet man would open his mouth not only to eat, but also to divulge some history and make known his character. Stridently, she set about setting her plan into motion.

32

When Craig awoke, he was at first confused as to where he was, but then he recalled the events of the day, and his new home was recognized for the safety it provided. This room in this modest house on Monroe Street in the scrappy little town of Walsh, West Virginia, was his refuge, his fort from which he might combat the numerous elements of the two deceitful armies which threatened him: one, the lie of his marriage with Dolores and the second, the larger lie of his quest for a life with Joan.

Yet again, the visions appeared in his mind. This time both women, flashing alternately in his brain, each offering a promise of some level of happiness, neither offering the likelihood that such a promise could be fulfilled. Would they never end? How much distance must he place between himself and the source of these promises? Would California be far enough? Would it help to place an ocean as a barrier, the largest of moats to stem the invasion? He grimaced as the realization hit home, an understanding he should have known from the beginning, that certainly no distance, and possibly no amount of time, would free him from his heartbreaking sorrow. He had escaped from his life in Peach Hill, but he could not escape from the expectations of his heart. That heart, capable of unwavering devotion, required commitments as well. Those to whom his heart established a bonding affinity were required to pursue continuously the virtues that had set them apart in the first place. Dolores's humility and good natured tolerance was less and less visible in recent months. Joan's tendency towards outgoing generosity had abruptly stopped when Craig had stepped into her path. The foundations of the best he had found on earth, if not crumbling, were at least shifting.

He recalled the short periods of relief he had known in Peach Hill. Occasionally when his mind engaged upon a problem solving exercise at Gilmore, Haskins & Cass, he found freedom from these haunting visions, a respite from the madness. He must set about finding an activity to occupy his mind and distract him from the madness, or he would surely go mad, if indeed his abdication were not already a manifestation of that condition. So with that thought he arose from bed, and with the visions still vividly playing in his mind, moved to the bathroom for a shower and a shave.

Craig emerged a short time later, refreshed and recharged, dressed for a spring evening with a sport coat to fend against the mountain chill. He descended the stairs almost silently, save for one creaking step, the aroma of Mrs. Stiles' fried chicken filling his nostrils. The smell beckoned memories of the homey comfort of his childhood, the meals his mother had prepared, spiced with love. This reflection caused him to pause, just slightly, before he stepped out the front door.

33

The Reverend Ebenezer Jordan concluded his hospital visit with Harmon Wilkins. He did so with a sincere smile and a slight glistening in his eye that served as his trademark demeanor, one of pleasantness and reassuring comfort. Tall and thin, his neck seemed to stretch out of his shirt collar as if to assist his long narrow nose to reach the air from a higher stratus of the atmosphere. Eb, the abbreviated name by which he was universally known, never left the impression of being distant, even from the most diminutive of his congregants. The bed-ridden Wilkins was suffering from a powerful kick to the abdomen from his mule, Solomon. Even from his bed Harmon actually looked down at the pastor, who, sitting in a nearby chair, had folded his elongated frame, pointed elbows on knobby knees, such that his eyes were slightly below those of the patient. Harmon would be returning home tomorrow, ending a thirty-six hour stay. For this good fortune, the minister had offered a prayer of thanksgiving, and to ease the farmer's mind, had related that a neighbor had offered to care for Solomon and Harmon's other livestock, and otherwise check on things until his return. It was this type of comprehensive pastoral care that had earned Eb Jordan the respect of his congregation and the community at large.

Leaving the mending farmer, Eb strode down the corridor of Walsh General Hospital, his long strides quickly eating up the linoleum tiles of the short hallway. For WGH was hardly an extensive facility, serving as a minimal care facility. Any case requiring more medical attention than what Harmon had needed was transferred to Covington, and the Reverend Eb devoted most of one day a week for the visit to that hospital to visit his more seriously ill congregants. The minister's thoughts then turned to another congregant, who, while not physically sick nor occupying a bed within WGH, was nevertheless not herself, and was not showing promising signs of improvement. His concern was for Sarah Stiles, the recent widow, who was having difficulty dealing with her loss. Eb had seen the look of detachment on Sarah's face immediately after Frank's death, but had not seen it change much in the succeeding weeks. In fact, her usually bright, intent eyes had become clouded, apparently focusing on nothing in the vicinity, but seeing instead another world, a world without passion and of few stimuli. Although she had attended church services regularly, she was clearly not engaged, and he had noticed that she was now absent from other church functions, which she previously had patronized. He was concerned for her mental well-being, fearing that depression might have set in. Eb decided he would stop and pay Sarah a visit on his way back from the hospital.

Eb drove towards the center of town with his car window open, enjoying the late afternoon of a gorgeous spring day. The trees were budding, and the hillsides were covered with the pinkish tint that the buds gave the trees. This tinge of color replaced the lifeless gray the leafless branches had given the mountains, providing an even colder appearance during the winter season. The promise of the coming of spring lifted Eb's spirits, and he reflected upon how he had grown to love this remote settlement in the Appalachians, with its sturdy miners and obstinate farmers who reaped the bounty of this country, from below the earth's surface and above. His assignment to the area eight years ago had been laden with apprehension, as he, a product of the suburbs of Richmond, Virginia, doubted his ability to successfully interact with people so alien from those he had known. His wife, always the adventurer, had encouraged him, praising his talents and discounting the perceived differences. As usual, she had been right. They both had been accepted quickly by the residents of Walsh, their spiritual needs proving to be little different from those of people anywhere. The remoteness, which so molded the character of the people here, had served to make him more independent as well, since professional support services were available to him only from the not so nearby capital city of Charleston. As he had become more confident with his independence, consciously he had chosen to pursue it, electing to decide more and more issues on his own, even shunning advice when volunteered by his superiors. He had enjoyed knowing that what he had determined often worked for his parishioners, and this had given him the confidence to become even more independent. This impact on his life had been profound. His scope of interaction had increased dramatically, and the extent of his involvement with others had grown, from what had been minimally required, to a full-fledged concern for many of the people with whom he came in contact. He had never remembered being so idealistic, even in his years in seminary. He had noted how his colleagues grew more and more cynical with the passing of time, while he, to the contrary, welcomed the opportunities to do the Lord's work, with the emphasis on work. Rather than becoming fatigued, he seemed to be energized with each new mission. The rewards, modest as they might seem to some--a smile, a nod of acknowledgement, a brief hand-written thank you note--were to him immensely gratifying and carried with them the utmost satisfaction.

    It was in this frame of mind that the pastor turned onto Monroe Street, and pulled to the curb across the street from Sarah's home. He was just shifting into park when the front door of the house opened and a middle-aged man came out and bounded down the stairs. Casually but conservatively dressed, he walked with a spring in his step, at a faster than average gait. Reaching the sidewalk, he gave a casual glance in the direction of the reverend, then crossed the street and continued towards the closest intersection, no doubt headed for town. Seeing the man exit Sarah's house was completely unexpected and froze Eb in his seat. He was curious about who this fellow was, and what his business was with Sarah. He thought better of stopping in now, uninvited, immediately on the heels of the unknown visitor. He would postpone this visit to another time.

34

It had been months since Sarah last prepared a complete meal in her kitchen. Though rusty at first, she soon instinctively recalled the little tricks that sped the process and was employing them to advantage. Rarely had Frank and she entertained guests, but she had a preferred format for such occasions, and planned to use a modified version for this one, a dinner to welcome her new lodger. She had considered serving the meal in the kitchen, so as not to make the meal appear too formal, but decided instead to use the dining room to keep things on a less personal plane. She chose her best china--she should use it some time, after all—and quickly set two settings, hers at the end of the rectangle table closest to the kitchen for ready access, her guest's plate centered along the longer table edge, his chair back to the doorway to the parlor. She placed and then removed candlesticks from the table, reconsidering the mood she wished to set. The somewhat glaring light from the modest brass chandelier would have to do.

Now for the difficult part—the invitation. After checking the stove, she hurried up the stairway. The squeaking step again announced her approach, this time louder than she had ever remembered. She stood outside the guest room door, and took a deep breath, and began to silently rehearse what she was to say.

"Mister—," what had he said his last name was? She was sure he had said it, but it clearly had not registered. There was no written lease, so she had not seen him write it, he had paid in cash, fortunately, so there was no bank draft to consult.

"Craig," oh, that sounds too personal. But what other option did she have? "Hey you!"? With the rehearsal proceeding so poorly, she decided to move along in *ad lib* mode.

"Umm, Craig?" she said aloud.

No sound returned from the room.

"Excuse me," she voiced, a little louder than before, followed by two taps on the door.

Again, silence.

"Craig," again, with elevated volume. Now four solid knocks struck the door.

More silence.

A slight panic gripped her. She imagined her new roomer had fallen and lay unconscious on the floor. No, worse than that, he had succumbed to some tropical illness he brought with him from wherever he came, and lay dead on the floor. She grimaced as her imagination fanned these flames adding the image of the stairs being climbed by a small army consisting of police, coroner and undertakers. She stood outside the door, wringing her hands, fearful of opening the door.

Something had to be done, though. Taking another deep breath, she slowly turned the doorknob and peered inside. Her guest was not present, neither alive nor dead. The bathroom door was open, disclosing his absence there, and the room was otherwise as neat and orderly as she could have wished. He must have left the house without her hearing.

Sarah closed the door and returned to the kitchen. The meal was nearly cooked, and her guest of honor had disappeared. She decided to try to keep it warm and hope that Craig would return shortly. She admonished herself for having the foolish idea and for executing it so poorly. Sarah immediately recognized that this self-inflicted assault on her self-esteem ran counter to the buoyancy she had experienced ever since Craig had rung the bell earlier that day. She had rejoiced in the resurgence of life, been excited by renewed awareness, fraught though it might be with uncertainty and fear. She was moderately pleased with herself for the proactive role she had played in dictating an outcome as opposed to the passivity that had characterized her life in the recent past. She sat at the dining room table and, using the room's street-side window to her advantage, awaited the return of her guest.

35

Joan found herself in a most unusual situation. Supper time was approaching, but with both her children away at friends' homes, she needed to prepare dinner for one. Lacking any appetite, she had no desire to prepare a meal or even to grab something from a fast food establishment. The second day at Gilmore, Haskins and Cass without Craig had proven more difficult for her on a personal level. The firm was staggering forward, as she knew it would, with temporary re-assignments and competitive jockeying for the coming promotion to fill the void his absence created. For her part, however, the realization of his abandonment of his position was becoming accepted, and her role in his decision to leave was becoming clearer as well. Walking away was so counter to Craig's approach to every task, that the unusual behavior was noted by everyone who broached the subject. That group including every employee of G. H. & C., with Joan being a direct party to many such conversations, or in a position to overhear those not directed at her.

From her pocket she withdrew the note she had received in yesterday's mail, and re-read the one word message for perhaps the twelfth time that day, as if there were a message to decipher from the non-existent words written between the non-existent lines. Once again a slight pang of guilt struck her, only to be immediately and thoroughly swept away as she again convinced herself that her decision was the only decision she could have made, the only decision she should have made. True enough, Craig had been kind to her and always respectful. Also probably true: his marriage was not as fulfilling as he would hope. But she had not been comfortable then, and was not comfortable now, with the idea of accepting Craig. To do so might bring pain to Dolores. Nor did she wish to position herself as a target for the animosity from someone, regardless whether well informed or not, who might conclude that her action was the cause of the marriage to fail, or of Dolores being injured.

At the same time she wondered what circumstances would have needed to be different to have resulted in a different response from her. There were times, though not frequent, when she would imagine herself remarried. A fleeting glimpse of a small, simple wedding ceremony would be immediately followed by images of a full, happy life as represented by a harmonious household, laughter and smiles, shared moments of confident silence. In these images, she saw herself as from a third party's viewpoint. Never was her new husband's identity revealed. But, she conceded, she would be hard pressed to name anyone better suited to the role than Craig.

As these thoughts were processed, conclusions drawn, findings filed away, on another level she began an investigation of the meaning of life—specifically, the meaning of meeting and loving her beloved husband, only to lose him so abruptly without warning or preparation. As always happened, her mind re-focused upon the enduring embodiment of that love, her two children to whom she had devoted her life and for whom she was willing to sacrifice anything on their behalf. These centers of interest clearly were the justification for all that life had presented and could present. This was forcefully underscored as she recognized Neal's mannerisms which were so reminiscent of her husband, and the sense of humor Cindy was developing, a reincarnation of another side of her late husband's personality. As her children again became the central focus of her thoughts, her other musings faded softly away, replaced by the need to telephone them to reassure herself that all was well and that they would be returning home on schedule.

36

Darkness came rather quickly on early spring evenings in the Appalachians—not as suddenly as in the winter, when it seemed to engulf the valley as soon as the sun dipped behind Knob Mountain—but still more quickly than in the summer when a period of twilight extended the day substantially. A gang of crows, their ebony forms silhouetted against what light remained in the evening sky, winged their way across the valley, with a purpose fathomable only to them. On a different vector, a red-tailed hawk glided towards a remote perch deep in the woods where he would spend the night and await another day of soaring and hunting.

Sarah sat nearly motionless at the dining room table, her eyes fixed on Monroe Street outside. Hunger was clawing at her insides. She was unsure why the impromptu little dinner party for her new house guest had become so important, and why the absence of her new tenant had assumed such an inordinate level of her concern. With the coming of darkness, confirmed by the nearby streetlight coming to life, the likelihood of the party assuming any of its planned appeal was called into serious question. The fallback position, to enjoy the fruits of her labor, alone, before the food lost its fresh-cooked goodness, became an increasingly attractive option.

She arose from the table, and, leaving the dining room lights on and the table set, moved to the kitchen where she set herself a simple place setting on the kitchen table and filled her plate. She attacked the meal with a vigor that she had not known for months and was rewarded with ample proof that she had not lost her culinary talents despite the extended period of dormancy. The chicken was surprisingly moist, given its extra time in the skillet, and the white gravy she had made from the chicken grease smothered a slice-and-bake buttermilk biscuit while the mashed turnip and vibrant green beans otherwise filled her plate.

As she ate, her mind raced through a list of projects that needed to be attacked. The clutter in the kitchen—unopened mail, grocery sacks that had been tossed aside immediately after they had been emptied, and an assortment of other items that had been carried to the kitchen for one reason or another and left there—this clutter had to go. She visualized her bedroom and shuddered as she remembered how various garments had been left draped on chairs, hung on bedposts, or tossed in a laundry heap but had never been directed further in that direction. And the yard. She had done nothing save shovel snow when required. Flower beds needed attention before the beauty that the spring brought would be obliterated by weeds and other undergrowth. The leaves from last fall that had accumulated in various pockets and recesses for the winter hiatus must be removed. And that gutter, which overhung the porch steps, had to be re-attached to its mating piece so that annoying drip would not strike her neck whenever it rained. And the garage needed to be cleaned out—no; no, the garage could wait.

Sarah finished her meal and sat back and admired her plate, cluttered only with a few chicken bones. Hastily, she rose and carried her dishes to the sink to be washed. She was about finished containerizing the leftovers when she heard the front door open. Dashing through the dining room, she brought herself up short, silently admonishing herself for such impetuous behavior, and entering the foyer at a dignified gait found Craig half way up the stairs.

"Good evening," she blurted, again silently checking her enthusiasm.

"Good evening," answered Craig, pivoting to face her.

"I fried some chicken, if you care for some. I made plenty."

"Much obliged," answered Craig, "but I grabbed a bite in town. But I thank you for the offer." Nodding, he turned again to continue his climb.

"Vegetables, too," she volunteered. Why was she pushing this agenda? Who was this person filling her skin and talking to this stranger so kindly? Whoever she was, she had been doing it all day. "Uh, green beans, turnip, biscuits and gravy."

Craig turned again, only part way this time, and smiled, "Again, I appreciate the offer, but I'm good. I have an early start tomorrow, so if you'll excuse me…"

"Oh, yes, of course. I'm sorry. Good night."

"No apology needed," he said. "Good night."

With that he turned, climbed the last few steps and retired

behind his door. Sarah remained at the foot of the stairs, somewhat perplexed with this turn of events, and considerably confused by the change in her attitude since the stranger had rung the doorbell earlier that morning.

37

Sarah lay on her back in bed, eyes focused on a dark ceiling with little visible detail. Physically she was exhausted from the day's activities. The shopping, cleaning, cooking—these exertions were much more than her habits of recent months had allowed. But now, in the quiet darkness, she focused on the questions that occupied her mind and postponed welcome sleep.

The lodger who was asleep just a few yards away, had rapidly, surprisingly and very completely altered her life. To what limited degree her contractual obligations required her to attend to his comfort, they had aroused her from a near dormant state, a self-indulgent immersion in pity and sorrow that was not only non-productive, but, she suspected, quite counter-productive to her mental and physical well-being. This awakening had been sudden, without warning, allowing her no time to consider or evaluate. Her revival had been complete, leaving her no opportunity to even consider relapsing into her previous state of automatic, mindless behavior.

Beyond that, there was a mysterious element to the stranger, which went beyond the uncertainty of his background. It was this aspect that captivated Sarah's imagination as she lay in the dark. Objectively, she outlined his attributes and her reactions, dare she say over-reactions, to them. Physically, there was little to remark favorably in his behalf. His stature was below average, and his bearing did not foster a memorable presence. His face was unremarkable, and the deep set eyes which appeared to take in everything but reveal little of their owner's thoughts or feelings, were nearly serpent-like in their lack of warmth. While readily granting that he had had little opportunity to reveal the full nature of his personality, he had demonstrated a proclivity towards politeness, although she would have to classify him more as reserved than outgoing.

Yet her reaction to him had been almost immediately one of outreach, which was surprising giving the reservations she readily numerated and was especially surprising given her reclusive nature since Frank's death. It was her reaction that troubled her, and which she attempted to analyze. But as objective criteria were alternately offered and dismissed, she was forced to conclude that some subjective powers were at work, and this proved only more disconcerting. She was, she reminded herself, a widow in mourning, and that status should preclude desires to entertain strange men at dinner, or for that matter, to obsess over why that desire surfaced in the first place.

But reaching no conclusion, despite asking and re-asking the same questions several times, Sarah succumbed to her fatigue, and drifted off to sleep.

38

With the first startling beep of the alarm from his wrist watch, Craig awoke and stabbed into the dark in the direction of the night stand. Grabbing the watch he silenced its insistent call to rise, then fell back onto the pillow and released the air he had gasped upon awakening.

He dared not lie for long, for were he to fall asleep he would certainly be late for his first full day of work. That thought excited him. It had been over two decades since his last "first day of work." He sat up and turned on the lamp, checking the watch to confirm that it was a quarter past four in the morning.

Out of respect for his landlady, Craig used extreme caution to prepare for his day as quietly as possible. Having laid his clothes out on the chair the night before, he was ready for departure within a half hour of waking, starting down the stairs at twenty to five. The silence of the house suggested that his efforts to move quietly had resulted in the landlady's slumber not being disturbed. But Craig whispered a curse as a loud creak, almost sounding as if it had been electronically amplified, came in response to his weight on one of the staircase steps. He froze on the next step down and listened. The house returned to its silence. He resumed his way down the stairway and exited the front door into the cool night air.

As it was in the house, it was eerily quiet outdoors, too. It was still too early in the season for the insects to conduct their overnight symphony. Having selected rubber soled sneakers in preparation for standing at a grill for the entire morning, Craig added little sound to the environment. Only the distant sound of a train horn, doubtless yet another of the endless parade of loaded eastbound or empty westbound coal trains, interrupted the silence.

Walking downgrade was nearly effortless, and Craig soon arrived at the front door of the diner as Carol rounded the corner, walking from the parking lot, the diner front door key at the ready. Upon seeing him, her face, illuminated by a nearby streetlight, brightened even more.

"Good morning!" she called.

"'Morning, Carol."

"This is the worst part of the job," she said, her smile

contradicting her words, "but you'll get used to it."

"If yesterday was any indication, I'm sure I will," Craig offered, as upbeat as he could be.

"On Saturdays, a lot of folks from the hills come into town, both to buy and sell. It's usually our busiest day for breakfast," she said as she pushed the door inward.

Craig was again impressed with the positive nature of Carol's personality. He could not imagine her getting angry at anyone for long, and it was certainly his intention to try to please her. He had secured this job very easily, but his observations in town and on his approach from the train suggested that that was not the norm. West Virginia's economy was struggling, and although he had not met many people yet to confirm that in their faces, the facades of the buildings—peeling paint on weather beaten-wood, sooty brick facings, cloudy windows, and gritty sidewalks—delivered the message just as clearly.

As Carol swung the door open to allow Craig entry, a teenage girl came around the building corner, headed in their direction. Wearing a navy blue sweatshirt and blue jeans, she carried a day pack on her shoulder, and her face betrayed a pouting, disinterested temperament which was verified by a distracted, leisurely gait. As the girl approached the door which Carol held open, the proprietor made introductions. "This is my daughter, Melinda. Honey, this is Mr. Miller, the new cook I was telling you about."

"Hi," was the adolescent's response.

"Nice to meet you," Craig said.

"I bring her to the diner on Saturdays so she doesn't spend the whole day in bed." Carol explained.

"Oh, Mom," her offspring moaned, eyeballs chasing eyebrows which had advanced upward on her forehead.

"Mostly she reads and does her homework, but she has been known to help out from time to time." This last information was delivered with a loving smile to suggest understatement. The daughter merely grinned as she walked past the adults into the dark diner.

Carol and Craig set about readying the kitchen for the day's business. Carol's instructions were clear, often anticipating Craig's questions, and as he set about completing the assignments she gave him, she left to ready the front counter and dining room. Occupied as he was, it did not seem that much time had passed before the bell attached to the front door began to jingle, announcing the arrival of the first customers. Carol walked in the first order, explaining her order short hand at the same time.

It was not long before Craig fell into a rhythm, turning out meals in response to Carol's orders, which followed the sound of the bell on the door only by a few minutes. Conversations from the dining room, while seldom audible enough to be understood by Craig, served as the background sound for his work. Occasionally an exceptionally loud laugh or Carol's banter would punctuate the undertones. At all times the sounds suggested that the diner was a comfortable place, and that the patrons were happy to be there, as clearly Carol was, too. Craig was beginning to sense that he could easily adapt to this environment, finding a sense of satisfaction and ease standing over the grill in the small kitchen.

As Craig was entertaining these thoughts, Melinda came into the kitchen and perched on a stool not far from the grill. The girl's closely cropped mahogany colored hair closely followed the contours of her head and served as the perfect complement to the dark brown eyes set deep in her face. Craig recognized the perfect match between the color of her hair and that of her mother, although Carol's green eyes seemed less intrusive. The youth regarded him quietly for a moment.

"Hi," she said.
"Hello."
"Mom says you started here yesterday."
"That's true."
"You like the job?"
"Yes, so far."
"You don't think it's boring? I'd be bored."
"Ah, the restlessness of youth!"

Melinda giggled. "You sound like my dad. He says the world isn't always 'high speed, intense heat, and fireworks'."

"Your dad's right. What grade are you in school, Melinda?"
"I'm a sophomore. I go to Greenbrier County High."

"Sausage sandwich on a hard roll," Carol shouted from the dining room. "Mel, you leave him alone!"

"She's okay, Carol; not a problem," Craig replied. As he

placed a pork patty on the grill he asked of Melinda, "What's your favorite subject in school?"

"Literature, I guess. I like to read. A lot of the kids don't like the books we have to read, but I don't mind."

"Oh? What's your favorite book?"

"I dunno. I liked *The Prince and the Pauper*. But I also liked *To Kill a Mockingbird*. I'm reading *Wuthering Heights*, now. So far I'm liking it."

"Wow, that's quite a variety!" he said, checking the grill side of the sausage.

"What's your favorite?" she asked.

"Hmmm. *The Count of Monte Cristo* is good. But I also like *The Hunchback of Notre Dame*."

"I read *The Count of Monte Cristo* last summer. Thought it was kinda slow."

"Ah, the 'high speed, intense heat and fireworks', again," he chuckled.

"I guess. I haven't read *The Hunchback* yet."

"Give it a try."

Craig flipped the sausage and began to prepare the roll. Melinda remained quiet, intertwining her legs alternatively around different legs of the stool. After several iterations, she spoke again.

"Where you from?"

"New Jersey."

"New Jersey. Capital: Trenton. The most densely populated state in the nation," she recited.

"Yep, that's the one. Although I lived out in the suburbs, lots of hills and trees."

"As many as we have here?"

"No, I don't think any place can beat West Virginia for hills and trees."

"Melinda, get back to your homework and leave Mr. Miller alone," Carol said, as she entered the kitchen for some silverware.

"See you later," the teen said, springing off the stool and out into the dining room in one motion.

"Nice kid," Craig offered.

"Thanks," Carol replied, her pride obvious in her smile. "Hope she wasn't bothering you."

"Not at all. I enjoyed her company."

39

"Two scrambled with bacon, rye toast," Carol yelled through the low opening above the high counter between the kitchen and the serving area behind the main counter.

"Comin' right up," Craig answered cheerfully. The breakfast rush was beginning to slow, but not before Carol and he had developed a comfortable rhythm in their interaction as waitress and cook. His short order cooking skills quickly returning, Craig had found his first full day at the diner ran smoothly, and Carol's tolerant personality and willingness to offer helpful suggestions only served to ease the transition period. He liked Carol's personality, her ability to evoke friendliness almost effortlessly, but with an underlying sincerity which enhanced its value. There was no doubt that this attitude was responsible for the success of this little diner, with repeat customers, some of whom Craig had recognized from the previous day, being common.

Craig was surprised at how much pride he was feeling as he tried to plate these typical American breakfasts with as much appeal as they would allow. A few extra seconds to drain off some excess grease from a pair of fried eggs, to pluck the best available sprigs of parsley, or to carefully balance within the oval circumference of the white china plate the main entree with the side order of hash brown potatoes: these were conscientious acts which he took seriously, both to please the eye of the customer and to symbolically thank his employer for taking a chance on him, a virtual stranger a little over twenty-four hours ago.

He was also surprised at how the requirements of this relatively simple job dissipated the extent to which Joan occupied his mind. Surely she had been in his thoughts as he had dressed in the early morning darkness, and descended the hill on foot into town. But now, standing over the hot griddle, she was able to commandeer his mind only for brief moments, as when he awaited the color transformation of pancakes from pale yellow disks of batter to rich brown flapjacks.

How soon, he wondered, would he tire of this diversion from his misery? How long until he would be compelled to exchange the conviviality of Carol for the prospect of once again grabbing a

100

glimpse of Joan, perhaps once more witness her warm smile, to catch the glimmer of her essence in her eyes? How many eggs, waffles and pancakes would he need to serve before his past was but a distant memory, available only in some shadowy corner of his mind, no longer accessible by retracing his rail journey in an eastward direction?

And what of his wife? Was she truly better off with him removed from her life? Was she brooding and sorrowful, lamenting his departure every hour that he had been gone? Was she sorry for her part in this drama, wishing that she could take back the hurtful things said, the painful acts played out? Or was she rejoicing? Was she dancing with the joy of knowing, even to the extent that she did know, that the lie was over, the game of pretend no longer required?

He had no answers. Indeed, he had not had answers for some time. It was this, the absence of solutions, which had led him to such a desperate response to the final exam.

40

Dolores began the second full day of being alone much as she always had. At times Craig's absence became apparent. There was no need to wait for him to finish shaving so she might use the bathroom sink. She only had to prepare breakfast for one. There was no need to inquire as to his evening plans to avoid any conflicts with hers. At these times she acted as if he were away on one of his infrequent business trips.

But this ruse quickly became ineffective in curtailing her curiosity as to where he might have gone, although she felt she had a good understanding of why. Apparently he had felt the same emptiness she had known. Only Craig had had the courage to do something about it. So after breakfast she rifled through his desk in the bedroom and found the business card of their financial planner, Nigel Williamson. Dolores remembered how Craig had been tolerant of Nigel, and the agent before him, because they refrained from frequently appearing with "investment opportunities" that were just too good to pass up. Rather, they were responsive to Craig's inquiries for life insurance, accidental disability coverage, or well regarded mutual funds.

Nigel's booming voice on the telephone was silenced by Dolores when she stated flatly that she wished to meet with him as soon as possible, that afternoon if possible.

"I'd like you to go over our financial position. Let me know where we stand," she said.

"Anything in particular you're looking for?" he asked. "You know, the market's been pretty strong the last couple of days."

"Nothing specific. I just want to know generally where we stand."

Characteristically Nigel would use small talk to identify an element of common interest which he would then try to turn into perceived concern to set the foundation for a sale. Mrs. Miller did not appear receptive, her manner being very matter of fact. Without that small talk he was nearly speechless, but arranged an appointment for half past two that afternoon.

"Will Mr. Miller be joining us?" he asked.

"No. No he will not."

41

With the departure of the last breakfast patron of the morning, Carol came back to the kitchen to assist Craig with staging the mid-day meal. Together they carried boxes of hamburgers, hot dogs, lunch steaks, French fries and other lunch fare from the refrigerated storage room. During one of these transfers, without looking up from the load in her hands, Carol asked, "So what brings you to the heart of West Virginia?"

Craig, keenly aware that this was the first venture into personal questioning in his two days on the job, decided to volunteer little. "It was time to move on," he said.

"Yeah, but why here? Why Walsh? This little town's hey day has come and gone."

"Oh, I don't know. We had a pretty good crowd for breakfast, here. Maybe Walsh will bounce back once again. Maybe Carol's Diner will be the heart of the renaissance." Craig sensed that his effort at humor would probably not distract Carol from her line of questioning. He was right.

"I don't mean to pry," she continued, "just hoping I could get some sense of what you're about. It might make it easier for us to work together."

"You've made me feel quite comfortable already. I appreciate that. For a first day on the job I must say I didn't feel much stress."

"You're picking it up pretty fast. I'll think you'll work out just fine."

Craig realized that he owed her some answers, if for no other reason than to repay her for the trust and kindness she had shown him.

"I've come from New Jersey," he said. "A small town in the northern half of the state. For years I worked in the real estate appraisal business. I was pretty good in the profession, made a decent living. But recently, I got very little satisfaction from my work, I sensed I could be, should be, doing more. That, coupled with some disappointments on a personal level, spurred me to leave and to seek out a new life."

Craig watched Carol for her reaction. Her personable nature, which was usually evident in her bright eyes and irrepressible smile, had changed. A furrowed brow and focused eyes indicated that she was trying to understand his story and his motivations. Craig wondered what success she would have, as much of his situation was still a mystery to him.

"Why Walsh? Why did you come here?"

"Would you believe me if I told you I closed my eyes and pointed at the page of an atlas? That's just about what I did. I was looking for some place as different as I could find from where I was. New York City was one option, but I chose to go in the opposite direction."

"Yeah, this sure ain't Manhattan." She paused, apparently in reflection. "And you expect to find satisfaction frying eggs in this tired old mining town?"

Carol's question was spot on. What would be his answer to such an inquiry? Her unabashed good nature encouraged him to be painfully honest. "I'm not sure what I'm looking for or where I'll find it. I just know what I'm trying to leave—what I had to leave."

"Had to leave? Are you in trouble with the law?"

"No. Nothing like that…I just couldn't bear it any longer.

"As for working here," he continued, "there is much to appreciate. You and your husband seem to be very kind people. Many, many people work for employers lacking that quality. In that regard I consider myself very lucky, doubly so in that I found a job here so quickly."

"That's very nice of you to say. Marc and I have a pretty favorable first impression of you, obviously. I just want to warn you not to hold out too much hope for this town. It can break your heart. It has sucked the soul out of many of the people who have lived here, driven others away. It can be a very sad, lonely place."

Craig watched Carol turn her eyes away, as if to look out of the kitchen, out the door of the diner, and out beyond the mountains on the horizon.

"You stayed here. You and Marc took a chance on this business. Haven't you found some happiness?"

Carol looked back at Craig with a sly grin, "Maybe there's more to frying eggs than most folks realize."

42

Nigel Williamson accelerated into the passing lane of Interstate 78 and then whipped back in front of the vehicle that had briefly obstructed his way towards Peach Hill. He appreciated the way his car maneuvered, and quick little moves like that made him think of his college days when he played right tackle for the Rutgers football team. He was one of the biggest players on the team back then, but had been extremely agile. His coach had told him he was quick enough to play guard, but the team needed his size in the tackle position. It had not always been the case. As a freshman at Barringer High School in Newark, he had just been big. He was so out of shape that he was cut from the freshman team before the first week's practices were concluded. His reaction to this failure had changed his life.

As a black boy growing up in the urban jungle, Nigel had been protected by his mother in every way that she could. Convinced that education would be his means to escape the downward spiral into poverty that so many in her family had followed, his mother had made sure that he spent more time in the library than on the street corner. She enrolled him in every Fresh Air program available so that he would spend a week or two of each summer in white suburbia to get a taste of the better life. By constant repetition she had him believing that he was going to go to college, the first in the family to do so.

By middle school, Nigel knew his aptitude for academic studies was sub-standard. But as he experienced the growth spurt that accompanied puberty, growing both up and out, he constantly heard from friends and family that he was looking more and more like a football player. This would be his ticket to college and the fulfillment of his mother's dream.

Failing to make the freshman team was a devastating blow to his pride, and it was weeks before he was able to tell his mother, forced to do so before she went to the first home game and not see him on the field. But those weeks she thought he was at practice were being spent to attain the ultimate goal. Following a weight lifting regimen provided by one of the coaches, followed by hours of running around the stadium, Nigel gradually transformed himself into a big, strong, and fast athlete. By his sophomore year he was a starting defensive lineman, and for the last two years of high school he played both ways, offense and defense, rarely leaving the playing field. He had learned a valuable lesson: find out what the people with power want, and give it to them. With the stubbornness he had inherited from his mother, it was then never a question of if, but only of when.

Now, eight years out of school, Nigel was well established in the financial planning field, thanks mostly to his ability to deliver what his customers wanted. Once Nigel established even the slightest connection with a potential customer, he began to employ two complementary tactics to promote his success. The circumstances that enabled these tactics had been learned by interacting with white students at Rutgers, and Nigel had noticed their reoccurrence on so many occasions that he began to believe they were nearly universally existent. The first was an aversion to any judgment or conclusion that would suggest that that decision, regardless of how well reasoned, may have been tainted by racism. Except in extreme cases, a fear of being labeled a racist would trump incompetence, laziness, even dishonesty. The second circumstance resulted from Nigel's discovery that a jolly black man was almost always welcome. An angry black man might be threatening. A somber black man might be perceived as scheming. But a laughing, joking black man was good for comic relief, a smile, eventually acceptance.

So Nigel assumed that role, announcing his arrival in a booming voice, never altering the smile on his face, even subjecting himself to self-ridicule, if necessary. He would seize every opportunity to morph a comment into a joke, a frown into a smile, a smile into a laugh, rejection into acceptance. Repeatedly he found himself leaving homes with signed contracts where originally the occupants were reluctant to allow him entry.

But such had not been the case at the Millers. Mr. Miller had sat, deadpan, through his first sales presentation, non responsive to any of Nigel's attempts at humor. He had asked a few specific questions, challenged Nigel to support some claims he had made, and then, without any emotion, had agreed to purchase one of the products Nigel was offering. Nigel recalled feeling uneasy having closed the sale without employing any trickery or showmanship, only to realize later that Craig Miller's actions had been a flattering testament to Nigel's competence, something he had rarely before experienced alone.

Even so, the fact that Mrs. Miller had called him was strange, as her husband had made all of the decisions previously. Nigel consulted his file to refresh his memory as to Mrs. Miller's first name, and considered how much of his usual role playing he should employ in dealing with her.

Immediately upon seeing her face as Dolores opened the door, Nigel canned his routine. The woman's expression was fearful and her frame seemed to be buckling under the emotional weight it was bearing. In a labored manner, she led him to a seat on the living room sofa.

"My husband left yesterday, quite probably never to return. He caught a train for Newark, and from there, who knows? I am totally ignorant of financial matters. That's why I called you."

"Perhaps he just left for a short time, an escape. He may be on his way back now," Nigel suggested, hoping to put her at ease.

"No, he is gone. He is not coming back. This I know," was her response. Then, "Can you tell me if there have been any changes to our finances?"

"For the most part, no. There was one liquidation, about two weeks ago, a relatively small amount. It was some miscellaneous funds from his mother's estate that we had bundled into a growth fund. You were not aware of that transaction?"

"No, I was not."

"I see." Nigel quoted the dollar amount from his records, and awaited her next question.

Dolores was silent, staring out the window towards the street. She remained this way for a minute or more, and then in almost a whisper, "Yes, that is how he would do it." Turning to Nigel, she asked, "I believe most of the investments are in our names, jointly?"

"Yes, they are."

"How limited am I in accessing the money?"

Nigel considered his response, then chose to err on the side of caution. "Permit me to make a phone call to our office. I really wish to give you the best answer from the beginning."

Leading him to the phone in the kitchen, Dolores stepped away and continued to stare out the window, hearing but not really listening to Nigel's side of the conversation, which was primarily affirmations of his understanding of what the other party was saying.

When the phone call ended, Nigel returned to the living room.

"In this short a time frame, it is difficult to conclude that your husband has abandoned you--"

"He is not coming back, Mr. Williamson. Of this, I am certain. I know Craig. He is gone."

"Okay, then, we'll work on that assumption. With joint accounts, you have a fair degree of freedom, as long as we assume you are acting in your joint interests, and that Mr. Miller's absence is temporary. You can move money around, cash out much of many accounts. A total liquidation of a fund, or a sale of the house—that could be a problem. Basically, under these circumstances, the law tends to leave everything in suspense. Should Craig return, everything would resume from where things were when he left. This tends to tie your hands in many ways."

"So things just stagnate, forever?"

"Well, no, there are presumption of death rules to handle long-term unexplained absences," Nigel said. Consulting his notes, he continued, "If Craig 'were to be missing from his home or usual residence for a period of seven years; such absence had been continuous and without explanation; persons most likely to hear from him had heard nothing; and he could not be located by diligent search and inquiry', then he could be presumed dead and the probate laws would come into force."

"Seven years," Dolores said flatly, continuing to stare out the window.

"You need to find him," Nigel said. "Get a private eye to track him down and have him come back, or pursue a divorce."

43

    Sunday's dawn in Walsh was masked by a light but steady rain, the thick clouds preempting the sun's first appearance so that there was no sunrise, only a gradual brightening of the sky to the extent that the grey cloud cover would allow. It had rained most of the night, and the dampness had saturated all things porous while water had pooled where it would not be admitted.

    The Sweetbriar River quietly flowed seaward, only slightly swelled by the precipitation. The velvet smoothness of the water surface was repeatedly dimpled by the striking raindrops, but only for an instant as the assaulting drops were promptly forgiven and accepted.

    On Mr. Huntington's railroad, creosoted cross ties repelled the moisture as best they could, with droplets coagulating on the level surface forming small clear domes which reflected the gloomy sky. The droplets transformed the gloom with glistening highlights atop the dark, somber tableau. Inside the cab of a throbbing diesel locomotive, the engineer hummed a Janis Joplin tune as his windshield wipers slapped time. The hundred hopper cars that trailed his engines were topped off with evenly rounded heaps of black diamonds which glistened with their newly acquired coating of moisture. Sensing that the locomotive wheels were close to slipping on the wet, polished steel rails, the engineer activated the lever controlling the sanders. Through the seat of his pants he felt the wheels dig in to the rails, the dry sand deposited before them providing the extra needed traction.

    On Main Street, nothing moved. The traffic light at the intersection of Depot Street displayed an inviting green, the welcome being repeated in a long smeared reflection on the soaked street. With mine activity slacking off over the weekend, truck traffic was gone. No commercial activity beckoned--even Carol's Diner was closed, to open later to serve lunch after church services concluded. It was too early for the churchgoers, too. Most of them were still in their beds, enjoying the extra rest that Sunday mornings afforded.

    Raindrops played a soft percussion on the window of Reverend Jordan's study, where he was quietly working even as his wife and children continued to slumber. Sitting at his desk, coffee cup cradled in his long, thin fingers, he reviewed his sermon which he had written two nights before. Always comfortable speaking before groups, Eb could easily ad lib a sermon on practically any topic, but he felt his congregation deserved, and he owed them, a well thought out, well rehearsed message. Thus the early Sunday morning review had become as much a ritual as the church service which would follow three hours later.

On the houses on Monroe Street, the rain that struck the roofs commenced a gradual cascade, from shingle to shingle to overlapping shingle, ever downward off the gabled slopes. Upon reaching the final tier, the water poured off the shingles into the aluminum gutters below, there to be channeled towards downspouts posted at building corners which expedited the collected flow straight down to concrete splash blocks on the ground below. This migration was repeated at each house along the tree-lined street, with one exception. At 43 Monroe, one of the gutters had lost its grip upon the house, the result of a gutter nail gone missing some months before. An especially violent wind during a January squall had forced a section of the gutter to abandon its parallel orientation to the roofline, placing it instead at an acute angle to its intended placement. This, in turn, had caused a fissure in continuity of the channel, said rift occurring directly above the steps that led up to the covered front porch. The wooden steps now served as a splash block for the errant stream of water which had found its short path to ground by way of the severed gutter joint.

The occupants of Number 43 were awake, but silent. Propped up on a pillow, Craig sat in bed looking out the windows at the rooftops of the town below, pondering how he might spend his first day off, hopefully in a purposeful but relaxing manner.

In her bedroom, Sarah sat in the upholstered chair in the corner, a post she had assumed an hour before sunrise after an hour of lying awake in bed unable to sleep. The events of recent days had dramatically altered her world. In many ways change had been for the better, but in other ways it had been disturbing. It had disrupted her lethargy but also had introduced subconscious rumblings which she felt but did not understand.

She was hopeful that Sunday would restore some normalcy to her existence. Sunday had offered her the sole anchorage in a life adrift. First came the preparation, attending to her appearance contrary to her practice the other six days of the week. Then there was the ritual of the church service itself. Even if she was less than attentive and found her mind wandering, she felt safe in the sanctuary, safe in the comforting words of hope and praise. This safety was reinforced by the organ music, be it prelude, mid-service hymn, or concluding recessional. Always it was the sacred music which had tied the loose strands of her life together, the weekly rebinding keeping her intact for another week.

On this morning, however, she was unsure that the tones from the pipes would be enough. She felt she needed some reassurance, perhaps some direction, at least an objective point of view. She decided that she would approach Reverend Jordan and see if he was up to the task of providing some of the spiritual reinforcement she felt she needed. Since her husband died, the pastor had made many offers to talk with her, to pray with her, to offer her counsel. Always she had politely declined, convinced that she was capable of working through her grief in her own way. But the new turmoil in her life had put her at a loss, and to counter her feeling of helplessness, she was now willing to reach out for help.

44

Craig had sat in bed for nearly two hours, a display of listlessness that was unusual for him. Perhaps it was the rainy weather, which made the prospect of going into town—on foot, of course—unappealing. Perhaps it was the weariness he felt as a result of the conditions of his new job, which, as opposed to the last two decades of working while sitting at a desk, now required him to be most often standing. Even with less than two days on the job, he felt fatigue in his legs. Certainly a major reason for his lack of enthusiasm was the aimlessness of his plan, if he even considered what he had was in fact a plan.

As he was coming to appreciate increasingly with each passing hour, his plan to escape his troubles in the north was incomplete and contained several flaws. These shortcomings were substantial, and not overcome simply through flawless execution, as, so far anyway, he seemed to be experiencing. He could now honestly admit to himself that his scheme had more overtones of a grazing animal's flight response than of a strategic algorithm to solve his problems. But like a wildebeest that spots a pride of lions at a watering hole, he had started to run and was committed to that course of action until he either outdistances the predators or was forced to succumb to their death grip on his windpipe.

As for the demon that preoccupied his mind, Joan was mocking his presumptions, was insulting his intentions. She was now joined by an unlikely ally. More and more his recalcitrant wife was occupying his thoughts, and with each occurrence he felt increased guilt for abandoning her. What had been the first and most easily supported reason for his course of action—a moribund marriage lacking only a divorce decree to serve as its formal death certificate—was now elevated to its formally sanctified position. The fact that he had turned away from it was a discredit to his moral character. To the extent he subscribed to this doctrine, and at many times he was convinced of its legitimacy, he felt sorrowful and repentant. But he was incapable of returning to Dolores, to once again face her dismissive passiveness, to have his entreaties greeted with disdain.

Painted into this forgotten corner of the world, Craig resigned himself to his fate, and choosing action—any action—over inaction, he resolved to make something positive of his day off. He determined to spend much of the day continuing to explore the town. Despite the rain, he would explore on foot, and let fate dictate what he would discover and how it might affect his stay in Walsh.

Thus were his spirits elevated to the highest altitude permissible given the gloomy weather and his depressed self-esteem, as he descended the stairs.

45

With high hopes for a positive experience at church—on both spiritual and practical levels—Sarah arose from the chair, showered and dressed. For the first time since before Frank's death, she passed by the black and somber gray dresses hanging in the front of her closet, and digging deeper into her wardrobe, selected a royal blue dress. She remembered buying the garment on a trip to Clarksville, and how Frank had said he liked the color on her. Standing before the mirror, she imagined seeing herself through her late husband's eyes. Objectively as possible she concluded that he had been correct, that it did become her, especially where her blond hair came to rest on the dress's shoulder.

She was not especially hungry, but chose some fruit and yogurt to serve as her breakfast. Once concluded, she busied herself with small chores to fill the time before leaving for the church. She had just completed watering some plants in the living room and was returning to the kitchen when she encountered Craig descending the stairs, wearing a jacket and ball cap and carrying an umbrella.

"Good morning," she said.

"'Morning," Craig replied, a cheery smile brightening his face.

"A gloomy morning out there, but 'April showers bring May flowers.' You're going out in that rain?"

"Yes, fortunately it's not raining too hard. I have a day off from the diner; thought I'd explore the town a little." A slight pause added emphasis to Craig's next comment, "That's a very attractive dress."

"Why, thank you. I haven't worn it in a long time, so I thought I'd wear it to church today." Sarah hesitated, then continued. "Services begin at ten. You're welcome to ride with me, if you'd like." She bit her lip as she finished, continuing to be surprised by her repeated overtures to this stranger. He was an imposition on her life, an intruder in her home, but for some reason, she offered to cater to him, again and again.

"Thank you for the offer," Craig said, "but I've never been much of a churchgoer, I'm afraid. Have a nice day." With that he smiled and went out the front door.

Sarah stood still, recognizing that her encounters with her

boarder thus far had been limited to brief vignettes, typically as he passed in or out her front door. Perhaps, if he remained as elusive, he might not be much of a burden to her after all.

She watched through the door sidelight as Craig started down the steps, taking care to avoid the trickle of water pouring from the gutter overhead. As he reached the ground he looked up at the defective gutter, seeming to study it for a moment, and then continued on his way towards the center of town.

46

Sarah could no longer tolerate the clutter that was slowly filling the house. From the living room she removed a book she had never started and a magazine that she had only partly read. She scooped up a pile of junk mail that had rested undisturbed in the foyer, and dispatched it to the trash. With these and similar tasks she filled the minutes until she had to leave for a timely arrival at the church. At the appointed time she donned a light jacket and prepared to make a dash for the car. Crossing the front porch, she began to search through her purse for her car keys, continuing without conscious thought down the steps towards the front yard. Suddenly a shaft of cold water struck the back of her neck, rapidly flowing down her spine. Letting out a high pitched shriek as a reaction to both the surprise and the cold discomfort, she spun around to stare at the piece of gutter hanging jauntily away from the house. To repair that gutter, she concluded, would be an action item of high priority.

Driving to the church, Sarah took in the beauty of the valley in early spring, an appreciation that had escaped her in recent months. Even subdued by the overcast lighting and lightly falling rain, the greens of the tree buds and revitalized grasses were alive with promise for the coming season of renewal. At the same time, the apparent rebirth of her soul, the revitalized interest in life with all of its related functions, of these, too, was she keenly aware. To what extent had her awakening made the obvious season change a new revelation? How much had the season changed affected her reawakening? And what was it about her new paying houseguest that at the same time was captivating, threatening, interesting, mysterious, annoying?

Entering the sanctuary, the organ music once again touched her heart. The composer of this Sunday's melody was unknown to her, as was the music itself. But the music enveloped her, its rhythm, melody and harmonious counter melodies grabbed her interest and would not let go. From the piercing high notes to the deepest pedal tones, the hymn spurred a complete sensory experience, being perceived not only audibly, but as though it touched numerous nerve endings all over her body. Although she had no training in the playing of any keyboard instrument, she sensed an involuntary response from various muscles as her arms seemed to thrust hands downward in forceful interpretations, she imagined her fingers stretched to execute rising arpeggios, and toes pretended to dance across foot pedals to urge the lowest bass notes from the largest of the organ's pipes.

She moved to her customary seat, but instead of the usual polite smile she typically shared with Kay and Sam, today's look was animated and engaging. Once out of her jacket, the regal blue of her dress radiated good cheer and all but completely overcame the gloom that the weather offered.

Nor did her elation end there. She became focused on all phases of the service, joining in the singing of hymns with an energy that she had not applied since before Frank's death. The Gospel readings held her attention, with even minor nuances leading her to deeper reflection. Reverend Jordan's sermon was the beneficiary of her new outlook, with her mind wrapping itself around the meanings of his words as well as some inferred ideas as well.

At the conclusion of the service, Sarah lingered near the end of the reception line, insuring that she would be one of the last congregants to greet the minister in the vestibule. When, in response to her inquiry, he indicated that, of course, he would be happy to speak with her for a few minutes, she returned to the sanctuary, sitting in a pew near the entrance to await the preacher's availability. Within a few minutes Eb Jordan made his way through the sanctuary en route to his office, and motioned that she should follow. She did so without speaking, taking a seat in the office that he offered as he proceeded to remove his robe and place it on a hanger. The office was Spartan in appointments, testifying to the fact that the reverend did most of his work in his home study. On the walls hung some photographs reflecting the history of the church building as it had grown in size over the years. A bookcase against the wall displayed but perhaps a dozen volumes, with several of them being a sampling of hymnals. On the desk were several pieces of correspondence, mostly invoices, and a working copy of the church's budget folded open to the operating expenses page. A manual typewriter occupied a central location on the desk, having been used most recently to prepare this week's bulletin. Eb placed a chair in front of the desk near to Sarah's chair and seated himself, leaning forward with forearms on his knees so as at once to both reduce his overbearing stature and project an aura of increased interest in his visitor.

"I'm glad you asked for this meeting," he said. "I've become increasingly worried about you."

"Oh. Why?"

"Sarah, everyone deals with grief in their own unique way. For each person it is different, and there is no one timetable that determines when one phase of grieving should end, and another begin. For many, a certain level of loss never ends. But even in those situations, they are able to get on with their lives—still missing their loved one—but not to the extent that they cease growing, cease actively participating in life. I will tell you frankly that I believe it is time you moved on to the next phase, to resume a more fulfilling life. I think it is what you need emotionally and spiritually. I think it is what Frank would have wanted you to do. I think it's what this congregation and this community need for you to do."

"Pastor Jordan, that's why I wanted to talk to you. I think I have moved to a new phase—was pushed to a new phase. I feel strange. Sometimes I'm exhilarated, sometimes I'm scared, sometimes I'm confused. But I feel alive again, I'm aware again."

"Pushed? What do you mean, 'pushed'?"

"I am renting out the spare bedroom in my house. To someone who's just arrived in town. I needed the money, and he seems to be a good tenant. But I have an uneasy feeling."

"What do you mean?"

"I don't know. I hardly know anything about him. He's very quiet, stays to himself. But I have this urge to find out more about him, while at the same time I feel uncomfortable, like he has some unusual power. I know my life has not been the same since he rang my doorbell. It's like I've awakened from a long sleep—a little groggy but much, much more aware than I was before. I feel good about the awareness, but uncomfortable about the directions it is tending to lead me."

"Are you scared for your safety?"

"No. It's not that. Craig—that's his name—Craig works at the diner. Carol seems to think he's okay. I trust her judgment. And he's done nothing to scare me. I just guess I'm used to having the house entirely to myself. He's like an intrusion. But such a mild intrusion, like I hardly know he's there sometimes. And other times…"

The minister waited for Sarah to continue, but she remained silent, biting her lower lip. "And?"

"And other times I have this strange desire to talk to him, as if I believe he is a messenger sent straight to me with an urgent message. But whenever I try, he's polite, but aloof. And before I know it, he's left."

Eb studied Sarah as he digested what she had revealed. Sarah knew she had averted her eyes frequently as she told her story. She realized that she was holding her arms close to her body as if to contain as much as possible, releasing information in carefully measured packets. Her hands were taking turns rubbing each other, as much to soothe her nervousness as to assign them something to do.

In response to the preacher's silence, Sarah spoke again. "I want to thank you for listening. I guess some of what I'm saying doesn't make too much sense."

Eb sat back in his chair, his erect pose forcing him to look down at his shorter congregant, cocking his head slightly as he spoke, "On the contrary, you are experiencing a number of significant changes, most of them, I would guess, not of your choosing. Because of these changes, things are new, different. It is natural that you would react with caution, curiosity, and sometimes, confusion. I see that as a good sign. For too long I have seen you plodding about with little interest for anything, your eyes nearly glazed over. And it's not just me. Kay has been worried about you for months—you should know you are constantly in her prayers. She has often come to me, urging me to do something, to talk with you. But I was hoping you would come when you were ready, although I will confess I stopped by your place the other day, prepared to take the initiative, when I saw a fellow—I assume your boarder—leaving. Thinking it may not have been the best time, I didn't stop. I'll also confess that may have indicated a little cowardice on my part."

Sarah smiled. It was so typical of Reverend Jordan to take a round of self-effacement as he parceled out his wisdom. "Until today I wasn't ready. Nothing to do with you, I just was absorbed in my loss. I miss Frank so much." Sarah closed her eyes as she sat silently for a moment before continuing, "But things have changed, I think for the better, I hope for the better."

Eb leaned forward again, capturing her full attention, "I believe you're right. Seize this opportunity, become revitalized!

Your shell has protected you through this storm of grief. But it's safer now. Safe to come out of your shell, to connect again, to live again. And yes, to take risks, again."

"Risk questioning my mysterious boarder?" she asked with a grin.

"When you feel comfortable. He may be a man with troubles of his own, fears we cannot know, in his own shell seeking protection from we know not what. In that case he might see your inquiries as threatening. On the other hand, perhaps such contact is what he craves most. You'll have to play it be ear." Eb paused for a second, then continued with a gentle smile, "Most often, it's a little of both, you know: fear and hope."

"Thank you, Pastor."

"Let us pray together: Father, Your child, Sarah, has been traveling in the darkness, missing her beloved Frank whom You have brought home to You. We ask that You help her not to be afraid of the light, to show her the way towards renewed life and the opportunity to do Your will. We pray that You will watch over her, and guide her uncertain steps in the days to come, as she returns to her rightful place in Your church and this community. Help her to bear the grief of her loss while dedicating herself to Your service so that someday she may rejoin Frank in Your kingdom. This, in the name of your Son, Jesus, we pray. Amen."

47

"Holy shit! Where did she come from?"

Jeff Downs threw his face into his car's passenger's seat, thrusting his camera and telephoto lens into the adjacent foot well, and lay still. Mrs. O'Connor, the subject of today's tail, had entered the pharmacy near the other end of the strip mall twenty minutes earlier, and as far as Jeff had known, she was still inside. Somehow she had left the drug store without him observing her and was now coming out of a gift shop at this end of the mall and was crossing the parking lot towards her car. Not wishing for her attention to be drawn in any way towards Jeff's silver Honda Civic, he had dived below the dashboard—hopefully before she had looked in his direction.

"I'm getting too old for this crap," he muttered aloud. At fifty-nine years of age, he was finding the job of private investigator to be more difficult than when he first started a little over twenty years ago as a means to supplement his disability income. He grimaced again as he recalled the sting of the nine millimeter round as it had entered his left leg, the result of stupid horseplay by a brother officer in Newark's South Ward. It had cost the idiot his job, and Jeff a permanent disability just a few years short of early retirement, and a limp which he still displayed today.

Too many mental mistakes were becoming commonplace. Like losing track of a tail in a small strip mall. Concentration, that's what was needed. Unfortunately, after nearly two decades of tailing errant spouses in hopes of capturing their illicit rendezvous on film, the job was not getting more interesting, and his mind was beginning to wander more often.

He slowly rose and peered over the dashboard to see Mrs. O'Connor entering her car. Jeff reached into the back seat and snared a bright red Cincinnati Reds baseball cap. He would change between this hat, a gift from his brother living in the Queen City, an imitation leather fedora and going hatless so Mrs. O'Connor would not see the same man in her rear view mirror too often. By adding and subtracting sunglasses, he could give her six different men in a car that was almost invisible in its commonality. He started the Civic and hustled across the parking lot to follow the mark out of the exit. No sense in losing her here. He would back off once she started to move in traffic.

By the time she made her second turn it appeared that Mrs. O'Connor was heading back home.

"What's the matter, Mrs. O., your panties aren't hot today?" Jeff was annoyed. Three days of tailing "the tramp", as her husband described her, and nothing to show for it. The husband's attorney, a newbie to matrimonial cases, was looking for a return on the dollars he was shelling out for Jeff's daily expenses.

Jeff considered the fragility of the marriage bond and how its weakness had sustained not only his basic needs but had allowed him to hold thirty yard line season tickets for the Jets, his life's true passion. There never seemed to be a shortage of people cheating on their spouses, of attorneys leveraging the infidelities to their advantage, of injured parties transforming into value-conscious recipients-to-be or conservators of threatened assets. As a participant in the enterprise, Jeff felt some shame before recalling what it was like during the time leading up to his divorce over twenty-five years ago.

When he and his wife had decided to call it quits, it was at first a relief, an abandonment of the arguments, accusations, defensive posturing. For the first time in months, they had agreed on something: that they both would be better off apart. Working together again in harmony, they began to function under the umbrella of an amicable separation, coordinating division of assets with amazing alacrity. Then, just to insure that their course would not be fouled by an overlooked legality, they sought out separate attorneys, and the adversarial process became just that. Entitlements established by legal precedents quickly became due and payable in their present case, enriched by bargaining strategies and to compensate for injustices now recognized, thanks to the guidance of respective barristers. The divorce became unnecessarily, but inevitably, bitter, making the previous arguments appear to be minor squabbles in comparison.

Perhaps it was rationalization, but Jeff reasoned that his role in the process was to bring some objective evidence—photographs, hotel registration documentation, credit card statements—to the subjective claims of suffering and injustice. He wasn't the cause of Mrs. O'Connor's screwing around, but if she chose to do it, Jeff's Nikon would enable Mr. O'Connor to make his case. But that would apparently not be the case today, as Mrs. O'Connor pulled her Buick into her driveway and Jeff continued past, taking up his position a block away, where he had a partially obscured view of the street in front of the O'Connor driveway. So the waiting and watching continued.

48

It was raining much harder as Sarah left the church. She wondered how the rain storm had affected Craig's walk into town. Then she marveled that this had been one of her first concerns. What was it about this man that captured her interest?

Stopping at the grocery store to pick up a few items, she was keenly aware of how friendly the cashier and sacker seemed to be. They were not new faces, she had seen them there many times before, but today they seemed especially friendly and outgoing, despite the increased gloominess into which the day had regressed. The sacker even volunteered to carry her bags out to her car, despite the heavy rain. Had they always been this friendly, and she just had not noticed? Maybe—just maybe they were feeding off her rejuvenated spirits? She felt a slight thrill as she pondered the prospect that the exciting new feeling she was experiencing might already be spreading contagiously. The reverend Jordan's validation of the feelings she had been experiencing had served to anchor her euphoria and was encouraging her to cast off in new, exciting directions from that newly established base.

Arriving home, she turned her jacket collar up against her neck, in preparation for the dash to the porch in the downpour with her shopping bags. This time, she thought, she would take more care as she passed under that errant gutter over the porch steps, for surely a small river must be tumbling out its lower end.

However, when she arrived at the steps, there was no torrent from overhead. Glancing up, she thought the gutter appeared to be back in its correct location, close to the eave. Acquiring a dry lookout on the porch, she saw this was so, with the sound of water splashing out of the downspout onto the splash block at the corner of the porch further validating the point.

Entering the house, she heard sounds from the apartment's plumbing fixtures that suggested Craig was home. After removing her jacket and putting the groceries away, she climbed the stairs, pausing outside the boarder's door.

"Craig?"

A moment later the door opened, revealing Craig who was leaning lazily against the door post. "How was church?" he asked.

"It was nice..." she said, and then, searching for a more descriptive adjective, added, "spiritually rewarding." The smile that accompanied the addendum was immediately returned by her tenant. "Coming in from outside, I noticed the gutter...?"

"Yes, I took the liberty of fixing that for you. The way it's raining now, you could get drenched passing under it the way it was."

"Yes, but how?" she asked.

"I picked up a couple of gutter nails in town at the hardware store. Found some tools and a ladder in the garage. Had the job done in no time."

Sarah felt a red hot flame ignite deep in her chest, the heat spreading rapidly to all extremities of her body, but especially to her throat, where it could not be contained. It erupted from her mouth in a volcanic blast that hurtled ashen words at her tenant. "You were told only to use these rooms," she roared. "The rest of the house is off limits. That includes the garage. Especially the garage!"

Sarah turned on her heel and stormed towards her bedroom. Over her shoulder she could here Craig stammering, "I'm sorry, I..." Whatever else he said was unheard and punctuated by the slamming of her bedroom door. She began to furiously pace the floor, saying nothing, but in no way limiting the rage that was building within her from boiling up to her head, to be vented in steamy exhausts through her nostrils. She stopped before her open closet door and kicked her shoes off in rapid succession. Their staccato ricochets off the closet wall added emphasis to her anger which she could not begin to effectively express as she continued to pace shoeless across the floor.

She continued to pace for nearly a quarter hour, her mind focusing on images of the stranger plundering the garage, her garage, *Frank's* garage. By what right had he gone there? Was there no limit to his audacity? How could she possibly tolerate this and continue their contractual agreement when he so readily ignored a major clause?

After some time, the rage began to cool, and then, as suddenly as the fire had been ignited, a chilling numbness raced down her spine. While the anger had demanded dissipation over as large an area as possible, this new feeling required containment, immobilized insulation against the chill and the empty feeling that accompanied it. She sought refuge in the upholstered chair in the corner of the room, drew her feet up onto the seat and wrapped her arms around her knees to clinch them possessively beneath her chin.

49

Craig had taken a step into the hallway to pursue Sarah in an effort to plead his case, but the slamming of her bedroom door proclaimed a finality with which he could not argue. Returning to his chamber, he closed the door, then sat down at the desk and stared out the window at the rain pelting Monroe Street.

His landlady's reaction to his morning's efforts was perplexing. On seeing how the gutter had discharged its contents directly upon the steps below, he had quickly determined the problem and its straightforward correction. His first stop in town was at the hardware store two blocks east of Carol's Diner. Acquiring the necessary nails, he left the store to discover that the pace of the rain had increased. He revised his plan of performing the repair later in the day, and returned directly to the house. He was not surprised to find an extension ladder to the rear of the garage, since Sarah had told him that her late husband was a carpenter. Inside the garage he found a workbench, upon which were a hammer and some other tools which might prove helpful for the task. Despite the rain falling harder, he had accomplished the repair in short order, and returned the tools to where he had found them.

Certainly he had meant no harm—quite the contrary. Her sudden anger was a new side of Sarah he had not seen before. He had considered himself twice blessed to have found Carol and Sarah—a job and place to sleep—so quickly upon arriving in Walsh. He certainly did not wish to jeopardize his situation. He resolved to beg for forgiveness at the first opportunity, and to that end he remained quietly in his room, attentive for any sound which would suggest that the offended party had left her room. Throughout the afternoon and into the evening he occupied himself with reading books he had checked out from the town library, skipping both lunch and supper. Not a sound was heard, however, and by nine o'clock he was asleep, his fatigued body having overruled his mind's intention of maintaining the vigil.

50

Sarah was surprised by her own capacity for anger, and its duration scared her a bit. Through the afternoon she sat or paced, silently going over again and again the simple request she had made, and her boarder's flagrant disregard of it. Was her request for privacy too much to ask? Was this typical behavior of visitors from the north, making themselves at home without invitation and in opposition to requests to do otherwise?

She paced back and forth across the bedroom, unable to avoid approaching the window which offered a view of the garage, the scene of the crime. Each time as she approached the window, she looked away, as if she were afraid the outbuilding had been transformed or desecrated by the acts of her house guest. On a few occasions she would pause near the window and extend her hand to part the gossamer curtains in order to provide a better view, only to turn abruptly away, daring not to look. Instead the window provided only the drab illumination of a rain soaked overcast day, and a misty view of the distant mountains. Now gloomy and foreboding, the dark trees which covered them served as yet another screen to conceal their essence. The bright green buds which had moved her in the morning had diminished in intensity, as much by her sour mood as by the increased precipitation.

With the coming of darkness, she became less restless, choosing to sit rather than pace. Perhaps in a protective attitude, her mind abandoned repeated analysis, offering instead a numbed, passive state of consciousness which Sarah had known so well in the last few months. Thus she sat, staring blankly at the darkened corners of the room, seeing little, thinking little. At half past nine, however, she became alert, aware that she was sitting alone in the dark and that she was very hungry.

Moving silently to her door, she quietly opened it a crack and looked in the direction of the boarder's room. His door was shut, but light escaping beneath its lower edge suggested he was awake. The rage in her chest having rekindled slightly, she was in no mood to have another encounter with Craig.

As quietly as possible, she entered the hall, closing the door behind her. She continued towards the stairs, still making no sound, and directed her stocking clad feet to avoid the creaking step on the stairs. Arriving on the first floor undetected, Sarah was relieved to have avoided another encounter even as her annoyance was increased by the need to move about like a thief within her own home.

Burning just the small light above the stovetop, Sarah prepared and ate the quietest meal she could devise, some peanut butter smeared on slices of white bread. She conceded that this offering was merely to silence an angry stomach, an organ which had quickly, and apparently irreversibly, adapted to the new regimen of scheduled meals, quite a change from the apathetic days prior to revitalization. For this she had the quiet little man upstairs to thank. She was thankful and regretful, relieved and angry, glad he had come but wished he would leave. She was totally confused.

What happened next was neither a cognitive nor a reflexive reaction. Sarah rose from the kitchen table and approached the kitchen window. Pressing her face close to the glass she peered into the night, focusing on the detached garage to the rear of the house. What few rays of light from a street lamp successfully reached the outbuilding's façade, were weakly reflected by its white clapboard siding. She continued to stare, her eyes slowly becoming accustomed to the low light levels, allowing her to recognize more detail with each passing moment.

Spurred by pleasant memories from what now seemed the distant past, she tried to imagine seeing the reassuring light escaping the garage through the small window. She longed for proof that Frank was busy constructing some project in the woodshop which had completely taken over the garage, making her automobile a permanent refugee in the driveway. Tonight, however, the garage was dark and lifeless, its specter having moved on, not ever to return. Confirmation of this fact was not at all unexpected, yet it left Sarah suddenly empty, a chilling sensation flooding her body. She promptly turned away from the window, extinguished the stove light, and retracing her steps, retreated to the safety of her bed. There sleep came rapidly, filled as it was with confusing dreams featuring her late husband in unfamiliar roles, while unknown thespians assumed vital parts.

51

The alarm sounded by Craig's wrist watch jolted him awake, but opening his eyes to the glare from the lamp on the nightstand and discovering that he was lying on the bed fully clothed was more disconcerting. The book lying on the floor by the bed reminded him of his earlier sentry duty and his hopes for an opportunity to apologize to his landlady. The flare up that his landlady had displayed once again became emotionally burdensome and was no closer to resolution, and his obligations at the diner meant that it would remain that way for most of the day.

He promptly prepared himself for work, additional motivation being provided by the emptiness in his stomach, the result of skipping yesterday's dinner. Leaving his room, he found the rest of the house dark and quiet. As he stepped out onto the porch, the smell of spring was especially fresh, scrubbed as it was by the rains of the prior day. The heavens were adorned with a spray of stars, their visibility proving that the storm clouds had disappeared and suggesting a sunny day was in store.

Arriving at the diner, he quickly fell into the morning routine, changed slightly by the preparation of three pancakes for his own consumption, a task whose completion he timed to coincide with Carol's routine English muffin popping from the toaster. As she set about buttering her muffin, he peeled the foil lid off two plastic syrup servings and began what he hoped was a nonchalant line of inquiry.

"Carol, how well do you know Sarah Stiles?"

"Pretty well, I guess. She and her husband used to come here regularly, and I got to know them as customers. We worked on a town committee together, once. Why?"

"Oh, I'm just trying to get a read on her personality. Is she moody sometimes?"

Carol eyed Craig with a directness that dismissed his attempt to disguise his question as casual talk to pass the time. That done, she continued, "She was very upset by the loss of Frank. He was so young, and apparently strong—still in his forties when he died. No one expected it, especially Sarah. She's taken it pretty hard. Maybe you're confusing her grief with moodiness?"

"Perhaps." Craig poured the syrup over his pancakes, his

concentration on that task relieving him of having to renew contact with Carol's eyes.

"Something happen?" Carol asked.

Craig found Carol's directness to be a critical element of her personality, and in a world of bravado and presumptive airs, a welcome change. He had expected this conversation might turn in this direction, and was almost relieved that it had.

"Yesterday, while she was at church, I took it upon myself to fix one of her gutters—it had pulled away from the house. It was a minor thing, just took me a couple of minutes." He looked at Carol to be reassured that she was following his story, then continued, "To do so I borrowed some tools from her garage. When she learned that I'd gone to the garage she lost it. Went to her room, slammed the door, and stayed there all night. She was really angry. I was just trying to be helpful. Didn't mean any harm."

Carol considered his words quietly for a moment. "I don't know why that would have set her off. Maybe she had a bad day. Maybe it was the gloomy weather. Why don't you try apologizing to her today? She's a rather forgiving person, I think."

"I was thinking of doing that. Just wanted to know if I should be prepared for something else. Until yesterday, she was very kind to me—as you've been, too. I really appreciate the contacts I've made since coming to Walsh; wouldn't want to sour them."

Being Monday, the breakfast rush was the slowest Craig had experienced in his three day tenure at the diner. The fact that he was becoming comfortable with the job helped as well. His mind was focused on the anger Sarah had vented in his direction, and he attempted to understand it by reviewing what he had done and what she had said, again and again. Even so, Sarah did not hold a monopoly on his thoughts. Joan entered his mind, and assumed a position of prominence to which she had grown accustomed. Likewise Dolores made an entrance, the hurt at times visible in her languid eyes, while at other times they expressed anger as they assumed a more sultry appearance.

At the height of the morning's business, Craig used the breakfast foods frying on his griddle to serve as icons for the three women who now occupied his mind. The mound of frying potatoes represented his wife, with all the fleshy substance symbolizing her most genuine standing and legitimate claims. The sunny side up eggs stood in for Joan, their near perfection and fragile consistency a suitable match for she who was so elusive. The sizzling and popping bacon, quite a lot of noise without much reason, was the metaphor for the newest addition to his banquet of woes: his landlady, no less. Craig moved his spatula from food to food, while his mind moved from vision to vision.

At one point it was clear that breakfast was over, the dining room was completely void of patrons. Seeing this, the cook asked Carol if he might leave for a few minutes to run a quick errand, to which she consented. Craig hustled out of the diner. In less than ten minutes he had returned, thanking his boss for her permissiveness, and returning to the kitchen to begin preparations for lunch.

52

Bright sunlight streamed into Sarah's bedroom and the chirping of sparrows flitting around in the trees and shrubs could be heard as she awoke. She rose promptly from the bed, excited by her newly found energy. But as her feet touched the floor, recollections of Sunday's pacing quickly came to mind, and she came to an abrupt stop. Rapidly the memories of Craig's trespass were recalled, and with them a certain degree of anguish. However, the anger had greatly subsided, and she paused to reflect on this. Could the weather have had such a profound impact upon her disposition? She remembered her rage from yesterday, and its apparent harmony with the gloomy, rain soaked afternoon. Today, though, the anger was quelled, incongruous as it was with the beautiful spring day just outside her window.

She moved towards the window, as if to perform a closer inspection. Once there, she turned deliberately towards the garage, as compelled to look in its direction today as she had been compelled to avoid looking at it the day prior. All seemed well. Its white siding glistened in the bright sunlight, the overhead door and the smaller hinged door suggested unaltered integrity—keeping the elements out and the outbuilding's contents safe within.

Without bothering to dress or even to wrap herself in a robe, she purposefully moved out the door and down the staircase, the tail of her nightgown trailing in the wind her rapid motion created. She moved through the kitchen and out the back door, the coolness of the mountain spring morning air and the chill of the damp slate stepping stones beneath her bare feet causing her a slight shiver, but having no effect upon her forward motion. She came to an abrupt halt, however, upon reaching the smaller door to the garage. She remained motionless, her hand resting on the door's knob. Closing her eyes, she took a deep breath, then opened her eyes widely and turned the knob. The door yielded and she stepped inside.

Her eyes had yet to adapt to the darkness of the garage, but they were quickly drawn to the only light present, a shaft of sunlight entering the small window and falling on the center of the workbench against that wall. Spotlighted like actors on a stage, a grouping of hand tools—a coping saw, a mallet, two or three rasps—revealed that they were at total rest, undisturbed in their informal arrangement just as their owner had left them, so many months ago. Gradually the rest of the room came into focus. There were the remainder of Frank's hand tools, hanging on nails and pegs on the wall near the bench. Leaning against the far wall was a table top, sanded smooth and ready to receive stain, the grain of each individual board proclaiming its singular attractiveness while making its special contribution to the beauty of the whole.

Nearby was the table saw, its fence rigidly awaiting to guide a piece of lumber mercilessly into the vicious teeth of the circular blade at precisely the measured width it had been assigned. Over there was the band saw, standing at erect attention in the corner. And here, almost within arm's reach, the lathe lay in gentle repose, snugly confining a length of cherry which was well on its way to being transformed into an elegant table leg, the pile of shavings on the floor representing what the wood had been forced to lose in order to achieve its elevated status.

Sarah's eyes absorbed these sights. Her nostrils took in the sweet aroma of the woods and sawdust. Her ears heard nothing except the beating of her heart which seemed to be amplified in the stillness of this sacred place, Frank's place. But Frank was not there. These were his tools, but his no longer, bound as they were to their earthly purposes, he no longer had use for them. While his spirit might still linger, she had felt it more strongly elsewhere, within her own heart, without the need to come here. Indeed, she had not entered this garage since before he had died, and now, having summoned the courage to enter, she had a keen sense of disappointment. With that disappointment came a sense of shame, a feeling of regret that she had reacted so strongly, with so much anger, to the actions of her boarder. She considered his motives, and quickly realized that he had tried to help her, to act out of kindness. It was unrealistic for her to have thought that he would have understood how holy she thought this workshop was, especially now that she herself found it wanting in that regard. She solemnly resolved to offer an apology upon his return. Scanning the room one last time, she turned, closed the door, and returned to the house.

When, an hour or two later, the doorbell summoned her to the front door, she knew instinctively the source of the flower arrangement being held by the freckle faced deliveryman. The small card that accompanied the flora needed no signature; it carried only the words "I am sorry. So very sorry."

53

Leaving Carol's Diner at the end of his shift, Craig was met by the glorious spring day that had been promised by the star laden sky during his pre-dawn walk down the hill from Monroe Street. Birdsong of numerous varieties floated on the air: sweet melodies of finches, agitated buzzing from titmice, raucous rants of a jay, syncopated chirps of sparrows. People he passed on the street displayed high spirits in their smiles and friendly greetings. Spring was as welcome to Craig as it was to the birds and citizens of Walsh, yet his heart became heavy as he turned his steps towards the hill to the south.

He had little hope that the flowers dispatched to Sarah would drastically alter her disposition. Seldom had he been lucky with flowers in the past. Once, years ago, a bouquet that he handed Dolores had brought a smile to her face and a change to her mood. But lately, neither flowers nor any other offering had softened her nature or cheered her heart. Yet he knew of no other way to break the silence and hopefully soften the heart of his landlady prior to his return to his apartment.

Chestnut Street crossed both the railroad and the Sweetbriar on the same overpass, and passing below Craig was a train of empty coal hoppers marching westward towards the mines. He stopped and leaned against the railing, peering down at the empty cars and their cavernous holds. The smooth motion of the train and the repetitive similarity of the string of freight cars soon produced a dizzying sensation. Craig refocused on a more distant spot on the train and began to imagine refilling this train. Quite likely it would be filled using strip mining techniques, where huge mechanical shovels would, in one scoop, gather enough coal to nearly fill a single car. Craig imagined, however, the efforts of more traditional miners, working on their hands and knees, perhaps even lying on their chests, in subterranean crawlspaces chipping and raking coal loosened from veins by localized explosive charges. He imagined how much of the mineral he might be able to gather in an eight hour shift, and visualized its small contribution to the filling of but a single car in the string of a hundred. Racing several hundred miles eastward, his mind pictured the output of his labors travelling up a conveyor to be discharged into a raging furnace, to be consumed in a matter of minutes, its output a conversion to steam, smoke and enough kilowatts to operate a few dishwasher cycles. His potential contribution to society seemed miniscule in this analogy. As his gaze continued on the empty hoppers hammering by, he sensed an even greater emptiness in his soul.

Crossing the river, another pause for reflection brightened his spirits somewhat, the eternal nature of the stream and all life that the waters made possible having a calming effect. He made his way to Maple Street, and after two nearly level blocks, began the ascent. By the intersection with Madison, the joys of springtime had all but left his consciousness, the effort of the climb and what potentially awaited him at the top of the hill having drained him. By the time he climbed the stairs to the porch, he was short of breath. A glance upward at the repaired gutter served as a premonition of the next act, one he anticipated would be filled with drama. Pausing briefly, he turned the knob of the door and entered with a feeling of resigned deliberation.

He was surprised to see Sarah sitting on the staircase. She was wearing a light pink floral dress, a reflection of the season. Upon his entrance, she looked up at him and meekly smiled.

"Hi," Craig offered, the shortest possible greeting seeming to be an exhaustive effort to extract from his vocabulary.

"Hi," she responded in kind, adding, "I got the flowers. They were lovely. Thank you."

"Listen, I'm sorry about yesterday—"

"No," she interrupted. "I was wrong to be so angry with you. You'd done me a great favor, and I exploded."

"You had a right to be angry. I crossed the line, I—"

"No," she interrupted again, "I owe *you* an apology." Sarah bit her lower lip momentarily, and then added, rising, "Come with me for a second."

She led him through the kitchen and out the backdoor, moving directly towards the garage. Without hesitation she opened the small door, and stepping aside, motioned him to enter as she offered a verbal entreaty, "Please."

Craig stepped into the dark workshop. The lone window was on the shadow side of the building at this time of day, and the reflected light that entered was feebly inadequate to illuminate the interior. Sarah flipped a switch on the wall illuminating two bare bulbs in the ceiling and revealing the contents of the workshop, which was unchanged from Craig's visit the day before. Sarah began to speak with a voice which was reverently soft but nonetheless determined.

"This was one of my husband's favorite places. He would come here as a way to escape the everyday. He once told me that after working with rough fir timbers all day, building crude frameworks that would be covered with sheetrock and sheathing, it was such a different feeling to work with hardwoods to build furniture with details and beauty.

"When I learned that you had come in here, my Frank's special place, I felt that you had intruded—gone where you didn't belong. I know that you didn't mean anything by it, that you were trying to help me. I overreacted."

"That's okay. You had your reasons. I should've asked first."

Craig took the time to study the room on this visit, an unnecessary task yesterday when he was merely searching for a hammer. The variety of power tools would offer the craftsman many options in pursuing his hobby. The legless tabletop and the leg locked in the lathe suggested that this was the last active project.

"Looks like he was working on a table," Craig ventured. "Look, there are three more pieces of wood here, ready to be turned into legs, to match the one in the lathe."

"Yeah, he enjoyed making furniture. Occasionally he'd sell a piece, but most often he'd give away what he made. He was making this table for a meeting room at our church."

Glancing at Sarah's eyes, Craig noted a tiny tear beginning to form. Looking away, he took a few steps deeper into the garage.

"I haven't been in here since before Frank died," Sarah continued. "Thanks to you, I got up the courage to come in here again. I should thank you for that."

Without a word Craig gave her a slight nod. He continued his tour, stopping to rub his hand across the surface of the tabletop. "Nice work," he said. "He was quite a craftsman. And from what I hear from people in town, he had a good reputation as a carpenter, too. He must've been quite a man."

"Yes, he was."

Craig moved past her to exit the workshop. "Thank you," he whispered.

This time it was Sarah's turn to nod knowingly. Closing the door as she came out behind him, she was immediately transformed by immersion in the afternoon sunshine. The pallor that imbued her skin in the dim light of the workshop was replaced by a warm, cheery glow as her flesh was caressed by the rays of the sun. Her dress, which had appeared Victorian and stately indoors, was alive with vibrant color outside. As much by the transition in her appearance as by the removal of the emotional burden he had carried for twenty-four hours, Craig felt empowered and free. He gave her a smile which he hoped would convey his understanding and appreciation.

Entering the kitchen, Sarah turned to him, "I once promised you a dinner. Can I whip something up for us tonight? My way of apologizing for my bad manners yesterday?"

"I have a better idea. Let me treat you to dinner down at the diner. I happen to know that the rookie cook is not working tonight, so we're guaranteed to get a good meal."

"It's a deal," she said, smiling at his self-effacing humor, "on the condition that you let me cook for you tomorrow night."

"Fair enough. Six good?"

"Six is fine."

Smiling, Craig turned and climbed the stairs, much relieved at how his fortunes, at least in this regard, had improved.

54

Nestled in a crease of the forested hills that line the north edge of Somerset County, was a small frame building, sitting just off the two lane highway that connects two small towns in the New Jersey countryside. From the outside the building was characteristically commercial in nature. Asphalt pavement flowed uninterrupted from the shoulder of the road to the building's foundation. With no grass lawn and only a few evergreens planted along one side offering any natural intervention to the man-made, it was a nearly maintenance-free environment. Conspicuously absent from the building and grounds was any kind of sign to identify the building or what activity occurred within. But each night in the early evening the parking lot began to fill with cars, with luxury vehicles such as Cadillacs, Lincolns, Mercedes and Jaguars well represented. The cars typically carried the license plates of the Garden State, although it was common to see a few of the vehicles bearing New York registrations.

A typical motorist passing by at fifty miles per hour would glean no olfactory clues as to the purpose of the building. Unless suffering the ill effects of nasal congestion, however, anyone stepping out of their car, as Dolores did that evening, would catch the scent of grilling steaks that rode the air. Her friend Barbara had suggested Michael's Restaurant as the meeting place when Dolores had called asking if they could get together, "just the two of us", to catch up. Dolores recalled visiting Michael's once before, when she and Craig had joined Barbara and her husband, Allan, there for dinner. The food was quite good, she remembered, if a little pricey, especially given the low key informality of the place.

Allan had been representing a client for whom Craig was preparing an appraisal, and Craig had suggested the two couples get together for dinner. Although they lived in northern Bergen County, Allan had suggested Michael's as a place he knew and liked.

The women had become instant friends, both having an interest in the theater, Barbara often performing in local productions throughout the northern half of the state. In every other way they could not have been more different. Barbara was a tall, large boned woman, with orange-red hair, cropped short and rarely venturing far from her skull. Her authoritative voice brought her attention from all corners of whatever room she was in. She was dramatic in voice and gesture, and her facial features were underscored by eye makeup and lipstick just to insure that no meaning would be missed from any downcast eyes, elevated brows or pursed lips. This, of course, was in stark contrast to the diminutive Dolores, whose shoulder-length brown hair presented a feminine frame for her gentle face with its understated expressions. She could move with feline fluidity often accompanied by a silent, almost secretive demeanor, which could well serve as an example to a stalking lioness. While Dolores exuded a fresh-scrubbed purity, Barbara reeked of cigarettes which she chain smoked.

These differences were in fact the bonds that secured their friendship. Each woman saw in the other traits to be coveted. Barbara was envious of a seductive, not ostentatious allure which she believed Dolores exhibited, while Dolores longed for a more forceful personality, a right-or-wrong dogmatism which scoffed at second guesses and reviews from varying perspectives.

The husbands, however, proved to have little in common. Allan, tall and trim in his early fifties, had always been athletic, and he continued to play golf, tennis, and racquet ball. Outside of law journals, which he read as a requirement of his employment, his idea of a good read was *Sports Illustrated*. His other passion was sailing, and he proudly boasted of the amount of money he spent on this hobby, keeping a boat moored at a marina near Mattawan. Craig's interest in sports did not extend beyond the television set, and then usually just for playoff rounds. Books and magazines were a staple of his diet, although sports periodicals would not be found among them. He had little use for the sea, and even less for sport craft upon it. Worse, Craig admitted to his wife that he found Allan a bit pretentiousness, which he conceded, was not unexpected given his profession. At the same time, he feared Allan looked down on him as a "number cruncher", not possessing much in creative potential.

Even so, each of the husbands, as a concession to the wishes of their respective wives, tolerated the half dozen or so evenings each year when the couples got together either for dinner or a show, on or off Broadway. On these occasions each man would linger on the sidelines of the women's conversation regarding theatrical performances, chiming in from time to time to prove they were being attentive. For their part, the wives would meet occasionally during weekdays to relieve their monotony without subjecting their spouses to additional stress, and at these meetings discussions would often turn to more personal concerns, confidences fully shared and staunchly safeguarded. Thus had Dolores reached out to Barbara, and except for the time of day, it was not an unusual request.

Dolores entered the restaurant and was greeted by Michael, a dark complexioned Italian with wide eyes and a pleasant smile just below the short, tight mustache that almost seemed to be painted above his lip. His well cut suit accentuated his thin frame.

"Bella signora, are you dining alone this evening?" he voiced with the thickest of accents.

"I'm meeting someone," Dolores responded, quickly scanning the patrons at the bar in search of Barbara's face. Not seeing her, she added, "I'll just wait at the bar until she arrives."

"Veddy well, signora."

Dolores assumed a bar stool closest to the doorway. Although her back was to the door, she had no fear of missing Barb's typical animated entrance. Ordering a Chardonnay, she made herself comfortable and focused her attention on the patrons to either side of her around the horseshoe-shaped counter.

Mostly they were couples, and in appearance, perfectly cast as if from an actor's guild to fill the needs for a cognac commercial. Hair, nails, attire—all were just so, to present not just the image, but the unquestionable certainty that they had arrived, that success had been achieved and so secured that only a cataclysmic economic crisis could pose any serious threat. If burdened by *noblesse oblige*, these people were bearing it well.

Dolores studied the faces of the patrons around her. How happy they seemed. At the far end of the bar a pair, younger than the others, sat near to each other, lost in each other's eyes. Dolores smiled in appreciation, not for the endurance for which their looks held such promise, but for the fragility, the temporal nature of the commitment that would be tried, and most likely found lacking, by passing years and overwhelming complacency. Next to them were the senior members of the group, basking in their own brand of complacency, where compromises had been negotiated, territories mapped, and tolerance of minor indiscretions and peculiar mannerisms had been offered. In exchange for these concessions, the contractors obtained financial security and the social comfort of an offered or accepted arm at the appropriate time. The others represented various phases of the transition between the extreme levels of acceptance: passionate adoration and resigned adaptation. See that? The look she gave him? He has yet to learn his place. And over there, that dismissive glance he gave his spouse for a comment she made to her neighbor? He has not yet come to understand how trivial so much of it is, how easy it can be ignored in exchange for a secure dependence when it really matters.

She was not of this group, this Dolores knew. Besides the obvious shortfall in the accountant's columned worksheets, she was missing a great deal of emotional capital. Somehow she and Craig had veered off the road between passion and complacency, between lusty possessiveness and fortified acceptance. As they had left the pavement, her husband had been thrown clear, while she remained alone in the vehicle, rocking unsteadily as it hung perilously overhanging the precipice.

"What's a pretty lady like you doing here, drinking all alone?"

Dolores was startled out of her silent study by these words. She looked up to see a man, just a few years younger than she, standing to her right, his back leaning against the bar rail, a scotch on the rocks in his hand. A full head of blonde hair streamed in large waves towards the back of his head, with the sides molded close to his head as if they had been blown there by the winds rushing by him aboard a motorcycle or at the wheel of a convertible. The leather jacket he wore fit this image of recklessness, while his tailored shirt suggested that he might well be a member of the exclusive set to which the patrons of this bar belonged. His bright blue eyes glistened like gemstones on either side of an unobtrusive nose. His pleasant smile floated in a sea of beard stubble.

"I'm waiting for a friend," Dolores answered, wondering if he had been drawn to her because of her looks or the fact that she was the only unattached woman at the bar.

"Mind if I wait with you?"

"Sure, why not."

"I'm Matt."

"Dolores."

"Pleased to meet you, Dolores. I've never seen you here

before, you're first time here?"

"My second. I take it you're a 'regular'?"

"I come here quite often. Food's really good, but the menu is rather limited—steak or lobster—period."

"Then I'll order the lobster tonight and experience all Michael's has to offer."

"Not quite. There's me," with this his grin widened into a full smile.

"You're on the menu?" Dolores smiled back, beginning to enjoy the banter.

"Special order only," he replied. "Can I buy you another glass of wine?"

"Okay, thanks. Chardonnay."

Matt ordered drinks for them both. After handing Dolores her wine, he clinked her glass with his, toasting, "Cheers!"

"Thank you, again," Dolores said. She was finding this situation much less awkward than she would have expected, and was flattered to be the subject of attention. "So what do you do, Matt?"

"Investments," he replied. "I manage not to spend all the money my father made. Rollins Sportwear, I'm sure you've heard of it. That was my dad's company."

"I own some of your clothes!" Dolores answered enthusiastically.

"Not mine. Dad sold the brand name years ago. Some prudent investing, and I'm set for life…at least I've made it this far."

Hmm, a playboy, and proud of it, Dolores thought. She couldn't deny that he had a certain amount of charm.

"What about you? Married?" he asked.

"I'm…separated," Dolores answered cautiously, her new status enunciated for the first time seemed unfamiliar but less awkward than she would have imagined.

"Sorry to hear that." Matt took a sip, and after some reflection continued, "If you don't mind me saying, your husband must be some kind of a jerk. I mean, you seem like a very kind, likable person. You certainly are attractive. I couldn't imagine walking away from you."

"No, I have had thoughts like yours. I've played through numerous variations of 'what ifs?'. What if Allan had become a partner of a large firm instead of maintaining his little private practice? What if he had become a great litigator, so that I could go see him perform in the public arena, listening to his carefully crafted and delivered closing arguments? What if he had become a prosecutor, advocating for victims of violent crimes? Oh, I've had those thoughts.

"But they're all just daydreams. A useless waste of time. We will never know how things would have played out differently had we made different decisions—things could have been better--or much worse. Then I started thinking of 'what ifs' in terms of the hand that I had been dealt, or more accurately, the cards I had chosen to play. What if I support Allan in whatever endeavor he chooses to pursue? What if I overlook his flaws and forgive him his transgressions? What if I take the stage—literally—and make public performances that make him proud of me, just as I had planned to be proud of him?"

Dolores looked at her friend and realized why she had always admired her. Barbara's ability to perform, on a stage at the Paper Mill Playhouse or on this little theatre-in-the-round table top in Michael's Restaurant, was always an outpouring from her heart and a revelation about the workings of her mind. "You're right, Barb. I was facing the wrong direction. I was looking back when I should have had my eyes forward. But still…"

"What?"

"I'm afraid that feeling might return—at the worst possible time. That I might not be strong enough to ignore it. That my weakness could put us right back in the same situation again."

"So it's not worth trying again? You want to strike out again on your own?"

"Funny you should say that. While I was waiting for you, a guy tried to pick me up at the bar."

"Was he cute?"

"As a matter of fact, he was," Dolores giggled.

"So?"

"So what?"

"So, you're free, unattached. Who knows what Craig's doing now? You don't owe him anything. He wasn't faithful to you, you don't have to be faithful to him."

"I don't know…"

"What do you mean, you don't know. Which one was it? The one in the leather jacket?"

"Barb, stop!"

"What's wrong? You said he was cute."

"Yeah, he was cute, but after you get past his looks, and the money he seems to have, he seemed a little shallow."

Barbara riveted her eyes on Dolores's, a gaze both unsettling and strangely comforting, too. "Do you hear what you're saying?" Barb was again at center stage. "You're admitting that you have more with Craig than you perhaps realized."

Dolores said nothing.

"Am I right?" Barb asked.

"Maybe."

"What do you want, Dolores?"

"I don't know. I told you, I'm confused. I need time to think."

"Honey, you said this has been going on for years. How much more time do you need?"

Again, Dolores had no answer.

"What do *you* want, Dolores?"

"I want things back as they were, the way I knew them, back when we both had dreams and were willing to share them."

"That's a starting point. But remember, you've both lived a lot since that time. The dreams you're talking about are young people's dreams." Barbara leaned closer to her friend. "What would you do if you went home tonight, and Craig was there?"

"I've imagined that. Of having the door swing open, and Craig stepping into the house."

"So what would you do if he did?"

"That's it, I'm scared of what I might do, what I might say that would drive him back out the door again. What would you do?"

"Honey, you don't want to know what I'd do. I'd kick his ass! But if you haven't noticed, you and I are different people, with different personalities."

"Okay, then, what do you think I should do if he comes back?"

"The way I see it, what you need to do is kick up your contribution to the relationship to insure its success. That is the giving part of love that truly qualifies it as love. For whatever reason, you got out of practice. Like an athlete in rehab—it will require some additional conditioning on your part."

"You may be right," Dolores volunteered. "No, I know you're right."

"But, do you think Craig's going to come back to you."

"I doubt it. Once he's made a decision, he usually doesn't change his mind."

"So what are you going to do about it?"

"I'm going to search for him. I'm going to find him. I'm going to ask him to come back. And the hardest thing, I am going to change. I'm going to appreciate what I nearly lost, and take steps to protect it. If I'm not too late."

55

The clock in the living room seemed to tick louder than usual as if to emphasize how each second was receiving its full measure, how time was going to pass as slowly as possible between now and six in the evening. Sarah had entered the room with a cloth to dust the furniture, more as an excuse to occupy her time than to perform a needed task. Her mind was full of conflicting thoughts and unfamiliar emotions.

Once again the stranger in her house was dominating an inordinate amount of her consciousness. It was not so much a fascination as a curiosity. What she had learned in the last few hours only served to pique her interest. He had reacted to her rage in a calm, deliberate way, and his apology, graced with flowers, seemed to be heartfelt. She was not sure why she had felt compelled to show him Frank's workshop, or, for that matter, why she suddenly had found the courage to enter the garage herself for the first time since her husband's death. Craig's response had seemed respectful, even reverent. As a result, the anger she had felt on Sunday had been completely dispelled by the same time on Monday. She no longer had any animosity about his crossing her boundary line and felt ashamed for having reacted as she had. The fact that he had taken on the gutter repair unilaterally suggested an innate kindness which, in spite of her initial reactions, she now found she was hoping to verify.

And what of their date this evening? No, it was not a "date." She was still a grieving widow. This wasn't dinner and a movie. That would be a date. This was just dinner, another apologetic gesture for his betrayal of her trust. Like the flowers. Flowers?! Dinner?! This was beginning to sound romantic. NO! She was not attracted to him. He was the complete opposite of Frank. Frank was big, strong, jocular, at times boisterous. Her guest was short, timid, quiet, almost secretive. Why, this was not romantic. Romantic would be a candlelight dinner at the Lamplight. This was supper under the harsh fluorescent bulbs at Carol's Diner. Just a meal shared by acquaintances.

Sarah picked up the framed photograph of Frank from the end table and stared at his smiling face and the blue eyes which seemed to pierce the glass and dive into her soul. What did he think of the plans for this evening? Was that smile his signal of understanding? He was always so good at understanding. Did he think she was betraying him? Did *she* think she was betraying him? No! But appearances? No!

"Oh, Frank, I feel so alone," she whispered aloud, as she held the frame to her breast.

Upstairs Craig lay stretched out across the bed, his arm over his eyes to block the afternoon sun streaming in through the window. Standing at the grill all morning was still an unusual muscular activity, and having Sunday off had not helped. Likewise, he was not accustomed to his early morning awakenings yet. A short nap would prepare him for the evening.

His landlady was proving to be a bit of an odd character. Clearly she was haunted by the memory of her late husband. This afternoon she had revealed a kind, almost nostalgic side of her personality, one that he found to be quite tolerable. But her mood swings had really caught him off guard. As difficult as it may be, he was going to have to try to manage her through future crises, as alternative housing options were few. The motel on the outskirts of town was probably the next best option, and he was sure it would be much more expensive and would require a longer hike to Carol's. Still, a few more extreme demonstrations could prove to be a real challenge. Even Dolores had never acted so erratically.

That thought returned the visions to his mind. Dolores was the first to appear, gazing at him pensively, her dark hair softly framing her face. Then, from the shadows, Joan appeared, standing akimbo, a slight smirk on her face suggesting a "take it or leave it" option. And with those images in his mind, at the same time both troubling and comforting, he drifted off to sleep.

With a full hour to go before the agreed departure time, Sarah stood before the mirror in her bedroom, conflicted with a wardrobe selection. The choice of a white blouse had been easy enough, but now she was alternately holding a red skirt or black slacks to her waist. Eventually she picked the slacks, their color reflecting the more somber mood she felt she should be portraying, although there was something she liked about the red skirt and the matching sweater that she would need to fend off the chill of the spring evening.

Somewhat reluctantly, she selected a gray sweater to complete the outfit, as no suitable one was available in black.

Decisions completed, she sat back on her bed and wondered how she was going to pass the next fifty-five minutes or so. A glance at the mirror confirmed that her hair would present no special problem, it seldom did. A few passes with a hairbrush was usually all that was required to coerce her blond tresses into obedience.

Pretending to be bored, she retrieved a magazine from a drawer in her night stand. From the cover of the magazine appeals to read the included articles were shouted in bold print: "Lose 25 Pounds in 4 Weeks!" "Hollywood Stars Reveal their Glamour Secrets" "Seven Surefire Ways to Ignite Him in Bed." A disgusted look streamed across her face as she wondered what impulse had caused her to purchase this issue. A glance at the cover date revealed that it was published the same month that Frank had died. With a disdainful flip of the wrist, she tossed the magazine into the nearby waste basket. Sarah fell backwards onto the bed coming to rest to stare at the featureless, blanched ceiling. Closing her eyes for a second to blot out this disappointing vision, she fell asleep.

The dream that seized her mind was as vivid as it was pointless. Sarah was walking through a forest at twilight. Behind each tree lurked a shadowy character, but as she ran from tree to tree to investigate, the shadows would be gone before her arrival. With each such disappointment, she would run more quickly to the next tree, only to be thwarted again. In this manner she dashed through the forest in ever increasing circles, until she collapsed from exhaustion next to a moss-banked brook.

At this point Sarah awoke with a start, her eyes immediately focusing on the alarm clock on the night stand, which read five minutes to six. In less than a second the import of this data was processed, and she sprang to her feet in one motion, the immediate result being a light-headed dizziness which forced her to seat herself again on the bed and await vascular equilibrium. This achieved, she quickly dressed, gave her mane a few dutiful brush strokes, and, checking herself one last time in the mirror, stepped out of the room.

From the top of the stairs she spotted Craig, standing at the front doorway, looking out the sidelight into Monroe Street. A tan sport coat covered a tie-less pale yellow shirt above brown slacks. He turned his head to face her, and the understated smile again made an appearance across his face as his eyes assumed a fiery intensity. Sarah began a stately, focused descent of the stairs, fully aware that her every movement was being studied, measured and cataloged by her boarder. Far from being self-conscious, she felt instead a flattering feeling of self-confidence. This, in turn, served to lighten her head slightly so that she gripped the banister with extra firmness so as to avoid a replay of the fainting episode that had just occurred in her bedroom.

"'Evening," Craig said, his smile warming a bit more.

"Hi," she responded, a little awkwardly, feeling her confidence waver slightly.

"You ready?"

"Yes. Should I get the car?"

"It's such a nice evening, would you mind walking?"

"Not at all."

No further words were exchanged as they moved down the walk towards the street. In the cloudless sky, the last light of day was rapidly losing its battle to the impending darkness. As they descended the stairs to the sidewalk, Craig broke the silence, "I usually take Chestnut Street, let's go down Maple for a change."

"Okay."

Sarah stole a sidelong glance at her companion, who appeared quite comfortable, walking along with his hands in his pockets, his eyes seeming to take in all the details of the houses they passed. She envied him his composure as she felt her heart beating faster, the silence they shared having no calming effect.

"You live in Walsh all your life?" he asked.

"Uh, no. I grew up in Lewisburg, about twenty miles north. Frank was a helper for a carpenter who did a job for my parents. That's how we met. He was from here. We dated for about a year, moved here when we got married." There I go, again, she thought, volunteering information so easily!

"So he impressed you right away?"

"Oh, yes. It was like magic. For both of us. He asked me out twice that first week. We knew right away it was the 'real thing'."

This revelation was met by a quiet nod, and they continued walking silently for several yards.

"Seems like a nice town," he said.

"It is. With several of the mines closing, we've fallen on hard times. But the people are good here. They support each other."

A soccer ball came rolling across the street, the result of an errant kick by youngsters playing in a front yard. Craig skipped ahead and intercepted the ball on the sidewalk, then adroitly spun and kicked the ball back from whence it came, all the while without removing his hands from his pockets.

"Thanks, mister!" cried one of the small athletes.

"Well played," added Sarah, unable to keep a smile from brightening her face. Craig offered a sheepish grin as he resumed his position at her side. Sarah believed she detected a slight blush in his cheeks.

"You were saying—about the people here?"

"They're supportive. The outpouring of kindness I received when I lost Frank—it was amazing." Sarah felt tears beginning to well up in her eyes, and to avoid embarrassment, looked away and attempted to blink them away. When she looked back in his direction, his gaze was directed across the street as if to give her time to recover.

"That's good," he said at last. "In the short time I've been here, I've sensed it, too."

"You mean Carol?"

"Carol, is 'top drawer'. Marc, too. The customers I meet at the diner--I can hear many of their conversations from the grill....You."

"Me? The crazy woman who flipped out on you for fixing her gutter?" a muffled laugh reinforcing Sarah's jest.

"No, no. I did cross a line. I admit that. And you know enough of what you want to define expectations and defend your position when challenged. I admire that. ...Sometimes I wish I had the courage to make a stand like that." He again turned his eyes to the opposite side of Maple Street, as if to close the topic and prevent any further leakage of the secrets he held.

Sarah recognized that this was the most the stranger had ever revealed of a personal nature. Although she was curious to know more, she would take this fragment for now and not press the issue.

Arriving at Washington Street, they turned west towards the recently illuminated streetlight which highlighted the intersection with Chestnut. At that corner they turned right to cross the overpass over the nearly silent Greenbrier and the equally tranquil railroad tracks.

Ahead lay Carol's Diner, an oasis of light in a quickly darkening town.

The supper patrons were few, not surprising for a Monday night. Marc stood at the counter, paging through a newspaper, his station at the grill unmanned. A young waitress waited tables. Marc looked up when the pair entered, then rushed to greet them near the door, assuming a big smile and a cheesy French accent.

"Welcome to *Chez Carol, Monsieur et Mademoiselle*," he quipped, bowing deeply and sweeping his right hand in a welcoming gesture into the interior of the diner.

The waitress gave Marc a look as if he had totally lost his mind.

"Dianne," the proprietor continued, "this is Craig, our new a.m. cook. And you know Sarah, his landlady?"

"Hi, Dianne," said Sarah.

"Good seein' you again, Sarah. Nice to meet you, Craig."

"Allow me to escort you to one of our finer tables," Marc interrupted, continuing his comic skit. He led them to the corner booth, farthest from the door. Handing them menus, he turned to return to the kitchen, "Dianne will be with you directly. Enjoy your meal."

"Marc seems to be in good spirits, tonight," Sarah ventured.

"I'm afraid I've only seen him that way. Consistently upbeat and happy, almost as much as his wife."

"Can I get you some drinks?" asked the waitress.

"Iced tea," replied Sarah.

"And regular Coke for me," added Craig.

The silence in the vacuum left by Dianne's departure for the soda fountain was again an awkward moment. Sarah felt obligated to speak.

"I want to thank you, again, for bringing me here. It's good to get out once in awhile."

"The pleasure is mine....If you don't mind me asking—and bear in mind I'm still in the process of learning my place—how long ago did your husband pass away?"

"Eight months. In some ways it seems like yesterday. At other times, it seems like a decade ago." Sarah again realized that she was being too forthcoming with her answers. Seizing the opportunity offered by Craig's silence following her last remark, she opted to both deflect additional questions and turn the tables on him. "You ever been married, Craig?"

Craig looked up at her with a hint of surprise on his face, then looked down at his hands, folded on the table in front of him. For the first time, Sarah now noticed a gold band encircling his left ring finger.

"Here you are," interrupted the waitress, placing their beverages and straws before them. "I'll be back to take your order in just a minute."

"Almost twenty years," Craig resumed, after the waitress had walked away. He stripped the paper wrapper off the drinking straw, adding, "Right now we're separated." Sarah detected an element of resignation in his voice. Her eyes met his as he glanced up at her again.

"You still wear your ring," she said, nodding towards his left hand, now resting alone as the fingers of his right hand were busy reducing the wrapper to a small paper ball.

"Habit," he said. "And a reluctance to accept certain facts."

A wave of remorse flowed over Sarah, and she began to back peddle. "I'm sorry. I'm prying. Please forgive me."

"No, it's alright. It's probably good that I try saying this explanation to someone real. The conversations in my head haven't gone too well." With this comment, the eye contact was more sustained, and Sarah sensed, more engaged. She received the smile he offered as a confirmation of what he had spoken.

As if to ease the tension, Dianne reappeared to take their orders.

Food became the new topic of discussion. The neutrality of the subject served to diminish the discomfort the two felt discussing absent partners. They talked of the offerings on the menu, and how each of their selections had been made. They spoke of favorite meals of the past, and the relative joys of cooking, whether in Sarah's kitchen or the grill just through the double doors ten yards away. They reviewed favorably the entrees and side dishes served, and the desserts offered at no additional charge. Craig suggested that was a clever marketing ploy, the Wilsons passing up the large profits that come from desserts in exchange for better chances for return visits.

Incidental to these discussions they learned that they were both from single child families, and that neither of them had parents living. A closer kinship was achieved when they learned that although Craig had done some domestic travel on business, most of his life had been spent in New Jersey, except for annual vacation trips to Maine, while Sarah had rarely left Greenbrier County, two notable exceptions being trips to visit family in Cincinnati and Norfolk. By the time the last sips of coffee crossed their lips, all of the stressful emotions of the last twenty-four hours had become distant, murky memories, with little chance that any action by either party could incite a revival.

No doubt buoyed by their newfound amity, and seeking to dispel the solitude that had characterized her days prior to her spiritual rebirth, Sarah sought to plumb the depths of her houseguest as they climbed the hillside back to the house. The slight chill of the spring night was soon forgotten with the exertion of climbing first the bridge over the tracks and river followed by the increasing steepness of the valley wall. Although their words were expelled with increasing forcefulness as the steepness of their climb mounted, the freedom with which they left their hearts was remarkably gratuitous.

"What did you expect to find here in Walsh?" she asked. "What made this place, of all the places in the world, your choice to begin your new life apart?"

"Carol has asked me the same thing," he said. "It's not so much what Walsh was as what it wasn't. It wasn't Peach Hill. It wasn't New Jersey. It wasn't the high strung rat raceway of the Northeast. Does that make any sense?"

"I suppose."

"I pictured West Virginia as offering something of a pristine environment, an affordable economy—that was important, not all that far away to get to, without too much of a culture shock, not to mention the mosquitoes, of, say, a Louisiana bayou. You might blame John Denver and his 'Country Roads' song "

"Oh, yes, our 'State Anthem'," she joked.

"He does make those roads sound inviting."

"Take the road out of Prince sometime, up through the New River Gorge. Let me know how inviting you find that!"

"Oh, what's that like?"

"One lane—no, make that two ruts. Huge rocks sticking up

from the road ready to tear the bottom out of your car. If you go off the road, well it's about four hundred feet straight down to the river. You're not likely to meet too many people along the road—there's only a couple of houses or trailers along the whole stretch—but you will definitely see deer, maybe turkeys and bear. And if you do meet another vehicle coming the other way, you'll need to negotiate how the two of you're going to get past each other without exchanging paint or removing rear view mirrors."

"'Almost Heaven, West Virginia!'" he sang.

Their shared laughter shattered the stillness of the night. It felt good to laugh. Oh, how long it had been since she last laughed!

They walked in silence until Sarah again spoke, "Do you know what you're looking for?"

Craig turned to her, but said nothing.

"Excuse me, if I'm being too personal—"

"No, it's a fair question. I'm not sure how to answer, though," he said. After a few steps he continued, "I guess I'm hoping to remove the pain, or at least reduce it. When love is not returned, when it is flatly rejected, that is very painful."

"I would think so," she said. "I know it is when it's taken from you."

"I wouldn't begin to compare our situations. Your loss was so—so final. I mean Dolores and I still have a chance, maybe a slim one, but a chance to get back together. With you, it's…" Craig's voice went mute.

"Dolores. That's her name?"

"Yes."

"Tell me about her."

Sarah could sense that Craig was searching his memory for the ideal anecdote to relate, flipping through a vast catalog of remembrances. At last, with a smile brightening his face, he began. "The first time I saw her she was acting a part in *Tartuffe*. I sat in the audience, mesmerized by her, envious of the male actor who was interacting with her in the story. After the show, I went backstage and met her, asked her out. To my surprise she agreed. We went out for dinner, afterwards walked around town, talking. Then we went to her place and talked some more until, like, two thirty in the morning." He paused for a moment, then added, "What I wouldn't give for talk like that again."

"What does she look like," Sarah asked.

"She has long dark hair, a gorgeous face, an understated smile that seems to grow on you, right before your eyes....Here, I have a picture." Craig opened his wallet to reveal a small portrait, giving it some study as if to reacquaint himself with her features before offering it to Sarah.

"She is beautiful."

"Yeah." Craig took back the wallet, slapped it shut and returned it to his hip pocket. Thoughtful silence again passed between them. It was Sarah who again posed a question.

"What do you plan to do? How long until you try to talk with her again?"

"You give me too much credit, suggesting I have a plan. I need some time to think, to decide what I'm going to do."

They completed their climb in silence, each absorbed in their own thoughts. Entering the house, Sarah turned on the light in the foyer, saying, "Thank you again for dinner. I had a good time."

"Me, too."

"Remember our deal, I'm cooking tomorrow night."

"I'm looking forward to it."

"How does pork chops sound?"

"Sounds great. I enjoyed talking with you…very much. But, if you'll excuse me, I still haven't got used to a five a.m. start."

"Sure. Good night, Craig."

"Good night."

She watched as he climbed the stairs and without looking back, entered his room and closed the door.

56

As Sarah undressed she was thinking of Craig. No longer did he seem aloof or alien. She could no longer imagine him as threatening in any way, and many of her questions of his past, his origins, had been answered. Given her compassionate nature, she was not surprised that she had sympathetic feelings for his situation. She tried to imagine what a breakdown in communication between Frank and her would have been like, but she had no context, for rarely had they even argued. This only served to deepen her concern for Craig's problem.

On another level, her new found comfort with her boarder heightened her discomfort with a deep seated emotion she kept trying to subdue. She was adamant in her insistence that while her relationship may have moved from professional to personal, it was still only casual. He was friendly, she would be his friend. Nothing else would come of it. Nothing else *could* come of it.

She turned towards her bed and squinted at Frank's pillow, trying to imagine him lying there on his back, his hands interlaced behind his head. The image was conjured easily enough, but the smile she saw on his face was strangely discomforting.

57

Craig lay on his back in the darkened room, with the streetlight outside his window making it anything but dark. Excusing himself from Sarah's company was more an attempt to bring the evening to a close than to meet a need for sleep, as it was not yet nine. Not that he had not enjoyed himself. He found her personality pleasant, her interests sincere. Having had the intent to cement their relationship as landlady/tenant, the evening had advanced a possibility of friendship, a kinship made more sound by her sincerity and his empathetic nature. But he was averse to taking on more risk than was absolutely needed. She had already proven herself capable of dramatic mood swings, and he had no need for another adventure into that realm. As it was he already had shared more about his personal life than may have been prudent.

Why was his good nature so readily accepted by all but the two women he loved most? That question itself brought to light a drastic change in his thinking. Months ago he had written off Dolores completely, figuring she would never again hold the prominent place in his heart that she had held for more than a dozen years. In Joan he believed he had found his true soul mate, He had fixated on her obsessively, confirming and re-verifying the validity of his conviction, confident that she would be unable to deny it as well. In her rebuff he believed that she had demonstrated less a rejection of him, more a refusal to accept incontrovertible conclusions, an abandonment of an honesty that would allow her to be true to herself.

But with each passing day Dolores was reaffirmed as a major, if not the preeminent person in his life. Clearly it was expedient to highlight her as his first, and only, love when talking to Sarah, but he had done so without any difficulty, for he believed the words to be true as much he hoped Sarah would. Almost as if to test this belief, he closed his eyes and brought forth an image of Joan, her bright red curls iridescent against the dark stage of his mind's theater. But as soon as she was in place Dolores stepped forward, eclipsing her rival with a nearly promiscuous display of readiness and offering. Craig's eyes opened wide, seeking focus on the shadows cast across the ceiling.

What was he to do? How tenuous was his grip on reality when he had such trouble holding onto a dream?

58

Carol was unlocking the door when Craig arrived at the diner the next morning. After the usual greetings, she said with a knowing smile, "So Marc tells me you and Sarah were here last night for dinner."

"Just repaying a small debt," Craig said, defensively.

"Well, for whatever reason, I'm glad you did. You were the first one to get her out of her shell, though several of us have tried. She took Frank's death really hard. Except for going to church, she stays cooped up in her house, just moping around as best as anyone can tell. It's good to see her finally getting out."

"I'm glad I could be of some service. I got to know her a little better. She seems to be a kind, sensitive soul."

"That she is," agreed Carol, "that she is."

Later, as they were prepping the kitchen for the noon meal, Craig motioned Carol aside. "I was wondering if you would object if I worked on the front window mullions when I get off today. That peeling paint has been bothering me since I started working here. The diner looks so good, otherwise."

"We've been putting off that paint job for months," she answered. "Yeah, we can pay you a couple of hours extra to get that done."

"Only if you're looking for an argument," Craig answered with a smile. "I'm not looking to get paid. Just want to do you a little favor."

Carol studied him intently for a few moments. "Okay, then," she said. Retrieving some bills from her apron pouch, she handed them to him, adding, "Let me buy the paint, at least. Give me the receipt for the paint and brushes, whatever you need."

"That works," he said, pocketing the cash.

"How's Michelangelo doing?" Marc asked as he handed his wife a plated tuna melt sandwich.

"I was just outside for a look," Carol said. "He's about two thirds done. Looks pretty good."

"Well, you could be sure Billy wouldn't have volunteered to

paint that window."

"No, and I didn't want to pay a painter to do it, although I was coming to realize *you'd* never get around to it."

"Hah! The way I paint? I'd be spending more time scraping the paint off the glass than putting it on the wood."

"Yeah, and the sidewalk, too, I reckon," she grinned.

59

Jeff Down's cell phone began to vibrate, and he saw his answering service was calling.

"Downs."

"Mr. Downs, it's Marcy at CDC Answering Service. A prospective client, Mrs. Dolores Miller called. Trying to track down her husband."

"Who's her attorney, did she say?"

"No attorney. She said she found your number in the Yellow Pages. Seems her husband took a train for parts unknown and she wants you to find him."

"Okay, do me a favor, Hon. Call her back and tell her I'm on a case right now, but I'll call her back today, after five. Send me her contact information as usual."

"Will do, Mr. Downs."

Well, now, he thought to himself, a "fugitive." That may be just a bit more challenging than usual.

60

Sarah emerged from the grocery store into the early afternoon sunlight. Walsh could look a little weary, a little run down sometimes. But today the town seemed to glisten in the springtime brightness, which was accompanied by warmer than normal temperatures. The window display at Kaufman's had been updated, and now featured apparel designed for the warmer days of the fast advancing spring season. The grocer had decided to display some produce on stands in front of the store, and the vivid colors of fruits and vegetables brightened the scene. Even the vehicular traffic on Main Street was refreshingly animated, and her attention was drawn especially to a bright blue coal truck stopped at the Chestnut Street traffic light. The young operator had his windows open wide, and the voice of Hank Williams yodeled from the radio, which was set at a volume sufficient to overpower the vehicle's husky diesel engine.

She had spent a good part of the morning reviewing cookbook recipes, and having found one for stuffed pork chops which sounded both tasty and challenging, she had driven to the store to obtain the ingredients she needed. Driving past the diner, she became aware of two simultaneous occurrences. She recognized Craig, standing on a ladder painting the trim of the eatery's main window. Then she felt her heart skip a beat as a result of that recognition. The latter troubled her immediately, and she turned her head, slightly surprised and slightly angry that she would have such a reaction. Her will, however, was not sufficiently steeled to prevent her from turning her head for one last look in her boarder's direction before he and the diner were obscured from view.

All the way up Chestnut Street her mind tumbled this revelation for repeated consideration, with denial, disbelief, apology and anger each having their voice. She called upon a vision of Frank to offer either chastisement or dismissal, but was further dismayed when his face assumed that accommodating look that had been so typical of his demeanor when he was alive.

Even carrying the groceries to the house felt more burdensome as they were now laden with the guilt she felt. She was tormented to realize that her bundles were destined to feed the man who had fueled such an inappropriate reaction. Arriving in the kitchen, she slung the bags onto the table and collapsed into a chair to stare at them.

Perhaps it was denial, that safety valve of the psyche, which took control. Perhaps it was cold, fluid reason that won out. In either case, she determined a plan of action. She would prove to herself, and anyone else in a position to observe, that Mr. Craig Miller had absolutely no effect on her emotions, that he had no chance whatsoever of winning the heart that would forever belong to her beloved Frank. She would demonstrate, beyond any doubt, by preparing the meal previously agreed to, serving it to her guest, and even by watching him consume it, that his force was infinitesimal. She would bravely sit in his company and by such proximity prove his powerlessness. Such was her conviction and confidence. With that resolve, she set about preparing the evening's dinner and setting a table that was elegant and tastefully chaste.

61

Craig climbed the steps to the porch of the lodging he was beginning to appreciate and accept as his home, and turned to look back towards the street and across the small front yard. With each passing day the vegetation in town was growing greener and fuller. Even this yard, which clearly suffered from Sarah's lack of attention over the last two seasons, was showing patches of thickening, vibrant grass. Perennials in the flower beds suggested their skeletal remains held promise for the months ahead. The few evergreen shrubs, while clearly in need of pruning, appeared to be in good health.

The appearance of this yard was a stark contrast to his property in Peach Hill. He pictured Dolores on her knees, attending to each of the extensive flower beds that filled their yard. Although he helped with many of the gardening tasks, especially the more strenuous tilling and mulch spreading, his wife was able to devote many weekday morning hours to the gardens' details while he was at the office. The result was that the garden reflected her personality, and, as a labor of her love, it was referred to as hers. The role of mowing the grass quite naturally fell on his shoulders. While the size of the flower beds greatly reduced the number of square feet requiring mowing, their irregular shapes and the requirement that cropped grass not be discharged into the beds, precluded any reduction in the time required to complete the chore. He wondered who would mow the grass this coming season, and the answer served again to shade his thoughts with melancholy.

Craig turned again, and entered the front door. His nose was immediately bombarded by a symphony of aromas from the kitchen. Pungent smells of roasting meat blended with more subtle vapors from vegetable steamers, over which rode the dry scent of toasted almonds. Finally, he smelled the unmistakable combination of apples and cinnamon, confirming that dessert had not been overlooked.

Reluctant to abandon these pleasant stimuli, Craig nevertheless climbed the stairs quickly. He washed up in the bathroom, taking special pains to remove spattered paint from his hands, arms, and even his face. He replaced his work attire with sports wear, quickly ran a comb through his hair, then descended the stairs, stopping in the foyer where he could look into the dining room.

The table had been set with matching bone colored china, with a simple blue accent pattern, resting upon a peach colored tablecloth, illuminated by a simple five lamp chandelier overhead. The silverware at the two place settings glistened, and the stemmed wine glasses were a lightly smoked gray. At each setting was a relish plate, containing pickles, olives, celery, carrots and radishes. This was the only food on the table, and introduced the only significant colors to an otherwise monochrome table, other than the two red carnations in a bud vase near the table center.

Realizing that his arrival had gone undetected, Craig spoke so as to be heard over the scraping of pans and the clatter of pot lids, "Hellooo? Sarah?"

Sarah was again pleased with how easily her culinary skills had been recalled. The recipe had not proven to be as difficult as she first had thought, and she congratulated herself on organizing her work flow so that cooking times were coinciding in such a way that everything would be ready at the same time, even allowing the chops to rest outside of the oven as the dinner rolls completed their browning within. Remembering that Craig had not appeared for the dinner she had planned just four days prior, she hoped that he would arrive soon, as the string beans were just now completing their time in the steamer. No sooner had she entertained this thought, than Sarah heard Craig's call. She experienced the same simultaneous reaction as she had on Main Street, earlier. *Just catching my breath,* she thought to herself, *a little startled by suddenly hearing a voice. Yes, that's all it was.*

Sarah poked her head around the corner, into the dining room while drying her hands with a towel. As she did so, she was suddenly aware of several strands of her hair which had banded together to hang before her eyes, from above the center of her forehead down to her nose, in effect bisecting her face. First giving the misbehaving fibers a brief, bewildered, cross-eyed look, she then looked at Craig, and smiling, greeted him, "Hey, come on in."

"This table sure puts Carol's Diner to shame," he said. "It's lovely."

"Thanks."

"And when I came in earlier, everything smelled delicious!"

"I didn't even hear you come in."

"You must have been busy, I know my nose was!"

"Well, I hope it tastes as good as it smells."

"I'm sure it will. It looks I got the better part of this bargain," he said with a widening smile.

Sarah smiled back. "Excuse me," she said, returning to the stove.

Craig walked to the doorway and was watching his hostess without actually entering the kitchen. Once again Sarah noticed the comfortable casualness with which he carried himself, such a striking contrast to his first appearance on her porch just a few days ago. She regretted that the room looked such a mess, with the table and all available counter space holding either completed dishes ready to be served or vessels that had held ingredients at an earlier stage. The sink was stacked high with bowls and other items waiting to be washed. Nevertheless, the clutter was a silent testament to the energy she had expended in preparing the meal. Standing at the stove, Sarah was tending to pots on each burner while at the same time sliding the rolls from the oven into a cloth draped basket.

"Dinner will be ready in a minute."

"Can I help in any way?" he offered.

"Sure. You can put these on the table," she responded, handing him the rolls and the previously tossed salad.

Dinner progressed much as it had the night before at the diner, but with Craig offering frequent, and, Sarah thought, sincere compliments on the foods she served. She was feeling increasingly comfortable in his company, and appreciated his quiet, but keen interest in any topic being discussed. She quickly felt at ease, no longer concerned with emotional overreactions.

No doubt influenced by this relaxed rapport, conversation began to drift in the direction of more personal subject matter, leading Craig eventually to ask, "Tell me about your husband. What is your most pleasant memory?"

It did not take much reflection on Sarah's part before she answered. "We had been married a little more than a year, and had just bought this house, using all of our savings and taking out a pretty big mortgage from the bank. Frank's business was growing, but was hardly secure. He had been hired to do a rather large job, an addition for a house here in town, the kind of job he had been hoping for.

"Several weeks into the job, the customer was laid off from his job at the mine. It was one of the first waves of layoffs to hit the mine, had not really been expected by anyone. Totally on his own, Frank re-negotiated the contract, barely covering his cost of materials. Well, when he told me, I was livid. This was our chance to get a little bit ahead, to add some security to our lives. I really tore into him."

"I can appreciate what that would have been like," Craig interrupted, with a grin to defuse his comment.

"Yes, I suppose you can," Sarah continued, unable to stop herself from smiling. "Anyway, he sat at the kitchen table, staring at a spoon he was twirling in his fingers, not saying a word until I finished. Then, he quietly looked up at me and said, 'I did what I did because that's who I am. I can't ignore my client's misfortune as long as I am in a better position. I'm a little surprised that you don't know me better by now, but I hope, with time, you will come to understand.'

"I admit that I felt a little ashamed, but I was too proud to show it. I just dropped the argument. Shortly afterwards, business began to flow in. In fact, he had to turn away a few jobs, although he hated to do so. Seems word got around town about what he had done for that one client, building an instant reputation. I rarely doubted him after that. And I came to appreciate that giving side of him as one of his best qualities."

Craig sat quietly, reflecting on her story, before saying, "That's a beautiful memory."

"Your turn. Tell me something more about your wife."

Craig twitched in his seat. He realized he should have expected this since he had started it. His curiosity had frequently put him in awkward positions, this was just another case. "Well, Dolores is a giving person, too," he began, "but in a different way. I've told you she was an actress when we met. She used to give so much of herself when performing. Before she even left for the theater she had assumed the role she was going to play—taken on the character completely. On stage she totally gave herself up, draining every ounce of energy out of her person, giving it to her audience."

He paused briefly before continuing, "After her acting career ended, she continued to apply herself in the same way to some of her interests. Gardening, for example. Shewill toil for hours to make her flower beds picture perfect."

"Why did she give up acting?" Sarah asked.

"You know, I'm not really sure. She complained about not having the time to truly devote herself to acting, but I'm not sure that was the case. I certainly would not have restricted her. I found her theatrical persona to be captivating. Maybe she wasn't feeling as comfortable on stage as she thought she should. I don't know. She never really opened up to me on this subject...or several others for that matter."

"You're missing her, aren't you?"

"Yes. Even more than I thought I would."

"Then why don't you go back?"

In response, Craig shook his head slowly, looking down at the plate in front of him. After a few seconds, he looked up at her. Sarah's look was unchanged, uncompromising. She envied him the opportunity he possessed, one which was unavailable to her.

At last he spoke. "You know how many love songs are written about rejection? So many you would think it is the most horrible emotional trauma imaginable. But rejection is nothing compared to dismissal. Rejection suggests some flaw, some incompatibility exists to prevent a romance, a bonding. Rejection is understandable, explainable. But dismissal is much worse. Dismissal is rejection after the romance, after the bonding, after the countless compromises and acceptances that facilitate a relationship. Rejection denies what has never been. Dismissal is destruction of what is. An admission that acceptance is no longer possible. It is extremely painful. For me, at least, unbearable."

Now Sarah was silent as she digested his words. As their meaning resonated with her, she felt a new level of kinship, a sincere empathy with her guest. With this feeling came the renewal of the fear of the attraction she feared she had sensed. But that fear was diminished with the growth of the spiritual bond she felt they now shared.

He went on, "As I approach so called 'middle age', or at least the 'approach to middle age', do you know what I fear most?"

Sarah was guessing the answer was death, but as that was too obvious, she shook her head.

"It's not death," Craig answered his own question. "It's not having someone there to hold my hand as I face death. Now, with this separation, that fear is intensified, and the probability of its likelihood increased."

A somber silence filled the room. Only the clock could be heard ticking from the nearby parlor. When Craig spoke again, his voice was upbeat and cheerful. "Well that's a horrible way to end such a delicious meal. I'm sorry, let's change the subject, shall we?"

Sarah was relieved by the suggestion, and offered a change of venue as well, "Let's go sit in the living room where it's more comfortable."

"Fine, but first there are some dishes for me to wash."

"Oh, don't be silly!"

"No, you worked hard making this meal, you should not be expected to clean up the mess. Unless Brillo pads are among the list of 'forbidden tools'?" Once again she found his smile disarming and against which it was impossible to argue.

"I'll wash, you dry," she offered.

"A poor compromise," he said, "but one which I will agree to—it was made in such good faith."

62

Jeff Downs pulled up in front of the unpretentious ranch home on a quiet street in Peach Hill. From the car he sized up the residence of his potential client. The front porch light burned next to the doorway and a few solar charged stake lights illuminated the sidewalk from the driveway to the front stoop. Even with this minimal illumination, which augmented the trace of sunlight left in the sky, it was clear that the property was well tended. Numerous flower beds lay near the house, along the driveway, along the curb and a large kidney-shaped bed in the center of the yard. The bright yellows of jonquils and forsythia announced the arrival of spring. Interspersed among them were white and violet crocuses, past their prime and beginning to wither. What was left of the yard for lawn, was nicely manicured and weed-free. A small stone cherub served as the only ornamentation to the setting, and this focal point was, like everything else about the landscape, understated.

Jeff eased his impaired leg gingerly to the pavement. Even injured so many years ago, it was still sensitive to certain stresses in certain positions. Clutching his clipboard, he walked to the front door, his slight limp adding a degree of awkwardness to an otherwise routine procedure. Arriving at the door, he adjusted his sport coat on his shoulders and straightened his shirt collar which was, as usual, free of a neck tie. This apparel and a pair of khaki pants constituted his usual attire for meeting a new client.

The chime of the doorbell was shortly followed by the appearance at the door of Mrs. Dolores Miller. Jeff felt an immediate empathy after his first glimpse of her face and reserved demeanor. A pair of flattering jeans and a plaid shirt defined a mature, but fit figure. Jeff thought he detected a sparkle in her eyes that promised ever so much more than the weak smile that was naturally formed by the line of her thin lips. At the same time, her eyes confessed that they had experienced more than their share of pain, and, though not weepy, belied a level of fatigue that some recent anguish had visited upon them.

"Mrs. Miller? I'm Jeff Downs."

"Won't you please come in, Mr. Downs."

Stepping inside, he noted how the modest tone that dominated the outdoor plantings spilled inside, reflected in the tasteful furnishings and accented by a few well placed house plants. Leading him into the living room, the hostess casually pointed to a sofa and then took her own seat in a nearby armchair.

"You have a lovely home," Downs remarked, making small talk to delay the inevitable discussion of the unpleasant. "You must have put a lot of time into the plantings outside. The flowers are lovely and beautifully maintained."

"Why, thank you," she replied, treating this common compliment as a most unusual and unexpected observation. "I am a member of a local garden club, and I enjoy working with plants."

A poor conversationalist under the best of circumstances, Jeff felt as if he had exhausted his verbal ammunition, and somewhat flustered, decided to get down to business. "How may I help you? We talked briefly on the phone, but I would like to have you tell me everything, from the beginning."

Dolores told of what she knew from the police investigation, of Craig's disappearance, the abandonment of his car, of him being spotted boarding a train for Newark.

Jeff listened silently, made a few notes in his notebook, then remained silent for a few more minutes as he considered what he had been told. His client sat quietly, her occasional fidgeting drawing attention to what must be her uneasiness caused by his failure to reply. At last he spoke.

"What could lead him to disappear in that manner?"

Now Dolores was silent. Jeff sensed that she was formulating her answer carefully.

"Our marriage has been shaky in recent months. We...I still love Craig; I believe he still loves me. But it's no longer the reckless love of our youth. It is measured, almost calculated. And it lacks the passion it once had. I know that's not uncommon. But we really made a mess of things—arguing about the most minor points, stone cold periods of silence, sulking at opposite ends of the house. Yeah, we had all that down pat. We've worked on making it better, but, I'm afraid, without much success. I'm sure that's why he left."

Jeff studied Dolores, again without speaking. Mostly his eyes were on hers, and he saw in them the pain that she had known, and the anguish she felt by confessing such personal information to a stranger. The intensity of his gaze seemed to disturb Dolores, and she averted her eyes.

"But why just leave? He apparently abandoned more than just you and your relationship. He left a long-time job, home, assets, friends."

"Yes," replied Dolores, "I guess I never realized how hurt he was. This was a drastic response, but the issues that triggered it have been around for a long time."

Once again the woman's eyes revealed a history of pain, and Jeff believed he saw tears welling up in her eyelids. This time, however, she returned his stare, a new found courage replacing her previous timidity.

"What do you wish to gain from my involvement?" Jeff asked.

"I guess I'm looking for some closure," Dolores said. "If he wants to end our marriage, then let's finalize it with a divorce. If he's looking for some kind of trial separation, I need to know what time frame is involved. If he's looking for me to chase him…well, then, to some extent, I guess I'm willing to do that, too. I…I just need to know something of what he's thinking, what his plans are, and what my reaction must be."

"What friends does he have here? Have you checked with them, do they have any idea of what Craig's intentions are?"

"My husband's closest friends are at Gilmore, Haskins and Cass. Everyone there was as surprised as I was."

Jeff looked down at his clipboard, but closed his eyes. After sitting like that for more than a minute, he looked up at Dolores and offered her a weak smile. "Your husband's trail leads to one of the most congested places on earth. In Newark, or New York City, a short distance away, he could be very difficult to find. In addition, transportation options exist to take him anyplace else in the world: planes, ships, trains, buses. I could spend a great deal of your money attempting to track him down. Even after just a few days, witnesses who may have seen him, if I'm lucky enough to find them, will have memories that are clouded by more recent, and probably more significant recollections.

"I propose," he continued, "to take a more passive approach. It'll take longer, perhaps, but will be much less expensive. Let me track him—more accurately, his financial transactions—electronically. When he surfaces, we'll have a better idea of where he's been and where he might be. I would not feel comfortable taking your money to spend weeks looking for him here in the metropolitan area only to learn that he went to Istanbul. Can you be patient? Again, this may take some time."

Dolores considered the proposal. Jeff hoped that she would agree. It truly was the best option, and he sincerely wished to help her. He enjoyed helping people as part of his job. But this time was different. He felt a connection with Dolores, and he wanted to help *her*, going above and beyond, if necessary.

"I put my faith in your judgment," she said. "Whatever you believe is best, I will agree."

63

"Hey, Sarah, how's it going?" Carol's greeting escaped from behind the counter over the clatter of a tray of dishes being slid into the dishwater.

"I'm well," responded her friend, assuming a stool at the counter.

"Cup of coffee?"

"Yes, please."

Carol placed the cup and saucer before her friend, then lowered her head to look her squarely in the face. "Feeling easier about your roomer?"

"My first fears were crazy," Sarah answered, "I realize that now." She took a sip from her cup, then looked up at the waitress and added, "But now I have new worries."

"Oh?"

Sarah added a packet of sweetener to her coffee, and gave it a stir with her spoon to buy time. She stared into the brew, still swirling in a counterclockwise motion, reluctant to start the conversation she had come to the diner specifically to begin. Taking a deep breath, she looked up and began, "I don't know. I'm feeling very strange. Almost like a schoolgirl, again."

Carol's look indicated interest, but was restrained enough not to interrupt and indicated that she was awaiting further comment.

Still reluctant, Sarah continued, "It's like every time I see him—Craig—my heart jumps. Early on I interpreted it as fear, but I know that's not it. He's proven to be a decent guy. He's feeling some pain, but means me no harm." She paused for a second before adding, "He thinks the world of you, too, by the way."

"Yeah, I know. It's like he thanks me every day for the job he has. Marc and I have often said how lucky *we* are that he's here."

"He's doing okay, then?" Sarah asked.

"Oh yeah, he picked up everything very quickly. Very willing to please. Even volunteered to paint the front window frames for us—off the clock! He's a sweetheart."

"Yeah, a sweetheart," Sarah repeated.

"So what's the matter?"

"I…I just feel awkward around him, like he's causing me to

feel…the way I shouldn't be feeling."

"You don't have a crush on him, do you?"

"No!...I mean I shouldn't. I don't *want* to."

"So do you or don't you?" Carol pressed, her eyes glistening more than normal, a slight grin pressing upwards on the corner of her lips.

"Oh, Carol, I don't know. It's not right. It's too early. I'm not ready."

"Not ready for what?" Carol asked. "Not ready to stop mourning, to move on with your life."

"I'm not ready to forget Fred," Sarah snapped, a little disappointed that her friend wasn't more understanding.

"Who said to forget him? You will never forget him. No one ever expects you to."

"But it just feels too early. The time isn't right. And, besides, Craig is married."

"Now *that's* a problem," Carol agreed. After a brief silence, she added, "Is he coming on to you?"

"No. Except for two evenings I've hardly seen him. He spends most of his evenings out, I don't know where. He comes home in time for bed, then leaves long before dawn. He's done nothing inappropriate. The problem is I feel that I'm inappropriate. The more I try to dismiss him from my mind, the more forcefully he shows up when I see him or think of him. I'm so confused."

"Look," Carol said, her intent gaze enforcing eye contact with her friend, "you're coming out of a really tough period of your life. You're out of practice with doing everyday things, of feeling everyday emotions. Once you get back into the swing of things, you'll feel more comfortable, things will seem more normal. Maybe you should push a little harder towards normal. You used to be active at church. Get active again. By reconnecting with people there, more normal relationships will present themselves, and the new, unusual situation of having a stranger living under your roof won't seem so awkward, or tempting."

"Maybe you're right," Sarah said. "Maybe it's time I broadened my horizons."

64

A week passed. Vibrant, light green buds were exploding on the trees' branches. Amongst the branches, birds added vocal testimony to the change of season. The measured mantra of the robin, repeated precisely again and again, was everywhere. Less common were the bright calls of the brilliantly crimson cardinal, whose song seemed to grow in intensity with each repeated stanza. Warblers, of various species, provided unseen harmony from their clandestine perches near the tree tops, while a mocking bird, performing from the top of the highest telephone pole he could find, put on an animated show with visual displays of his striking white patched wings and a repertoire of imitated songs that numbered almost a dozen. All the while, sparrows and finches flitted about providing chirped undertones.

Sarah had begun to re-channel her newfound energy into new directions. She began to review the help wanted advertisements in the paper with the hopes of finding employment, not only to add needed income but to fill her days with activity and absorb her new energy. She soon realized that if not properly expended, her drive would exhaust her. She made herself available to the church, and was quickly accepted as a member of several committees as an agent to get things done.

She saw very little of Craig, his pre-dawn departures for work were often matched by late evening returns. She had no idea where he spent his afternoons and evenings, but rarely was he on Monroe Street between those hours. She was aware that he had adopted the practice of carrying a small portfolio when he came and went, although its purpose was a mystery. Few as their encounters were, they were always cordial, if also brief, Craig most often alluding to the late hour as a reason he should choose to retire over all other options.

On one afternoon, however, upon returning home from what were becoming more frequent trips into town, she found her houseguest standing in the front yard, hands thrust securely into the hip pockets of his jeans. A puzzled look adorned her face as she approached, and she was met by his observation, preceded neither by salutation nor good tidings.

"I think it's time we got these flowerbeds planted and dressed up. The lawn is greening up pretty good, but it needs the help of some flowers and shrubs to really make this yard look great."

With her agreement, he was soon using a spade from the garage to turn the soil, pausing only to drink the lemonade she brought him as relief against the unseasonably warm afternoon heat. The following afternoon found them working together, planting the selections from an expedition she had made that morning to a garden center in Ronceverte. A third day found him spreading mulch around the base of each plant, at the conclusion of which the flower beds took on a finished appearance which complimented the general appearance of the entire property.

They had conversed little during these sessions, other than exchanging information to get the jobs done. Sarah was especially conscious not to fan flames of dormant emotions, although she was unsure of what those emotions may have been. At the same time she was finding Craig's assumption of the role of instigator and director to be new and slightly uncomfortable. It did not help that in this self-appointed directorship he seemed to become even more quiet, more focused, more aloof.

Towards the end of the third afternoon, Sarah sensed a lightening of Craig's mood. As she paused to survey the outcome of their labors, her gaze included Craig emptying a wheelbarrow of the balance of its load of mulch. He was working on this project, but he did so without losing his signature smile, flashed at her from beneath all-seeing eyes, in the company of a knowing nod. She was unable to restrain a smile in return. Not only was the yard assuming a new beauty, exceeding what had been known in years past, but the promise of a return to normalcy, telegraphed by that smile, relaxed the tension that she had felt the last few days.

65

Arriving at the diner on Saturday morning, Craig once again found Carol accompanied by her daughter. This time, however, Melinda was less perky and said little before retreating to a corner booth where she emptied the books from her back pack.

"She okay?" Craig asked Carol.

"Yeah, she's got a term paper due Monday, and she's stressing."

"It's mostly done, Mom," objected the teenager, "I just don't like parts of it. I gotta see how I can fix it to please old Mr. Crenshaw."

"If you want, bring it in to me later and I'll give it a quick read," Craig offered.

"Really? You think you can help me with an English paper?" Melinda countered.

"I'll give it a go. I seem to remember that I wrote a few of those in the past. Besides, writing is writing, regardless of the subject."

About thirty minutes later, Melinda came into the kitchen and placed several sheets of loose leaf paper next to Craig's station. The paper was filled with prose in carefully penned script. "Here," she announced. "When you get a chance. And, thank you." She smiled and returned to the dining area.

When a lull in cooking duties permitted, Craig read Melinda's work. Afterwards, he stepped out of the kitchen and motioned Melinda towards him.

"What do you think?" she asked him, seeing that he held her work in his hand.

"It's a train wreck," he answered, flashing her a grin.

"Jeez, you're harsher than Mr. Crenshaw!" Melinda said, sagging her shoulders and dropping her chin onto her chest.

"You asked my opinion. Do you want the analysis or do you just want to sulk?"

"Let me have it," she said with resignation.

"Okay. Your introduction is long winded, but doesn't really set up your main idea. The topic sentence is well written, but you fail to support it with the rest of the paper. Some of your examples actually argue against your premise. And your conclusion is just a repetition of your topic sentence—several times."

"That's all?" she said, sarcasm congealed on her words.

"No, actually. You make use of too many idioms and your vocabulary seems too elementary for a high school paper."

"Great," she said, with all hope seeming to rush out of her body.

"Let me see your outline," Craig continued, dismissing her attitude.

"I don't have one," Melinda confessed.

"'When you fail to plan, you plan to fail.'"

"I don't need one. It's not that long a paper!" she protested.

"Long enough for you to lose your way," he countered. "Get a piece of paper and let's write one. It doesn't have to be extensive, as long as it lists the major points you want to cover."

They continued to work through the breakfast period, the sizzling of bacon complementing the heated exchanges between reluctant student and patient mentor. Methodically and deliberately, Craig met each of his pupil's objections, founded as they were in laziness and complacency, with solid reasoning supporting why corrections were required, and why some alternatives were superior to others. As they worked he believed that her objections were becoming less frequent and obstinate, an indication, he hoped, that she was beginning to recognize the need for an organized, disciplined approach and that his suggestions were in that vein and in her interest.

By the time Craig was scheduled to leave, the paper had been significantly rewritten. Craig was confident that Melinda understood what she needed to do to complete it. As he prepared to leave, Melinda approached him from her workstation in the corner booth.

"Thanks for all your help," she said. "I really do appreciate it."

"You're welcome," Craig said. Over her shoulder he saw Carol, occupied with one of her countless tasks, but with her eyes and gentle smile directed in his direction, serving to second her daughter's gratitude.

66

Completing the cleanup in the kitchen following her evening meal, Sarah stepped out onto the front porch and sat in one of the chairs that faced the street. Her day had been a busy one, and it felt good to get off her feet. Even so, the slight muscular fatigue was a pleasant replacement for the weariness that came with the listless boredom that had been a defining feature of her life in the recent past.

Pastor Jordan's words that afternoon had touched her, and reflecting upon them now rekindled the warmth they had brought to her heart.

"Sarah," he had said, "you've brought a new level of energy to each committee you've joined here at the church. And I'm not the only one to notice, either. Several members have mentioned it to me. They are grateful for your enthusiasm. Martha even said she'd been considering stepping down as chairwoman, due to lack of interest by the committee members. But now, she says, she is challenged to keep ahead of you, saying she sometimes feels she has to rein you in as your ambitious ideas sometimes exceed the capabilities of the group."

Sarah knew that Pastor Jordan was not inclined to offer gratuitous praise; that his honest depictions were responsible for the high regard most parishioners had for him. She was also aware that her contributions had been genuine, and well received. They seemed to flow easily now that she had a fresh perspective. She thought of Frank, and how she was sure he would have been proud of how improvements in her life had quickly been magnified and passed on to benefit others.

The street light came on, a meek attempt to duplicate the sun, which had taken its leave beyond the mountains to the west. Walsh was entering its transition into quiet dormancy which it adopted every evening at this time. Far off to the east, chime horns announced another train's approach to the crossing of Fowler Road. A handful of boisterous robins formed a choir in nearby trees, their repetitive songs seeming to serve as a demonstration against the ending of this day.

Craig's appearance a half block away was sudden, and

immediately recognizable. His carriage, gait, and somehow, his disposition, were all instantly identified. And with the identification came the tiny infusion of adrenaline which she found to be both uncontrollable and unwelcome. Rationally, Sarah would insist that she had no special feelings for her tenant, that emotionally he could elicit no feelings different from any other town resident or casual acquaintance. Yet each encounter seemed to be accompanied by some chemical reaction within her body, which accelerated her heart rate even as the organ seemed to be forced upward within her chest. She was conscious of becoming a little light headed, but far from diminishing her mental capacities, this state seemed to elevate her awareness as she consciously and pointedly focused her attention on his every movement.

By the time he reached the porch, she had regained control of her emotions, and her greeting was offered in a restrained, proper manner, "'Evening."

"Good evening, Sarah."

"You're back earlier than usual."

"Yes, I made it a short night, tonight," he said, flashing his characteristic smile.

"And what, if you don't mind me asking—it's none of my business, excuse me if I'm prying—"

"No," he interrupted, smiling once again, "it's no big secret. I spend most afternoons and evenings at the library, doing research."

"Researching what?" she pressed.

"I'm reading about the history of this county, and the town of Walsh, in particular. It's pretty interesting."

"If you say so," she said, a slight grimace expressing her doubts.

"No, it is," he insisted, taking a chair next to hers. "The first pioneers here were a pretty rugged group. But civilization quickly followed with the building of the railroad and due to the proximity of the well established civilization in Virginia."

"Fascinating," she said, her grin revealing the intended sarcasm. "What do you plan to do with this research?"

"I don't know; write an article maybe. Or possibly a book. I'm digging up quite a bit of information," he said, patting his slightly bulging portfolio. "I've made contact with the newspaper and they're going to give me access to their archives."

"And you find this enjoyable, writing historical books?" she asked, somewhat incredulously.

"In many ways, yes. And it keeps my mind off other things," he added, averting his gaze towards the porch floor.

"Like what?" Sarah asked.

"I'm afraid that now you *are* prying," he replied, his offered smile falling short of softening the remark.

They sat silently for several minutes, each looking out into the street. The birds had become quiet. In the distance a dog barked. At last, Craig broke the silence. "I'm sorry, I didn't mean to be so abrupt."

"No," she countered, "I crossed the line. I apologize."

"Then no hard feelings?"

"Not from my side."

"Good." He paused briefly, then continued, "I seem to keep jeopardizing what I have here, and I don't really mean to. I appreciate—really appreciate—your hospitality. I couldn't ask for better accommodations than what I have here."

"Then I'm pleased," she said. "You have been a model tenant—after I got to know you."

Craig nodded and turned again to look towards the street.

Sarah considered her next words carefully. Craig's last remarks suggested that it might be difficult for her to offend him, and she would use that to her advantage. "Again, I don't mean to stick my nose where it doesn't belong, but if something is bothering you maybe you should consider talking about it with someone. I don't mean me, I mean someone who is better equipped for that kind of talk."

Craig turned towards her again. "You have someone in mind?" he asked.

"The pastor at my church is a good man—kind, well-meaning. I'm not trying to push my religion on you. But he has helped me through several tough times in my life. I'm sure he would try to help you. If you're interested, I'm just making the offer."

Sarah's eyes met Craig's, and the intensity of his gaze seemed to scour every corner of her being. Unlike before, she felt no discomfort from this inspection, for she knew the purity of her heart, the sincerity of her intentions. She was prepared to reveal her inner self to him, to peel back as many layers as he required to understand her willingness to give him whatever she could to promote his well-being, to anchor his soul which she sensed was adrift.

"I'll keep that in mind," he said. "Thank you," he added, once again flashing that smile which was promptly replicated on her face.

67

It was a Tuesday afternoon when Craig left the diner, stepping into the bright sunlight and the warmth of a glorious spring day. Like cold blooded beasts energized by the sun's rays, traffic on Main Street was more active than usual with a short procession of loaded coal trucks causing Craig to wait on the curb before he could cross. Across the street, two coal trains passed in opposite directions. On the near track, a long string of empty hoppers plodded west, their cavernous shells serving as sounding boxes that amplified and broadcast the crashes and booms as the coupler slack was compressed and then stretched. Going in the opposite direction, coal loads moved more swiftly, more quietly, their weight causing the track structure to creak and groan. A low joint responded to the mass of the paired axles, beating out a syncopated rhythm separated by pauses as the center of the cars soared overhead until the next two pairs of wheels arrived: BA-BAM-BA-BLAM...... BA-BAM-BA-BLAM...... BA-BAM-BA-BLAM.

Craig directed his steps towards the public library on Washington Street to continue his research. The portfolio under his arm had grown in thickness with each day he spent there, his note cards and full sheets of paper filled with his notes were like visa stamps in a passport book, authenticating his visit at the same time they secured the gleanings of his research.

This day, however, his steps lacked the usual drive, his legs less devoted to achieving the usual purpose. Perhaps it was the sunlight, filtered by fresh leaves recently emerged from the buds that had imprisoned them. Perhaps it was the clear, bright song of the oriole just in from the south. Having announced his arrival orally, the songster proceeded to dart from tree to tree so as to flash his orange and black feathers to leave no doubt that both he and spring had arrived. Whatever the reason, Craig found himself walking cheerfully but without clear destination on the sidewalk along Jefferson Street, approaching the school bearing the same name.

The building was a typical example of late-1950's school construction, a large brick-clad block enclosed the multi-purposed room. Here, assemblies, meetings, and indoor athletic events were invested with the same time-share contract as the irrefutable need to prepare and deliver the mid-day meal daily to the student body. Extending from this thoracic hub were two long, low blocks of classrooms. Each had a central hallway: long arms extended not to support digital extremities, but amputated at the wrist, and terminated with identical glass exit doors. The building possessed virtually no architectural embellishments or beauty marks. The only break to the austere, efficient and practical design was the multicolor sheets of construction paper taped to the windows, the students' futile attempts at beautifying their daily existence.

As depressing as the building appeared, Craig experienced a deeper sadness once he passed the building and his eyes beheld the athletic field. It was clear that in better times the baseball diamond had once shone with the residents' pride and the hope for their youngsters. Behind the backstop stood a frame refreshment stand topped with a second story sportscaster's booth. At one time the hills would have echoed an amplified voice announcing: "Now batting for Walsh, number 13, Roger Johnson," as the smell of popped corn and broiled hot dogs wafted upward over the valley. Now, however, weathered plywood strained to hold what remained of its whitewash, and the shutter enclosing the outlook overlooking home plate was about to be released by the one hinge making a valiant effort to hold on.

The chain link enclosure designed to separate athletes from spectators had numerous breaches where the stretched webbing yearned to return to its rolled form of distant memory and was allowed to do so when guardian hardware had abandoned their posts. The skinned infield was bleeding profusely into the outfield through numerous wounds. Meanwhile the grass of the outfield had abdicated, with a wide variety of weed types having taken over. These had ventured into the infield as well, their colonization effort proving to be quite effective. The field reminded Craig of a forlorn version of the ball field where he had played as a child.

Within this amphitheater, six youngsters in their early teens struggled to pay honor to the National Pastime. The largest one brandished a bat beside home plate, entreating the dirty-blond lad standing in the center of the diamond to offer him a pitch within the confines of his larger than normal strike zone. The runt of the group, a carrot-headed boy lacking any protective equipment, cowered near the backstop. Making no pretenses of serving as a catcher, he was content to be a retriever of any errant throws from the ace who stood submerged in the wallow where the mound should have been. The three other players had dispersed themselves deep into the outfield, in deference to the potential strength of the batter.

What came over Craig at that instant was as brilliant as it was insane, as carefully planned as it was unpremeditated, as undeniably reasoned as it was uncontrollably impulsive. He took a step forward, only to freeze and then reverse direction, the foolishness of the concept that was forming in his mind acting as a bucket of cold water in the face of inflamed passion.

It was in this position, with his back to the field, that he heard the sound. No longer a "crack" of seasoned ash striking the leather orb, it was the new sound, the "thonk" of machined aluminum put to the same purpose. Instinctively, he pivoted round, his eyes trained on the sky above, scanning, seeking, and promptly finding the tiny cream dot sailing upward. He dropped his portfolio to the ground, and started to move instinctively to intercept the parabolic trajectory of the ball as it succumbed to gravity's force. Although dormant for three decades, his instincts proved keen, and a dozen steps later he was positioned beneath the ball. Craig was a kid again, playing under the lights at the little league ball field, camped under a high fly to right field. Out of that night into this day, the ball fell into the basket formed by his cupped hands. The sting of the cowhide on his palms was tempered by the satisfaction of having made the catch, a feat that was acknowledged by the three outfielders converging near his location.

"Good catch!" exclaimed the lanky lad coming from left field.

"Bet that stung!" sympathized the chubby centerfielder, offering his glove as a target to receive the ball.

"That kid can hit!" Craig said, as he tossed the baseball back over the fence.

"Yeah, Tommy got all of that one," remarked the right fielder, his black framed eyeglasses giving him a scholarly look. "He's the best hitter we got."

"You boys play in a league?" Craig asked.

"Nah, not any more. Ain't nobody wants to coach us."

Craig heard the sadness in the boy's voice. Perhaps because he was especially attuned to the emotion, he also heard the implied sense of rejection. The words sliced his heart, reopening the unhealed wound. He would want no one to feel such pain.

"That's a shame," Craig lamented, looking up to see Tommy cutting his home run trot short near second base and starting to walk towards the centerfield fence. The pitcher was following at a distance while the boy stationed near home plate chose to remain there.

Again, the crazy thought returned to him, and again he was prepared to dismiss it. What was the likelihood that he could transform this little acre of Walsh, make a material improvement in a corner of his personal purgatory? Why should he make an attempt here, where it was apparent so many who lived here had given up? The image of his wife flashed into his mind, her disapproving look seconded by a shake of her head. No, she would have discouraged this idea as too idealistic, too naïve. Because of this mental image, Craig became more galvanized to move forward, if only with caution at first.

"So there is a league in place?" he heard himself ask.

"I guess so," the scholarly looking boy said. "Ronceverte has a team. So do a few other towns."

"And you just need a coach?"

"Guess so. My dad still has the equipment in our garage from last year. He can't coach this year, he's too busy at work."

"What's going on?" inquired Tommy upon arrival.

"This guy's asking about coaching a team," the centerfielder volunteered.

"Really?" Tommy asked, looking at Craig with imploring eyes.

"Well, I'm just thinking about it at this point. How many boys you think would be interested?"

"Well, we had fifteen guys last year," answered Tommy.

"And Homer wanted to play, but signed up too late," added the leftfielder.

Like closing his eyes and stepping off a diving board, Craig spoke again. "Tell you what: get anybody who's interested to meet here tomorrow afternoon, about this time. It would help if one or more parents could come, too." Craig said, still not believing how this nutty idea was taking root. "Depending on the turnout, I'll make a decision."

"Why'd you want to do anything for us? You don't got a kid playin'" asked the pitcher, his arms folded across his chest.

"Shut up, Jesse!" Tommy barked, turning about to face his friend. "If this fella wants to help us, let him." Turning back towards the stranger, he added, "My dad's willing to help coach. He just didn't think he could do it all by himself."

"I'm worried, too," Craig said. "It's a lot of work and I won't do it if I don't see commitment from you guys. Do you think your dad could come tomorrow?"

"I think so. He was really sad when the team broke up last year."

"Good. Let me tell you, what I'm thinking is a little crazy. I'll admit that. But if you and your friends really want to play, then I'm willing to invest my time to helping you do so. As for Jesse's concerns," Craig smiled at the light haired boy who maintained his distance and clutched his arms more tightly against his chest, "let's just call it 'community service', okay? I feel I owe this town a little 'thank you', and this would be my way of saying it. You guys look like you could use some help. Maybe I can give it to you."

The red haired catcher was approaching the group now, his curiosity aroused by the lengthy delay in their play. All of Jesse's friends had turned toward him, silently beseeching his acceptance of the stranger's altruism. With a trace of reluctance, Jesse repositioned his hands to his hips, the stance still projecting some defiance to preserve his dignity while also signaling his acceptance. "Okay, Mr. - -,"

"Mr. Miller. I live on Monroe Street. I'll see you boys tomorrow, then?"

"What's going on?" the catcher asked.

68

Craig approached the Jefferson Street School with both excitement and fear. He had left his portfolio behind in his room, replaced by a notebook, with a page already filled with questions. Late into the night he had reviewed his plans, convincing himself in the process that a successful outcome was possible, if not necessarily probable.

His strides down Jefferson Street were deliberate and fast paced. As he passed the school building and got his first glimpse of the ball field. His spirits rose as he could see about a dozen boys sitting on or clustered around the bleachers. Standing nearby were a man and three women, who looked in his direction when one of the youths excitedly pointed that way.

"I'm Craig Miller," he said, extending his hand to the lone man.

"Pleased to meet you," the heavyset fellow answered. "I'm Tom Potter, Tommy's dad," nodding his head towards the home run hitter of the day before. Tommy was swinging a bat near the backstop and grinned weakly at Craig. "He told me of your interest in coaching the team." He paused to look across the ball field, then added, "It's a lot of work. Are you sure you're up to it?"

"I'm willing if the boys are interested. But only if they're interested. It's *their* team, I'm just willing to coach it."

"I can appreciate that," Tom replied. "I just don't want to see them get their hopes up only to be disappointed. When the team fell apart last year, many of the boys were crushed, especially Tommy."

"I understand," said Craig. "You're going to have to believe in my sincerity. I've only been in Walsh a few weeks, probably don't have much of a reputation." He sensed that the three women were intently listening to the conversation, and he turned to include them in his audience. "But my job offers me afternoons free, and I am willing to commit that time to working with your sons."

"Oh, sorry, let me introduce you. This is Donna Blanchard, her son is Jimbo. Marie Nielson, Jesse is hers. And Anita Thompson, Billy, over there in the green tee shirt is her boy."

"Pleased to meet you all. I'm willing to do as much as I can, but I could use all the help I could get from anyone. As it is, we're starting pretty late in the spring."

"When Tommy came home last night and told me about you, I made some calls. It took a little pleading, but the league is willing to include us in their schedule. But opening day is two weeks from Saturday."

"So we can get insurance through the league?" Craig asked.

"Yes, we can reenter the league with all the benefits we had when we dropped out last year."

"Well that's really good news. That could have killed the whole deal. What about the field?"

"That shouldn't be a problem. The school has supported the program for years. I'll make some calls tonight to confirm that. But--" Tom turned his eyes towards the infield, "the school budget has always been tight with field maintenance. They'll cut the grass, but everything else is pretty much up to us."

"Another challenge!" Craig said, grinning, turning his eyes to the field as well.

"Have you ever done this sort of thing before?" asked Mrs. Thompson.

"Coaching a baseball team, specifically? No. Overseeing corporate projects—I've done that for years. I'm not saying they are the same, but desire, planning, commitment, execution—those are all the same in just about every endeavor, at least that's my experience."

"I'm a little puzzled why you want to do this," stated another mom. "I've heard that you're new to town."

Craig could see the concern in the woman's face, and addressed the issue head-on. "It's true. I've been in Walsh only a short time. But in that time I've met some great people, people I'm proud to call my friends. It's in that spirit—a spirit of respect and fellowship—that I'm offering to do this. If you knew me, you'd know that I finish things I start. But you don't, at least not yet. If you give me a chance, I know you'll be pleased with the effort I put forth. If you ever have any concerns, please, contact me either at the diner during the mornings or at Sarah Stiles's home on Monroe Street, where I rent a room."

Craig scanned the parents' faces for signs of acceptance. The woman who had spoken last appeared to be softening somewhat. He regretted that the world was such that he felt obliged to make an addendum. "If any of you still have concerns as to my motivations, that's understandable, especially with some of the strange stories we hear on the news. Let me say that all my interactions with your sons will be scheduled so that Tom will be present, too. And all of you are welcome at every practice, every game, whatever. But be warned, if you show up, I may try to put you to work!"

The smiles and chuckles assured Craig that he had been convincing.

"He's our last hope for having a team this year," Tom said, addressing the women. "If I thought I could do it, I would have done it again this year. But there's no way I could do it by myself. Between the two of us, though, there's a good chance it'll work."

Sensing general acceptance from the four parents present, Craig said, "Let's talk to the boys."

Tom called for the young players to return to the bleachers, as they had gradually dispersed while waiting for the new coach to arrive and during the grownup discussions. Craig had their attention when he began to speak. "As you no doubt heard, I'm seriously considering coaching a baseball team this season—if there is real interest on your part. The fact that so many of you showed up today is a really good sign. If you are willing to make the commitment to the team—show up for practices, field maintenance sessions, and games, then I am willing to make the commitment to coach and handle the behind the scenes details. Am I correct in assuming that you are making that commitment?"

There was subdued, but generally positive assent, indicated by nodding heads and murmured responses, until Tommy spoke up, "We want to play. We're ready to go."

"Okay, then," Craig said, opening his notebook, "let's get started."

69

It would be an understatement to say that the boys had been surprised by their new coach's first announced practice. They were to leave balls, bats, and gloves at home. They were to bring shovels and rakes, instead. This was to be a mandatory practice. No player would play who had not participated in the field revitalization.

The day was especially warm, and the players appeared lethargic when they first arrived, but Craig quickly assigned them to small teams with specific assignments. He urged them to stay focused on their tasks, with appeals to their pride and likely rewards. He occasionally offered some advice: "This is our home field. We want our rivals to recognized our pride, and be a little intimidated when they step onto this field. ...The smoother we make the infield, the fewer bad hops, the more double plays. ...Hold the hoe like this, and use the long edge to make wider cuts."

Craig spent most of his time moving from group to group offering encouragement and support. A father of one of the boys arrived in a pickup truck loaded with tools, including a much needed wheelbarrow. Craig asked him to put his carpenter tools to work to repair the press box.

By the end of the afternoon, a group of tired, sweaty boys gathered on the bleachers. Craig addressed them enthusiastically. "Gentlemen, look at that ball field! Who would have believed that this could have been created from the sorry mess we found when we got here earlier today? If you guys are as good as ball players as you are as groundskeepers, then we're going to have a terrific season. Now, if you can find the energy to walk a few blocks down to Main Street, I'll buy each of you a soft drink at the diner."

"What's this?" Carol asked, as Craig marched his small army into the diner to occupy all the available booths.

"Just drumming you up some business," Craig said with a smile. To counter the look of bewilderment that remained on her face, he added, "Better get used to it. This is Walsh's Little League Baseball team, and we'll be stopping in for a treat after every win, which I suspect will be often."

Still somewhat perplexed, Carol began to take their orders.

After delivering the drinks, she joined Craig at the counter, serving him his cola with a slight flourish. She needed to say nothing, as her look alone was enough to elicit an explanation.

"They needed a coach," Craig said, grinning. "I had free afternoons, so …"

"That's a lot of work. You've done this kind of thing before?"

"Actually, no," Craig paused, turning to look at his charges. "They're good kids. Today they worked hard to whip the ball field into shape. It should be a great season. I'm looking forward to having a lot of fun."

Craig was aware that Carol was studying him intently, but chose to divulge nothing more. For sure, his own motivations were not all that clear to him. Perhaps he saw Joan's son, Neal, in some of the boys. He missed the time spent with Neal more than he thought he would. Beyond that, Craig had felt an unexplainable yearning to act in a selfless way, to provide a community service but with specific members of the community to be directly targeted. He sensed that this compulsion had religious or mystical overtones, but where they originated, or why, was less clear. No doubt his life was in need of some redemptive acts, especially given the guilt he felt for his abandonment of his New Jersey life and the people in it. Additionally he felt an obligation to these people, the residents of his newly adopted home, to show respect for their acceptance of him thus far or ease his future acceptance. And to a certain degree, this trend towards altruism was a marked contrast to the pragmatism of his career and the constantly practical approach to everything that marked his marriage.

He looked at Carol, whose face continued to reveal some lingering cynicism, and flashed her a grin. She smiled back, shook her head gently, and returned to her duties.

70

In an effort to cool the house on this hot afternoon, Sarah had put some electric fans to work, placing one on the desk in Craig's room next to the portfolio he had left there. What did it contain? Her fingers rested gently on the cover. A quick peek was possible. He would never know. Quickly, she brought her hand to her mouth. She was ashamed of the temptation to peek into Craig's private things. She was relieved that she resisted, that her dignity was not impeached.

Why she was so interested in him was still a mystery. Repeatedly she had rationally examined details of his character, personality and physical appearance, finding nothing to warrant more than a friendly, business relationship. Yet each time she but caught a glimpse of him, Sarah felt a stirring deep within, a feeling that was both exciting and disturbing, a stimulus that had motivated her actions even as her fear of the feelings immobilized her.

The sun was descending towards the top of Knob Mountain when Sarah stepped out onto the porch. As if on cue, she spotted him turning the corner onto Monroe Street and felt her heart jump upward in her chest as her stomach began to churn slightly. Dressed in tee shirt, jeans and sneakers, he appeared as he had the day they planted her flower beds, although as he approached, she could see that his clothing was considerably more soiled this time. He never seemed to mind getting dirty if the work required it.

"Howdy," he greeted her.

"Hey! What have you been up to?"

"You're looking at Walsh's new Little League coach. Today our team resurrected the baseball diamond over at the school. It needed a lot of work, but we got most of it done."

"When did this all happen?"

"Just a couple of days ago. The season starts in a little more than a week. We've got lots to do before then."

"Wait. You just walked in off the street and became a baseball coach?"

"That's pretty much the way it happened. The boys needed a coach, I have afternoons free—Presto! They seem to be good kids, should be fun."

Sarah leaned back against the wall, a look of mild disbelief on her face.

"What?" Craig asked.

"Nothing," she replied, as a smile shouldered its way onto her face, and she felt the stirring within once more.

71

"Hi Dolores, it's Barb." Her voice from the phone receiver exhibited the same clarity and resonance as if she were on stage. "I'm waiting for Danielle's dance class to finish. Thought I'd call to see how you're doing."

"I'm okay. I've been focusing much of my time on the garden club; they're really busy this time of year. Oh, and I got a job! I start next week at Van Nest's Lawn & Garden. I'm looking forward to that, and they seem to be glad to get someone who knows something about plants."

"That's great news! Have you heard anything from the investigator?"

"No, not yet. He said it might take some time. It's been about two weeks since I met with him." Dolores fell silent for a moment before continuing. "I keep imagining that Craig's going to call. I've come up with scripts for what I'd say when he does. But the phone never rings." Dolores paused again, then continued, "I must have really ticked him off this time."

"Think of the future, not the past," Barb countered. "Sooner or later you're going to hear from him. It's important that you be as positive as you can when that happens."

"I know, I know," Dolores said.

"Here comes Danielle, now. I have to run. But first, are you still interested in getting back into theatre?"

"Yes! I really want to try again."

"Okay, great. The Black River Playhouse is having auditions next Wednesday for *Da*. I know Beth Rosen, the director. Already put in a good word for you."

"Barb, you're the best! I'm going to give it a shot. Thanks so much!"

72

The fan on the desk oscillated, each change of direction punctuated by a loud click. In an almost futile effort, the device sucked warm air from outside the open window and spewed it into the stagnant air that filled the bedroom. Freshly showered, Craig lay on his back on the bed, the roster of his new ball club clenched in his left hand. Sequentially he went through the names, closing his eyes to better picture the face and body type of each player he had met that day. He had scribbled notes as reminders as to stated preferences or deduced probabilities regarding a given boy's aptitude for a particular field position.

Today's field rehab effort had gone better than he had expected, and his team seemed more cohesive as a result. It just might be possible that his whimsical decision to coach this team could prove to be a positive experience for all concerned.

Justin. Which one was Justin? He again closed his eyes to try to recall this particular boy from all the others. The image was blank. But not for long, as the gentle curves that defined Joan's face appeared before him, yanking him out of the sports world back into the unreal reality that defined his turmoil.

Craig recognized that he had enjoyed the relief from the torment that accompanied the visions. Unlike working at the diner, where the routine tasks seemed to encourage the apparitions, his time spent with the team, focusing on the needs of each member, had served to banish the haunting specters. Was this the solution? To throw himself into serving others in order to subdue his personal ghosts? How long would that strategy prove successful? Would he be able to muster the energy to sustain it? Or would Joan and Dolores eventually invade that territory as well, not only proving the distraction ineffective but also subjecting his latest effort to possible failure—yet another instance to add to his growing list.

Craig was suddenly overcome by a sense of helplessness. Like an immense weight placed on his chest, this feeling had a crushing effect on his spirit and his confidence. Daunting organizational challenges boosted his drive, seldom were they intimidating. However, he found these personal challenges to be unfathomable and thus unsolvable. Perhaps, he thought, it was time to recruit some external assistance.

73

The Saturday morning walk to the diner was more cheerful than usual. In one of the yards he passed every day, an inconspicuous shrub revealed its identity this morning by scenting the air with the unmistakable fragrance of lilac. Although it was hours before sunrise, robins were up and vocal, serenading Craig as he moved downhill. So loud were their songs, it was surprising the town residents, sleeping with windows open, were not awakened by these singing thrushes.

"Good morning, Coach," was Carol's tongue-in-cheek greeting. Standing beside her outside the front door, Carol's daughter gave her mother a confused look. "Mr. Miller is now coaching the Little League team," Carol explained.

"'Morning Carol, Melinda. Actually, it's a Babe Ruth team, older boys."

"How did your practice go?" Carol asked.

"It went well. We have another one this afternoon. We don't have much time to prepare. The opening game is next Saturday, so we're practicing just about every afternoon."

"Do you think you'll have a winning season?" asked Melinda.

"I hope so. They seem to be in good shape. Better than me, that's for sure. Pitching BP yesterday just about killed my arm. How about you? How'd you do with that composition?"

"I got a B plus. Thanks again for your help."

"You're welcome," Craig said, holding the door open for both of them.

It was a typical Saturday morning breakfast crowd, and Craig quickly adapted to the pace. Once again he was visited by his ghosts. Although not negatively impacting his work, again and again he struggled to understand what meanings had been missed, what words misunderstood, why promises had been broken. Carol seemed even more cheerful than usual, interacting with the customers in her trademark fashion. Melinda, sitting in the corner booth, quietly worked on her homework.

A mid-morning lull gave Craig an opportunity to step away from the grill to sweep the kitchen floor, when Carol poked her head through the doorway.

"Craig, there's a fellow here who wants to talk to you for a minute. I'll watch the grill for you."

Stepping into the dining area, Craig saw a tall man, in good physical condition, standing by the counter. Muscular arms protruded from his sleeveless shirt and a ball cap rested high on his head that featured deep set dark eyes and an angular jaw.

"Mr. Miller? I'm Joe Lorenzo. I coach the Alderson Eagles. We're playing you next weekend."

"Nice to meet you. It's Craig." A bone-crushing grip caused Craig to wince slightly as the two shook hands.

"Craig. Great. Yeah, well we just drove over to check out the field. When the revised schedule came out we couldn't believe there was a game scheduled in Walsh. Your field was nearly unplayable last year. I must say, though, it looks pretty good today. Still a lot of weeds, but at least they're mowed."

"We've done what we could."

"Yeah, well I understand you guys just reorganized. You're getting a late start."

"I think we'll be ready, though. The boys are working hard."

"Okay, then. Well, I don't want to keep you from your work. It was good to meet you. See you on Saturday.'

"Nice meeting you."

Attempting to return feeling to his right hand, Craig returned to the kitchen to Carol's grin. "So, you've met the competition."

"Yep. Word travels fast."

74

Sitting in his small boat near the center of the Greenbrier River, a fisherman cast his line as a pair of mallard ducks swam away from the shore into the central current. Overhead, a great blue heron ceased his laborious flapping, locking his wings into position to glide down to his landing spot along the river edge.

On shore, the coal conveyor which extended over Main Street sat silent, brought to a stop at the end of Saturday's second shift, to remain quiet until the first shift commenced at seven the next morning. Main Street was quiet, too, except for an occasional automobile passing through town. The double track main of the Chesapeake & Ohio was still as well, save for the occasional metallic pop of the rails expanding in response to the morning sun's warmth.

On the porch of 43 Monroe Street, Craig sat in one of the two chairs, his elbows on the arms, thumbs under his chin, his index fingers resting along either side of his nose like a steeple. He was dressed in the better garments from his wardrobe, including a light sport jacket, and tied around his neck, the only necktie he had brought with him in his exodus from New Jersey.

His eyes were concentrated on a search of the treetops for the tiny yellow warbler that was repeating its spirited call. Craig was convinced that warblers were the ventriloquists of the avian world, able to throw their voices to distant branches to confuse anyone inclined to search for them. This one was no exception, and with vision unaided by binoculars, Craig knew his only hope of spotting the bird was when it took to the wing.

Sarah came out through the front door, dressed for church. Seeing Craig, she lurched slightly as a startled expression took command of her face.

"I'm sorry. I didn't mean to scare you," her boarder said, rising from his seat.

"No, I just didn't expect you to be there. Good morning."

"Good morning. It's a beautiful day. And the warblers have arrived! There's a yellow in one of those trees over there. I've been trying to get a glimpse of him."

"If you haven't seen it, how do you know it's there?" Sarah asked, furrowing her brow.

"By his song. Listen. ….There. 'Sweet, sweet, I'm so sweet.' Hear it?"

"Hmm hmm. So you're an expert on bird songs?"

"I wish. Unfortunately, I don't hear the rarer ones often enough to make a big enough impression on my memory. The whip-or-will was the exception. I've only heard it once, but I'll never forget it."

He watched her looking at him with an expression between disbelief and admiration. The ends of her lips showed the slightest upward curl, suggesting a smile was waiting for the right moment to escape. For the first time that morning he looked beyond her face, finding her body—more shapely than he had previously noticed—tastefully wrapped in a pastel blue and white floral print dress.

"Do you always dress so formally to go bird watching?" she asked.

"Actually, I was hoping—if your offer still stands—to accompany you to church this morning. Again, I don't mean to impose. If you'd rather not—"

"Sure. I wouldn't mind. You're always welcome."

"Thank you," he said, sensing the words inadequate in expressing his gratitude even as he realized to say more would approach overkill. The silence that followed proved awkward. He regretted accepting her offer, realizing too late that she might not be as comfortable with the situation as she first suggested.

He was relieved when at last she spoke, "Shall we go, then?"

Silence marked most of the drive to the church. Craig, never the conversationalist, could think of nothing profound to say. For her part, she seemed especially intent on driving the car, or perhaps her thoughts were elsewhere. Craig directed his gaze out the windows. As Sarah's house of worship was a late comer to Walsh, it was located on the eastern outskirts of town as buildable downtown real estate was all spoken for. Being off the routes he traversed daily into town, Craig valued the new vistas and was content to take in their details quietly.

Walking from the lot towards the church, the two were greeted by three separate pairs of parishioners, each finding it necessary to pause for a formal introduction of Sarah's guest. With the first encounter, Craig sensed a discomfort on Sarah's part, and he regretted that his presence would make her ill at ease. He silently vowed not to repeat such a pilgrimage for her sake, if not also for his own. In this frame of mind, the names that Sarah pronounced in introduction left his mind before the handshakes were completed. He made an exception, however, when Sarah introduced him to Sam and Kay Simpson, for two reasons. First, he recalled Sarah speaking of them when they had gone to Carol's for dinner, as having been especially helpful to her following Frank's death. More significantly, Craig noticed that when Sarah had introduced him as the boarder in her home, that Kay had offered her an especially sweet smile. That smile was accompanied by a noticeable aftertaste, which he detected, seemed not to sit well with his landlady.

    Entering the sanctuary, the pipe organ was fully engaged in rendering a lively tune, by Bach, possibly, though played at low volume. Glancing at Sarah, Craig saw that she had stopped walking, and stood, eyes closed, as if she were absorbing the music through every pore of her skin. He paused, too, to observe this osmosis, until, after a moment or so Sarah opened her eyes, giving him the warmest smile that he had yet seen adorn her face. She then led him down an outside aisle to take a seat next to the Simpsons, leaving the aisle seat for him.

    A short time later the organ began the processional, at full volume. The gangly minister, accompanied by two church elders, approached the altar ceremoniously, and the service began.

    Craig tried to remember the last time he had attended a church service, but no vivid recollection surfaced. With the singing of the first hymn, however, he became positive that whatever the date of his last church attendance, it surely coincided with his last attempt at public singing. His voice stumbled about in an attempt to match the notes the organ produced. He noticed that Sarah, to the contrary, sang confidently, with a lyrical voice full of expression, a dramatic contrast to her usual reserved demeanor.

    Craig found the pastor to be interesting. His elongated frame and stork-like limbs visually suggested a clumsy, awkward man. But his words, well chosen, carefully and clearly spoken, denoted not only an educated mind but also a person who had put his faith into practice and appreciated the practical limitations that must apply to idealism.

Although he made salient references to the scriptures, he did not overuse or stretch their applicability as Craig had heard some preachers do. His sermon was to the point, founded on one scripture reference, supported with three anecdotes from life, two pro and one con. Far from the tranquilizing effect that most sermons had upon Craig, Reverend Jordan's was engaging and enlightening.

Following the service, Sarah and Craig's routes of escape were blocked by several members curious to learn the identity of the stranger in their midst. This resulted in another half dozen introductions before they reached the front portico where they were greeted by Eb Jordan.

"So Sarah, I see you have a guest with you this morning," began the reverend.

"Yes. Pastor Jordan, I'd like you to meet Craig Miller. Mr. Miller is renting a room in my house. He wanted to come with me to today's service."

"Welcome, Mr. Miller. I hope you enjoyed your visit and will come again, soon."

"Thank you, I did. I enjoyed your sermon. A very good presentation."

"Why, thank *you*. You're definitely welcome to return!"

Sarah offered Craig a pleasant smile as they re-entered her car. After they pulled out of the church lot, Craig said, "I want to thank you for bringing me along, today."

"Anytime," she replied.

"I also want you to know how much I enjoyed your singing. You sing beautifully."

"Now you're stretching the truth, I'm afraid."

"No, I'm serious. It was very melodic."

Sarah flashed him a doubting smile, before refocusing on the road ahead.

"I also noticed how you were listening to the organ prelude. You really seemed to enjoy it."

Sarah again turned toward him, as if checking to ensure he was being sincere. "I don't know what it is about organ music, but I've always loved it. It does put me in a kind of a trance. But a very alert trance. I feel more in touch with everything when I hear that music." She paused for a moment and then continued, "I think organ music may have saved my sanity after Frank died. It was about the only thing I cared about. I only lived so to make it to church the following Sunday to hear the organ again."

Craig said nothing, touched by the confidence she had shared. They continued the rest of the ride to Monroe Street in silence.

75

Two overhead spotlights were the only illumination in the theatre, beating down on an oval at center stage. Had Dolores been there, she would have noted the intensity of the light, how it would sharply define each line of her form and cast dark shadows to emphasize the definition. Had she been there, she would have seen by the reflection of a few stray rays how the seats in the empty theatre were vaguely described, and seen the three pale faces seated together in the center of the room. Had she been there, she might have felt what those who had gone before her, and those still waiting in the wings, must have felt. She might be aware of the uneasiness in her stomach, the bristling in her brain, as she recalled memorized lines, inflicted accents, repeated practiced nuances.

But Dolores was not there. Charlie's mother had taken her place. Gone was her Jersey Girl accent, replaced by a heavy Irish brogue. Dolores's shoulder length hair had been confined within a tight bun, her straight spine arched slightly forward, her confident, sensual gait replaced by heavy, deliberate strides. Such were the tolls of traveling the turnpike that defined Charlie's mother's life. A road bordered by her rebellious son to one side, and the obstinate man to whom she was married, the man whom her son called affectionately, in spite of himself, "Da."

The woman carried a copy of Hugh Leonard's play in her hand, but for no particular reason. Paper clips marked the pages where her parts began, but the passages had been committed to memory along with gestures, inflections, facial expressions—all had been seared into the flesh and soul of her being. She approached the bright spot with the confidence of a matriarch accustomed to bringing order to a household against the inclinations of her family members. That was who Charlie's mother was. At the same time, she approached the spot with the measured tempo that an extended engagement in this crazy household dictated. Arriving there, she turned to face the three seated figures.

"Miss Miller, we'd like you to begin with the pantomime

scene on page 17, the scene where you and Da are welcoming Mr. Drumm to your home."

"But, of course," replied Charlie's Mother, with the Irish accent sounding through. Turning to her left, she mimed the greeting, head cocks, genuflections, smiles, eye brow lifts, hand clasps—all exaggerated to just the necessary degree. When completed, she turned again to face the three, a slight, confident smile—not exaggerated this time—gracing her face. She stood for a few moments as the three nearly faceless heads exchanged whispers until finally the center head spoke again.

"Very well. Now, on page 20, we'd like you to recite beginning with the line 'I took him out of Holles Street Hospital…'. Continue to the end, ignoring all other parts."

Charlie's Mother nodded. This section had been anticipated, as it was one of the more significant speeches of the role. This would be somewhat challenging, as the speech was interrupted numerous times by Charlie of the future and once by Da. She would present it as she had rehearsed it, offering brief silences for each interruption. And so she did, concluding with the line that proffered great pride in Charlie while not hesitating to conceal the magnanimity of her numerous sacrifices as his parent.

Again the heads came together and exchanged hushed comments. This time the wait was longer, and in spite of herself, the woman on stage strained to hear what she could of the whispered comments. At one point she heard, from the deeper voice, which carried better, "…could've been done better." These words were troubling, yet she detected a positive tone in the voice. Perhaps he had said, "I don't think it could've been done better." Now she was second guessing her second guess. No doubt that was why listening in was such a bad idea—too much room for misinterpretation. She had done her best. She should leave it at that.

Once again the middle head spoke. "Okay, now on page 44, beginning with 'Don't you pull *me* up.'"

Also expected. Indignation surfacing, another dimension to the role. She nodded once more, then, thrusting her fists to her hips, began to give Charlie the comeuppance he deserved. The words merged into a short tirade towards Da, and ended with satisfied acceptance of Young Charlie's accommodation to her will, although she was oblivious to the extra measure of satire with which it was served.

The heads huddled again, and Charlie's Mother waited patiently, not caring to hear what muffled words reached the stage.

"Thank you, Miss Miller. We will be in touch."

76

It had been a long practice, extending into the evening until the failing light had threatened to make the outfield drills unsafe. Batting practice had been first, and this session had enabled Craig to finalize a batting order with confidence. The little second baseman, Billy, would lead off. With his speed he hopefully could steal second on occasion. Buzzie would bat second. A good athlete, he was unquestionably the starting shortstop. Jesse, the doubting centerfielder, had fully signed on. An excellent contact hitter, he would bat third. Tommy would bat in the cleanup position, playing third when not pitching. Max also would field third, or would pitch on Tommy's days off. Tommy's spot in the order was protected by Homer, the tall first baseman with a strong swing. The quiet left fielder, Justin, would bat sixth, followed by the catcher Jimbo, Max, and finally Willie, whose thick glasses did not seem to be effective in helping him see pitches well enough to hit them, although he was a decent defensive player in right field.

Craig had been happy with the infield practice that followed. Billy was unquestionably the soft spot at second—he just wouldn't consistently keep his glove low enough. That was something they would have to work on. But Buzzie sucked up everything at short, and had great range. Nothing seemed to get past Homer at first base, neither hot grounders down the line nor errant throws from the far side of the diamond.

Jimbo was learning his leadership role as the backstop, but clearly deferred to the *de facto* team captain, Tommy. From his roost at the hot corner, Tommy was constantly offering encouragement to his teammates, especially the pitchers. As a pitcher himself, Tommy's brief visits to the hill served the pitcher and the team well. Craig imagined that such chats might save him many a mound visit.

During the outfield drills, Craig concentrated on cut-offs and base coverages, keeping the infielders involved with each play. Orchestrated by Jimbo at the plate, various runners-on-base scenarios were set up and appropriate defensive tactics deployed. The boys seemed to grasp the varied assignments, based upon the situation, and adapted to them well, if not yet quite automatically.

Following the practice, Craig piled the equipment into the bed of Tom Potter's pickup truck, and politely declining a ride home, began walking uphill towards Monroe Street. As he approached the house, he could discern Sarah on the porch, her form silhouetted against the illuminated living room window. As he drew closer, he could see the pensive expression on her face in the dim twilight. She seemed to be mentally detached, her mind visiting some distant vista. It quickly returned, contemporaneously with a startled expression in response to his greeting.

"Oh, hi," she said. "Your practice just finishing up?"

"Why, yes," he responded, a little surprised. He had not mentioned anything more of the ball team to her. "How do you know about that?"

"It's all over town. Several of the boys' mothers were talking about you after a meeting at church today. 'Seems the boys are all excited to be playing this season."

"I keep forgetting about how there are no secrets in a small town," Craig remarked, flashing Sarah a grin.

"Except for me," she countered. "I had to play along as if I knew all about it when they started complimenting my tenant for his 'civic mindedness.'"

"I told you I was coaching the team."

"Yes, but folks in town are thinking it's quite a big deal. You're doing much more than they expected, devoting a lot of time."

"I'm doing what I think needs to be done. Nothing more, nothing less. Didn't mean to keep you in the dark. Guess I haven't seen you much the last few days."

"It's your business, not mine. But I admire the fact that you're devoting time to the kids. I'm impressed." With that she smiled. It was a smile that he looked forward to seeing each time they talked, as it seemed to grow larger and warmer with each occurrence.

It was then that he felt it, that sensation he had known only a few times before in his life. Physically, it felt like a heat source near the center of his chest. The warmth radiated from this source, but remained localized, as if it were incapable of being diluted to any significant degree. Emotionally, the sensation was all encompassing, surpassing and repressing all other feelings. At the same time it was both tranquilly calming and electrifyingly exciting, complete in its certainty, under frantic reinforcement unless its fragility be revealed, its temporal essence proven to be but a momentary illusion.

He had experienced the feeling most frequently during his courtship and through the many years of marriage with Dolores. It had recurred most recently in response to Joan. That such a feeling should surface at this time, an attraction to his landlady with the potential to be as powerful and enduring as previous similar events, was as surprising as it was fascinating. Now his mind responded to the stimulus with awakened zeal, courses of action proposed, scenarios imagined and played out, reactions predicted and addressed. While in the background, the part of his mind that had not totally succumbed to the force, applied cold rationality to analyzing the inconvenient, less than practically prudent nature of this development. At the same time he was fully recognizing the futility of defying it, the impossibility of it being reversed.

Granting this rational analysis the respect it deserved, Craig promptly excused himself, and wishing Sarah a good evening, retreated upstairs to his bedroom.

77

"Fellas," Craig addressed the team seated on the bleachers before him, "Tomorrow we play Alderson. We haven't had as much time to prepare as they have, but we have used our time wisely, and you have all worked hard. Coach Potter and I are pleased with what you've accomplished. Remember the fundamentals, execute the plays as we practiced them, and we should do okay tomorrow afternoon."

Craig saw a few of the boys looking at each other, some bewilderment present on their faces. Clearly, he wasn't used to speaking to such a young audience. But soon, these boys, like the rest of their teammates, turned back to him with what he interpreted as looks of respect for him, self-confidence for themselves.

Tom Potter continued, "Guys, you need to be here by noon tomorrow. ..."

As his assistant provided final reminders, Craig could see over Tom's shoulder the unmistakable form of Eb Jordan leaving his parked car and walking towards the fence along the first base foul line.

"... Get a good's night rest, and come here ready to play tomorrow. We'll see you then," Tom wrapped up.

"You walking home again tonight, Craig?" Tom asked.

"Yeah, I think I will. Thanks." Craig took a seat on the bleachers as the players dispersed with waiting parents or on nearby bicycles. The minister still stood by the fence, but he seemed not to be noticed by anyone but Craig.

"Okay, I'll see you tomorrow, then."

"Right. Good night."

It had been a light practice, concluding earlier than usual, and the players were eager to move on to other things. Within a couple of minutes Craig was alone except for Eb who remained standing by the fence about thirty yards away, gazing at the outfield grass. Craig rose, and began to walk in his direction.

It was amazing how quickly the ball field had been transformed. From a noisy, animated theatre of play, it had transformed into a quiet, pastoral setting. Magically, a cottontail had appeared in left field and began to crop the vegetation there. Craig approached the minister somberly, as if the ball diamond he had just commanded were now an open air cathedral falling under the purview of the long-limbed preacher. In a way, it was a kind of surrender, a relinquishing of command. But Craig felt no loss. The transition seemed as natural and proper as retiring the colors at a military base at sunset. Nor did he feel apprehension. The mannerisms of this man seemed to be in keeping with the easygoing nature of this little mountain town, and he felt as comfortable approaching him as he felt when interacting with Walsh's citizens.

"'Evening, Pastor."

"Good evening, Mr. Miller."

"Please, call me 'Craig'"

"Your team ready for tomorrow?"

"As ready as we're going to be. If you came to offer a prayer, though, I'm not going to turn it down." With the last comment Craig offered the minister a grin.

Eb Jordan leaned forward, resting his arms on the waist-high fence. "I didn't come by to pray for you, necessarily. I came to thank you."

"Thank me?" Craig asked, thrusting his hands into his pants pockets.

"You've made quite an impression in the short time you've been in town, taking on the coaching of a ball team."

"Somebody needed to do it," Craig said, leaning back on his elbows on his side of the fence, looking out onto the field with Eb.

"Is that why you came to Walsh, to coach a little league team?"

"Could be," Craig answered, turning his head to look into the outfield. After a short pause, he continued, "I came here not sure what I was looking for, or why. Coaching this team has given me a focus. It's been good for me. Hopefully it's been good for the kids, too."

"Apparently it has been. The parents seem to be impressed with how the team is coming together. There's always a skeptic or two. People curious as to why you'd being doing this with no child of your own on the team."

"What? They think I'm some kind of pervert?" Craig said, the incensement clearly expressed by his voice. He stepped away from the fence and squared to face the minister.

"I said they were skeptical, not that they were right," Eb said,

215

without changing his position. "These are the times we live in, I'm afraid."

"Hmpf," Craig grunted.

"You have kids, Craig?"

"No."

"Married?"

A simple question. Why was it so hard to answer? Craig looked at the minister, sizing him up. How much should he reveal to this man? Craig was impressed with his intellect. He had come to that conclusion after hearing only one sermon. Sarah had high praise for him, and that was worth a great deal. He desperately longed to confide in someone, as if just talking about his troubles would relieve some of the burden. He would give it a try. Chances were it would stay confidential, he was talking to a minister, after all. And it just might help. Craig returned to lean on the fence and look onto the ball field.

"We're separated," Craig answered. "After nineteen years we spent more time arguing than anything else. The more I tried to change things for the better, the worse they got. As things continued to go downhill I didn't believe it was doing either of us any good, so I split."

When Craig turned his head to face the pastor, the reverend was looking at him intently, but made no verbal response. Craig looked away again and continued, "I'm not saying I'm proud of leaving, but it was something I felt had to be done."

"What's your wife's name?"

"Dolores."

"Let me ask you, do you love Dolores?"

Craig turned to face the minister, "Yes, I do. That's what makes it so painful, the failure to have the love returned. Disappointment. That's the main feeling: disappointment."

"So you left her, and came here?"

"That's right."

"Has your escape helped relieve this feeling of disappointment?"

"I can't say that it has."

"Running away usually doesn't solve anything."

"I won't argue with that," Craig said. "But coming here has introduced me to a simpler type of life, some very kind people, and the ability to focus on what really is important."

"And what's that?" Eb asked.

"Commitments. Like honoring obligations to employers, landlords. Informal commitments—but still important--to community and society in general, I guess. Trust. In yourself. Even in your belief system, I suppose, regardless of how many people fail to measure up to your standards."

"Who's failed to measure up?"

"You want the short list?" Craig asked, sarcastically. "Employers willing to cut corners for some short term profits while putting the long term sustainability of the firm at risk. Politicians—of all stripes. Educators who substitute a few facts for knowledge. Clergy—present company excepted, of course—more concerned with a trendy political agenda than universal truths."

"You sound angry, Craig."

Craig turned his head again towards Eb Jordan. "No! Far from it! There are enough good people in the world to offer hope for salvation from the curses of the charlatans. It's not a one-to-one ratio, but it doesn't have to be. My perception is that the good done by a Carol Wilson more than offsets the harm done by my former boss. That one excellent teacher can inspire a class of students despite what her counterparts do the other hours of the school day. As for politicians, well, I guess we're still running deficits there."

Craig returned his eyes to the outfield. "No, I'm not angry. Like I said, I'm disappointed. Sad, sometimes, but I don't think I'm unduly pessimistic. I try to project a positive image. Think I've been pretty successful: at the diner, with the kids on the ball field."

"Maybe you're expecting too much from others," the clergyman suggested.

"I've considered that, especially when I realize how many times I've felt let down. But it always comes back to the same comparison: often I feel that I fall short of my own expectations of my potential. At the same time, I feel—and I try to be as objective as I can—I feel that I have easily attained more than so many others who appear or claim to have exerted so much more effort. I have no delusions about my performance. I suffer from laziness, carelessness, inattentiveness—all the character faults all men have to some degree or another. But I usually feel I put forth an honest effort and often obtain a positive result. It's just that the reciprocity—the matching effort, the same honesty, similar results—I don't always see it from others, particularly people I very much care about. These people, these special people, are special because I have high expectations, a heightened appreciation for their qualities or potential. When they let me down, then my disappointment is even greater."

"What about your wife?" Eb asked. "Didn't you let her down by taking off?"

Craig looked over his shoulder to see the clergyman's intense interest. Nothing else was important, not the birds calling from the trees, nor the breeze that had kicked up. He was only interested in this conversation, and Craig appreciated that. "Of course. Don't think that hasn't been eating at me ever since I left. But I left in reaction to her actions. I believe I gave her many opportunities, but we just couldn't make it work. I'm not saying two wrongs make a right, but neither do a dozen wrongs." As he said these words, Craig's looked at the grass at his feet.

"So where does that leave Dolores?"

Craig looked up meekly at the minister. The pastor's words were not profound; indeed Craig had moved towards a similar conclusion since he had left Peach Hill, and that, in turn, had tormented him. Yet somehow, hearing them from this independent observer had made the meaning more clear and had affirmed Craig's guilt. "You're right, of course. I acted out of fear. And that fear blinded me as to what was right."

"What are you afraid of, Craig?"

"Heh," Craig laughed, to soften the force of his self-condemnation, "I'm afraid of failure. Of admitting those failures. I'm afraid of the finality of the decision I need to make. I'm afraid of hurting people I love. Even though I hurt them by my indecision."

"Besides Dolores, who else are you hurting?"

Craig looked at Eb, a slightly startled expression on his face. "Oh, you're good. Sarah said you were good." He returned his gaze to the outfield and said nothing for a moment. It would be easy to leave it at this, to say nothing further, reveal no more secrets. However, he was finding this discussion helpful, an unanticipated result of a chance meeting. Or was it by chance?

Without turning his eyes from the left field foul pole, Craig continued, "There is another woman, a close friend. Nothing adulterous or scandalous, just someone I admired tremendously."

"Are you trying to convince me or yourself?" Eb asked.

"Don't go placing a Puritanical harness on me, Reverend. I know my heart. There was no maliciousness—in thought or action. But once again there was a rejection of me, and with it, disappointment. I was probably running away from the disappointment at the rejection of what could have been as much as I was running away from the destruction of what was."

The two men stood in silence. The sun had dropped below Bald Knob, and the long shadows that had stretched across the ball field were replaced by the uniform shadow world that foretold the night. A pair of killdeer noisily announced their arrival as they flew in close to the ground, alighting on the infield. The birds began to walk about, in part a patrol of their territorial grounds, in part a ceremonial dance with exaggerated head and neck movements, and occasional displays of partially spread wing feathers.

Craig jerked his head in the direction of the fowl and queried the pastor, "Do you think they're happy?"

"I'm not sure such creatures experience emotions as we know them," Eb replied, with a matter of fact tone.

"Well, if they do, just think how little they require to find their happiness. If he flies to another field, she flies after him. Maybe he helps with feeding the young in the spring. He hopes she is bedazzled when he displays his wing feathers. That's about it." Craig turned back towards Eb, "Sometimes I think my requirements are almost as simple, and yet so seldom met."

"You sound very sad and lonely. It has been my experience that faith can bolster people in such a position. Have you turned to God?"

"Now comes the commercial part of the discussion," Craig quipped. "Mind you, I know it's your job, and I fully expected you'd get here sooner or later. Please, don't take my cynicism as an attempt to discredit in any way the good I believe you do. Yes, and of the good that Sarah has told me you do."

Craig continued, "I'm afraid my faith is not as personalized as many people I know claim to experience it. Oh, I believe in a Creator. The universe is much too complex and organized to have been the result of random mutations and chance developments. But I think He just set things in motion, and it's up to us to carry on, as He looks on with bemused interest. I don't perceive of God as sitting in waiting, ready to launch a lightning bolt to change the course of history, to right a terrible wrong, certainly not to act especially on my behalf. So you see, I'm even lonelier than you thought."

"What if you're wrong? Jesus said 'I am the way and the truth and the life. No one comes to the Father except through me.' Even though there are various interpretations of this text, it still suggests to me a personal relationship between God and individual men."

"I could very well be wrong," Craig said. "I have a tough enough time figuring out earthly matters without being so brash as to claim an understanding of the workings of heaven. But if He shoots one of those lightning bolts in my direction, I'm sure there's no way to avoid the consequences, anyway."

"I think you may have given up too easily in your search for answers from God. You admitted that the questions are complex. Perhaps you need to ask the questions again, in different ways, at different times. I would also suggest that the answers you seek may not be as clear to understand as you may be expecting. God speaks to us in mysterious ways. We must first be open to receive His answers. Then we need to interpret them intelligently in order to act upon them confidently."

"All right then—and please, I'm not trying to be difficult or obstinate, here—but suppose it was God's idea that I abandon my old life and come to Walsh. I certainly acted confidently on a plan that, looking back, was half-baked. Maybe He's leading me to something—something new, something rewarding and fulfilling. I never volunteered to coach a ball team in New Jersey. I never volunteered to do much of anything. Oh, I'd make out a few checks each year to a few charities—but give of myself? Not until just recently."

"So you're saying that once you came to West Virginia, you became a giving person?"

"No, actually I went through some kind of change up north. It happened after I met that second woman, Joan. I gave a lot of time to her son, who was going through some tough times." Craig turned to look directly at the pastor. "It was time freely given, I expected no *quid pro quo*."

"And yet, you felt that she rejected you. What did she reject?"

"I guess I felt that she rejected my giving. She rejected the selflessness of it, its honesty and purity. Being so new to me, I never felt better than after I gave of myself. To be rejected by someone who I admired so much—when I fully expected my actions to receive her approval—that was devastating."

"Are you sure she didn't think that perhaps you were looking for more?"

"And what if I was?" Craig answered, somewhat sharply. He was off the fence now and animated. "If you have three unhappy people, and by a simple realignment the result may be two happier people, possibly even three happier people, is that such a bad thing? Must we adhere to some civil contract drawn up decades ago, the terms of which are constantly being breached?"

"Aren't you mocking the bond that holds the society together—a union not just sanctioned by civil government but consecrated by God?"

"I'm not mocking anything other than a sham and a hoax. Dolores seems to want to float along even as I'm shouting that a tsunami is coming. She revels in the *status quo* even as she moans about how boring it is. Any efforts I take to make life more interesting—and believe me, I have tried often—are rejected out of hand before I finish the proposal. She wasn't like that in the past. When we met she was an actress—and a very good one. I fell in love with the dramatic Dolores, the Dolores who could put forth a different persona every day. But no matter who she was, the constant was that she loved me. Now... Now, everything is constant. Wake up at the same time, eat the same meals, putter in the same garden, watch the same TV shows, pack off to bed at the same time. Not only does she not act anymore, she doesn't even care to go see a show."

"Why do you think that is?" Eb asked.

"I'm not sure. I've tried to ask. I've tried to encourage her. Over and over again, all I got was rejection. It gets tiring, getting the same, constant response.

"Did I say everything is constant? Well, not quite. That constant love has been replaced. On a good day it's replaced with toleration, on worse days with disdain.

"Still, I think I love her. No—I *know* I love her. I love her not only for what she was but what she still could be. But she refuses to be either."

"I don't see how running away solves anything."

"Of course, it doesn't. I didn't leave seeking a solution. I was looking for relief. You can bang your ahead against a stone wall only for so long before you become senseless. When I turned in another direction—and met another stone wall—it became too much. I took off for fear that I was being boxed in, that the walls were closing in on me."

"So you plan to return to New Jersey? To seek a solution?"

"I'm sure I will. But I'll be honest with you. I'm really enjoying the relief. What I've found in this little town…well, it's what lots of people look for in a prescription bottle. As long as I continue to find acceptance here—from Carol at the diner, from Sarah, and especially from this bunch of kids: from the eager-to-please Tommy, to the hapless Willie, and yes, even from the cynical Jesse—as long as I find acceptance like that, it's going to be hard to leave."

The two men fell silent. The killdeer flew off toward the west. In the distance a dog barked.

"Thanks for stopping by," Craig said. "I appreciate the fact that you led the discussion, but didn't force it in any direction."

"I believe there is a difference between a preacher and a minister," said Eb, smiling.

"It may not have sounded like it from some of what I said, but you've made me rethink my position."

"And what did you conclude, if anything?" asked the minister.

"I'll let you know when I get it figured out," Craig answered.

"Can we pray together?" Eb offered.

"Sure," Craig said as he smiled at the reverend with appreciation.

78

Saturday's chill seemed especially severe following the heat wave of the previous days. There had been little improvement by the afternoon, the cloud cover and brisk wind only added to the cooling effect.

At the Jefferson School field, the Alderson Eagles and the Walsh Pirates were engaged in a stand-off through five innings. Although the wind had adversely affected some of the pitches of both team's hurlers, the contest had been primarily a pitcher's duel, with neither team scoring.

"How's your arm feel?" Craig asked his pitcher as he started out to the mound in the top of the sixth.

"I'm good, Coach," Tommy replied.

"I wouldn't expect you to say anything else. The mature pitcher knows when he's done, and when it's best for the team that he step off the mound."

"No, coach, I got two more innings in me, easy."

"Uh huh. Jimbo!"

"Yes, coach," said the catcher, trotting over to join the two by the backstop.

"They've all seen Tommy's stuff at least once. Time to mix it up a little. Call for some change-ups, especially if they're on his fast ball. Tommy, you shake off the curve if you don't think you can throw it with some bite. You leave one hanging out there today, and with this wind, Jesse'll be fetching the ball from across Jefferson Street. Now, mow 'em down!"

As Craig walked back to the bench, Tom Potter flashed him a grin before glancing down at the scorebook then calling out the opponent's batting order to his battery, "Eight, nine, one, fellas. Let's sit 'em down, one, two, three!" Then, to Craig, "They're playing a damn good game."

"That they are, Tom, that they are."

Craig looked across the infield at Joe Lorenzo coaching third base. His cockiness had disappeared after the top of the third, when his number three and four hitters had reached base with no outs, only to be stranded there as Tommy struck out the next three in a row.

Based only on appearances, this game belonged to Alderson.

Their white uniforms, trimmed in royal blue, were bright even on this cloudy day. The blue socks with white stripes added a finishing touch as they stretched up the players' calves to meet the white pants. His Pirates, by contrast, wore black tee shirts with matching hats. In deference to the temperature, many of the boys were playing with sweatshirts of various colors covering their jerseys. Those that were visible displayed the word "Pirates" in white across the front, with a large numeral on the back, just below the sponsor's name. Blue jeans completed the outfit, with many boys wearing sneakers, unable to afford a pair of cleats.

But the Pirates were playing well, putting them on equal footing with the Eagles. A ground out to short and another strike out for Tommy, and it looked like the sixth inning would continue as the earlier innings had. Then Alderson's lead off hitter laid down a bunt that looked like it would go foul, and Jimbo hovered over it, watching it finally die on the fair side of the line. The next batter went with an outside pitch, lining it to right field for a single.

Tommy quickly got ahead of the number three hitter. First a curve caught the outside corner for a call strike, and a change up was missed, the batter way out in front. Tommy then tried two curves, but both just missed the plate. His fifth pitch was inside heat, and the hitter stepped into it and drove it down the third base line for a bases clearing double.

The pitcher looked toward the bench, half expecting his afternoon to be over. From his dad came a shout of encouragement, and from Craig, two index fingers pointed at him accompanied by a confident nod.

From the coach's box, Lorenzo shouted, "Okay, Allen, let's keep it going!"

Tommy looked homeward to see Alderson's clean-up hitter, a tall, strong farm boy, digging in. Besides being a head taller than the next tallest player on their team, the hitter displayed well defined muscles on his upper arms—bright pink arms due to their bared exposure to the chilling wind.

With a runner on second, Jimbo gave a series of signs, with two fingers thrust downward as the only one that mattered. From the stretch, Tommy checked the runner, then went to the plate, his wrist snapping downward to give the spin that would cause it to curve. The ball moved towards the plate, then seemed to hang like frozen long johns on an arctic clothes line.

Tommy watched the batter's eyes grow large and the powerful swing of the bat make a loud, forceful contact with the ball, shooting it skyward. The pitcher's head jerked upward, following the ball's path—higher, longer, and higher still. His eyes dropped to the outfield, where Jesse had arrived near the center field fence and stood, his hands waiting overhead, calmly, patiently. The ball smacked smartly into Jesse's glove, and Tommy heard the sighs from the infielders. The batter, halfway to second, kicked the dirt in frustration, as Tommy pumped his right fist with an audible, "Yes!" Coach Lorenzo walked toward his bench, shaking his head.

Arriving at his bench, Tommy looked up at his coach, with a little more relief than remorse.

"You were *so* lucky he got under it," Craig said.

"Yeah, I know."

"You held them to two, though. Their best hitter beat you. If you're going to get beaten, that's the way to do it." Craig smiled as he rubbed Tommy's right shoulder, then, louder for the team to hear, "Okay, let's get those runs back. Everyone hits!"

"I'm still good for another inning, coach," Tommy said, a little meekly.

"Buzzy, Jesse, Tommy," Tom cried out the batting order.

"You did a good job, Tommy. You got through the meat of their order, with minimal damage. You'll play third next inning."

"Aw, coach."

"Don't argue. Max will close it out. The junk he throws is so completely different from your heat." Looking under the brim of the hat on Tommy's downcast head, Craig added, "Why don't you help the team out, now, with your bat?"

Tommy couldn't stop the grin from forming. "I'm on it!" he said, picking up a helmet.

The big farm boy came in to pitch in the bottom of the sixth, and he was slow to gain command of his pitches. Buzzy walked on five pitches, then Jesse stroked a solid single to left. Just that fast, Tommy came to bat, representing the go-ahead run. He had been studying the pitcher during the previous at bats, and saw that he telegraphed his curve ball by exaggerating the overhand arc his throwing hand described. Tommy forced his helmet firmly onto his head, then looked up at the pitcher, who stared at him sidewise, from the stretch position. Receiving his sign from the catcher, the pitcher allowed the smallest of smiles to pull at his lips. Then he lunged towards the plate, his right arm reaching for the sky. *It's a deuce!* Tommy realized.

The ball sped towards his head. Tommy resisted the urge to jump out of the way, held his hands high behind him, his bat motionless and erect. *Come on, break!* At last, the ball changed direction, dipping towards the strike zone. Tommy released. All the strength in his arms, legs and back let go, all focused on forcing his aluminum bat to streak through the strike zone.

He was a split second late, and a fraction of an inch low. Just like the last pitch Tommy had thrown, this one exploded off his bat, heading out high, but this time, in the direction of right field. Tommy started to run towards first, picking up his speed as he saw the right fielder, a chunky kid, begin running towards the fence. *It's going out or it's gonna drop!* Tommy rounded first and looked up. Jesse was racing for third, convinced that the outfielder would not get to the ball in time. Buzzy was prancing towards home, beginning the celebration for the Pirate's first run halfway down the foul line. Approaching second, Tommy looked towards Coach Miller, who was windmilling his arm near third, signaling both Jesse and Tommy to continue advancing.

Halfway to third, however, the umpire motioned Tommy back to second, and directed Jesse, who was hugging Buzzy near home plate, to return to third base. "Ground rule double!" the ump shouted. Although Tommy had not been looking in that direction, apparently the ball had landed in the outfield and had bounced over the right field fence.

Tommy had come so very close to tying the game. The Pirate's first run remained their only run, as the Eagle's pitcher gained control of his pitches and the following Pirates proved to be no match. Max did well in the top of the sixth, allowing only one base runner. But the Pirates could get nothing going in the bottom of that inning, going three up and three down.

Ceremoniously, the teams lined up at home plate, the lines passing each other to exchange hand slaps and chants of "Good game." Craig and Tom shook the hands of the opposing coaches at third base.

"A well played game," Lorenzo said, unable to hold back a satisfied smile.

"Your boys did a great job," Craig responded.

Afterwards, Craig addressed the team, complimenting them on their good defense, and lamenting that the difference in the score was just a few inches. "More important than the score, was the character you displayed—each and every one of you—throughout the game. I am so very proud to coach this team." Craig looked to Tom to continue.

"You guys make me proud, too." Tom said. "It's no big secret that Coach Lorenzo was bragging that he was gonna embarrass us here today, beat us by ten runs or more. Now he has to explain how he escaped with a 2-1 win."

"It was a secret to me," Craig muttered for Tom to hear.

"'Guess I left that out of my scouting report," Tom apologized, softly.

79

Jeff pulled his car to the curb in front of the Miller house. In the weeks since he had last seen her, he had had no reason to contact her. He had warned her that he wouldn't be calling unless he had some news. But that did not mean that she had been out of his mind.

He wasn't sure what it was about Dolores Miller that was intriguing. She was attractive. So were many of his clients, but never before had he looked at any of them in anything but a professional manner, never more than a means to pay the rent or buy some groceries. She was vulnerable. Ditto, again, for most of his female clients. If anything, the disappearance of this loser, Craig, might be a good thing. With luck he'd help get the financial situation clarified so she could get on with her life. If she wanted Craig back, well, he'd see what he could do about that, too, if maybe a little reluctantly. The good news was that the opportunity had presented itself, and he was confident that something was about to give.

She met him at the door in designer jeans and a light sweater, her hair pulled back into a pony tail, revealing a graceful neck. Her eyes contacted his directly, as if she were attempting to read the news he carried before he could tell her. This eagerness translated promptly into the two moving to the living room, assuming the same seats as they had on his prior visit.

"Are you familiar with Walsh, West Virginia?" he asked.

"Never heard of it," she replied.

"How about Marc and Carol Wilson?"

"No. What does this mean?"

It was clear from her face, that his questions were confusing Dolores.

"According to Social Security records, Craig works for them, or more accurately, their corporation: Marcar, Inc. They do business as Carol's Diner."

"Wow. Craig's working in a diner? In West Virginia?"

"Apparently."

Dolores uncrossed her legs as she looked at Jeff with a puzzled expression. Crossing her other leg, she leaned forward in her seat, as if to focus her next question.

"In a diner? Are you sure it's him? He was a cook in the

National Guard, but I *never* thought he'd want to work in a restaurant!"

"He didn't make any effort to hide the fact. Used his legitimate social security number, his real name."

"So you're saying he wants to be found?"

"Dunno. Maybe he didn't think about it. Maybe he got careless. Maybe he didn't think you'd have the ability to track him down."

"Do you have an address where I can contact him?"

"I've got an address. But I don't want to spook him. If he thinks he's safe—and holding down a job suggests he's put down some roots—hearing from you might drive him deeper into the weeds. Could be more expensive to find him a second time."

Dolores seemed to consider this for a moment. "So what do you suggest?"

"There's several ways we can proceed." Jeff considered her expression. It continued to display the same level of trust she had shown at their first meeting. "From the beginning I've tried to do this the most economical way for you. Mind you, typically I don't mind making a decent salary off of other people's troubles. My clients have plenty to spare. I'm happy with the scraps the attorneys leave behind. I see a different set of circumstances here."

"I'm willing to pay for what needs to be done," Dolores said.

"I understand. But there's no reason to make that bill higher than it needs to be. What do you think of this? I've got a brother in Cincinnati. I owe him a visit. Figure I'd take some vacation time and drive out there. If I go off the route a bit, I can swing through Walsh, look up Craig, get a read on the situation. Depending on his reaction, I can do what needs to be done, or get a private eye to pick up the case there. I'm only licensed in New Jersey, so there's only so much I can do. I'd be working 'off the clock', so to speak. You'd owe me just some gas money, and I'd talk to you before committing to the expense of another p.i."

"Why are you doing this?"

Jeff could see the skepticism on her face, the cute way the skin wrinkled between her eyebrows. "Like I said, I see different circumstances here. I'm guessing a simple misunderstanding. Or else Craig's the biggest fool I've ever known." Jeff caught her modest smile, so he knew she was aware he was flattering her. "Either way,

I'd like to see this to completion. Would hate to farm it out to some hillbilly. Besides, I owe my brother a visit. This may be the best excuse I have for taking that vacation."

"Do you always take your cases so personally?" she asked. She was looking at him out of the corner of her eye.

"Yes," he lied.

"And what will you say to him when you find him?"

"I'm going to have to play that by ear. Like I said, I don't want to spook him. On the other hand, the guy's not ignorant. He has to know he's left you in a bit of a bind. Probably expects he's going to have to do something to make it right. If I'm right about that, then I should be able to talk to him calmly. I expect we'll reach an understanding."

Dolores's face was nearly expressionless. Jeff could sense she was imagining her husband in West Virginia. Trying to imagine what his life was like there. He enjoyed looking at her face, he almost hated to interrupt her daydream. "So what do you think of my plan? Do I go to West Virginia?"

"All right, then."

"I have a few other cases I have to wrap up or stabilize. It will take me a day or two. I hope to leave on Thursday morning."

80

Craig was happy to enter the house after walking home from the diner. The wind had picked up. The chilly gusts cut through his jacket, adding to the chill he had felt on the field. He was somewhat out of breath from the brisk walk home. He closed the door with a shiver, and heard Sarah call from the kitchen.

"So how'd you do?"

"It was close. We lost, 2-1."

"Aw, I'm sorry to hear that," she said, appearing in the doorway.

"No. The boys played well—very well. Nothing to be ashamed of." Seeing her standing there, leaning casually against the door jamb, Craig was reminded of the feelings he now felt for her.

He felt extremely comfortable in her presence. He no longer needed to be cautious of causing another outburst as he had experienced after the gutter repair. That period was far behind them.

Beyond that, he had come to see she was a caring and compassionate person. He liked that, and wanted to claim for himself however much of that outpouring she was willing to offer him.

He also sensed a level of loneliness in her life. That was a void that he wanted to fill. It was one that he felt obligated to fill, if for no other reason than he had landed upon her doorstep and had maintained a nearness without being challenged. He knew it provided him no legitimacy, but he would be more than willing to try to build upon the opportunity.

Countering these emotions was the guilt he felt for falling for Joan in almost the same way. Additionally, there was the guilt he felt for giving up on Dolores for Joan as an alternative. He owed it to Dolores to try again, and to do so, he could not harbor strong feelings for Sarah. So he suppressed them.

"So, you think if you'd a little more time to practice, you might've won?"

"I don't know. We could've hit better. That's always the case. More batting practice might've helped. But otherwise, I don't know what else I could've given them." He looked at her eyes and saw they were focused on him. That directness: that was what he had come to admire about her.

"Not selling yourself short, now, are you?" she asked with a smile.

"Not making false claims," he answered. He liked her smile; he was glad she was doing it more often.

"And where'd you learn what you know?" she asked, moving towards him in the hall.

"Most of what I know I learned from my little league coach and a few coaches in school. There are some fundamentals, and then the repeated drilling of them until they're second nature."

"Care to sit down?" she said, motioning towards the parlor.

Craig paused for a second. His first instinct was to decline, to avoid feeding this newfound hunger. But he did not wish to be rude, and, yes, he enjoyed her company. He must keep it at that alone. "Sure."

Sarah took a seat on the sofa; Craig sat opposite her in an arm chair, draping his jacket over his knee.

"I've heard," she continued, "that baseball is such a complex game, with a lot of strategy and psychological moves and countermoves."

"It can be. But don't forget we're dealing with kids, here. They usually aren't developed enough intellectually or emotionally to appreciate most of that. Few of them have learned how to be subtle, much less coy. Even physically, there is often no explanation for what might happen. A kid can throw eight strikes in a row and then launch one over the backstop. You look at him and he looks back at you and shrugs his shoulders."

Sarah chuckled softly, looking away. Craig admired her profile. She had a "down home" look about her: simple, but solid. It was not the elegant beauty that Dolores possessed, nor the ethereal presence Joan's face suggested. He was struck by it just the same. Then, remembering his place, he checked himself, turning his gaze towards the floor.

"So you've got no regrets about taking on this challenge?" she resumed.

"No. In fact, I regret that I even hesitated as much as I did. They're a good bunch of boys. With luck they will learn some of what baseball taught me."

"And that would be…?"

"Teamwork. Cooperation. Relying upon someone else.

Doing your best when it's your turn to do your part. Afterwards, sharing the joys of victory, or just as important, sharing the disappointment of losing."

"And you experienced this, when you were young?"

Craig looked at her inquisitively. Did this question have any special significance? Was she directing the conversation towards personal revelations on purpose, or just making conversation? Sarah's face provided no clues.

"I was never a star player," he began. "Not very strong or coordinated--I barely made the starting team. But one time—it was while I was in middle school—I come up to bat with a runner on second. It was late in the game and there was no score. Old coach Furman called time and came over to talk to me, to encourage me to try to get a hit. Now while on deck I had noticed that the third baseman was playing way off the bag, and I had recently read a library book that included a chapter on place hitting. I told the coach that I thought I could pull a ball down the line, and maybe get it past him. Coach Furman just nodded his head, and said, 'Yeah, yeah, just try to hit the ball.' I don't think he had hopes of me making contact, much less hitting it where I wanted to.

"Well, on the very first pitch I 'stepped in the bucket', you know, stepped with my lead foot towards third, which leads the bat to make contact towards the left side of the field. The pitch was a little inside, and my timing was perfect. The ball bounced down the third base line, bouncing fair, right over third base. It continued bouncing down the line, finally rolling to a stop deep in the outfield before the left fielder could get to it. I made it to second and the runner scored what turned out to be the winning run.

"I looked over at Coach Furman, and he just shook his head. I don't think he really believed it happened."

"You must have been proud!" Sarah said.

Craig had not told this story to anyone since it happened. He was moved that Sarah would appreciate the event and its significance in his life. With every minute he spent with her he felt a stronger bond. "It was great. But it really hit home when the game ended. My teammates hoisted me onto their shoulders and carried me off the field. Unforgettable!"

Sarah smiled again, and Craig basked in its radiance. He could easily get used to talking with her every day, just watching her smile.

"A nice story," she said. "I guess it shows you don't have to be a home run hitter to score when it counts."

Craig looked down again, not to give himself away. But unable to keep his eyes away from her for long, he looked back at her. He found her eyes both forcefully attracting and a comfortable place to focus. "It's like I said: it's about doing your best when it's time to do your part."

Perhaps his gaze was too intense, for she looked away. But she soon turned back to him, speaking in a more matter-of-fact tone. "Craig, can I ask a favor?"

"Sure," he said, looking once again to her eyes, "what do you need?"

"I don't mean to take advantage, I…" Sarah hesitated.

"What is it?" he prompted.

"I want to clean out the garage. I'd like to sell Frank's power tools. Could you make a list of what's there? I'm afraid I wouldn't know what everything is called, exactly. I want to make a list for an ad."

"That's all? Sure. Be glad to."

"I don't want you to think you have to. You can say no."

"Don't be silly. I'd be glad to help."

She smiled that smile again, and Craig became fearful of staying any longer. "I'll start on it tonight. If you'll excuse me, it was good talking to you, again."

"Thank you," she said, as they both rose. Craig had started up the stairs when Sarah added, "Were you planning on coming to church again tomorrow?"

Prudence would cause him to decline, but Craig rejected the warnings. "I'd like that. If it's not too much trouble—"

"No trouble at all," she said. "I'd enjoy the company."

81

Again, the ride to the church had been nearly a silent one. Sarah had attempted to start conversation several times, but Craig had responded with one word answers, killing her attempts.

Once they arrived, her companion had seemed to warm up a bit, returning greetings from other parishioners with vitality. Over the past month, he had appeared regularly, and was being accepted by the congregation. Once seated in the pew, however, his eyes became distant, his manner even more reserved. When the first hymn was sung, Craig seemed to study the words in the hymnal, but made no attempt to sing. He remained as just a spectator during the entire service, although he appeared to be more engaged during Eb's sermon.

Craig smiled meekly at Sarah at the end of the service, and followed her to the portico where the Reverend Jordan was greeting the congregants. "Hello, Sarah. The Lord has blessed us with a beautiful day, today. If still a little breezy."

"Yes, Pastor Jordan. I'm so glad it's warmer than yesterday. You see, I'm still bringing Mr. Miller along."

"Hello, Craig. It's good to have you with us, again."

"The pleasure is again mine," Craig responded. "I enjoyed the analogy in your sermon today. At first I thought it was a stretch, but you brought it all together very effectively."

"Why, thank you. I hear you came up just one run short in yesterday's game."

"A squeaker. But the boys played very well, and that's what's important."

"Apparently your opposing coach was served a slice of humble pie," Eb said with a grin.

"So even you heard of his bragging? Was I the only one who didn't?"

"Some of the fathers around here have been known to take youth sports too seriously, especially as it pertains to their own egos. It's refreshing to see the emphasis where it belongs."

"Thanks. I'm trying."

"So how are things otherwise?" the pastor asked.

"A little better, thank you. I've thought a lot about what we talked about the other night."

Sarah's attention was aroused by this comment, and as Craig glanced in her direction, she eyed him with interest. "Thank you again for sharing your time with me," Craig said, looking back towards the pastor.

"My pleasure, Craig. Thanks again for coming. Enjoy the rest of this glorious day!" Eb said. "And good luck in your game next Saturday," he added.

As she pulled the car out of the church driveway, Sarah glanced at Craig, just as he did the same. Their eyes made contact for a second, before Sarah's returned to the road. "Pastor Jordan is easy to talk to, isn't he?" she asked.

"Yes, he is. You called that one right. I should thank you for the suggestion."

"Well, I'm glad you went to speak to him," she said.

"Actually, he came to me," Craig answered. "The guy makes house calls. Or more accurately, *field* calls."

"Really?" she said, surprised. "Well, I hope it was useful."

"It was," he said. "Very much so."

82

"Hi, it's Beth Rosen from Black River Playhouse."

"Oh, hi," Dolores said, her heart suddenly beating faster.

"I'm calling to let you know you got the part. We were all impressed with your audition. Great stage presence!"

"Oh, thank you, *so* much. I can't tell you how much this means to me."

"So, listen, our first rehearsal is Thursday night, seven o'clock."

"Thursday at seven; I'll be there. Thank you, again."

83

Near the west end of Walsh, a little less than a mile from Carol's Diner along the main highway, stood Blake's Service Station. The glare of the lights was reflected by the whitewashed building, making it appear as an oasis of light in the growing gloom of the spring night.

Craig approached on foot, walking along the road's shoulder, unlike the typical customer who stopped to fill his gas tank or sought repairs to his car or truck. The remedial work Craig was seeking was not mechanical, but emotional. It would not take place in the garage bay, but in the enclosed phone booth in the corner of the lot, next to the road.

On the walk over, Craig had rehearsed what he would say, how he would begin a conversation with Dolores after all these weeks. Upbeat. It had to be upbeat, positive. If she had grown accustomed to his absence, had learned to prefer it, well, he was ready for that. If, however, she wished for him to return, that was his preference. He owed his marriage, and Dolores, one more chance. Pastor Jordan's rather pointed remarks had driven that realization home, although Craig would be the first to admit that he had known this all along. Until the option to return home was unquestionably dismissed, he dare not say anything that might jeopardize it.

Arriving at Blake's, Craig saw that the phone booth was occupied. Illuminated by the harsh overhead light, a teenage girl, wearing a leather jacket and aggressively chewing gum, was having an animated conversation inside the closed booth. Craig loitered on the opposite side of the lot, drawing a suspicious glance from the young attendant working the pumps. Eventually she hung up and crossed the highway and began walking west. Craig moved to the booth and entered, closing the door behind him and activating the overhead light.

In the stark light Craig confronted the payphone, his left hand massaging a handful of quarters. The phone, its stark blackness, standing chest high at 'present arms,' was intimidating. Not that its operation was foreign, but that the message it might deliver could prove to be without mercy, too cold, too abrupt. Craig had thought he would be prepared for that message, an understandable reaction to his cruel disappearance. But now, facing the imminent possibility, he was afraid. Afraid of the painful truth that might be announced. Afraid of the finality that his desperate act had only caused to postpone. Afraid that the pain he had hoped he could relieve would be revisited with more intensity.

The phone booth shuddered as a dump truck rumbled past. Craig stood and stared at the phone, frozen with apprehension. He did not want to think of walking back into town with nothing to show for this excursion. He stood there motionless for another full minute. Then he dialed the number and deposited some coins.

Craig closed his eyes and imagined the phone hanging on the kitchen wall. He visualized Dolores rising from a seat in the family room and moving to the phone. As if it were a soundtrack to the movie in his head, he heard her voice, unmistakable in its soft clarity.

"Hello?"

Panic seized him. None of the rehearsed lines seemed right. No sentiment seemed adequate. He returned the receiver to its cradle, dropped his head against his hands and closed his eyes. The vision of Dolores appeared, walking away down a fog-shrouded street, turning briefly to throw him a shunning glance. Craig watched her disappear into the fog, her footsteps resolute, never giving him a second look. When the image finally left him, he stepped out of the phone booth, and walked back into town.

84

It was early Monday afternoon, and Sarah was preparing several meals for the week. She had completed the shopping in the morning with ease, the mild spring day in the mountains enhancing the experience.

While cutting vegetables, the knife suddenly met little resistance, and sliced into her left hand.

"Fuck!" she said aloud. Immediately she took herself to task for using such a vulgar expression. *That was not like her. Surely there were more meaningful, appropriate and more effective words she could choose.*

She looked down at the wound which grinned back at her, then defined itself with a sharp line of blood. Quickly, the cut opened, and more blood escaped, now serving to hide its source. With it came the stinging pain, which had been missing just a second before. *No, there was no better word.* "Fuck!!" she said again, this time with more conviction.

"Sarah? You all right?"

Fuck!!!! What a universally useful word! Apparently Craig had returned home, unheard. "In the kitchen!" she called. Within seconds he appeared at the doorway. "Cut myself," she explained.

Craig stepped forward, grabbing a handful of paper towels as he passed the dispenser under the cabinet. "Let me have a look."

When Sarah removed the pressure of her other hand, the blood flow began to quicken. Craig wiped the area quickly to examine it before it again became flooded. "It's pretty deep," he said. "Better get you to the hospital for some stitches. Here hold this tight, don't let up on the pressure. Where are your car keys?"

"In…my…purs…", Sarah had started to motion towards her purse on the table, when she became faint.

She regained complete consciousness almost immediately, or so it seemed. She had not moved from where she was standing, but her head was resting—quite comfortably—against Craig's shoulder. His right arm was holding her to him, his left hand now applying pressure to the wad of blood-soaked towels on the slice. She was aware of his strength, and this surprised her. Somehow he seemed stronger than she would have imagined. Yet another one of the surprises that he constantly seemed to offer her.

"Here. Sit down," he commanded. "You almost passed out."

Dropping to his knees, Craig gently extricated his arm as Sarah leaned back against the chair. It was a poor substitute for his shoulder.

"You going to be okay?"

"Yes, I think so."

"Hold this again."

Craig jumped up for more towels, and returned to re-cover the wound with fresh ones. Another jump to the sink, and he used a wet towel to clean the blood from the floor. "You going to be able to make it to the car okay?" he asked.

"Yeah. I don't know what happened, why I blacked out."

"Come on, let's go."

Sarah stood at the counter at the emergency room admissions desk, pondering the huge bandage on her hand, only half listening to what the nurse was saying.

"...The stitches will dissolve in a couple of months. This sheet describes what I just told you."

"Thank you, nurse," she heard Craig say.

"Sarah? What happened to you?" said a familiar voice. Sarah turned to see Eb Jordan taking large strides down the hospital corridor.

"Oh, Pastor Jordan!" Sarah said. "Cut myself with a kitchen knife. Lucky for me, Craig had just got home and brought me here. Took three stitches."

"I'm sorry to hear that, said the reverend. "Man, that's quite a bandage! How long will you have to wear that?"

"A couple of days, probably," she responded. "What brings you here?"

"I was just here visiting Ruth Harmon."

"Oh, right. How is she?"

"Much better. Will probably go home tomorrow. Are you okay?"

"Oh, just fine! Although I'm pretty much one handed for awhile." To the nurse, she said, "Are we done?"

"You're all set."

"Okay. Good seeing you, Pastor," Sarah said.

"Take care of yourself, Sarah. Bye, Craig."

"Again, I'm thanking you for helping me," Sarah said, as they entered the house.

"Don't mention it," Craig replied.

"If you hadn't been there and I passed out, I could have bled to death."

"A little over-dramatic, don't you think? I'm glad I was there to help."

Craig looked at his watch and grimaced. "I've got a practice in twenty minutes," he said, "but I'm not comfortable leaving you here alone."

"No, I'm okay. Go on ahead."

"Here's an idea. Come along and hang out there, and I'll take you to the diner for dinner after it's over."

"No, Craig, I'm fine. Go to your team."

"Are you sure you'll be okay?"

"Go!"

She sounded angry, but Craig knew better. He *had* heard her angry. Now, the slight upturn at the corner of her mouth, and more significantly, the tenderness in her eyes, revealed her true feelings. He wondered if anything less than his commitment to his boys could have torn him away at that moment.

85

Craig lay on his back on his bed, his eyes focused on the ceiling. It had been a busy six hours since he had held the fainting Sarah against his body. He had walked to and from the school, had swatted grounders to his infielders for a half hour with a fungo bat, pitched batting practice to the entire team, and downed a spaghetti dinner at the diner. Even so, the nerves in his shoulder registered a residual heat where her head had rested. His brain was interpreting this false report, certifying not only its accuracy but offering it as evidence to the special nature of that warmth, a warmth that was quickly replicated within his heart. In an effort to dismiss this line of thought, he tried to recall similar sensations.

He remembered the many times he would embrace Dolores from behind, feeling simultaneously the softness of her hair on his cheek even as it transmitted her body heat at the same time. Then he recalled the numbing reaction: the icy chill that pierced his heart as she turned away from his advancing lips, while her comforting body heat remained, just as she remained passively in his grasp.

How often he had complained of her tepid responses, had demanded explanations, had volunteered to shoulder blame for unknown transgressions? Her responses, increasingly predictable, were never informative: this day, a quiet shake of the head, the day before, eyes moistened by tears, the week before that, a silent retreat to the bedroom. How many times had he endured this performance? How many times had he tried different approaches? How often had he been heartened by events, perhaps an especially productive afternoon where they had both toiled in the garden, only to experience the same frustration?

Out of nowhere, the image of Joan filled his mind. She offered no answers, only more questions. What would have been the intensity of her body heat? How long would it have lingered on his shoulder? At least one thing was known. The virtue, compassion and good sense that had made her attractive to him had defined her rejection of him. For that unwavering integrity she continued to intrigue, to retain his respect, and, yes, to be the subject, if not the recipient, of his love.

Joan was right, of course. Rejection was as logical a reaction for her as it was illogical and impulsive for Dolores.

On cue, the image of Eb Jordan appeared, his lanky form leaning against the chain link fence of the ball field. Providing a voice for the obvious, a plan for the inarguable, he should have been totally superfluous. But only when Craig's words echoed off of the reverend's unflinching countenance were their hollowness revealed, their unsustainable nature made clear. He must contact Dolores, asking her one last time what it was she wanted, what it was he might do to make her happy. This time he would have to speak, to hear her response, to gain an understanding.

Craig was tired. The shift at the diner, the hospital ordeal, the practice, even lying on a bed with his thoughts—all were tiring. But he knew he could not sleep. He glanced at his watch: the library would close in thirty minutes, no refuge there. He got up and moved to the desk and began to review his note cards on the history of Walsh.

86

"Hey, Jason!"

"Jeff? I don't hear from my little brother for months at a time, and he calls me twice in one week? Anyway, Phyllis and I are looking forward to your visit, seeing as how it's so unusual for you to leave New Jersey."

"Yeah, well about that, I'm going to be delayed," Downs said.

"Delayed?"

"Yeah, a trial date got moved up, and I have to testify on Friday. I'll leave from the court house, probably blow into Cincy on Sunday afternoon."

"Still taking the scenic route?"

"Yeah, I've got some business in West Virginia. Hopefully that won't take too long. It would have worked better if I got there on Friday, like I planned, but I still hope to be done quickly and get back on the road. I'll call you if that takes a turn for the worse."

"Hope it doesn't."

"Me, too."

87

After Sarah's accident, Craig made it a point to return to Monroe Street after work rather than proceeding directly to the ball field. For the first two days, when he had asked if she needed help with anything, she had declined, thanking him for asking. On Thursday afternoon, he entered the house, his breathing labored following the climb up the hill. He found her in the kitchen, preparing to knead bread dough on a counter top dusted with flour.

"I thought I'd bake some bread for a change," she said.

"That's a bit challenging for someone who's one-handed," he teased.

"One-and-a-half," she countered, holding the bandaged hand up for inspection. "It's not totally useless."

Craig grinned. "You're amazing. Anyone else would have postponed such a chore for a week or so."

"I'm not a procrastinator. At least not any more." Sarah dropped the dough to the counter, raising a small cloud of flour. "I felt like some homemade bread, and I shall have it!" She thrust the heel of her hand repeatedly into the dough, driving it into the flour bed. Her exertion was noticeable in her speech, "And it helps me relieve my frustrations."

"But does it relieve more frustrations than it creates?" Craig joked.

Sarah rolled the dough together with her good hand and raised it to shoulder height as she turned her head to glance at Craig. She released the dough with a bit of acceleration, as if to punctuate her argument with a solid strike to the counter. The flight of the dough, however, was slightly off course, and struck the handle of a wooden spoon resting in a nearby bowl of flour. The spoon began its own flight, backspinning into the air, spewing its contents into a small white cyclone, most of which soon came to rest on Sarah's hair and face.

Stunned silence filled the kitchen. Craig saw the look of surprise on Sarah's face, her open mouth a spot of darkness on her whitened face. Attempting to hold back his laugh, he failed, emitting a loud snort as his body began to quake with derision. For an instant he saw anger in her eyes, perhaps a tinge of red glowing beneath the heavy white powder that covered most of her face. Then he saw that cherished smile conquer her face in spite of herself. Her shoulders began to shake as laughter, surging upward from below, found no outlet through her mouth, but was quickly vented through her nose. That sound only served to increase Craig's laughter, and he embraced himself in an attempt at containment.

Sarah was unable to control herself any longer, bending at the waist as laughter, humility, and even some self-respect all escaped at once. Craig felt pain in his sides. Sarah's release granted him permission to laugh freely, and when he saw two small tears describe channels in the flour landscape of her cheeks, yet a higher level of frivolity was reached. He, too, bent forward, releasing chortles, snorts and spurts, as even then he tried to contain his entertainment at her expense.

Feeling lightheaded, Craig breathed deeply as he attempted to bring his laughter under control. Sarah's face was just inches away, she beginning to gasp for air as well. As part of his mind tried to slam on the brakes, another part of him—or was it some outside force, some demonic possessor—moved him forward. When their lips were but a hair breadth apart, some gravitational force overpowered him. The kiss was soft, more a tender brushing than an emotional lock, more an inquisitive reconnoiter than a staking of a claim.

Immediately, the disciplined part of Craig's mind regained control and he retracted his head. "I'm...I'm sorry..." he stammered.

The intensity of Sarah's cerulean eyes was magnified by the field of flour in which they were now set. Craig became focused on her eyes, distracting him from his hasty apology. But this focus was short lived as Sarah grasped his head with her wrists and engulfed his lips with her own. It was all that he had imagined it could be, and more—forceful yet gentle, possessive yet not domineering, a surrender yet not unconditional.

Craig's brain continued to be divided, an increasing portion enjoying this taboo experience, the minority faction continuing to fight for control, to struggle to wrest him free of her. Sarah again grasped his head, this time with her good hand, and pulled him more tightly towards her. In reaction, Craig pulled away, holding her shoulders at arm's length. "Sarah, we shouldn't..."

She stared at him, her eyes disbelieving. Her face, behind the flour mask, displayed no emotion. Only her eyes were communicative, but they delivered a message more strongly than Craig had ever seen from her before. "I thought you wanted me," she said at last.

"I'm sorry. It was impulsive.... It wasn't right."

"Not right? It *felt* right. For so long I denied it, rejected it. You came into my life, turned it upside down. Only I found that it was right-side up, that *I* had been upside down and didn't even know it. I attacked you, and you showed me kindness. I recognized your goodness, and you showered me with more. And now, 'it isn't right?'"

"No, stop, please. You are beautiful, wonderful. You deserve better than me. I will only bring you pain." He released her, retreating a step towards the door. He could no longer bear to look into her eyes.

"Is that it then? You tempt me and then pull away when I surrender to the temptation?"

"Sarah, I'm sorry." He left her, escaping out the front door and down the porch steps, his heart pounding. Briskly he walked down Monroe Street, putting distance between himself and the disaster he had created. He was ashamed of his weakness. He was uncertain if he could ever make anything right again.

88

Arriving at the ball field, Craig found many members of the team throwing warm-up tosses. Tom was emptying the equipment from the duffel bags, and looked up to greet him. "You didn't get changed today?"

"No, things have been... hectic."

"What's that in your hair?"

Craig followed Tom's gaze with his hand, until it found the tacky bread dough plastered to his hair. "Oh," he said, "a risk you take working in a diner." Craig grinned, hoping he had covered for that hard to explain detail. "Say, Tom, would you mind running the practice today? I'm a little out of sorts."

"Sure, no problem."

"Thanks." Craig's mind had not left Sarah since he had departed her house minutes before. How could he have been so stupid? How could he have been so thoughtless? Her reaction was totally unexpected. Her open, honest acceptance had been briefly gratifying. However, quickly the shadows of the ruins of his life began to cloud not only the promise of any relationship with Sarah, but they also conjured foreboding images of a probable reunion with Dolores. His indiscretion had now jeopardized all that he had gained in Walsh, and that potential loss, combined with the actual loss of his previous life, made him feel emptier still.

He was in a near stupor, immobilized by remorse for his impulsive behavior, when Jesse cycled onto the ball field, nearly striking him. Grabbing his glove, Jesse dismounted on the move, allowing the bike to coast on its own for a dozen feet before crashing to the ground.

"Hey, Coach!" the boy said as he rushed by.

Craig smiled at the enthusiastic youngster. Jesse ran through the opening in the fence and then intercepted a toss between two of his teammates before throwing the ball back and taking his place along one of the complementary files. If Craig left Walsh, and that seemed increasingly likely, he would miss this team, these boys.

Craig remained nearly motionless, on the spectator's side of the fence, his mind racing. Tom picked up a bat and walked to home plate, giving Craig a quizzical look as he did.

"All right, fellas! Let's play out some situations! Take your positions! Max! You and Tommy alternate at third! Here we go!"

The *THONK* of the aluminum bat jarred Craig from his thoughts, and he slowly began to walk onto the field, circling behind third base.

"Okay, one out, nobody on!" Tom shouted, as he swatted a grounder towards third.

"Bend your knees, Max," Craig encouraged. "Field the ball as if you're sitting on a toilet!" Craig recalled how his own coach had used the same expression when coaching his infielders. And now he was carrying the tradition forward. And the toilet—a perfect metaphor for where his life had landed.

"Still nobody on, one out!" Tom shouted again as he lined one into center field.

"Get your hands up, Buzzie! Don't give Jesse any doubt where his target is." Throwing his own hands up in despair seemed to be what should come naturally to Craig.

"Left, left, right there!" shouted Billy, lining up his cut-off man. "Let it come!"

Buzzie stepped aside and let the ball whiz past, skipping once before landing in Billy's glove.

"Way to line him up, Billy." Craig yelled, his enthusiasm growing.

"No one out, runner on first!" yelled Tom. His bat directed a single to right field.

"Left! Left!" shouted Tommy.

"Move Billy! The throw's to third. Listen to Tommy!" Craig's direction was focused. He had forgotten his problems as the intricacies of baseball now consumed him.

"Hold up a second, guys. If your relay throw is going to be close, move your feet so you receive the ball like this. You see? Then your feet are lined up towards the base and you're ready to throw—all in one fluid motion. Tom, do that last one again."

A *THONK*, and another ball bounced into right field.

"Right there!" yelled Tommy. "Cut it!"

Billie executed the catch and throw as Craig had demonstrated, his throw reaching Tommy's glove ankle high.

"That's it, Billy! Willie—way to hit your cut-off man!" Craig smiled back at Tom, his satisfaction evident on his face. Tom returned the smile as Jimbo tossed him another ball.

"Okay, one out, first AND second. Play it to home!" *THONK,* and a line drive dropped into right field.

Now it was Jimbo's voice ringing clearly over the field. "Left, Buzzie. Right there! Cut it!"

Sarah sat at the dining room table, her checkbook and a short stack of bills before her. They served as her reason for sitting there, but paying them was the farthest thing from her mind.

Initially she had been elated by the events earlier that afternoon. Craig's kiss had aroused a passion, another in a stream of such emotional uplifts that she had experienced since he had entered her life. His consistent, easy-going manner had become the trademark of their relationship, and had lulled her into a comfort level that permitted her to admit her feelings for him and even pronounce them to him. Now, it was like a horrible secret had been told, and her trustworthiness as guardian of such secrets was in question.

Sarah turned to look at the framed photograph of Frank resting on an end table. He smiled back at her with the assurance she so adored and the confidence he had always demonstrated towards her decisions. What would he think of this decision?

Sarah dropped her face into her hands and exhaled heavily, her warm breath reflected back from where it came. Withdrawing her head, she again looked at the portrait. For the first time she saw details in the eight-by-ten, especially the tiny creases around Frank's eyes. At the same time she recognized some truths emerging. Frank was gone, never to be replaced. She would always love him and cherish the time they shared. Simultaneously, she was alive, and now felt alive forcefully. That force could be enhanced—no, enriched—if it had a focus. She longed for a partner, not to replace Frank, or as a substitute for him, but as a complement serving an original role in the unique new chapters of her life to come.

She closed her eyes again and remembered Craig walking through Frank's woodshop. He had done so reverently, not as a trespasser or transgressor, but as an honored and respectful guest. It was that display of respect that had first altered her view of him.

She closed her eyes once more, and this time saw Craig struggling with the overloaded wheelbarrow, trundling shrubs and topsoil to where it was needed. He had done so to improve her garden, a garden for which he had no claim. That lack of a personal stake had served to magnify the selflessness of his offer to help, just as the beads of sweat that formed on his brow seemed like jewels in his crown.

Sarah looked again at the photograph of Frank. He was still smiling. He understood.

A buzzer from the kitchen startled Sarah and she smelled the baking bread to which she had been oblivious before. After removing the bread from the oven, she returned to her bills. As she sat down, Craig entered through the front door. Sarah felt her heart skip and her mind race as she considered what to say. She pursed her lips to speak, to say anything to delay while she framed the perfect sentiment, the convincing appeal. But she was too late, for Craig spoke first.

"I'll be moving out as soon as I can find other accommodations," he said, "hopefully in a day or two. Naturally, the rent for the remainder of the month is yours. Again, I'm sorry. So sorry." With that, he dropped his chin, turned and climbed the stairs.

Stunned by yet another reversal of course, Sarah remained speechless as she watched him reach the top of the staircase and disappear into his room. She dropped her forehead into the palm of her hand, closed her eyes, and sighed.

89

"Guys," Beth Rosen said, stepping forward from the edge of the stage, "I know this is only the first reading, but I expected a little more passion. Did you hear the emotion in Mother's voice? Dolores, read that last line again."

Dolores re-read the line, much as she had before.

"Hear that?" Rosen repeated. "She knows she's about to lose Charlie to manhood; that she's never going to have her same little boy again. Tony! She also knows that she's married to a strong-willed, weak-minded man. She loves him, but she knows what trouble that combination is going to bring her in the coming years. You, and you, too, Frank, need to convince us! Frank, you have to show that you've outgrown her mothering. Tony, you have to be more passionately stubborn! Without your parts, Mother's passion will be over played."

90

After stopping for coffee in Lexington, Jeff Downs drove north on the Lee Highway to the I-64 interchange and headed west up into the mountains of western Virginia. It was after two o'clock in the morning, and he was tired. He had left the courthouse in Somerville about the time he had planned, but everything since then had fallen apart. Stopping back at his office and returning a few phone calls had cost him an hour. Hopping into his Civic, he had turned the key, and—nothing! The car had refused to crank, though the battery seemed to be strong. A tow to his mechanic and a great deal of pleading on his part had resulted in the new starter being installed, with Jeff paying for the Friday evening overtime. It was after eight before he got on the road.

Jeff had had no choice but to nap in the rest area off I-81 just over the Maryland state line, he had been so exhausted. He got his second wind after sleeping, but that had not lasted for long. Maybe the coffee would sustain him for the next two hours until he reached Walsh.

It was a cloudless night and the moon was bright. The trees that covered the hills were awash in the blue light. Their fresh leaves gave them a smooth, rounded shape, as if they had been deposited by a huge ice cream scoop, which made for a scalloped effect. The Honda's four cylinder engine was giving its all, attacking the grade up the Blue Ridge at a very stately forty-five miles per hour.

Occasionally, an open field or a farmstead would appear along the road, the moonlight revealing many details, but casting just enough shadow to obscure some secrets and make it clear that this theatrical lighting was no substitute for full sunlight.

When at last he crested the hill, his tachometer dropped as the car plunged downhill. Soon, though, the car was upward bound again, attacking the next ridge.

Near Lewisburg, Jeff left the interstate, striking off towards Ronceverte. The tree-lined secondary highway offered few of the vistas available from the four lane road, but artificial light supplementing the moonbeams and the sealed beam headlights switched on high, painted quick vignettes of the countryside and the small towns through which he passed.

It was nearly four when he passed the roadside sign welcoming him to Walsh, WV, Population 1,386. Driving under the conveyor belt on the east end of town, Jeff coasted down Main Street, where there was no visible activity of any kind. Near the stop light which glared green, unchallenged by any traffic from the side streets, Jeff spotted a whitewashed building. The name "Carol's Diner" was printed in large blue letters over the front window. Stepping out of his car, Jeff walked up to the dark building to read the hours posted on the door which indicated that the diner would be open at six.

Jeff followed a side street towards the river, and found a small gravel lot, probably used by fishermen. Parking the car, he reclined his seat, pulled the bill of his Reds ball cap down over his eyes, and quickly fell asleep.

Across the river and up the hill, Craig was startled awake by his wristwatch alarm. He groaned as his head fell back on the pillow. It had not been a restful night. He was sure that he loved her. He was just as sure that he could not act on that love. While there might be enough room in his heart for three women, it was a certainty that there was not enough room in his life for more than one.

His decision to move out had been made hastily while walking to the ball field, and he had announced it to Sarah before he searched the newspaper he had picked up on the way home. Later, in his room, he had scoured the paper for advertisements of available lodging, but had found few listed. These were either inconveniently located or considerably more expensive than what he was presently spending. The interim alternative, checking into the Cherokee Motel west of town, would also be a long walk from the diner and the ball field, and also prove prohibitively costly.

Nevertheless, he could not remain on Monroe Street. The feelings he had for Sarah were a complication in his life, a complication he could not afford. Her response, as evocative as it was unexpected, could only provoke him to act in a way he was sure to regret. What was to come in his relationship with Dolores remained an open question, one he had been unable to ask. Surely he must resolve that matter before anything else. Today he would call her, would talk to her, would seek closure.

Thinking of Dolores, he was squeezed by two feelings. His love for her, the years that they had shared—this he longed to renew, to reignite, and hopefully, one day to bask in the comfortable heat they had known. In opposition was the heartbreak and sorrow that her repeated rejections had brought him, his certainty that he could not bear another occurrence, could not stand the bitter cold of banishment. Today he must know which it would be. He would force himself to face the possibility of one more icy blast, or, perhaps, the promise of a reinvention of a more positive, more lasting relationship. Today he must know.

Within the tight confines of the shower stall, Guilt paid Craig another visit. As on the train, the spirit immediately began a silent cross-examination, so incisive and pointed as to stun Craig where he stood beneath the shower's spray.

"Is there no limit to your selfishness? Yet another woman becomes the victim of your desires?" Guilt asked.

"Guilt, your assumptions are wrong, again. My goal is for harmony, wherever and with whomever it can be nurtured."

"Harmony? By preying on a widow still in mourning?"

"I have preyed on no one. I have offered kindness and compassion, aid and understanding."

"Yet she fell for you, was entranced by you, like a snake to the tune of a *pungi*."

"That I regret, because it was premature. I am in no position to make new commitments, when prior commitments remain unresolved."

"Ah, yes, uphill from here, along your path of devastation!"

"They will be resolved. And soon—beginning today. And it could be that I may find contentment, here, with Sarah, someday. I am not sure of anything. Now get lost, spirit! I have a job to get to."

Jeff awoke to the sound of doors slamming. Two men had arrived in a pickup truck, and were dragging a canoe out of the truck's bed. Soon the boat was afloat, and they and their tackle were aboard, gliding out into the steady current of the Greenbrier.

Jeff got out of the car and stretched. His watch said six thirty, and the sun had risen above the mountains, throwing into sharp focus all the details of Walsh. Countless birds were making a racket he would have thought impossible to sleep through, but somehow he had.

The detective struck off towards the diner on foot, his injured leg more rebellious than usual at that hour of the morning after a nap in the car. Jeff let out an audible sigh, as he began his foot patrol, the bane of a cop's existence, but so useful for getting a detailed understanding of his surroundings and what he might encounter.

91

Dolores awoke more excited than she had been in weeks. She was looking forward to going to her job at the garden center. She was comfortable there, the owner liked her, and she was working well with the other employees. She was developing her own following with customers who sought her out for advice. The success or difficulties she had had planting various species was information they appreciated.

Play rehearsals were going well, too. Beth seemed to appreciate her talent. At the same time, Dolores was learning from her. Beth's suggestions helped Dolores explore her role more fully. Even more than usual, Dolores was getting into the skin of Mother, and feeling emotional ties with the character. Particularly, Mother's relationship with Da was mind opening, even inspiring. Would she be able to model her own character on the part she played when the curtain rose on the next important chapter of her life—her life with Craig?

If that curtain was going to rise. Today, most likely, she would hear from Jeff. The results of that communication would finally define what her relationship with her husband might be. Anticipation, fear, hope, regret, loss--all of these emotions were swirling within her—and materialized as excitement for the new day, whatever it was to bring.

92

Jeff walked two blocks east of the diner on the railroad side of the road, then crossed Main Street and headed west along the sidewalk, taking time to view the windows of the businesses along the way. If the buildings, in their general state of disrepair, were not depressing enough, the window displays would suffice. The apparel hanging on the headless manikins in Kaufman's was neither stylish nor appealing. Jeff had the impression that this display was anything but recent, and even when it had been created, the message was "necessity" not "style."

The banks were at war. Cardboard signs in each window proclaimed the interest rates offered for home mortgages or personal loans, with a cocky assuredness that the one-quarter of a percent difference was not only enough to lure an applicant across the street, but to close the deal as well.

The diner was an island of clean white in a sea of dusty bricks and weathered clapboard. Jeff passed by without pausing, noting that every parking spot in front of the establishment was occupied.

Continuing on, he passed the grocery store, where produce was being placed on sidewalk stands in anticipation of the store's opening. The food looked nutritious enough, but the gritty setting did little to make it appetizing. Jeff walked around behind the store, past the rankly sweet dumpster and the stacked milk crates, and moved down the alley common to the market and the diner. The screened rear door of the diner was emitting the smells of frying breakfasts mingled with the clatter of cooking and the whir of the exhaust fan. Jeff circled back around to the front and entered.

The peacefulness of the morning outside bore no resemblance to the activity within. Every stool at the counter, every booth, every table was occupied. The clientele was talkative and animated, with some conversations spreading over several tables. Jeff was tuned to what was being said, but quickly realized that it was mostly banter between old acquaintances that suggested an artificial, non-serious competition in the realms of intelligence, cunning, and via innuendo, sexual prowess.

Hovering around them was a waitress, coffee pot in hand, who seemed even more animated and engaged than the customers. She looked up and smiled at Jeff, then quickly scanned the interior before turning back to him. "Just a second," she said. Directing her attention to a teenage girl sitting in the most distant booth, she called out, "Melinda! Grab your books and move to the kitchen. I need that booth."

The youth looked up from the book she was reading, assumed a look of resignation, and began to gather her things.

"No need to move her," Jeff said. "I don't mind sharing the booth, if she doesn't mind."

"It's no bother," the waitress said. "My daughter can find another place."

"No, really. I would enjoy the company. Been driving all night, tired of talking to myself. Ask her? Please?"

The waitress gave Jeff a curious look, then addressed the girl. "Melinda, this gentleman is willing to share the booth with you, if that's okay with you."

The girl had gathered all of her belongings by this time. She again gave her mother a resigned look and responded, "Sure. Whatever."

The waitress looked back at Jeff, cocked her head slightly, and said, "Right this way." He followed her to the booth. "This is my daughter, Melinda. She can be very pleasant—when she wants to be. If you change your mind, just say the word, and I'll clear her out of here."

"I doubt that will be necessary."

"Coffee?"

"Yes, please."

"I'll be back in a sec."

Jeff took a seat as Melinda and her mother exchanged looks—an unspoken admonition, perhaps linked to a subtle threat, answered by submissive compliance. "Melinda, my name is Jeff. I'm pleased to meet you."

"Nice to meet you, too."

"You're sure I won't be bothering you? Don't want to interrupt your reading."

"It's okay. I don't have much to read, and all day to get it done."

"You're spending your Saturday here?"

"Almost every Saturday. The family business. Mom brings

me in to help, but then usually doesn't let me do much. Tells me studying is more important. Dad works nights at the mine, so he needs quiet at home so he can sleep."

"So, your mom is Carol?"

Melinda gave him a strange look.

"From the sign," he said, motioning to the exterior.

"Oh, right. Yeah, that's my mom."

Carol returned with a coffee cup and menu. "You still okay? It's no problem to move her."

"We're getting on famously," Jeff said, giving Melinda a smile.

"Be back for your order in a minute," she said, giving her daughter a repeat of the previous look.

"Business looks good," he said, looking around the dining area.

"Yeah, I guess."

"That's a credit to your mom. She must be a good business woman."

"I guess so."

"She seems like a good mom, too. Just based on what I've seen in the few minutes I've been here."

"Uh huh. Where you from?"

"I'm from New Jersey. Heading to Cincinnati to see my brother."

"New Jersey? Our cook is from New Jersey. Mr. Miller."

"Really?" Jeff looked at Melinda with new concern. Ethics had always presented him with many gray areas, especially in the sewer of matrimonial discord. He felt he was now on the cusp of an ethical issue. But he hadn't created this mess, he was just trying to clean it up. The quicker he could do this, the better. If she could help him, so much the better. And how could it do her harm? "This town sure is different from New Jersey."

"That's what Mr. Miller says. He says he likes it here because it's not a 'rat race.'"

"I bet it isn't."

"'Rat race'. I imagine lots and lots of rats running around everywhere."

"That would be Jersey City."

"What?"

"Never mind."

"What do you do in New Jersey?"

"I, uh, help people find things."

"What kind of things?"

"All kinds of things. People, misplaced things, proof that something happened. Mistakes mostly."

"And you get paid to find these things?"

"Yep."

Carol reappeared. "What can I getcha?"

Jeff turned towards the waitress, but his eye was attracted to a man behind the counter. He wore the white outfit of a cook and there was no question that he was the man in the photo Dolores had given him. "Uh, two eggs, scrambled, white toast."

"Bacon or sausage?"

"Sure, I'll have some sausage, too. Melinda, would you like something?"

"No, thank you."

"Coming right up," Carol said cheerfully, as she spun around to leave them.

Jeff continued to watch Miller until he returned to the kitchen.

"That's Mr. Miller," Melinda said. "Do you know him?"

"Huh? No. New Jersey's a small state, but it's got a lot of people. Sometimes you can live next door to someone for ten years and never meet them."

"Wow! That could never happen here."

"No, I suppose not. Mr. Miller, for example, how long has he been here?"

"Oh, a few months, I guess."

"And you know he's from New Jersey. Of the three families that live in my building, I think I only know where one of them is from. And they've lived in my apartment building for a few years. This Mr. Miller, did he tell you much about himself? You think he's an okay guy?"

"Uh huh. He's nice. He's helped me with my homework a few times."

"What else do you know about him except that he dislikes New Jersey rat races?"

"Not too much. He's kind of quiet." Melinda moved her head closer and her voice became more hushed, "I think he's really sad about something, but he won't talk about it. Sometimes I see him staring as if he's seeing something, but it's nothing close by."

"Lots of people have problems," Jeff offered. "Many times they gotta work them out themselves."

"Hmmm."

Jeff sensed that Melinda was drifting away from the topic. She had begun to page through one of the books on the table. He'd try to make one more inquiry, without being too obvious. "Is Mr. Miller the only cook here at the diner?"

"He works in the mornings. My dad comes in around ten and covers lunch and dinner," Melinda volunteered.

"I see," Jeff said.

Saturday mornings were always busy, but this one had been busier than most. Craig could tell that Carol's demeanor was feeding off the activity, and her enthusiasm was always contagious. Their quick exchanges at the window between the kitchen and the dining room had been upbeat and spirited. The chatter, combined with the additional cooking, had caused the time to pass quickly, and Craig was surprised to look up and see Marc putting on an apron.

"Wow, is it ten o'clock, already?" Craig asked, glancing at his watch.

"Yep. Carol said you guys were really busy today."

"I'll say. I broke into our last dozen eggs!"

"Yeah, Carol called me earlier. I stopped by Hofsteader's on the way in and picked up a case. You got a game today?"

"Sure do. We're playing at Ronceverte. I gotta get over to the field to catch the 'team bus'"

"Good Luck. Both at the game and surviving the ride in Tom's truck!"

Craig stepped into the bright sunlight and allowed his eyes to adjust to the glare off the windshields of the cars parked along the street. He was about to step off the curb when he heard a voice.

"Craig Miller?"

Craig turned to see a man approaching, walking with a slight limp. Maybe a few years older than himself, the man had square shoulders and a muscular build, which a little extra weight around the mid-section and the limp did not invalidate. He was upon him in an instant. It would have been impossible to flee, even if Craig had had that reflexive reaction. His response was a weak, "Yes?"

The stranger extended his arm which held credentials visible through a plastic window in a small leather case. He held the documents available for Craig's inspection as he introduced himself. "My name is Jeff Downs. I'm a private investigator, hired by your wife to find you."

Craig felt a rush of heat fill his body and rush to his face. He had imagined the possibility of such an encounter, but now that it had occurred, he felt resigned, overcome with a strange sense of relief. As his shoulders visibly dropped, he tried to regain his composure, eventually asking, "How is Dolores?"

"She is well, not that I believe you care."

This guy was wasting no time in pissing him off. "What?!?"

Downs put up his hands defensively. "Sorry. You're right. That wasn't a very professional remark."

"I guess not."

"It's just that, the way you left, sneaking out of town…I'm surprised you give a hang about Dolores."

"Believe what you want. I'm glad she's fine."

Downs returned the case to his pocket and the two men stared at each other in silence, sizing each other up. Craig felt intimidated, not only by the man's size and build, but by whatever authority his license carried, and the fact that he was competent enough in his craft to have tracked him down. He didn't care for his attitude. After the beatings he had given himself in recent days, the p.i.'s snide remarks were just piling on. Craig reacted to the intimidation with an aggressive offense, like a water snake striking at an enemy many times its size.

"So you've found me," Craig said, "What do you want from me?"

"You might start with an explanation," Downs said, his eyes narrowing slightly.

"Dolores is confused as to why I left?" Craig questioned sarcastically. "Maybe she should review our last twenty-five arguments for some clues. You can help her. Private detectives are supposed to be good with clues, right?"

Downs said nothing, just continued to study Craig. Craig felt like that snake, coiling its body in anticipation, neither gaining nor giving ground. After a time, Downs moved his hands to his hip pockets, a relaxation of his aggressive stance, opening himself to a sucker punch.

"Can we go somewhere to discuss this? Someplace more private?"

"Actually, I'm on my way to an appointment." Craig laced his next words with as much venom as he could summon, "Why don't you just give me the bottom line. What does she want? Money? She can have it all. What I've abandoned was worth more than all I ever earned or saved. Send me the papers. I'll sign anything she wants."

These final words were spoken especially viciously, and a woman passing by on the sidewalk gave Craig a strange look, which he found to be disconcerting.

When Downs spoke, his words were even tempered. "Mrs. Miller has some regrets regarding her conduct in recent months. If it matters any, she's sorry."

Craig was taken aback by this revelation. Unanticipated, it threw him off guard once again. He understood that his selected stance was too aggressive, and tried to adjust his tone. "So what does she want from me?" he asked.

"She wants you to come home. She wants to try again. To try harder." His gaze was intense, and Craig again felt intimidated, even more so after the detective's next comment, "I think Mrs. Miller is an attractive, kind woman. Frankly, I don't know what she sees in you. You appear to me to be a real loser. But I'm just a messenger, and that's the message."

Craig felt his fists clench, his teeth grate. Anger was activating every nerve, coursing through his body with a pent up pressure he hadn't experienced in some time. Just as suddenly, his anger was gone, dissipated through an audible exhalation. His focus moved from the messenger to Dolores. He was surprised, and pleased, that she was interested in saving the relationship.

"Again," Craig said, "I don't care what you think. But I appreciate you giving me Dolores's message. I'll call her tonight. Maybe we can straighten this all out."

"I'm afraid I am going to need more than a simple assurance," Downs said. His arms were now crossed across his chest, an obvious demonstration of his power and authority. "I'm going to need to know how to reach you."

"I understand, " Craig said. "I'm living at 43 Monroe Street—at least for the time being. Give me your card and I promise to let you know if I change my address."

"How can I be sure that address is good?" Downs asked. "Nothing personal, but you did choose to disappear before."

Craig considered this for a second, and then said, "Follow me."

Stepping back into the diner, Craig called out to the waitress, clearing a nearby tale. "Carol, could you tell this gentleman where I live?"

The woman looked in turn at the two men, then, with a puzzled look on her face, said, "You rent a room from Mrs. Stiles up on Monroe Street."

"Thanks, Carol." To Downs, "That work?"

"Fine," Downs said.

Back outside, Craig continued, "You know, I dialed Dolores a few nights ago, but got scared when she answered, scared of what she might say. So I hung up without a word. I can't tell you how happy I am to hear what you told me today. I will absolutely make that call. You have my word. Now, if you don't mind, I really have to go."

From the same phone booth Craig had used a few nights before, Jeff filled the payphone with coins from his pocket. Dolores answered the phone on the third ring, her voice bringing an involuntary smile to Jeff's face. "I made contact with your husband," he told her.

"How is he? What was his reaction?"

"He seems healthy enough. I got the sense that he was surprised that you wanted him back. His first comments were about signing a divorce agreement—with no objections to anything you asked for."

"But now?"

"He says he will call you tonight. Gave me his word, for what that's worth."

"Thank you, Mr. Downs. I appreciate what you've done to find him."

"You're welcome. Your husband also said that he called the other night, but got gun-shy, and hung up without saying anything."

"Yes. I did get a call, and whoever it was hung up when I

answered."

"So maybe he is telling the truth."

When Dolores made no comment, Jeff chose to move on from his awkward comment. "So, I'm heading on to Cincinnati. You still have my brother's phone number I gave you?"

"Yes."

"Good, because this portable phone I have isn't worth much here in the boonies. I'll check in with you tomorrow, if that's okay."

93

The ride to Ronceverte was a background for the thoughts racing through Craig's mind. Craig hardly was aware of the old pickup's struggles to make it up the mountains as it journeyed east. He felt no discomfort as part of the sandwich consisting of the meaty Tommy sitting between his dad at the wheel and his coach against the passenger door. Rarely did he glance down through the holes in the rusted out floor to watch the pavement whiz by below them.

Instead his eyes were focused out the windshield, at the ever-present mountains on the horizon. Beyond those hills, back up I-81 and I-78, could his life in New Jersey be revitalized? Was Dolores up to the task of changing, of accepting him again? Just as importantly, was he prepared to accept her love, if that's what she offered? Could he overlook her faults? Could she overlook his, beginning with his willingness to abandon all? Did the simple word "sorry" have enough power to overcome all the pain they had inflicted on each other?

The chatter in the cab was mostly about baseball, and thankfully, mostly between father and son. Craig considered it his good fortune that when the conversation did veer his way, he was able to deflect it with a casual affirmative grunt or a nearly mumbled "don't know."

Once on the field, however, and in the presence of the members of his team who had piled out of parents' autos charged with energy, Craig returned to the immediate mission, to make a respectable showing at their first road game. Batting orders, game ball contributions, ground rules, confirming that his players felt good after warming up—all of these things and more occupied his time and his mind.

Gathering his team together on the bench prior to the first pitch, Craig saw the anticipation on their faces, awaiting his words of encouragement, support or inspiration. Unlike adults, for whom doublespeak, innuendo, false promises and platitudes were interchanged freely and shamelessly, these innocent faces expected more. Shallow propaganda would be unacceptable to these kids who traded in genuine feelings. He hoped his conversation later that evening would be as genuine and as accepted as what he was about to say now.

"Boys," he started, a new confidence swelling within him, "you have practiced hard, you have paid attention to Coach Potter's and my instruction. You know what to do and how to do it. Your bodies are in good shape so you *can* do it. Seeing you perform in other games, I *know* you can do it. The only question now is whether you *will* do it. That depends on each of you. It's nothing Mr. Potter or I can do for you. *You* have to want this win, and to play like you want it. You have to be thinking all the time—before the ball is pitched, after it's hit, after you field it. You have to remember the fundamentals, things we have practiced so much that I hope they come to you without thinking. Eye on the ball, glove on the ground, feet in position, weight back, bat high. By themselves they're just words. Combined with a will to win, they are the secret to success."

Craig smiled at his team that sat silently in front of him. Would they recognize his air of confidence for the sham that it was? He was confident of nothing in his own life. Career and marriage--a musty mural from the past. Friendships and relationships--teetering uncertainly or lying about in ruins. Even the hopelessness of his love for Dolores was in question, based upon the news that the private detective had brought him this morning. Only this team, this unlikely bunch of strangers, served as a focus for his life. He was as confused about what bound them to him as he was about what attracted him to them in the first place. Nothing had developed beyond their relationship on the baseball diamond. He knew them only as ballplayers. But that had been enough. Some chemistry had cemented their relationship, had made them such a significant part of his life that abandonment was outside the realm of possibility. He, who had abandoned so much and so many, would have to see this season through.

When Jesse stood up, Craig looked at him in baffled amusement, but was willing to yield him the floor. If he had asked. With hardly any recognition of his coach's existence, the boy spat on the ground then turned towards his teammates.

"Guys, we can do this!" Jesse said. "We nearly beat Alderson, and they creamed this team earlier this season. Look at 'em over there. A bunch of city sissies! Why, even Willie's got more muscles than their biggest kid! At least Willie knows what it's like to really work on his parents' farm. I'm surprised some of them can even open their refrigerator door! If we can't hit better, pitch better, run better and field better than that bunch of wimps, then I'll be ashamed to go home with you guys and admit that I play on the same team!"

The sandy haired boy sat back down, spitting once again. Murmurs of agreement rose from the bleachers, and Justin squeezed Willie's biceps, mockingly inspecting the muscles featured in Jesse's speech.

Craig felt this was a good way to close the meeting. "Okay, Billie, Buzzy, and Jesse, lets get things started. Everybody hits! And guys, check for signs—every pitch."

94

Spirits were high on the ride back from Ronceverte. Tommy, basking in the joy of his first win, repeated accounts of the game as if the other two truck passengers had not been there to see it. Critical at bats were described, with Jimbo's pitch choices or Tommy's occasional override given high marks for cleverness, wisdom and timing. Outstanding defensive plays were lauded for their game-saving importance, while Walsh's hitters were acknowledged for racking up the runs that led to the 5-3 win.

Tom's pride in his son and the team led him to add to the descriptions, underlining the events' importance, crediting the players' good judgment or athletic prowess. A few times he would point out how Craig's coaching had led to a particular player being in the right position to make the critical play or how time spent alone with Jimbo had been devoted to developing strategies of calling an effective game.

Craig would defer Tom's accolades, granting the team members credit for skills regardless of where they were positioned, and offering assurances that Jimbo had a good head on his shoulders. "I didn't really have that much to teach him," he confessed. "He instinctively knows what pitch sets up another, and what a batter is least likely to suspect. And he knows just which hitters are prone to 'climb the ladder', and raises his mitt higher and higher to oblige them!"

The post-game celebration dulled Craig's focus on the morning's meeting with Downs, but did not obliterate it. Dolores's request for him to return was as unexpected as the detective's arrival. If she wanted harmonious coexistence, she certainly had failed to demonstrate it in the past few months. However, he could not deny that he would welcome such a relationship, and bring an end to his refugee status. The small room on Monroe Street would be easy to leave. He was already in the process of finding a replacement. Likewise he would miss the job at the diner, along with Carol, Marc and their genuine friendship.

He knew further that the bond that had formed between Sarah and him was more permanent than many people, including Sarah, could imagine. That a simple physical separation—across the width of Walsh or the leagues to New Jersey—would prove ineffective in banishing her from his mind or excising her from his heart. That whether a self-imposed exile for her benefit or the honoring of a superior obligation to Dolores, neither could serve to negate Sarah's importance to him. Dolores possessed this aura. So did Joan. Their three names were written with indelible ink upon his soul.

As the pickup truck neared Walsh, Craig's thoughts again began to focus on the phone call he had to make later that evening. The uncertainty surrounding his wife's purported state of mind, what she might say, how he would react, went right to his gut, where his stomach attempted unusual contortions, challenged as it already was by the task of digesting two hot dogs consumed earlier at the ball field.

95

The quarters and dimes echoed loudly as they rattled into the pay phone, bringing to mind a pin-ball machine as they clinked, chimed and clanked into the machine. Craig drew a deep breath as he heard the phone ringing on the other end. *She wants you to come home. She wants to try again. To try harder.* So the detective had said. Again he tried to put himself in Dolores's place, to try to imagine how she felt, how she might think. After all his attempts at reconciliation, now she was willing to be responsive, to be proactive? He didn't understand. Once again, or still, he didn't understand.

Three rings. Four rings. Was she not home? Five rings.
"Hello?"
Craig's heart jumped to his throat. That voice, that precise diction, the undercurrent of grace and loveliness—all that he had long loved and admired—came through the wire so clearly. What words would that voice speak, and how would they influence the rest of his life?

"Hi, Dolores," he stammered.
"How are you, Craig?" she asked, in a very matter-of-fact tone.
"I'm okay," he replied, then hesitatingly, fearing the recriminations that might be unleashed, he added, "And you?"
"I'm okay, too. I've missed you."
Neutral enough. Almost inviting. If only they could maintain this tone. "I've missed you, too. I'm sure it's been hard for you. I'm sorry to have…to have left you like that."
"I guess you believed you had to."
Apologetic? Submissive? "I may have overreacted."
"Oh, you think so? You leave without so much as a 'good-bye', leave me worried sick, without any idea of what was going on?"
The sarcasm was familiar. It was like old times. "How many months did you leave me in the dark? Refusing to explain your thinking, your feelings or why you hurt me again and again? I just couldn't take it any more!" Craig stopped short. This was not the way he had wanted the call to go. Why did he always react so forcefully to her taunts?

A short silence followed. When Dolores spoke again, her

voice was again soft and controlled. "Look, I don't want this call to be about blame or name calling. I am willing to try to understand. I would hope to get the same from you."

"I appreciate that. I've always tried to be understanding. I'm sorry if I didn't try hard enough. To be honest, I was surprised when the private detective said you wanted me back."

"Surprised? We've been together for so long. What else do we know? What else is there?"

"This separation..." Craig searched for the perfect words, and then settled for much less, "being away from you—but I was never away from you. You were always there with me. It's like you said: 'what else *do* we know?'"

"But you were willing to let it all go? Or at least try to?" she asked.

"At the time, that was a risk I was willing to take. I'm not saying I was faultless. But I just couldn't seem to change course. To stop the bickering, the anger,...the loneliness."

"I realized that when you left. That you felt much more helpless than I realized. That I had been less understanding than I should have been."

"Dolores, I left you. I take the blame. I'm sorry. Once I left I realized it was a mistake. That I missed you. But I couldn't turn around. Partly because of pride. Mostly because of fear—fear that you'd reject me, again."

"So come home now, Craig. Let's work on this together. I've changed. At least I think I have. I've thought about the last few years. What I should have said. What I should have done."

"I want to believe you, Dolores."

"No, I have! I've thought about what happened. I was stupid. I pushed you away and then was surprised when you were gone. Please. Give me a second chance."

"I should be the one apologizing. I abandoned you, our life, my job. If you feel this way, obviously I should have tried harder, made more attempts."

"We messed this up together. Let's fix it together. Come home, Craig."

Craig made no answer, the silence echoing within the small glass booth at a deafening pitch. At last, he spoke again, "Okay. I'll come home. But..."

"But what? What's the matter?"

"I've made some commitments here. I'm going to need a few weeks to see them to completion. I hope you can understand, but I need a little time."

"What kind of commitments?"

"You probably wouldn't understand. As I'm thinking this, I know it sounds crazy. But if you know me, you know I can't go back on what I said I was going to do."

"Is there…someone else?" she said, with hesitation.

"No, it's not like that. Actually there's a whole bunch of somebody else's, and I've made a commitment to them individually and as a group. Please, just be patient. I'll call you every night until I come home. I promise."

Craig waited for her response, and again heard nothing for a few moments.

"I don't understand,… but…but I'll wait—for a while. How long are you talking?"

"I'll check and give you an exact date tomorrow. This obviously means a lot to me or I wouldn't ask. Once again, I owe you so much."

"Just come home. That's all I ask. Oh, and when you call, can you make it earlier? Between four and six? I'm rehearsing for a play, and usually won't be home at this time."

"A play? You're back in the theater?

"Yes, I tried out for a part at Black River, and I got it."

"That's great! I never wanted you to quit the theater. You seemed to enjoy it so much."

"I didn't realize I missed it so much until I got back into it. …Sort of like the way I found I missed you. … I'm really enjoying being on stage again."

"I still love you, Dolores. Do you think we can make this work?"

"I hope so. I really want to start over. Start fresh. To love you again like I did years ago."

"That sounds good, babe. Too good to be true."

96

It had been a long walk. And he still had to walk back into town and up the hill to Monroe Street. But he believed it would be worth the trouble.

The porch light was on next to the front door of the two story frame house adjacent to the church. Craig deliberately climbed the steps to the porch and rang the bell. Soon a girl in her early teens opened the door.

"I was wondering if Pastor Jordan might have a minute for me?" Craig asked.

"He's next door at the church," the girl said, nodding her head casually in the general direction.

"Thank you," Craig said, "sorry to bother you."

He picked his way across the lawns. Darkness had fallen, but the fluorescent bulbs in the sign in front of the church offered some illumination. Above the Sunday School and Worship Service hours, the sign read "Exercise Daily. Walk with God. Run from Sin."

Entering the church, he found only a few lights on in the sanctuary, a spotlight on the large cross on the rear wall being the brightest of them. Too timidly at first, he voiced a "Hello?" which went unanswered. After calling again, louder this time, a nondescript door in the rear of the sanctuary opened, and the tall, gaunt form of Eb Jordan emerged.

"Craig!" he called, "Please, come in!"

The two men met near the center of the church and shook hands, after which Eb motioned him to follow him towards the rear of the sanctuary. "How have you been?" the reverend asked.

"I'm good."

"And the team?"

"Even better. They won their first game today against Ronceverte."

"That *is* good."

Eb led the visitor back through the door that led to his small office. Offering him a chair, he asked cheerfully, "What can I do for you?"

"I just wanted to let you know the news...I called my wife tonight. We're going to get back together."

"I'm pleased to hear that. You are happy with that prospect?"

"Yes, yes I am. A little surprised, I'll admit. I never expected Dolores to be so forgiving. That has not been her nature recently. But that's a turn for the better. Maybe it's what we needed."

"Forgiveness is an essential element of living a good life. We should be willing to forgive more often: 'Not seven times, but, I tell you, seventy-seven times,' as Jesus said. I hear the positive tone in your voice. Maintain that positive attitude, and all will work out for the better."

"I hope so. I'm really looking forward to us getting a second chance."

"Of course, your gain will be Walsh's loss. I venture to say that you will be missed here. The boys on the ball team, I'm certain, will be sorry to see you go. Maybe you'll be able to recruit a new coach before you leave."

"I would like to—for next season. But I'll see this season through to conclusion."

"You intend to delay your departure—to reunite with your wife—in order to complete a baseball schedule?"

"To honor a commitment to a dozen boys. I saw how disappointed they were the last time their season was cut short. I couldn't do that to them. I couldn't break my promise."

"Hmm, that sounds like an honorable gesture. Still, I can't help but think that your first obligation is to your wife, to your marriage. You wouldn't want to squander this opportunity for the sake of a few boys you hardly know."

"Ah, but I do know them! I know Tommy Potter has a heart as big as his body; that once he sets his sights on something he is unstoppable. I know that Jimbo Blanchard is a quiet leader, assuming no credit but earning the respect of everyone who works with him. I know that Jesse Nielsen can be cynical, but that only disguises an open mind, and that he is steadfast once he is committed to something. I know that Willie Moran took constant teasing in exchange for acceptance in the group, and as a result, the others have become more sympathetic to him, and the teasing has become less common, and certainly less vicious. Oh, I know these boys—individually and as a cohesive unit. I will never forget them. And it would be impossible to betray them."

"And Dolores understands this?"

"I hope she will. At any rate, it's not for that long a period. If our relationship can survive my departure for so long a time, it should be able to stand another couple of weeks."

"And if it doesn't?"

"Then it really wasn't so strong after all. In which case, returning could be as big a mistake as I now believe leaving was."

"So you see this as a test of Dolores's commitment?"

"I see it as being true to myself. I made a commitment to this team. While few understood why—honestly, I didn't understand it myself at first—and some jumped to totally wrong conclusions, I always understood what I needed to do and what I must finish. My commitment to Dolores has a long history, and is open-ended. Only when I was certain there was no reciprocal commitment, that my presence was doing more harm than good, did I decide to leave. Now she is challenging my perceptions. If she is right, then we'll move to a better relationship. I've always admired her integrity. If she says we should get back together, I have no doubt that she is right. To whatever extent we can return to the way things were, I would be thankful."

The climb to Monroe Street was especially tiring that evening. The air was heavy with humidity and no breeze stirred the leaves of the trees that lined Willow Street. As he had done on his first night in town, Craig stopped by the large oak tree half-way up the hill, resting against the solid trunk to rest. He attuned his ears to listen to the town beginning to relax after a busy Saturday. A few cars stirred on Main Street. Through an open window, a television could be heard: multiple gunshots, hopefully in pursuit of justice. From far away, the shouts of playing children soared over head.

Craig was going to miss this town. The calm atmosphere, the peaceful evenings, the unpretentious neighborliness, even its unkempt grittiness—he would miss all of it. He also would miss the people: Carol and Marc, Tom and the boys, and Eb Jordan. And Sarah. He felt his heart ache as he thought of her, of how she had made such an impression on his life and how she had moved him to think beyond himself in so many ways.

He also recognized that his scheduled departure from Walsh would aid him in removing himself from Sarah's house and her life—a move necessary for both their sakes. With his residency no longer being open-ended, the move to the motel on the highway now could be financially affordable. Even the longer walk to and from the diner was tolerable as it was closer to level than the climb to Monroe Street and the toll being extracted as he repeatedly found himself short of breath. He would make the arrangements tomorrow, and move out as quickly as possible.

Closing his eyes, the vision of Dolores appeared, a young Dolores, in costume for *Tartuffe*, possessing all the loveliness and promise that had compelled him to fall in love with her those many years ago. In the theater wings stood Joan in her ruffled blouse and Sarah, wearing jeans and a plaid shirt, quietly admiring the actress. Like understudies for a star with perfect attendance, they stood, resigned to their fate.

Craig continued the climb, noiselessly entering the quiet house where the light from under Sarah's bedroom door indicated that she had retired there. He slipped into his chamber, thankful an encounter with his landlady had been avoided.

97

Sarah awoke in a panicked state after hearing the sound, a thunderous rumble like an August afternoon thunderstorm rolling through the parlor. Springing to her feet, she dashed into the hallway. Dawn's first light was illuminating the foyer, where she could see Craig lying on the floor at the base of the staircase. She scrambled down the stairs to kneel by his side. Craig's face was compressed in a grimace, his hands embracing his ribcage.

"Heart," he murmured.

"Hold on!" she commanded. "Hold on!"

Sarah ran to the kitchen phone and dialed the emergency number. Impatience mounted and mounted as each ring went unanswered. In turn she agonized as each ponderous question of the dispatcher was asked. When she could take it no longer, she shouted, "Please, just hurry! 43 Monroe Street! Come quickly!"

Returning to the hallway, she threw open the front door and flipped on the porch light. To Craig she pleaded, "Don't move. Just hold on!" Then she rushed up the steps again, only to return with a bottle of aspirin. The bottle's safety cap proved to be a challenge, handicapped as she was by the bandage on her left hand. When the cap finally opened, many of the tablets rained onto the floor. Shaking out two that remained in the bottle, she pressed them through his lips.

"Chew these," she implored.

Craig looked up at Sarah's face, her resolute countenance commanding his respect. Her warm fingers forced the tablets into his mouth, where they came to rest between his molars, to be crushed with a single chomp of his jaw. She was on her knees now, bending over him like an angel of mercy, tears welling in her eyes.

The pain in his chest had subsided, and he released his hold on his ribcage. As the acrid powdered aspirin burned its way down his throat, he felt her right hand take his. As if they were independent units, their hands undertook their own embrace, squeeze met by reciprocating squeeze, each curve and crevice melding into matching contours.

With one of these compressions, the pain surged again within his chest, as he attempted to disguise the resultant grimace with a hopeful smile. A look at her face and he imagined once again the flour covered head that had surprised them both a few days prior in her kitchen. Into this white tableau were imprinted in stark contrast her bright eyes and opened mouth. The vision brought a true smile to his face that proved superior to the wave of pain rising within his core. That hallucination was his last conscious thought.

98

In the twilight, the white stucco walls of the cottage had assumed a lavender tint. The shaded vegetation that surrounded the dwelling was no longer a vibrant green, but rather, a cool, greenish blue. This coolness was offset by the warm light that escaped from the sole window in the building's front elevation, and a wisp of smoke spiraling skyward from the chimney, originating, no doubt, from an inviting blaze in the fireplace.

Sarah knew no one in this cottage. Indeed, the setting was totally foreign to her. Still, she wished to enter the house, to make the acquaintance of its occupants, to listen to the numerous tales they unquestionably had to tell. She need only walk up the flagstone path and knock on the door. Surely she would be admitted.

"Mrs. Stiles?"

The voice interrupted her concentration, her focus on the framed painting hanging on the wall in the hospital corridor. She started to rise from the bench, when the woman, a stout brunette wearing a white lab coat, extended her hand to Sarah's shoulder and kindly, but firmly, bade her to remain sitting.

"Mrs. Stiles," the woman continued, "I'm Doctor James."

Sarah looked at the physician with intense concern. No words could find their way to her mouth, but none were needed, as her pleading eyes said all there was to be said.

"When Mr. Miller arrived at the E.R. we immediately began to treat him as if he had had a heart attack, as the symptoms manifested suggested that was the case. We placed him on a heart monitor and obtained an EKG reading, which again suggested that our treatment plan was appropriate. Mr. Miller was never fully conscious, so we were unable to communicate with him. While under observation, he went into cardiac arrest. The emergency room staff initiated cardio-pulmonary resuscitation and attempted defibrillation. Unfortunately, although every attempt was made to revive him, we were unable to do so. I am very sorry."

99

Tom Morgan pulled his patrol car to the curb in front of the house. The mid-morning sun was bright, showing off the vibrant colors in the flowerbeds that surrounded the residence. What were the odds he would get this assignment? He took a deep breath and stepped from the car, the soft breeze carrying the sound of the Catholic Church's bells in the distance, announcing the conclusion of the morning mass.

The doorbell was answered by Dolores Miller, her soiled jeans and tattered shirt a strange contrast to her radiant face, glowing as if freshly scrubbed. A few strands of her dark hair had escaped confinement by the red kerchief on her head.

"Patrolman Morgan!" she said, with a smile of recognition. "What brings you here?"

"Good morning, Mrs. Miller. Um, may I come in?"

"Sure, please." Tom removed his hat and held it over his chest as she directed him to the sofa in the living room. He guessed that she had detected something in his manner, for, as she seated herself, her eyes narrowed, and tiny valleys appeared in the center of her brow.

"Mrs. Miller, I am very sorry to have to tell you this. Our department received a call from Greenbrier Valley Medical Center..." Tom glanced at his notes, and continued, "...in Ronceverte, West—"

"No!!"

"...West Virginia. Your husband had been brought there. They believe he had a heart attack."

Dolores had covered her mouth with her hands, and her eyes appeared to plead for an alternate ending. Tom could not bear to look at her directly. He dropped his head and forced the final words from his mouth as if he were expelling poison. "I'm afraid he did not make it."

Dolores's body began to quake as her hands slid up to cover her eyes, her head dropping forward, supported by arms resting on her knees. Tom dropped to a knee and slid towards her, placing a hand on her shoulder. Her body was heaving as the sobs became more audible, and rather than merely ride the waves of her grief, he administered firm pats which he knew in advance would be futile in providing comfort.

Less than a minute later, although it seemed like much longer, Dolores pulled herself erect and began to daub her eyes with a handkerchief that Tom had produced from a rear pants pocket. Tom accepted without question yet another of the many ironies of his profession, that he should carry a patch of cotton for compassionate purposes in the same pocket as his lead weighted leather billy, designed solely to knock a combatant senseless.

"I'm sorry," she said. "I'm sure you have more important things to do."

"No, ma'am, I'm here for you. Is there anyone you'd like me to call?"

"No. No, thank you. You've been very kind…considering… Do you have to do this kind of thing often?"

"Fortunately, no. Although, no matter how much you practice, it's something you never get good at." Tom had seen this before, the rapid lapse into small talk, the body's way of taking bad news in small doses. Dolores was yet to understand the full meaning of this notification. He felt obligated to play along. "The hospital had attempted to contact you directly, but got no answer when they called."

"Oh, I was working outside in the garden. Must not have heard the phone ring."

Tom offered her a weak smile as he retreated to the sofa. Fumbling for something to say, he thought he might be less grim. "Your flowers are beautiful."

"Thank you," she said.

He could see tears gathering again, but she blinked them away and then rose. He stood also.

"I appreciate you letting me know," she said. "But you can go now, I'll be okay."

"You're sure?"

"Yes." She returned the handkerchief, her contorted face expressing the awkwardness of handing him his possession now crumpled and soggy due to her use.

"Okay. Here is the hospital phone number. If our department can be of any assistance, please, call us. I'm very sorry for your loss."

100

Sarah entered her house in a trance. She could not remember any part of the drive back from the hospital: traffic signals, speed limits, hills or sharp turns. Quite unlike the trip there, where she had been keenly aware, as well she should have been, pushing the limits in an effort to catch up to the ambulance. Not that she thought she could catch up, given the head start they got while she threw on some clothes. Still, she had hoped to round a bend to see the red flashing lights ahead, to be that much closer to Craig, at least one more time.

Once again Death had been the victor, and she felt herself a victim, perhaps even more so than Frank, and now, Craig. She cast her eyes downward to the spot on the floor where last she saw him. It was bare now, of course, except for the sprinkling of aspirin tablets and some sanitary wrappers the EMT's had discarded in their haste to administer to him. That, and the bunched throw rug on which she stood, thrown into disarray by the gurney's rapid exit from the foyer, was all that remained to suggest the morning's events.

She looked up the stairs, towards Craig's room, and pictured him standing there, that smile she had come to admire gracing his face. She felt a tear stream down her cheek, as out of place as if it had been placed there by an eyedropper held by a Hollywood makeup artist.

She had not cried at the hospital. She had stoically received the news and then had asked softly if she might see him. When Dr. James had taken her behind the curtain she had seen him lying there, restful, at peace. She had never seen him so. He had always been alert, active, and, she believed, troubled.

Sarah smiled as she remembered Craig digging in her yard, preparing a flower bed for planting. She remembered the look of alarm on his face as she had begun her rant after he had repaired the gutter. She remembered him striding off to baseball practice, full of confidence and pride. She closed her eyes and remembered the kiss, its moist warmth offering promises of growth and blooming. A second tear retraced the path of the first.

She opened her eyes and wiped her cheek with the back of her hand, took a deep breath, and bent to straighten the rug. She picked up each aspirin tablet and scooped the wrappers off the floor and stuffed them into the pocket of her jeans, then climbed the stairs towards Craig's room, a chill racing up her spine when the creaking step offered its lament.

101

Sarah stepped from the parking lot up to the station platform, her footsteps echoing in the late night silence. She stood and listened, amazed at how sounds traveled so easily in the stillness of the night. The rhythmic clanking of the coal conveyor provided percussion accompaniment to the cricket chorus singing in the weeds just beyond the tracks. Down the platform a small huddle of waiting passengers was being orbited by a young boy brimming with energy even though he was awake much earlier than usual.

Headlights raked across the columns supporting the canopy, and when the car parked and its occupant emerged, Sarah recognized it as Eb Jordan, his form unmistakable even in the dim light.

"Thank you for coming, Pastor Jordan," she greeted him as he approached her.

"It is my pleasure," he said. "I'm an early riser, but even this is early for me. Still, there's little I wouldn't do for you, Sarah. I hope you know that."

"I do. When you offered to meet me here, I was surprised. The hour is hardly convenient."

"Yes, we should have a talk with the railroad about their scheduling."

Their conversation was interrupted by another set of headlights, which drew close so as to blind them with their glare. Then the lights veered away, inscribing a circle around the parking lot, before being extinguished, the long dark vehicle backing solemnly towards the platform. Simultaneously, a baggage handler pulled a cart over to the hearse as two men exited the vehicle and opened the rear door. In short order, the three men had lifted a coffin from the car and placed it on the cart, the lacquered oak box shining faintly in the sparse light, resting high on the cart above its spoked steel wheels. Amid hushed whispers, paperwork was exchanged, and then the driver of the hearse approached Sarah.

"Mrs. Stiles, I trust all has been done in accordance with your wishes and those of the deceased's wife?"

"Yes, I wish to thank you for all you've done."

"And thank you for dropping off Mr. Miller's belongings. You have our heartfelt condolences. Good night, ma'am." Nodding at Eb, he added, "Good night, Reverend Jordan."

The hearse drove off as the baggage handler wheeled the cart noisily across the platform. Then he offered Sarah a sheepish smile before walking back towards the station, leaving her and Eb alone with the coffin.

Nodding at the pastor, Sarah bowed her head.

Eb Jordan removed a small book from his jacket pocket and read, "O God, You gave us your servant and our friend, Craig Miller, and in Your wisdom and love have called him home to You. Please listen to our humble prayer: pardon his sins and faults, and grant that we may be reunited safely in Your Presence. Through Your Son, our Lord, Jesus Christ, we beg this of You. AMEN."

"Amen," she said softly, as the sound of horns to the west announced the approach of No. 2.

The two remained silent for the next few minutes. Eventually, the train's headlight flooded the platform, and the silver streamliner glided into the station, coming to a stop with the baggage car door next to the waiting cart, the heavy smell of heated brake shoes filling the air. The door opened and a trainman and the baggage handler, who had silently reappeared, slid the coffin into the baggage compartment. Shortly, the door closed, the traps of the coaches behind them slammed shut, the locomotives growled to life, and the train began to move. The limited had nearly attained track speed as the last car passed them, towing behind it a gust of wind that pressed against their backs. They watched as the train was sucked into the void of the night, the two red markers finally disappearing around a curve, as the whistle for the Fowler Road crossing echoed back off the hills.

"I loved him, you know," she said, still staring eastward down the tracks.

Eb offered the softest of rumbles from his throat as an acknowledgement.

"He was always kind to me, even after the time I laced into him. But there was something else. It was like he was looking for something, searching as if…as if he could look into my heart for it. At first I found it unnerving—intruding. But slowly I came to realize he wasn't trying to capture anything, to seize it, or take it away. He seemed only to want to recognize it, to honor it. For just a brief moment I thought that he had found it in me."

Sarah covered her eyes with her hand and began to cry. The reverend placed a comforting hand on her shoulder and she curled into his shoulder and began to sob, releasing all she had held within for the past few days.

"Look at me," she said at last, pulling away from him and wiping a tear with the sleeve of her blouse. "Bawling like a schoolgirl. I'm sorry."

"You have nothing to apologize for. It is right that we mourn the dead. You probably knew Craig better than anyone else in town. You will grieve in your own way, at your own pace."

"At first I was angry. First Frank, and now Craig has died. It's like anyone who gets close to me is taken away. But I keep seeing Craig's face, his upbeat nature, always looking for a way he could make things better. And I remember how he jerked me out of my depression, made me—in his weird way, with his strange powers—want to live again. If I were to betray that for self-pity, to go back into the stupor I was in after Frank died, then what would have been the meaning of Craig's life? God brought him to me for a reason. I truly believe that."

"Perhaps. I have long believed that it is folly for men to guess at God's intentions. But we must have faith that His will is for the best."

"Thank you, Pastor Jordan. For coming here, for listening to me."

Eb smiled and nodded in return.

"You know, when I was getting his things together to send back with him, I found the story he was writing on the history of Walsh."

"Really? I didn't realize he was writing something."

"He had told me he was working on it, but I didn't realize he had written as much as he had." Sarah paused before continuing, "God forgive me, but I didn't send it with the rest of his things."

"No?"

"I felt it belonged here. No one in New Jersey is going to care about it. I thought, maybe in a few weeks I'll write his wife and get permission to have it published here, you know, maybe in *The Herald*?"

"I doubt that she'd object...I wonder how she is taking this? The night before he died, Craig told me he was going to return to New

Jersey, to try to make his marriage work again."

"He did?"

"After baseball season ended, that is."

"Yeah, that was Craig."

"Yes, yes it was."

"Can I ask you another favor?"

"Certainly, my dear."

"Could you perform a memorial service?"

"Ah, you are not the first to make that request. I've tentatively scheduled a service on Friday morning."

102

North winds brought a chill to the mountains, not unusual for springtime in the Appalachians, but perceived by many as being especially cool when contrasted to the warmer than normal days already experienced. The Reverend Jordan had considered turning on the heat in the sanctuary, but decided that the sun rising higher in the clear sky and the limited funds in the church's bank account argued against it.

Those in attendance that morning tried to maintain a somber tone, but the bright sunshine and the goodwill that provided the common theme to their shared remembrances of Craig worked against them. When they took their seats in the church, Sarah sat with Carol and Marc, who had closed the diner for the occasion, as well as the Simpsons, who seemed to be present at every church service and affair. In front of them, filling the entire first pew, were a dozen young teenage boys, Walsh's Babe Ruth team, looking out of place in jackets and ties. A few parents of these boys, including Tom Potter, unsuccessful in arguing that they shouldn't miss a morning of school, had driven them here and were now dispersed throughout the chapel.

Eb Jordan's remarks were brief; generalizations about the positive aspects of Craig's character that he had come to know in their few encounters. An invitation for members of the congregation to step forward, brought Marc to the lectern, speaking on behalf of Carol, himself, and the diner as Craig's employer. Tom Potter followed, relating what it was like to work with Craig, how he believed the boys had benefited, and committing himself to completing the season as best he could.

"Anyone else?" Eb asked.

Restless shuffling came in response. Though she felt she had much to say, Sarah chose to keep her memories selfishly to herself. The pastor was opening his hymnal in preparation to announce the closing hymn, when Jesse Nielson stood, and walked directly to the lectern, as the minister yielded.

The boy turned to face the congregation, only his head and neck visible above the lectern, it being unclear whether his ruddy complexion was due to his farm boy's sunburn or asphyxiation from the tie encircling his neck under a starched white collar.

Eb Jordan returned to the lectern to adjust the microphone down towards Jesse's mouth, the creaking of the mike's gooseneck being amplified over the speakers.

Jesse cleared his throat, giving a quick grin to Tommy below him.

"The first time I met Mr. Miller I thought he was crazy and a liar. I thought he was crazy to think he could put our ball team back together. I thought he was crazy thinking he could fix up our ball field where Tommy and Buzzie and Billy and me would hack around.

"I thought he was a liar, 'cuz we'd been lied to before. Not by Tommy's dad, he's always done all he could. But other coaches said they'd coach the team but then got 'busy' or had 'problems at home' and on and on. I figgered this guy was gonna let us down, too.

"But I was wrong 'bout Mr. Miller. Oh, he mighta been crazy—to spend so much of his time with a bunch of kids like us. But he weren't no liar! He came back the next day—like he said he would. And he kept coming back. He helped us turn that patch of weeds into a baseball field. And he helped us turn into a team—all working for the same goal.

"No, I was wrong about Mr. Miller. And I'll never forget him."

103

Joe Lorenzo swung his leg hard, his foot hitting the bucket, sending it careening against the fence, scattering the baseballs it contained in several directions. His Alderson Eagles were being thrashed by this ragged team from Walsh. When the Pirate's number nine hitter beat out a bunt for a base hit, Lorenzo knew a win wasn't likely today.

Across the infield, Tom Potter grinned at Dave Nielsen, his new assistant coach. "Now everyone's gotten a hit, right?"

"Every single one of 'em," Dave said, scanning the scorebook. "'Course, Tommy's homer really sent the message that we came here to win!"

"No, Dave, every one of these guys is playing his heart out. I've never seen them so focused as they are today."

"You know, if I had known this was so much fun, I would've offered to help long ago."

"Well I really appreciate you stepping forward. Your help couldn't have come at a better time, whatever your reason."

"Are you kidding? You were there. You heard Jesse's words at the memorial service. I had no idea he was going to say anything or that this fellow, Miller, had made such an impression on him. Afterwards I began to think how unimportant so many of the 'important' things in my life were. And how it wouldn't be all that tough to give some of my time to my son and his friends. Jesse's fourteen. I came within a few years of missing the opportunity of a lifetime."

"I've been coaching Tommy most of his life," Tom said, then to the team, "Buzzie! You're on deck!" Turning back to Dave, "I guess I've sort of taken it for granted."

"Don't, man!" Dave urged. "What you have with your son is special. Never forget that."

104

Joan sat at the cluttered desk in her bedroom, writing out the last check for the bills that had accumulated there. She really needed to clean this desk. She reached forward and grabbed a small stack of papers randomly. Falling from her grasp was a small note card, that landed open in front of her, its single word message: "Adieu", visible before her.

She picked up the card and stared at it for a moment, then, turning off the desk lamp. turned to look out the window at the moonlit yard.

How many billions of human interactions occurred every day? How many faceless workers toiled on her behalf in a factory somewhere making something she would one day use? And the truck driver who delivered it to the store. The anonymous clerk who rang up her purchase. A retiree somewhere living off the dividends that her purchase so microscopically influenced.

How many relationships were more personal, more recognized? How many are cultivated but yield minimal or even negative rewards? How many are dismissed so quickly, with little thought, a tiny distraction in a world of blaring calls for attention.

Joan looked back at the card, and returned it to its spot on the desk. She would clean the desk some other time.

105

The bottom of the curtain touched the stage floor, and members of the company dashed in all directions. Dolores, whose final exit had occurred several minutes before, had had plenty of time to reach the wings at the rear of the stage, where she had observed the final moments of the final act from a unique perspective.

From there she had watched the back of Charlie's head as he realized, perhaps too late, the impact that Da had made on his life. The parallels with her life struck home. Craig had been laid to rest a little more than a week ago. Da had died tonight, the last two nights, and would die again during Sunday's matinee. Was the mere repetition of his death and post-mortem analysis the reason why the meaning of Da's life was so clear, and the meaning of Craig's so much less so?

The curtain rose, and the minor part actors quickly stepped to stage center for their separate and group bows. Dolores was next, her prominent role acknowledged by the audience by louder and more intense applause. Taking her bow, she moved to stage right as Charlie bounded forward, greeted by a raucous crescendo of applause. In turn, he moved to stage left, as Da came forward in a deliberate, stately gait. Now the applause was thunderous, augmented with calls and whistles.

His bow complete, Da turned to her and extended his hand. She joined him, as did Charlie from the opposite side, and they bowed as one, then again individually, and as one once more, as the curtain dropped a final time. The company scattered to dressing rooms, stage hands began muscling scenery into place for tomorrow's Scene 1. While Dolores remained motionless for awhile, thinking of Da and Craig.

In a row near the rear of the theater, Jeff Downs returned to his seat from where he had stood for the ovation. His ailing leg made known its discomfort, both from the long time sitting and the sudden call to rise. He was unsure of what he should do next, so he remained seated and watched the theater empty. When all but a few patrons had left, he rose and left the theater to go home.

THE END

Acknowledgements

I extend my sincere thanks to members of the Montville Writer's Group, namely David Reuter, J. D. Rule, Tina Book, Christine Balne, Gill Otto, Kate Matta, and Robert Lefkowitz. Their critiques, comments, suggestions, objections, and praise provided encouragement, challenge, and competent guidance.

Thanks also to Gail Petriello and Frank Gregory who so generously responded to my request to use a photo of their home for the cover illustration. Frank even went so far as to change the house number for the photo shoot!

My special thanks to Rebecca Curcio, who, assisted by Landers Watson, made the author look his best in the portrait.

Finally, the patience of family and friends during this writing process is gratefully acknowledged.